The Orphans *of* Bell Lane

The Orphans of Bell Lane

Ruthie Lewis

ZAFFRE

First published in Great Britain in 2019 by
ZAFFRE
80–81 Wimpole St, London W1G 9RE

A CIP catalogue record for this book is
available from the British Library.

Paperback ISBN: 978–1–78576–129–4

Also available as an ebook

1 3 5 7 9 10 8 6 4 2

Typeset by IDSUK (Data Connection) Ltd
Printed and bound in Great Britain by Clays Ltd, Elcograf S.p.A.

Zaffre is an imprint of Bonnier Books UK
www.bonnierbooks.co.uk

To Alice and Arthur and all the Holbrook relatives. Hope you can forgive me mining our family history for plotlines.

Prologue

December, 1849

Waking with the familiar warm feel of her sister's body next to hers gave Grace a few moments when she could pretend that nothing had changed and they were at home in Rotherhithe. The cold air in the workhouse dormitory was familiar too, as waking up in winter cold had been normal throughout Grace's young life. It was the sharp smell of other bodies than Rosa's that reminded her, even before she opened her eyes, that home was a long way away, and they would never be going back.

The girls quickly dressed in their thin woollen dresses and rushed to the dining hall. Grace sat shivering next to Rosa waiting for the meagre portion of porridge which, along with a bluish glass of skimmed milk, constituted breakfast. Usually the porridge was warm, but it was very seldom hot and always very thin. Many of the others in the hall tried to warm their hands over the bowls for a minute before starting to eat.

'Now Gracie,' said Rosa, 'you remember that I will not be in lessons with you anymore from today? But you must pay attention to the teacher, and work hard and learn as much as you can.'

'Yes, Rosa,' replied Grace, her eyes beginning to fill with tears. 'But couldn't you ask them to stay on longer in the school? I shall miss you so much.'

Rosa smiled sadly. 'No, now that I am ten they say I have no more need to go to school. I can read and write and do sums. I need to learn how to sew clothes for the workhouse. Maybe I will make your next dress, Gracie. Wouldn't that be lovely?' And she gave her little sister a quick hug.

'Will I see you at dinner time, Rosa?' asked Grace. 'I want to see you before they take us to pick clothes.' After the midday meal, the younger children were put to work picking old clothes in order to make rags that the workhouse could sell. The older children had a variety of other jobs, the lucky ones getting to work in the kitchen or the laundry. Half of Grace's day was spent in the finger-shredding work, and after the first few weeks of bleeding and sore fingers her little hands had toughened up and looked like those of a much older person.

'I don't know whether we will be here at the same time or not. I want to do well at the sewing and learn as much as possible so that I can find a good job when I am older and can get us out of here.' She gave Grace a kiss on the forehead. 'So I will do just as I am told and hope that they think I am a good worker. If they say to stay I will stay, Grace, my dear. But don't worry, I shall see you tonight. You know I shall always be here for you, Gracie.'

Grace gave her a rather watery smile and went to join all the younger children who were going up to the schoolroom on the top floor of the workhouse. Sara, one of the others, pinched Grace and said softly, 'You better be nice to me today, or else. Did you bring some of your bread from last night's tea?'

'I'm sorry, Sara,' said Grace, 'there was no bread left at our table. I didn't get any at all and there was none to keep. I tried, really I did.'

'That's what you say,' hissed Sara, 'but I don't believe you. You are a greedy little pig and you stuffed your fat face with it. I can tell. You will pay for this.'

Sara was nine and ran an extortion racket among the younger children in the workhouse. Her technique was simple: do what I tell you to do, she demanded, or I will beat you. Beatings with a thick rattan cane were part of workhouse discipline, but Grace was always well-mannered and had so far avoided punishment. The first time Sara had struck her, the pain was so intense she had almost forgotten to cry.

Sara was particularly fond of preying on newcomers, either cowing them into submission or, when she spotted a like-minded urchin, gathering them to her to form part of her gang. She was careful and cunning. Sara never bothered anyone older, bigger or smarter than herself and was always sweetness and light to the workhouse staff who rewarded her with such small tokens of favour as were possible in this place. These included placing her at a table nearest the kitchen so she had the first choice of food, the best of shoes that were donated, and other small but significant things that eased the life of the staff's favourites.

The bully kept well clear of Rosa, and her first act of terror was to make Grace swear on her mother's grave not to tell Rosa about anything Sara did. She threatened to get Rosa moved out of Grace's dormitory, to have her beaten up and all manner of other threats. Grace would do anything to keep Rosa safe, and to have her big sister by her side at night. Rosa was her only refuge. So, she kept quiet when Sara tormented her, pinching her and slapping her and shouting at her, knowing that if she tried to defend herself it would only make matters worse. Grace had never experienced bullying before, and she found Sara terrifying, even the sight of the older girl could make her shake and tremble.

Trying not to cry and make Sara despise her even more, Grace followed her tormentor up the three flights of stairs to the cold classroom on the top floor. Despite the cold, the room had little of the damp that permeated the lower floors and its high windows let in plenty of light. Grace made her way to her usual seat next to Nellie, a pale gingery-blonde child who sniffed a good deal, but was not unkind to Grace.

For the next three hours Grace was happy, as happy as she could be in this place where she and Rosa had been flung after the terrible weeks of illness and death had left them orphans. Three hours of learning. Although she was only five years old, Grace loved to learn. She particularly loved the letters of the alphabet and how, when they were put together, they made words, almost like magic. Words, Grace knew, even in her five-year-old brain, were powerful things and she hungered to gain mastery over them. Secretly, when the teacher wasn't paying attention to their part of the class, Grace would try out combinations of letters to make up her own words; Grace's special words.

But Grace knew that the teacher did not approve of her making up her own words. The teacher was interested in neat handwriting to the exclusion of almost everything else. Poor Nellie was always being told off for messy letters, for she had never held a pencil or chalk until she came to the workhouse, and her first instinct to use the slate pencil in her left hand was violently dealt with in her first week in class. The bruises on her arms and fingers lasted for many days. Struggling to form letters, she looked at Grace's quick writing in awe.

Midday meant the end of education for the workhouse children. Three hours of basic reading, writing and simple arithmetic was considered to be enough, why would orphans and abandoned children need more? Workhouse education was a pragmatic investment meant to create useful workers, and to the governors of the workhouse, the children were nothing but a potential workforce.

For Grace though, the period of work that followed the midday meal was a nightmare. She was not a physically strong child, and the workhouse food had made her more frail still.

Rosa, she knew, was eager to work. Rosa was determined to learn a skill or a trade that would get her a job outside the workhouse and allow them to leave this hellish place where they had been confined since their parents and brothers died of cholera. But Grace herself could hardly imagine life outside the workhouse. Already, memories of her parents were beginning to fade. There was only Rosa, five years older than herself, her big sister and only protector. She would do whatever Rosa said, but she had no real hope for the future. Some of the adult inmates had passed their entire lives in the workhouse, never setting foot outside, never feeling the sun on their faces or the wind on their cheeks, and Grace was sure that this would happen to her.

As the children rattled down the stairs in their heavy, ill-fitting clogs and boots to the work room, Sara came up close behind Grace and hissed in her ear. 'I haven't forgotten you owe me one, you know.' Then she shoved past Grace and out to the yard, going towards the laundry. Older and stronger than Grace and able to do more physical work, Sara had a job in the warm wash house, another mark of the favour shown to the young bully.

Grace and Nellie, along with many more of the smaller and weaker children, found their way to the picking room, and found a seat together. Nellie didn't talk much, but she was a kind little person and would leave Grace to her work and not make a stream of complaints which were bound

6

to bring the attention of the head picker down on them. As the afternoon wore on Nellie and Grace began to look forward to the evening meal, meagre though it would be, usually just a piece of bread and thin soup.

There was a small commotion at the door to the picking room, and then the head picker shouted, 'Grace Perrow, get yourself over 'ere!'

Grace looked up in surprise, but she ran quickly to the door, fearing that something had happened to Rosa. It always seemed like something was happening to one of the children.

'A treat for you, young Grace,' said a thin, hard-faced woman. 'You'll have the rest of the day in the nice warm laundry. They are short of a hand or two and you've been picked. Goodness knows why,' she said looking Grace up and down, 'can't see you'll be much use heaving laundry about, but it ain't up to me.'

Grace was surprised and a bit worried at this change. She gave Nellie a quick glance of enquiry, and then followed this strong-smelling and faintly steaming woman across the workhouse yard and into the thick, hot and noisy room. ''Ere you,' shouted a stout red-skinned woman standing by a big copper boiling pot, 'Come 'ere and get a wiggle on. There's bags to do and we're behind.'

The stout woman gave Grace a searching look. 'Sara didn't say you were such a titchy thing . . . well often the small ones are the nippiest. Here's your hook, luv. Just reach into this bloody pot and sling the hook and clothes onto

7

that pile for Big Sal to put through the mangle. An' don't you go anywheres near that mortal mangle. Pulling you out of there would muck up the day good and proper.'

Grace took the hook and gingerly prodded in the copper, bringing out a small wet article that she turned and added to Big Sal's pile of work. The smell of lye soap caught in the back of her throat and made her eyes water. The copper was full of bubbling, boiling water and looked to Grace like a living monster. Grace was afraid of boiling water, having nearly been badly burned in her mother's kitchen last year, but she was even more frightened of Big Sal who kept shouting at her to 'get a flaming move on'. Now Sal shoved a wooden box towards Grace. 'You'd better stand on this if you are going to be any use at all. We need all that laundry out, not just the bit on the top.'

Grace held on tight to the wooden top edge of the copper to reach as far down into the cauldron as she could. She used her sleeve to try and keep her hand from burning. Behind her she heard Sara's voice.

'How do you like your new job, lazy-bones? Time you did some proper work like the rest of us,' and she slapped Grace hard on the back. Grace staggered and clutched again at the edge of the copper, trying to use her hook to regain her balance. She righted herself, frightened and resentful at the same time, and thought, *Proper work? I'll show her.*

For the next half hour she worked like a demon, grabbing clothes and flinging them onto the pile like a little girl possessed. As the amount of laundry in the copper decreased, she had to lean further and further over the edge, her balance as she stood on the wooden box growing more and more precarious, but she was determined to drag out every single piece of laundry.

Fishing with the hook in the boiling depths, she dragged up an enormous quantity of clothing. The weight made her arms and shoulders ache and she struggled to lift them. She gave another heave, but the weight was too great and she lost her balance. Her feet slid out from under her, and then she was falling towards the rim of the copper, her legs kicking in the air. She knew she should drop the hook and use her arms to regain her balance, but she could not bring herself to do so.

Steam blinded her. She screamed and in her own ears it seemed particularly loud and piercing. She screamed again, but to no avail. She lost her balance completely, and began to fall towards the boiling water.

Then all at once someone grabbed her lower legs and hauled her back. Flailing, she managed to shed some of the clothes from her hook. Released from the weight, the hook and the remaining clothes flew backwards over her head as she was dragged to safety. The hands holding her legs let go and she fell, stumbling off her box and collapsing on the floor. She landed on something soft and realised after a moment that she could see Rosa's skirt under her. It was Rosa who had grabbed her, and it was Rosa who was underneath her now, crying out in pain.

Scrambling to her feet, Grace saw that the boiling hot clothes that had remained on the hook had hit Rosa and were still wrapped around her upper body. Grace grabbed the clothes and began to pull them free. They burned her hands but she didn't care; she was desperate to get them off of Rosa. It was mere moments before Grace had removed the clothes but already she could see that Rosa's arms were terribly burnt. Almost worse than the burns, Rosa had fallen with her leg underneath her and was struggling to get up, biting her lip to avoid crying out in pain again.

Finally Big Sal turned and saw what had happened. Moving swiftly, she pulled Rosa up with strong arms. 'Can you walk, then?'

Rosa replied through gritted teeth, 'My left leg. It hurts.'

'Hmm.' Accidents in the laundry were commonplace; Big Sal had seen almost everything during her years of service here. 'Reckon you've twisted your ankle and all,' she said. 'And the skin on your arms looks dangerous red. Right you, hop along to the infirmary. Grace, go with her.' She turned and began shouting at the other girls. 'Don't just stand there, get a flaming move on!'

Later that evening, Grace was allowed to go and see Rosa in the infirmary before bed. Her big sister was lying with her left leg raised and her right arm bandaged to the shoulder. Grace tiptoed to the side of the bed. 'Rosa, Rosa, you are hurt, all because you saved me,' she said in a soft voice. 'I am so sorry, Rosa. Please don't die.'

'Gracie, dear Gracie,' said Rosa, smiling through her pain. 'I am not going to die. It only hurts a bit and I am nowhere near dying. I wouldn't leave you on your own. I will always be with you, Gracie. Remember it's me and you, together for always.'

Chapter 1

June, 1867

'Oh, look, Grace! Who is that ever so handsome man?'

The young man, who was indeed a rather pleasing sight in grey frock coat and fawn trousers, looked around and saw the two young women. Realising he was the object of their attentions, he removed his top hat and bowed solemnly in their direction. Grace and Mela curtseyed and then turned away, hands over their mouths to cover their giggles. 'He's still watching us,' murmured Grace. 'I think he likes you, Mela.'

'I think he is looking at *you*,' said Mela Clare. She twirled her parasol and then reached up to adjust a stray lock of her fair hair. 'Oh, look. Now he is talking to Lady Ringrose. I wonder if he is one of that family? If so, he will make a very good catch for someone.'

'I thought you vowed you would never marry,' said Grace.

'And so I did. But one can walk past a shop window and admire a fine gown without desiring to try it on.'

'Mela! You are quite shocking,' said Grace, laughing. 'Come, let us go and find your mother, before you get into trouble.'

They linked arms and walked across the grass. Around them, the trees of Hyde Park glowed vivid green beneath a blue spring sky. Little groups of picnickers were scattered across the grass, eating cold chicken and pies. Two little girls in pretty dresses were playing with a ball. They looked like sisters. The younger was about five, Grace saw, the same age as she had been in the workhouse.

She was twenty-three now, and that terrible year in the workhouse was for the most part a distant memory, although sometimes she dreamed of it still. Only last night she had woken in a panic, remembering the laundry, the boiling water and heat and steam and fear. She had dreamed of slipping, falling towards the boiling water, and Rosa's hand dragging her back, Rosa's cries of pain as the hot fabric scalded her skin.

Grace had become convinced that she would be in the workhouse forever, working and enduring Sara's bullying. They were rescued in the end by their Aunt Edith, their mother's sister, who had combed every workhouse in London and finally found them in faraway Chelsea, where they had been taken after the cholera epidemic. Aunt Edith had secured their release and brought them to live with her at her home in Bermondsey, south of the Thames. She was a widow who worked in a factory that made clothing; her husband had been a soldier who had been killed far away in Afghanistan at a place called Gandamack. Her only son, Charlie, had run away to join one of the street gangs that infested that part of London, and had never been seen again. All the love she might have given her own family was poured out instead on Rosa and Grace, and her death, when Grace was fourteen, had broken Grace's heart.

Once again the two of them were orphans, but Rosa was already working in a garment factory back in Rotherhithe – the district in south-east London where they had been born – and had a little money and could support herself. Grace could have gone to live with her, but then fortune stepped in. Before her marriage, Aunt Edith had been in service with the Clare family, who had remained in contact with her and supported her after her husband was killed. When Mr Clare learned of Aunt Edith's death and discovered Grace was alone, he insisted she come and join the family as Mela's companion. Rosa had remained in Rotherhithe, working for a few more years and then meeting and marrying a bricklayer named George Turneur, while Grace had gone north of the river to live a life of comfort in the Clare household.

The laughter of children pulled Grace from her musings. The mellow notes of a brass band sounded in the distance. More heads turned to watch the two young women, smartly dressed in ruffled hooped skirts and bright silk jackets; Grace all in lavender, Mela in a rich blue and crimson outfit that made her look faintly military. Mela smiled. She liked being the centre of attention.

'Did you enjoy Mr Forster's speech?' Grace asked.

Mela frowned. 'I am not sure that *enjoy* is the word I would have chosen, but certainly his proposal of a new education bill was very interesting. And informative, too. And it was wonderful to hear Mr Charles Dickens speak. What an admirable man he is! Not just his writing, but all the social causes he engages in. He is an example to us all.'

'He is,' said Grace. 'Do you suppose it will ever happen, Mela? Will we see a day when education is open to all, even the poorest pauper child? What was the phrase Mr Forster used: when knowledge and science become freely available, and poverty and hardship are swept away? It sounds almost too perfect to be possible.'

'Nothing is impossible,' said Mela firmly. 'But we must put our shoulder to the wheel. Nothing will happen unless we work for it.'

She turned her head to look at Grace, her face serious. 'And, you see, that is why I shall never marry. Marriage would be a distraction, and I will let nothing stand in my way. Before I die, I want to see free schools established the length and breadth of the land, open to both boys *and* girls, no matter what their station in life might be. This is a great cause, Grace. And I for one intend to devote my life to its service.'

'And I also,' said Grace, and she squeezed her friend's hand.

They found Mela's mother beside the Serpentine, a tall woman in green silk talking to Mr Forster; or rather, lecturing him, wagging a finger firmly in the air while the MP nodded in response. Grace thought he looked rather worried. Swans drifted slowly past, necks arched and wings lifted like sails shining in the sun.

'This bill must pass through the house, Mr Forster,' Mrs Clare was saying as the two girls came up. 'The situation is desperate. Half the children in the country have no access to education at all, and their number is increasing. Lord Shaftesbury's Ragged Schools are gallantly attempting to stem the tide, but they cannot educate every child in need. The government must take action.'

'I agree, I agree,' said Mr Forster, nodding again. 'But the matter is not in my gift, Mrs Clare. I have done all I can; I have talked myself hoarse trying to persuade the backbenchers, but the truth is, unless the Prime Minister signals his support for the bill, it may well fail. Mr Disraeli's own party will not dare to stand against his wishes, and the rest are not strong enough to force the bill through.'

In the distance the band was tootling again. 'Then the National Education League must press Mr Disraeli to lend his support,' said Mrs Clare firmly. 'And you must do all you can to assist them, Mr Forster. We are counting on you.'

'Yes, ma'am,' said the MP. 'We shall do our utmost, I assure you.'

Mrs Clare turned her head and saw the two girls. 'Ah, Mela, Grace, there you are. Come and meet Mr Forster. May I present my daughter Pamela? And this is her companion, Miss Perrow.'

Mrs Clare was the only person in the world permitted to refer to her daughter as Pamela. No one ever called her Pam; at least, not if they knew what was good for them. Mr Forster raised his hat and bowed, and Mela and Grace curtseyed. 'My daughter and Miss Perrow both teach in our works school,' said Mrs Clare.

'Do you, by Jove?' said Mr Forster, grateful for the distraction. 'I have heard of the Clare School. By all accounts, it is an absolute model for public education. I believe your husband founded it, as a free school for the children of his employees?'

'We founded it together,' said Mrs Clare firmly. 'We now educate more than sixty children.'

'How splendid! And I understand you yourself are the headmistress, Mrs Clare?'

'I am indeed,' said Mrs Clare. 'And I am flattered that you should have heard of our little establishment. May I ask if you would honour us with a visit one day?'

'I should be delighted.' Mr Forster pulled his pocket watch from his waistcoat and checked the time. 'And now, my dear Mrs Clare, I fear I must abandon your company. I must be in the House this afternoon, for the debate on the situation in Abyssinia. But I shall take up your invitation, most certainly. My secretary will contact you.'

The MP bowed and departed. Mrs Clare beamed fondly at the two young women. 'Well, my dears. Did you hear him? Recognition at last for all our hard work.'

'For all *your* hard work, Mother,' Mela corrected her. 'You and Father have carried the burden of this school for many years. Grace and I are merely your helpmeets.'

'I would call it a duty, not a burden,' Mrs Clare said. 'Nevertheless, we shall continue to bear it. Unless, of course, Mr Forster's bill succeeds in passing through the House of Commons, and the government really does provide free education for all.'

'Do you think the bill will pass?' asked Grace.

'Of course not, my dear. It will fail at the first attempt, that much is plain to see. Failure to enlist Mr Disraeli's support was their first mistake.' Mrs Clare clicked her tongue. 'Honestly, I would sooner entrust a matter of important public business to a haddock than to Mr Forster. Now, it is time we were away. Mela, dear, go and find your father; I will summon the carriage.'

Mela and Grace found Mr Clare with Sir Hector Ringrose, a prosperous cloth manufacturer from Bedfordshire. Mr Clare owned a textiles trading concern and the two men often did business together. Now they stood talking earnestly, discussing prices. Lady Ringrose, a matronly woman in a dark old-fashioned gown and hair pulled up in a bun, smiled at Grace and Mela.

'They are discussing matters of commerce,' she said. 'They will be finished shortly, or so I devoutly hope. How are you, Miss Clare? And you, Miss Perrow?'

'We are very well,' said Mela as they both curtseyed.

Lady Ringrose beckoned to someone standing nearby. 'Allow me to present my nephew, Walter Ringrose.'

It was the young man in the grey frock coat and top hat. More bows and curtseys were exchanged. 'Very pleased to meet you, Miss Clare, Miss Perrow,' said Mr Ringrose. He had a gentle, rather cultured voice. 'Are you also supporters of the National Education League?'

'We are,' said Mela firmly. Grace smiled, content to let her friend take the lead. 'We are both teachers at the Clare School.'

'Ah, that splendid institution.' Mr Ringrose looked impressed.

'The Clares are an example to us all,' pronounced his aunt. 'As are you yourselves, young ladies. I have no doubt that you, Miss Clare, will one day succeed your mother as headmistress.'

'I do not think Mother intends to step down any time soon,' said Mela smiling. 'At least, I hope she doesn't. But when she does, then yes, I hope to follow in her footsteps.'

'And you, Miss Perrow?' Lady Ringrose asked. 'What is your intention?'

Grace smiled too. 'I am content to serve,' she said.

Mr Ringrose looked surprised at this statement. 'Have you no ambitions for yourself, Miss Perrow?'

'My ambition, sir, is to be the best teacher I can be and help children to learn and grow. The Clare School is a good place to be.'

Mr Ringrose, smiled warmly at her. 'That is a noble ambition indeed. I feel sure your ambition is well on its way to being realised.'

Grace returned his smile. 'I do hope so, sir. There are so many children to help.'

'Hmm.' Lady Ringrose surveyed Grace. She knew that she had been a child pauper before coming to live with the Clares.

'You should think of your prospects beyond the Clare School, my dear,' said her ladyship. 'As it happens, I am establishing an endowed school for girls in Sevenoaks, in Kent. I need talented young women to serve as teachers. The post would command a good salary, plus all found. Are you interested?'

Grace blinked. 'Me?' she said.

'Yes,' said Lady Ringrose. Her nephew stood to one side, watching Grace with interest. 'Will you consider the offer?'

'I . . . I will, of course,' said Grace, starting to blush, and she curtseyed again. 'Thank you, my lady. You are most generous.'

'Good,' said Lady Ringrose, as if the matter was settled. 'Ah, here come Sir Hector and Mr Clare. Goodbye, my dears. It was a pleasure to see you again. Come, Walter, we must be away.'

The following day Grace taught as usual at the Clare School in Hackney, a solid brick building overlooking the marshes where wild ducks quacked among the reeds. She taught reading and writing to a class of twenty girls – as in most schools, boys and girls were taught in separate classes – in a simple room furnished with wooden chairs and desks and shelves of books. Her pupils, faces shining and scrubbed, beamed at her as she moved around the room, correcting the work on their slates. They adored her, and she them. But today as she worked she was restless, her mind wandering.

The bell rang for the end of lessons and the children streamed out, chattering like little birds. Grace remained behind for a moment, gazing out of the window while silence settled in the room around her. The fine weather of yesterday had passed, and dark clouds drifted over the marshes. She heard a distant rumble of thunder.

The interest in her own career by Lady Ringrose and her nephew Walter was at the heart of her wandering thoughts and she was pondering the scene and the offer again when the classroom door opened and Mela came in, skirts swishing. 'Penny for your thoughts,' she said smiling.

"I was just thinking about Lady Ringrose's offer,' Grace said. 'I cannot make up my mind what to do . . . Why did she ask me, of all people? Why not you?'

Mela came across the room to stand beside her. 'Because she knows Mother wouldn't let me go,' she said. 'And she knows you are clever and bright and very hard-working. She has spoken to Mother about you, several times.'

'But why should Lady Ringrose take an interest in me?'

'It is as she said. She thinks you have prospects, and Mother agrees. You could go far, you know.'

Prospects, thought Grace. *I am not even sure what that means* . . . 'What do you think I should do?' she asked. 'I would value your opinion, Mela.'

Mela wrinkled her nose. 'An endowed school for girls? Do you really want to teach the pampered children of bankers and lawyers and merchants, people who can fully afford to pay for education privately? What about the people who cannot pay? Remember yesterday, when we talked about education for all?'

'Endowed schools take in poor children too,' Grace pointed out. 'And I have been thinking that I need a change. I cannot stay here forever, living off your parents' charity.' She sighed. 'The truth is, Mela, I don't know what I want to do, beyond helping children to learn.'

Mela smiled. 'Then stay here, you silly goose. Stay with the Clare School, until you decide what you really want. Heaven knows we need you.'

She kissed her friend on the cheek. 'Come along. It's time to go, and we mustn't keep Mother waiting.'

Arm in arm, they walked through the school and outside towards the coach. In the distance, thunder rumbled again. 'I was also thinking about my sister and her family,' Grace said. 'It has been a month since I visited them. The children are growing so quickly now.'

'Then you must go and see them,' Mela said. 'You have a day off tomorrow, why not go then? Shall I accompany you?'

Grace smiled. 'You are kind. But no, I shall go on my own.'

'Have care,' said Mela seriously. 'According to the news-papers, the gangs south of the river are growing increas-ingly dangerous.'

Rosa had said the same thing. But Grace was not wor-ried about the gangs; she knew the streets of Rotherhithe well, which streets were safe and which to avoid. She squeezed her friend's hand. 'Don't worry about me,' she said. 'I will be fine.'

The following morning Grace took the train from Hackney into the city and then walked across London Bridge teem-ing with people and horses and wagons, seeing the river Thames crowded with ships and barges below. At London Bridge station, another train took her to Rotherhithe. She sat on the train watching the streets of London slide past, thinking.

She was still undecided about her future. As Mela's companion the Clares had housed her, fed her and edu-cated her until she was eighteen, and then offered her a teaching post at the school with a small salary, making it clear that she could continue to live with them for as long as she wished. More than anything else, they had given her their unstinting affection.

The thought of leaving them to go and live and work in Sevenoaks felt like a betrayal. But at the same time, Grace was growing restless. She had meant what she said to Mela. She felt she was living off the Clares' charity, and it was time this stopped. She needed to make her own way in the world, as Rosa had done.

She gathered her things and got off the train at Rother-hithe. Even though it was only a month since she had last been there, Grace found the area had changed. More houses and warehouses were going up, blotting out the green fields, and from everywhere came the sound of hammers and the rasp of saws. Wagons loaded with brick and timber rumbled past her, the harness of the teams jin-gling like bells. In the distance she saw the brick arches of the South Eastern Railway viaduct, a train shooting white plumes of steam into the air as it ran up towards the City. Turning her head, she saw the cranes and warehouses of the Surrey Docks rising over the rooftops, clouds of smoke billowing among the tangled masts and yards of sailing ships. There was a sweet tang of freshly sawn wood in the air, mingled with acrid coal smoke and the heavy aroma of brick dust.

Bell Lane was a cul-de-sac, two rows of small rough-and-ready brick houses with tile roofs separated by the lane which oozed foul-smelling mud. Grace knocked at the door of number twelve. A woman in a faded blouse and skirt and fraying apron opened it. She had dark circles under her eyes and her fair hair was coming down from its bun.

'Grace!' Light came into the other woman's tired eyes and she hugged Grace, clinging to her, arms around her neck. 'Oh, come in, come in! Oh, my dear, you look so fine! How are you?'

'I am very well, Rosa.' Before she could say anything more the children, three little shapes in threadbare clothes, launched themselves at her, squealing with delight. She knelt down and hugged them each in turn; Albert, a sturdy boy of eight, and the twins, Harry and Daisy, just turned five, planting grimy kisses on her cheek. She reached into her pocket and pulled out a handful of sweets. The squealing intensified as the children pounced on these, stuffing them into their mouths. 'What do you say?' instructed their mother.

'Thank you, Auntie Grace!' three small voices chorused. The children sat down on the floor, faces a picture of concentration as they sucked on the sweets, determined to extract every last ounce of satisfaction, and Grace rose and faced her sister again.

'How are you?' she asked quietly. 'Are you still feeling unwell?'

'No, I am much better,' said Rosa. She turned to the fire, where a cast-iron pot full of stew bubbled on the hearth. It was nearly noon and George, her husband, would soon be home for his midday meal. 'It's just a cough, that's all. It will go away. Some fine weather this summer would help, but I suppose that is too much to ask for.'

Fine weather in this part of London usually brought a blanket of smoke and foul air from the river, which would hardly help a woman suffering from a persistent cough. Grace watched her sister for a while. They did not look much alike. Grace was small and neat with a round, serious face, while Rosa was tall and fair. The difference wasn't particularly surprising, as the two weren't related by blood. Grace had been adopted at birth, taken in by Rosa's parents after her birth mother – a dear friend of the couple – had died in childbirth. That fact that Grace was adopted did not matter. Rosa was her sister, her family, and Grace would do anything for her.

'How is George?' she asked.

Rosa smiled. 'You know George. Always the same. He never changes.'

Yes, thought Grace, *and that is part of the problem*. She was very fond of George Turneur, her brother-in-law, but she was under no illusions about him. He had kindness bred in the bone, but although he had steady work as a bricklayer, money never seemed to stay long in his pockets. His salary should have been enough to sustain the family, but George was forever lending money to someone. Before she married George, Rosa had been a fine seamstress, one of the best in London. Her ambition as a young woman was to save money and start her own business, but then she had met George and realised their lives lay together. But she still worked part-time from home, making and mending clothes for the well-to-do, and it was largely her income that enabled the family to put food on the table.

Rosa picked up a bowl of potatoes and a knife and sat down at the wooden table. 'Let me help you,' Grace said. She took off her coat and laid it on a bench, rummaged around for another knife and then sat opposite her sister and began to peel potatoes. They worked in silence for a while, and she could see her sister struggling not to cough. She saw too the old red mark on Rosa's arm – the scar from the boiling water – half-covered by the sleeve of her blouse, and once again the memories swirled around her.

Rosa laid down her knife and leaned over and took Grace's hand. 'It is wonderful to see you,' she said smiling, her voice warm with love. 'You do look so elegant and fine. How I wish Aunt Edith could be here to see you.'

They smiled at each other. 'Never mind me,' Grace said firmly. 'Tell me about yourself. Tell me every little thing that has happened since I was last here.'

So they gossiped about the area and its people, who had married and who had produced children and who had died, who had fallen out with whom and who the vicar's wife had offended this month, what new buildings had been built, and the activities of the gangs. 'It really is becoming quite dreadful,' Rosa said. She coughed again. 'Most distressing of all is a group of girls, some of them only eight or nine. They call themselves the Angels. They're orphans, or if they do have homes, no one knows where. They live in the rough lands over by the railway line, and spend their days stealing or getting into knife fights with other gangs. Lord knows what will happen to the poor little mites.'

She glanced at her own daughter, sucking earnestly on a sweet. 'Every time I see them I think about my little Daisy, and how horrible it would be if she ended up on the streets like that. It breaks my heart to think about it.'

George Turneur came home an hour later to find them still talking. A gentle, softly spoken man, clothes red with brick dust and hands grimy with mortar, he gave Grace a brotherly kiss on the cheek and then knelt down to hug the children. Albert climbed onto his back while he tickled Daisy and Harry until they both shrieked with laughter. Even when he sat down at the table the twins continued to clamber over him, laughing and giggling until Rosa shooed them away to take their seats. She dished up stew and bread, serving George first, and then the children, who held out their bowls one by one, and finally Grace and herself. She ate very little, Grace saw, not enough.

They talked again about the gangs. 'It's getting quite bad,' said George. 'It's not just street urchins, not anymore. There's one really bad lot, called the Bull Head Gang. They started out up around Bull Head Dock, but they're all over the place now.'

'What do they do?' asked Grace.

George spread his hands. 'You name it. Thieving from the docks and warehouses, robbery, arson. They've started asking for protection money, too, from shops and businesses. The firm I work for pays them off. I heard the foreman say as much, just the other day.'

'Can't the police stop them?' Grace asked.

'Can't, or won't,' said George. 'The fellow what runs this gang, he's bad and dangerous. No one wants to run foul of him, not even the coppers.'

'Who is he?'

George shrugged. 'Calls himself the Captain. No one knows his real name.'

He mopped the last of the stew from his bowl with the heel of a loaf of bread, then leaned over and kissed his wife. 'Be good, you little rascals,' he told the children, ruffling their hair, and then kissed Grace on the cheek again. 'I'm off back to work. Good to see you, lass. Come again soon. Rosa misses you.'

'I know,' said Grace.

The door closed behind George. Grace helped Rosa clear the table and wash up while the children went into the next room to play, and then Rosa made tea and poured it into two chipped cups. 'I'm afraid there's no sugar,' she said.

'It doesn't matter,' said Grace.

They sat and sipped their tea. Rosa coughed again. 'I'm worried about you,' Grace said. 'I think you should see a doctor.'

'Dear, you know we can't afford it.'

'I could find a doctor for you.' Mr Clare's company provided free medical care to its staff and their families; perhaps one of the works doctors or nurses could be persuaded to see Rosa.

Her sister patted her hand. 'That's very sweet of you, Gracie, but I really don't need a doctor. I'm telling you, it's just a cough. All we need is a good warm summer and I'll be right as rain.'

Silence fell again. Rosa watched her. 'There's something you want to tell me,' she said. 'Isn't there?'

'Yes,' said Grace after a moment.

'What is it? A man?'

Grace thought briefly about Walter Ringrose and smiled, but said, 'No. Not a man. It is a job.'

She told Rosa about Lady Ringrose's offer, and her sister's eyes opened wide. 'Are you going to take it?' she asked.

'I don't know yet.'

'Oh, don't be silly, Gracie, you *must*! Don't you see? This is your chance to spread your wings! No more Rotherhithe mud for you, my dear. You'll have the entire world at your feet.'

'But I would be so far away,' said Grace.

'Oh, nonsense. Sevenoaks is only half an hour from London Bridge by train. You can come back and forth whenever you like.'

'I still don't know,' said Grace.

'Well, I for one will be very cross if you don't go. You might never get another chance like this. When would you start?'

'The end of September.' The secretary of the new school had sent a letter, confirming Lady Ringrose's offer and giving details, including the salary which was far more than she earned with the Clares.

Rosa took her hand again. 'I am so happy for you,' she said, and her eyes were shining now. 'I think it is wonderful, Gracie. It's nothing less than you deserve, you know.'

Rosa is right, Grace thought later, riding on the train back to London Bridge. *I should take the job. I am still not certain where it will lead me, or what I want to do with my life, but this is the chance to make a new start. I love the Clares and I always will. But it is time I stood on my own two feet.*

That evening she sat down at her writing desk and wrote a reply to the secretary, accepting the offer of the post. But even as she dusted the letter with sand she remembered Rosa coughing, and heard again her voice on that day long ago.

I will always be with you, Gracie. Remember it's me and you together, for always.

Chapter 2

Returning to her home in Hackney after visiting Rosa, Grace was unable to stop worrying about her sister. It was not just the cough, but the lack of appetite. Both, she knew, could be symptoms of consumption. But there was nothing she could do for the moment. Her duties at the Clare School kept her busier than ever, and she loyally supported Mela and Mrs Clare as they threw themselves into campaigning for Mr Forster's Education Bill. It was three weeks before she could escape and visit the house on Bell Lane again.

When she next saw her sister in early July, she was horrified. Rosa had stopped eating almost entirely and had wasted away to nothing, skin stretched tight over her bones. Her face was like a death mask, and she was coughing up blood.

Racing back to Hackney, Grace had sought out Mr Clare and begged him to let the works physician see her sister. Mr Clare had agreed at once and sent the doctor down to Rotherhithe that very afternoon. After a brief examination of the sick woman lying in her bed, the doctor had beckoned to Grace and they went downstairs to the parlour.

'Is it consumption?' Grace asked directly.

The doctor nodded. 'I am afraid so. And what is more, the disease is very advanced.'

Grace stared at him. 'How can that be, sir? She has only had the cough for a few months.'

'She has been ill for much longer than that,' the doctor said. 'She has been concealing the signs from you, and from her husband and children.'

'Can she be cured?'

The doctor shook his head. 'I am sorry, Miss Perrow. Your sister is beyond the help of medical science.'

Even though she was half expecting it, the shock was still numbing. 'Is there anything that can be done?'

'Make her comfortable,' the doctor said gently, 'and wait for the end.'

She wrote to Mr Clare, who responded by return of post, telling her to stay as long as she was needed. In the house on Bell Lane she cared for Rosa as best she could, trying to coax her to eat, changing her bedding when she soaked the sheets and blankets with sweat, wiping the blood from her lips. She looked after the family too; the children were silent and frightened, not really understanding what was going on, and George walked through each day like a man trapped in a nightmare, silent and dull-eyed. He adored Rosa, had done so since the day they met, and the prospect of losing her terrified him.

'I don't know what I will do without her,' he said once Rosa was asleep. They were talking in whispers so the children would not hear. 'She is everything to me.'

'You have to carry on,' Grace said. 'If nothing else, the children need you. You must go on, George.'

'I don't know how,' George said. There was a sob in his voice, and he was shaking like a man in a fever. Grace put her arms around him. 'I'll help you,' she said. 'I will do everything I can. I promise.'

Now, ten days since the doctor came, she sat watching the desperation in George's face as his wife slipped away from him. In the lamplight, Rosa's breath wheezed and bubbled as her ravaged lungs fought for air. Downstairs on the mantelpiece the clock ticked softly, the seconds counting down to the end. 'It won't be long now,' Grace said quietly.

Rosa reclined on the bed, propped on pillows and bolsters to help her breathe more easily. Her eyes were closed, her cheeks sunken, her skin waxy and pale. There was a little dribble of blood at the corner of her mouth. Grace reached out with a handkerchief and gently wiped it away. The July night was hot and humid, and the oil lamp made the air in the room hotter still, but Rosa's skin was cold to the touch.

George Turneur sat on the other side of the bed, staring at his dying wife. He clasped Rosa's hand tightly in both his own, as if he was somehow struggling with the forces that were taking her away from him, trying to drag her back into life. Like Rosa herself, he was losing the battle.

Grace was surprised at how calm she was herself in the presence of death. She had already had her time of grief, a shattering storm of tears when she realised that Rosa was about to die. But Rosa *would* die, and no power on earth could prevent it. She had to come to terms with this, and quickly. It was Grace's duty now to care for the others and be strong for them. When the end came, George and the children would need her strength. And so she had wiped her eyes and squared her shoulders, and taken the advice she had given George; she had carried on.

Rosa coughed again, her breath whining in her throat. Her eyes opened for a moment. George gripped her hand hard as she struggled to speak. 'Where are the children?' she whispered.

'Asleep in the other room,' George murmured. 'Do you want to see them, love?'

'No. Let them sleep. I don't . . . want them to see me . . . like this.' Rosa's voice was no more than a sigh. 'Gracie . . . Are you there?'

'I'm here,' said Grace, taking her other hand.

'Thank you,' the dying woman whispered. 'For everything. I don't know . . . what we would have done . . . without you.'

'You promised you would always be here,' Grace said softly. 'And I am here for you.'

Another cough, shallow and painful. Rosa closed her eyes again. Her breathing was calmer now, her pulse weak and fluttering. Her mouth moved a little, and Grace leaned forward to hear the ghostly whisper coming from her blood-stained lips. 'Love . . . you,' Rosa said.

Whether she was speaking to George, or to Grace, or to both of them could not be told. They sat in utter silence, watching her face and listening to her struggling for breath. An hour later, her breathing stopped. Her pulse flickered one last time, and then was still.

Quietly, George reached out a gentle hand and closed his wife's eyes. Then he sat for a moment, staring at the sunken face lying on the pillow. Grace waited for a few minutes, and then touched him softly on the sleeve. 'Come away,' she said. 'There is nothing more to be done.'

The strength seemed to have gone from George's limbs. Taking the oil lamp in one hand, Grace helped him rise and go down the narrow stair, leaning heavily on her. In the little parlour he sank into a chair and then sat immobile, staring at the wall. Her heart a solid mass of pain in her chest, Grace went into the kitchen. The cast-iron stove was still hot. Despite the summer heat she had kept the fire going, just in case Rosa should want anything. She made two cups of tea and carried them into the parlour. There they sat for a while without speaking.

'Will you tell the children?' Grace asked finally.

'Yes,' said George. His voice echoed the pain she felt. Rosa was gone. The sister who had looked after her, cared for her and loved her when everyone else who loved her had died, was gone. There was a hole in her heart, in her life, that could never be filled.

But she had been granted twenty-three years of Rosa's love. The children had been cut off just when they needed their mother most. In years to come, Daisy and Harry would barely remember her. That thought was the most painful of all.

Grace swallowed the lump in her throat. *I must not cry again*, she thought. Now more than ever, she needed to be strong. She looked across at George.

'The vicar must be told,' she said. 'The funeral will have to be soon.'

The summer heat made this a grim necessity. George said nothing, staring down at his hands. 'The vicar is also secretary of the burial fund, isn't he?' Grace said.

For a moment she was not certain he would answer. 'Yes,' George said finally.

Grace nodded. 'I'll go to him in the morning. I will make the arrangements. You look after the children.'

'Thank you.' George fell silent again, lost in his pain. They sat together in the lamplight, while outside the sorrowful night drew to an end and the shadows began to grow pale.

Dawn came with cruel brightness. The sun, shining red through the haze of smoke over the docks, reminded her of lost hope. George sat slumped in a chair in the parlour, asleep at last. The children were still sleeping upstairs. Grace waited until the clock struck eight and then, as quietly as possible, lifted the latch and let herself out into the hot, foetid morning.

Even at this hour, Lower Road was busy with traffic. Wagons loaded with bricks and timber rumbled past, kicking up dust. Clouds of sulphurous steam rose from the vitriol works near the Albion Dock, and more steam billowed from the wash house further down the street. Passing the parish workhouse Grace heard a hymn being sung, the usual morning service after breakfast, and she repressed a shudder as the memories crowded in again.

All Saints was a foursquare stone building topped with a spire, solid and lacking in grace. Its architect had been a noted designer of warehouses, and the church looked a little like a warehouse itself. The vicarage was a big, lumpen brick building next to the church, set well back from the road. A servant answered Grace's knock at the door. 'The reverend is at his breakfast, ma'am.'

'I will wait,' said Grace.

Fifteen minutes later the servant returned and ushered Grace into the vicar's study. The Reverend Elijah Hobbes, a white-bearded man in his fifties, sat behind his desk, hands clasped across his waistcoat. 'Miss Perrow, is it? Sit down.'

Grace sat, looking around a little enviously at the shelves full of books. 'How may I be of service?' the vicar asked.

'My sister died last night, sir. Mrs Turneur, of Bell Lane.' Saying it brought the lump back to her throat, and tears welled up behind her eyes. She fought down the rush of emotion as best she could.

'I am sorry to hear it,' the vicar said. 'Bell Lane. Turneur. Yes, George Turneur has an account with the parish burial fund. Let me see.'

He reached into his desk and pulled out a black ledger and opened it, leafing through the pages until he found the one he wanted. Frowning, he ran his finger along the page and then looked up.

'The account is in arrears,' he said. 'Mr Turneur is behind on his payments.'

Oh, George, Grace thought in despair. The contribution to the burial fund – an insurance scheme that provided money to cover a family's funeral expenses – was only a few pence a week. 'How much in arrears, sir?' she asked.

'Four shillings and tuppence,' said the vicar. 'A considerable sum.' His frown deepened. 'How did this come to pass?'

'Mr Turneur is not very good with money, sir,' said Grace.

'I see. What does he spend it on? Drink?'

'No, sir. He . . . He is a man of gentle nature. Others take advantage of him.'

'He allows himself to be gulled, you mean. Very well. You may have the money, but I shall deduct the arrears from the amount I pay out to you.' The vicar looked at her sharply. 'That is only fair, don't you think?'

'Yes, sir.' She would make up the difference out of her own pocket. The vicar opened another drawer in his desk and took out a small iron-bound strongbox and unlocked it. He counted out a small sum of money onto the desk and then, very ostentatiously, took back the four shillings and tuppence and returned the coins to the strongbox.

'Warn Mr Turneur to keep his accounts more carefully in future,' he said. 'You may inform Mr Jevons the undertaker that I will conduct the service at twelve noon. Tell him to be punctual. If the arrangements are not complete, I shall not wait. I am a busy man.'

Putting the money into her reticule, Grace rose to her feet. 'Thank you, sir. I shall be sure to tell him.'

As she departed the vicarage Grace glanced into the churchyard behind All Saints. A flicker of motion caught her eye. Four children, barefoot girls in tattered smocks or shifts, were crouched down beside one of the larger tombs, tearing a loaf of bread to pieces and stuffing it into their mouths. A small boy knelt beside one of the girls, holding her hand, and every now and then she turned to feed him as well.

She saw too that all four girls had knives at their waists. One of them turned her head, and saw Grace. She whistled like a bird, and in a second they had snatched up the remainder of the bread and were running out of the churchyard, taking the little boy with them.

Grace watched them go. She remembered what Rosa had said about the gang, the Angels, and wondered if these girls were part of it. The knives in particular frightened her. Repressing another shudder, she walked on.

∾

The moment I saw her watching us, I thought, we have to run. I didn't know who she was, or why she was watching, but I thought she meant danger. She might tell someone she had seen us, and then we'd all get put back in the workhouse. I'd been there once, and I wasn't never going back, not me nor my little brother, neither. We ran out into the marshes where no one would follow us and waited all day, hiding.

I kept wondering who she was. I didn't recognise her from round these parts. And why was she staring at us like that? I didn't like it, not at all. I touched my knife. If she comes near us again, I thought, I'll stick her. That'll teach her.

∞

The offices of Mr Jevons the undertaker were in Jamaica Road. Mr Jevons himself did not look much like an undertaker. He was short and jolly, and wore a flowered waistcoat with bright brass buttons that strained over his rotund belly. 'Hot today, isn't it, miss?' he said, wiping his forehead with a blue handkerchief. 'Don't you worry, we'll have everything arranged. I'll send Mrs Pegler around now to lay out the body, and I will bring the coffin later. I can let you have our best hearse today, but I'm afraid there's only the one horse. Do you want the black ostrich feathers? It's three shillings extra for the hire.'

'Yes, sir,' said Grace. She would pay for these out of her own pocket too. There must be no pauper's funeral for Rosa. She would have the same dignity in death that she had in life. 'Where might I find the gravedigger?'

'Harry and his mates are probably in the White Swan right now. You don't want to go in there, miss, it's no place for a lady. I'll find Harry for you. His fee is two shillings. Leave it with me, and I'll pass it on.'

A few hours later, everything was done. The physician from the workhouse, the nearest doctor, had come to the house and examined the deceased and written out a death certificate. A black ribbon hung from the door knocker, and she had purchased black armbands for herself and George. The hearse stood waiting in the lane, the horse shuffling in its black-plumed harness. Rosa had been dressed in her best gown and laid out in the coffin, pale wood with brass mounts, and was resting now in the parlour. In daylight, her face looked less sunken and haggard than it had last night. She was at peace.

People came and went, neighbours and friends coming in to view the body and speak softly to George. He barely noticed them, but he looked up when Grace fastened the black band around his arm. 'Thank you,' he said.

'Are you all right, George?'

Mute with grief, he shook his head. 'Where are the children?' Grace asked.

'In the kitchen. I thought it best to keep them out of the way.'

Exhausted and sleepless, Grace went into the kitchen and found the children sitting at the table, looking frightened. She kissed them all. 'Have you eaten?'

'No,' said Albert. His lower lip was trembling, and he was doing his best not to cry.

There was bread and cheese in the larder. The bread was a little stale and she had to pare mould off the cheese, but she managed to lay out some food for the children. Unable to contemplate the thought of eating herself, she made a cup of tea.

'Why is Mummy sleeping?' asked Daisy. Her little face was anxious, her blue eyes clouded with puzzlement.

Her heart aching, Grace kissed the child again. 'She's not sleeping, my sweet. She has gone away.'

'But she is here,' said Harry, equally puzzled. 'She's in the other room, with Daddy.'

Oh, lord, Grace thought in despair, how do you explain death to a five-year-old? She wondered what George had told them. 'Her spirit has gone away,' she said gently. 'In a little while, they will take the rest of her away too. They will lay her in the churchyard.'

'Why?' asked Harry.

'So she can be near to God,' Grace said. 'That is where her spirit has gone. To be with God.'

'But why does God want to take Mummy?' Harry asked.

To that, she could make no answer.

She was just finishing her tea when the clock in the parlour struck noon. In the distance she could hear the tolling of church bells. Someone knocked on the front door, hard and peremptory. George opened it, and she heard the vicar's voice.

'Come along, my sweets,' she said. She ushered the children upstairs to their room, then took a deep breath and walked back downstairs.

The funeral took place in the parlour, a dozen people crowded into the little room around the coffin with more in the lane outside listening through the window, while the vicar read the service in a deep, sonorous voice. Afterwards Mr Jevons and his assistants carried the coffin to the hearse and loaded it aboard, and then the procession set off towards the church, the hearse leading the way, the vicar and George and Grace walking behind with a few of the neighbours following. In the street, people turned and bowed or curtseyed as the hearse passed, the men removing their hats, and then stood and watched as the procession moved down the street.

At the graveside in All Saints churchyard there was a short service of committal. Grace did not really hear what the vicar said. She stood, gripping George's hand tightly and watching as the coffin was lowered into the newly-dug grave. Moving forward, she knelt and picked up a handful of soft earth and sprinkled it gently onto the coffin. A fresh wave of grief and shock washed over her, and she rose and turned away. She felt George's arm around her shoulders, comforting her, but nothing could hold back the tears. Standing in the hazy sunlight she wept for the end of joy, for the end of a love she had thought would never end.

Grace remained at Bell Lane for another two days. She wrote to Mela, telling her what had happened, and received a letter in reply so full of love and sympathy that Grace started to weep again. Mela asked if she could come and help, but Grace wrote back to say no, she could manage.

She packed away Rosa's clothes, and then cleaned and aired the house thoroughly to get rid of any last lingering trace of illness. Leaving the twins with Mrs Berton, one of the neighbours, she took Albert with her to the market and bought bread and potatoes, salt fish and beans and cheese, good nourishing food that would keep even in the heat. Back at Bell Lane she cleaned the kitchen and polished the pots and pans until they shone.

Apart from the visit to the market, all three children stayed close by her. Daisy and Harry were always playing around her feet, and several times she nearly tripped over them, but she had no heart to scold them. Albert offered to help her when he could, but otherwise sat quietly and watched her work, saying very little. The twins, she saw, were already beginning to forget, but poor little Albert was suffering.

'He is taking the loss very ill,' she said to George on the second evening, when he returned home from work. He had gone back to his job the day after the funeral, his employers having allowed him only a single day off. Now they were in the kitchen, she preparing supper and he washing the dust from his face and hands. 'You must be careful of him. Comfort him, and give him plenty of love. He needs it.'

'I know.' George was still hollow-eyed with grief himself, struggling to come to terms with his loss. Grace watched him sit down at the table, a mug of tea in his hand. 'I can stay a few more days,' she said. 'No one will mind.'

George looked up at her and smiled his kind smile. 'We can manage,' he said. 'You must go, love. You have work to do. Rosa told me about your new job.'

'I have made lists of what needs to be done,' Grace said. 'Mrs Berton and the other neighbours will keep an eye out for the children, and help them if they get into distress, but you must take care of them and make sure they are safe and well fed. You will need to feed them in the morning before you go to work, and again at midday as well as their evening meal. I have left some recipes for you to follow.'

She handed George a sheaf of papers. He peered at them doubtfully, and Grace felt a twinge of misgiving.

'Rebecca will come in once a week to do laundry,' she said. Rebecca was Mrs Berton's daughter, an industrious girl of about twelve. Grace was paying her a couple of shillings a week from her own purse. 'I will come again as soon as I can.'

The school holidays were about to begin, and the Clares were going as they did every year to the seaside in East Anglia. Grace had volunteered to run a nursery at the

Clare School so she could stay in London to spend time with the children. Her job in Sevenoaks would not start until September.

'Thank you.' George looked down at his tea for a moment, embarrassed by his poverty, and then looked up again. 'You must not worry for us,' he said quietly. 'We will get by.'

Grace watched him for a while longer. Her misgivings grew stronger. 'The landlord's agent called today,' she said. 'The rent was in arrears. Did you know?'

The embarrassment deepened. 'Rosa looked after that side of things,' George said. 'How much do we owe?'

'Nothing, now. I paid him. But George, you must learn to keep accounts, and make budgets and stick to them. There is the rent, and food, and the coal merchant to be paid, and of course there is the burial fund to be kept up. You must not allow yourself to fall into debt.'

'I will try,' said George. 'The truth is, I'm not very good with numbers.' She started to speak and he held up a hand. 'But I will do my best. I will care for the children and make sure they have a good home. I'll do it for them, and I'll do it for Rosa, too. I won't let her down.'

She wanted to believe him. She was deeply fond of George; there was no kinder or gentler man in the world. But it was no secret that Rosa had been the strong one in the family, and without her as his prop and mainstay, George might well begin to crumble.

In the morning she departed. George had already gone to work. The twins clung to her, one to each leg, and Albert's lower lip trembled once more. She kissed them all, holding them close while her heart ached for them. 'Be good, little ones,' she said, caressing their hair. 'Do as your daddy tells you, and be kind to him, and each other.'

'We shall,' said Albert.

'I will see you soon,' she said. She kissed them again and turned away to the door. Outside, she walked towards the railway station, surrounded by the clopping of horses' hooves and the rumble of wagon wheels, the shouts of workmen and the clack of machinery from nearby factories, the air full of coal smoke and steam with the sun shining through a dull orange haze, and she felt the tears on her face once more.

She knew what she was going towards. But she also knew, painfully, what she was leaving behind.

Chapter 3

In August the Clares departed for the seaside as planned, and Grace remained behind in Hackney, alone in the house with a single servant for company. She spent as much time as possible with her niece and nephews, travelling each day by train to Rotherhithe, going against the tide of workers less fortunate than her who flooded in from the newly burgeoning suburbs to the south-east to work in the hot, quickly expanding city. Sometimes on fine days she and the children went further on the train, up to Greenwich Park where the air was cleaner and clearer and occasional breezes blew through the trees.

In the park, the children ran about like young lambs in fresh pasture. Their usual playground was a muddy street or a tiny yard at the back of their Rotherhithe house, and the green grass was a novelty for them. Here they could really be children and Grace took great delight in throwing balls and playing hide and seek with them. Together on such days they could, for a short time, forget the tragedy that was the loss of their mother.

'Look, look, Auntie Grace, I can come down this big hill so fast,' cried Albert as he rolled over and over down the steep incline from the top of the park, up near the observatory. Grace watched in some alarm at first, thinking that the younger twins would want to follow where their older brother led, but they both clung to her as they watched Albert whizz down the hill and then race back up again until he got tired halfway to the top.

'I think Albert is very brave, Auntie Grace,' said Daisy. 'This hill is so very high. I would be scared to go down it so fast.'

Harry said, 'I'm not scared to go down it, but I don't want to climb back up.'

'That is a sign that you are still too young to try rolling down,' said Grace. 'I should wait until you don't think it is such a great climb back up.'

'I think they should have a train to bring you back up,' said Harry.

'I think even a big steam engine would have trouble climbing that hill,' responded his aunt, 'but engines are doing such magic new things all the time that maybe one day they will make an engine that can. Would you like to make such an engine, Harry?'

'I want to make an engine that can fly,' replied Harry, and they all laughed as they imagined what a flying steam engine would look like.

'I think that being up on this hill is a bit like flying in the air,' said Daisy.

Grace smiled at the little girl. 'I think you are right, sweetheart. If you go to the brow of the hill and look out over the city, you can see it as if from the air.'

They walked slowly up to the summit of the hill. 'Hold on to your hats, children, it is rather windy,' she told them. 'But at least the wind has cleared the dust and smoke from the air, and that means we can see a long way. See how many church towers you can count?' Rosa, when she was well, had been teaching the children to count and read, Grace knew, but she was not certain how much they remembered.

'You can see everything from up here, Auntie Grace,' said Harry. 'You can see the whole world from up here, can't you?'

'Well, maybe not the whole world, Harry, but you can see all of London. Look, there is the tower of All Saints church near your house. And you can see all the docks, too. there is the new dock that your father is working so hard on.'

'Fa comes home late and very tired from work,' said Albert, running over to join them. 'Mrs Berton says he works too hard because he misses Mum. Do you think that is true, Auntie Grace?'

'I think he works so hard to make a good life for you all,' said Grace, 'but I know that he misses your mother very much, as do we all.'

The little group stood for a few minutes looking out over London, each wrapped in their own memories of Rosa. The twins moved closer to Grace and Albert reached out and took her hand.

51

'Is Mummy really never coming back?' asked Daisy. 'Some mothers go away, and then come back. Maybe our mummy will come back too.'

Grace hated to spoil her young niece's hopes, but knew what she had to say. 'Your mummy has had to go to be with God and he needs her to stay with him, so she won't be coming back to us. She was so very sad to leave you all, but she will be waiting with God in heaven for you and she is looking down on you from heaven too.'

'I think God is mean to keep Mummy,' said Harry. 'I said so to Mrs Rev'rend at Sunday school and she was very angry with me and said I was wicked to say such things.'

'You really shouldn't say such things in Sunday school, Harry,' said Grace seriously, 'Mrs Reverend will think you have been brought up a heathen.'

'What is a heathen?' asked Albert.

'Someone who does not believe in God, Albert, and you know that your mother would want you to love God. She believed he was a kind and gentle God and would want you to think so too.'

'Mrs Rev'rend makes God sound scary rather than kind,' said Harry. 'She is always talking about how he will punish us if we don't behave.'

Grace hugged the youngsters close to her. 'Well, I prefer your mother's kind of God to Mrs Reverend's, don't you? But don't tell Mrs Reverend I said so, if you please.'

In later years, Grace would remember those three weeks she spent with the children as a gift. The four of them explored the Tower of London, and St Paul's cathedral and climbed the many steps of the Monument to get a different view of London. Grace regaled them with stories of Old London that she had learned from history books, and they tried to imagine the city below them as it would have been after the Great Fire two hundred years before. 'How could fire have destroyed such a huge area?' Harry had asked, and Grace explained how the fire had started. Albert said it was a lesson to be very careful with the kitchen fire at home.

On Sundays, after church and Sunday school, George joined them on their rambles. On those days he dropped his worries and his sense of fun was partly restored by his children. Grace saw once more the gentle, kind and often funny man that her sister had fallen in love with and married. She wondered if she would ever find a man to love, as Rosa had loved George. She hoped so. Unlike Mela, she wanted one day to fall in love and be married, and she had high expectations of what married life would bring her.

These Sunday outings with George and the family were happy, but they were also tinged with an inevitable sadness as they all felt the absence of Rosa. Often, though, they sensed that Rosa's spirit was with them, especially when Grace and George spent hours talking about her. Grace told some simple stories of the happy days before she and Rosa were in the workhouse. She also talked to them about their aunt Edith and how she had plucked them from the workhouse and made a happy home for them. She wanted the children to know about their grandparents and their aunt, not only for the children's sake but so that she could keep their memories alive in her own life. Telling Albert, Daisy and Harry about them meant she had others to help keep their spirits alive now that Rosa and Edith were gone.

She and George also told the children about Rosa and her work as a seamstress working in a garment factory making uniforms. Rosa, as she had wished, had become able to earn her own living and was trusted by her employers with 'specials', making one-off uniforms for senior army and navy officers and sometimes even for Queen Victoria and her daughters when they wanted to dress for military occasions.

All of this was new to the children, who did not know about Rosa's working life before her marriage to their father. To them she was Mummy, so clever with her needle and scissors that people came to ask her to make things for them. Their eyes opened wide when Grace and their father told them how their mother used to go to Buckingham Palace to fit her feminine uniforms. The Queen and her court liked them to look as real as the men's uniforms and hence they wanted to use the same cloth and buttons and decorations. Rose 'uniforms' were very popular. Her talent for making feminine versions of regimentals brought her acclaim in her firm, and some special presents from the Queen and members of her family.

'How did Mummy meet Fa?' asked Daisy. 'Were you at Buckingham Palace too?'

'Were you a soldier?' asked Albert. 'You never said you were a soldier. Were you, Fa?'

'No, no,' chuckled George. 'I've always been a bricklayer, lad, and I've never been out of work what with all the building going on in London. I met my Rosa while we were building a new part of the uniform factory. She was always shooing me out of her workshop, saying I made her fabrics dusty. She kept me in line even then,' he said smiling.

'But what were you doing in her workshop, Fa?' Albert asked.

'Well, part of the new building had a door into the corner of her work-room. So we had to go in there in order to knock through and build the door. My mate Bert asked Rosa out several times, but she weren't interested in him. Goodness only knows why, but she took a shine to me.'

'I know, why, I know why, Fa,' said Harry. 'It's because you told the best jokes.'

They all laughed at this for George was very fond of telling silly jokes and playing gentle tricks on the children. His love of fun had indeed been one of the things that had attracted Rosa, Grace knew. It had reminded Rosa of her own late father who had been a great joker. Physically, Grace knew that her brother-in-law had little in common with Fred Perrow who had been a big bluff man with reddish hair. His size and the hair was all the impression that she retained of her father.

Grace was glad to see George recover a bit of his old self on these outings, but she was much more concerned about how he was coping on a day-to-day basis. Rosa had kept their little house spotlessly clean, partly so that she could continue to work at sewing and bring income into the household, and partly as a matter of pride. She and George might have lived in a poor area, but Rosa had been determined that their home would always be a haven from the mucky world outside. And so it had remained until her illness made keeping the house to her own high standards, even with the willing help of the children, no longer possible.

Thus, those three weeks were not solely a time for fun, frolics and exploration. Grace also spent several days bringing the little house in Bell Lane back up to the standard of order and cleanliness that Rosa had maintained when she was healthy.

The children helped. Albert took on the task of keeping the tiny cooking space clean and tidy. He was very keen to learn how to make food for the family. 'But I like to feed people,' he said when Grace expressed surprise at his keenness to help her shop and cook. He didn't even mind cleaning up, saying, 'I like to see it all clean, just like Mother kept it.'

Harry was more of a dreamer and would often be found part way through a task such as making the beds, sitting and humming a tune to himself. He was always sorry that he hadn't finished his job and would hurry to complete it once he was found. He was just not always connected to the world around him and the other people in it. He clearly had a vivid daydream world.

Daisy was a miniature version of her mother and always keen to be busy doing the best that her little hands could manage. She followed Grace like an enthusiastic puppy and copied all that she did. Grace knew that she was too young to keep the house clean on her own but hoped that she, along with her brothers, would keep it in some semblance of order once she moved to Sevenoaks

Some of Grace's time was also spent in making George a budget that he could follow. She listed what she knew of the family's expenses against George's income. His pay was just enough to cover the basics, and with what Grace could send from her own new salary they would be able to get by comfortably. George protested at her spending her money on his family. 'But you will have all sorts of new expenses yourself. New clothes, books and all manner of things.'

'Nonsense, George,' said Grace. 'We are all in this together.'

'Well, you mustn't spend all your free time coming up to Rotherhithe,' George said. 'You'll make new friends down in Sevenoaks, and you'll want to spend time with them. You mustn't worry about us, we'll be just fine. Albert is a real little man by now and won't let any harm come to the twins, and Mrs Berton from next door will see them at lunchtime.'

'They should be at school,' said Grace. 'Is there nowhere that they could go? I know Rosa taught Albert his letters and numbers, and I have given him some books to keep up his reading, but they should be in regular school. I only wish they were close enough to go to the Clare School. I know Mrs Clare would be happy to have them,'

'There's no school closer than Lambeth,' George said. 'I reckon they're too young to get there by themselves, and I can't leave work to take them. None of the other local children go either.'

'Sometimes I think that it would be better for me to stay here in Rotherhithe and start a free school myself,' Grace said, 'rather than swanning off to Kent to teach young ladies.' She sighed. 'But goodness only knows where the money to do that would come from.'

'Rosa would never have wanted you to live here in Rotherhithe, Grace. You know she always had bigger plans for your future and you always did too. Don't worry. We'll do just fine here, you'll see.'

'I'm sure you will,' said Grace. 'Just don't let your employers and your foreman take advantage of you. They would work you all hours until you dropped down, if they could. And, I am sure you know this, but you need to keep a close eye on the money and don't go lending out to friends like I know you have in the past. You are a soft touch, George. The rent and food and clothes are more important than doing favours for friends, especially when they seldom pay you back.'

'Yes, yes, I know,' replied George. 'Rosa was always saying the same.'

Grace said a silent prayer that her brother-in-law would listen to the voice of his dead wife and not let himself be taken advantage of. She had no real choice but to trust his word. She left the little house clean and tidy, just as Rosa would have liked, hugged the children hard, and took her leave.

At home in Hackney at the end of these three bittersweet weeks, Grace began to pack up her belongings. Her new life beckoned to her, and she looked forward to it, but her heart and mind continued to be with George and the children. She would miss the children terribly and visits would perforce be less frequent. She had written to the new headmistress to ask for permission to spend one Saturday and one Sunday per month out of school, but she had not yet had a reply.

The Clares returned from the seaside, and Grace prepared to say goodbye to them. Mrs Clare passed on books and some excellent advice and reminded her to write and ask for more if she needed it. Grace had a great respect for the knowledge and advice of Mrs Clare and knew she would find it helpful in her new role. Mela helped her pack, and then walked with her to the railway station.

'Goodbye, my dear friend,' she said, embracing Grace on the platform. 'Be sure to write to me often, and tell me all your news. Nothing will be the same without you here.'

'I will,' Grace promised. 'I wish you could come as well. I shall miss you terribly.'

Excitement was her predominant emotion when she climbed onto the train to take her to Sevenoaks. A new adventure awaited and her mind was a whirl of plans for her new life and questions about how she would get on. But she knew that a little part of her heart had been left behind with George and the children in Bell Lane.

Chapter 4

The headmistress in Sevenoaks was grudging, but she accepted Grace's need to keep in touch with her family so gave her the time away from school that she asked for. In late September, three weeks after taking up her post, Grace travelled back by train to Rotherhithe and walked through the muddy streets to Bell Lane.

It was Saturday and George was at work, but the children greeted her with shrieks of delight. Grace kissed them and surveyed them critically. They looked clean and well fed and the house was in good order; not quite as immaculate as when she left it, but still very clean. 'And what have you been doing with yourselves?' she asked. 'Albert, have you been reading the books I left you?'

Albert nodded vigorously. 'And you,' Grace said, ruffling Harry's hair. 'Have you been a good boy?'

'I have been making up songs,' declared Harry.

'He sings them all day,' said Daisy. 'Over and over. They don't make any sense.'

'They make sense to me,' Harry asserted.

'I'm sure they do,' said Grace laughing. 'Come, your father will be home soon. It is time to start dinner, and you can all help me.'

George came in an hour later, covered in brick dust as always, and kissed her on the cheek before going out back to wash up. 'You must tell us all about your new school,' he said, and so over dinner Grace described her new life, the grumpy headmistress and the other teachers, the big brick schoolhouse and her pupils, the daughters of bankers and solicitors and prosperous farmers. She struggled to describe Sevenoaks, so different from Rotherhithe that sometimes she thought it might as well be a different world.

All seemed well, and she left the next day to travel back to Sevenoaks reassured that the family were getting on well. But her next visit in October was not so comforting. The children were in foul moods; the twins had been quarrelling, and Harry had torn the pages of one of Albert's books. 'They have nothing to do,' Grace told George that evening. 'Rosa always kept them occupied, but when they're home on their own they grow bored, and that's when they cause mischief. Oh, how I wish we could get them into a school.'

But there was nothing to be done. There was no school in Rotherhithe, and even if there had been, there was no money to pay the fees. Grace was being well paid, but even her salary would not stretch that far.

Worse was to come. On the next visit Grace found Albert walking around the house barefoot, his feet covered in mud. 'What are you doing?' she scolded him. 'Where are your shoes?'

'Please don't be cross, Auntie Grace,' Albert said piteously. 'My feet are too big now to go in my shoes, and I don't have any others.'

'Your father was supposed to buy you shoes,' Grace replied.

'Fa says there isn't any money,' Albert mumbled.

That evening Grace said nothing until the children went to bed, but then she took George into the parlour room of the little house and sat down facing him. He hung his head, knowing what was coming.

'What happened to the money for Albert's shoes?' she asked. 'I made sure there was enough in the budget to afford them.'

'I don't know, lass. The money just seems to disappear. It's like trying to hold water in a sieve. It don't matter how fast I make money, it just drains away.'

'Have you been lending money to your mates again?' Grace demanded.

'I couldn't help it, lass. The poor fellow was in a piteous state. He couldn't pay his rent, and he and his kiddies were about to be evicted. So I lent him five bob to help him out.'

Five shillings was a quarter of George's weekly wage. 'You lent your friend money, and now your son has no shoes,' Grace said.

'Please don't be angry with me,' George pleaded. 'He said he would pay me back, and I believed him.'

'I know. You always believe people, because you want to see the best in them.' There was no point in getting angry, Grace thought. Nothing was going to change George's nature now, and anger would only hurt him. 'There's not much food in the larder either, and the coal bunker is nearly empty. And have you paid the rent?'

'I'm a little behind,' George admitted.

'I'll leave you some money before I go,' Grace said. 'George, you *must* look after your finances.'

'I try, lass. I really do.'

In her reticule, Grace had her first pay from her new school. She left money to pay their bills and buy Albert a new pair of shoes, and she travelled back to Sevenoaks the following day, full of misgivings. Three weeks later, just when she was planning another visit, a letter arrived in the evening post. The writing was childish and shaky, with many mistakes and misspellings.

Dear Auntie Grace
   Daddy asks me to write and say we have no munny and cannott pay the rent or by coale. Pleasse help us.
   Your loving nefew Albert

Grace gasped with horror. George was hopeless with money, but she had never dreamed things could get this bad. Without coal, the family would have no heat and could not cook their food, and if the rent could not be paid, they would be evicted. If they were made homeless they would have just two choices; the street, or the workhouse.

She knew she should be angry with George, but all she could feel was sorrow for him. For all his gentle nature, George was a proud man. He had never learned to read much, or to write at all. Asking his son to write that letter must have been one of the hardest things he had ever done, and was a measure of his despair.

She slept little that night. Instead, she lay on her bed gazing at the shadows on the ceiling and wondering what to do. She loved her new job, despite the grumpy head-mistress, and she did not want to leave. But it was clear, now, that despite the help and money she provided, George could not manage alone.

The decision was painful, but she knew she had no choice. In the morning after prayers and breakfast she knocked and entered the headmistress's study. 'Ma'am, I am sorry. But I fear I must hand in my notice. My family needs me, and I must go to them.'

'Your notice?' The headmistress stared at her over the rim of her spectacles. 'In the middle of term? It is out of the question. Who will replace you?'

'I am so sorry, ma'am,' Grace said. 'But my family needs me.'

'You are a talented teacher, Miss Perrow. Even though you have been here only a short time, the governors have already taken note of your qualities. If you stay here, you are certain to advance. A fine career awaits you. '

'I am sorry,' Grace said. 'But I have no choice.'

'Very well. You may go at the end of the week. Make sure you pack all your belongings, and do *not* expect a reference for your next employer.'

She wrote to Lady Ringrose, apologising for her decision and explaining her reasons, and received a very kind letter in return. She wrote to Mela, too, who wrote back at once.

My dear friend, are you certain? You know that whatever you do, I will always support you and be your friend. But my dear Grace, it is the friendship and love I have for you that compels me to tell you my true feelings. You have such talent, Grace, such energy and such zeal for teaching, and you are giving it up to look after your sister's children? Is that truly the right thing to do? I cannot believe that it is.

Mela's letter was written from the heart, and Grace took no offence. On one level, she knew Mela was right. The desire to teach was embedded deep in Grace's soul, and she knew she could not give it up entirely.

The nearest school was in Lambeth, George had said, too far away. Perhaps, thought Grace. But in the back of her mind, an idea slowly began to take form.

On Friday afternoon after lessons, Grace packed her bags and said farewell to her fellow teachers. Most thought she had taken leave of her senses, but a few understood. A carriage took her to the train and she rode up the line to Rotherhithe, arriving as dusk was falling. She hired a porter to bring her bags, and walked through the streets to Bell Lane. Smoke drifted heavy in the autumn air, and the stinks from the glue factory and the vitriol works were as strong as ever. Mud squelched under her feet.

Through the window she could see an oil lamp burning in the parlour. She knocked at the door and George opened the door in his shirtsleeves, eyes wide with surprise when he saw who it was. Grace drew a deep breath. 'You need me,' she said, 'so, I have come to stay.'

'I make one condition,' she said later that evening. 'I am in charge of paying all the household bills. When you receive your salary, George, you must bring it straight to me. There must be no more loans to your friends. Is that understood?'

'Yes,' said George humbly. 'Oh, Grace, I am so sorry. I didn't mean for things to work out like this.'

'Well, they have, and we shall make the best of them,' Grace said briskly. 'I am determined that good come out of this. I can start teaching the children, and maybe attract a few other pupils too. In the morning I shall go to market and stock the larder, and in the afternoon we can have some lessons.'

The children, who had come tumbling shrieking downstairs at the sound of their aunt's voice, were delighted by the idea of lessons. They were overjoyed to see her, and happy to assent to anything that would keep Auntie Grace with them. Looking at their shining faces, Grace was certain that she had done the right thing.

'We need to make some changes to sleeping arrangements,' she warned. There were only two bedrooms upstairs. 'Albert and Harry, you can go in with your father. Daisy, you and I shall share.'

'Goody,' said the little girl, clapping her hands with delight.

Grace looked at her severely. 'Do you snore?'

'No!' said Daisy indignantly.

'Hmm. Do you bite?'

'No!' squeaked the girl, beginning to giggle.

'Good. Mind you don't do either of those things, or there will be trouble.' She looked at George. 'It's all right,' she said. 'I am here. Everything will be fine now.'

Life at Bell Lane settled into a routine that Grace did not find unpleasant. George had clearly learned his lesson; he brought his pay home each Friday and counted it into her hand, and there was never a penny missing. His gratitude to her for lifting the burden of financial management from his shoulders was plain to see. And once she had control of their finances, she found that with George's wages and her own small savings they could comfortably get by.

She woke each morning early, lit the fire in the kitchen stove and made breakfast for the children and George before he went off to work. Most mornings she went to the market, sometimes taking the children with her; when the weather was bad she left them at home, and kindly Mrs Berton kept an eye on them. In the afternoons, she gathered the children in the parlour and gave them lessons, teaching the twins to read and setting Albert to doing sums.

Mrs Berton noticed this. 'I don't suppose you could teach my daughter?' she asked. 'Rebecca is twelve, and I've taught her a little, but I don't have much lettering myself.'

'I would be delighted,' said Grace. 'It would help to repay the many kindnesses you have done for the family.'

Word began to spread. Another neighbour, Brigit Doyle, had a brood of three, two young children and a boy called Billy, close to Albert's age. The two lads were friendly, and Billy began joining in the lessons.

In the market one day she saw a thin little girl, barefoot in a ragged dress, selling matches. On impulse she stopped and bought some. 'What is your name, child?'

The girl curtseyed. 'Lettice, ma'am.'

'Where do you live, Lettice?'

'In Jamaica Road, ma'am. In a loft above a stable.'

'In a loft . . . Do you not have a home?'

'No, ma'am.'

'Do you go to school?'

'No, ma'am.'

'Would you like to? I can teach you to read and write and do arithmetic, and then maybe one day you could get a job and you wouldn't have to sell matches anymore. Would you like that?'

The girl looked up at her, innocence beneath the layer of grime on her face and hope in her dark eyes. 'I'd like that very much, ma'am.'

'I live in Bell Lane,' said Grace, not entirely sure what she was doing or why she was doing it. 'The fourth house on the left. Come this afternoon and we will begin.'

She was not at all sure Lettice would come, and indeed they had been at their lessons for half an hour before there came a timid knock at the door. Grace opened it to find Lettice along with two boys, aged about eight and ten, barefoot like her and in ragged trousers with the knees worn through.

'These are Gabriel and Isaac,' said Lettice. 'They lost their parents too. They live in a shed in Cherry Gardens. May they come too?'

Grace smiled at them. 'You are all welcome,' she said.

'Honestly,' she said to George that evening, 'I don't know what came over me. I just saw them, and had to help them.'

George smiled. 'And you say I'm a soft touch. You can't walk past any waif or orphan without wanting to help.'

'I suppose that is true,' Grace admitted. 'But every time I see a child like this, I think of the workhouse. I don't want any child to have to endure that. I do want to help them, George, and teaching them is the only thing I can think of to do. It's all I know.'

'You talked once about starting your own school,' George said.

'I have thought of it, but I don't have the money.'

'Maybe the church would help,' George suggested. 'You could talk to Reverend Hobbes, the rector at All Saints.'

Grace agreed, though she had not been favourably impressed by Reverend Hobbes when arranging her sister's funeral. Nevertheless she called next morning at the rectory and a maidservant showed her into a parlour where the vicar and his wife – Mrs Rev'rend, as Harry had called her – sat drinking coffee. Mrs Hobbes had a lined, wrinkled face and a very short neck, and she reminded Grace of a turtle poking its head out of its shell. Another woman was with them, a tall, plainly dressed woman with a severe face. She and Mrs Hobbes both looked as if they disapproved of just about everything.

'Miss Perrow,' said the vicar. 'Yes, I remember you, of course. How may I be of service?'

'I wish to start a free school here in the parish,' said Grace. 'I am an experienced teacher, having taught for several years at the Clare School, and I would like to give lessons to the poor children of the district. I feel it important that they receive an education to give them a chance to better themselves in life—'

'Better themselves?' interrupted Mrs Hobbes, looking more like a turtle than ever. 'What is the use of that?'

Grace blinked. 'Even the poorest child has hopes and dreams, ma'am, but lack of education is holding them back. I want to remedy that. I understand the Church of England often supports free schools. Is there any chance that the parish would assist me now?'

'"Even the poorest child has hopes and dreams?"' repeated Mrs Hobbes, incredulous. She looked at the other

71

woman. 'My dear Mrs Lane, did you hear? What an utterly absurd notion.'

'There is no harm in education,' said Mrs Lane, looking more dour than ever.

'No harm in education?' said the rector. 'My dear Mrs Lane, you mean well, but I fear you are much mistaken. Education, in the wrong hands, is the very work of the devil. You might as well put poison in the hands of a child. There is no knowing what mischief they will get up to, wittingly or not. By educating the poor you are playing into the hands of those agents of Satan, the communists and anarchists and trades unionists and Methodists, all those wretches who are determined to pull the house down around our ears and reduce civil society to ashes. No, Mrs Lane; the ignorance of the poor is the only thing that stands between us and anarchy. The poor must be kept in their place.'

'Sir,' said Grace, 'I am shocked to hear you speak so.'

'Oh, she is shocked!' declared Mrs Hobbes. 'Goodness, Mrs Lane! Do you suppose she herself is one of these agitators? Come to preach about communism, or votes for women, or some such pernicious nonsense? Perhaps *that* is what she plans to teach at her school.'

'My aim is only to teach them to read and write, ma'am, but I can see that we shall not agree. I will detain you no further,' said Grace, and she curtseyed and marched out, fuming.

She was still seething when she returned home. Over lunch George tried to calm her.

'Don't fret, lass. He's not going to help you, so you'll have to go somewhere else.'

'That's not the point, George. He talks about keeping the poor ignorant, when he is one of the most ignorant men I know.'

By the time lessons began that afternoon she was calm once more and absorbed in the task of teaching the children. They had been working for perhaps an hour when someone knocked at the door. Frowning, Grace moved to answer it.

A boy stood in the street, looking at her. He was about ten, she reckoned, ragged and thin. His clothes were dirty, but his face and hands were clean. 'Pardon me, ma'am,' he said shyly. 'But are you the lady that is giving lessons?'

'Yes,' said Grace. 'I am Miss Perrow. What is your name?'

'Jimmy, ma'am, Jimmy Wilson.'

'And why have you come, Jimmy?'

'Begging your pardon, ma'am,' said Jimmy nervously. 'But I really want to learn. I want to read and write and study and do all them things. There's nothing I want more in the world, ma'am. I don't want to live in Rotherhithe. I want to go someplace else, but I heard tell that the only way you can get ahead in life is to study. Please teach me, ma'am. I'll work ever so hard, I promise.'

There was no mistaking the appeal in the boy's voice and eyes. Grace smiled. 'You wish to learn?' she said. 'Well, Jimmy, you have come to the right place. Come and join us.'

From the moment he walked into the room, Grace was glad she had accepted Jimmy. She had never had a pupil like him. He soaked up knowledge as a sponge soaked up water, and his enthusiasm for his lessons infected the others, even poor Lettice who was often too tired to concentrate properly.

But she could take no more pupils. Nine children plus herself could barely fit around the coal stove in the little parlour room. If she accepted any more, she would need more space. She was brooding on this on her way through the market one morning, when a sudden commotion interrupted her.

Up ahead was a butcher's stall, and out of nowhere a swarm of small figures erupted, climbing onto the stall shrieking like banshees and brandishing knives. To Grace's astonishment they were all girls, dirty and ragged with tangled hair, and she realised it was the group she had seen in the churchyard a few months ago, only this time there were more of them. Some waved their knives at the butcher and his assistant, who backed away hastily with their hands in the air, while others grabbed joints of meat and strings of sausages off the stall and then ran, haring away down the street. People were shouting, and in the distance Grace heard a police whistle. She stepped behind a wagon to get out of the way, but then came a sudden patter of running bare feet and a girl hurried around the end of the wagon, holding a little boy by one hand and clutching a shin of beef in the other. She had already started chewing on the meat, and there was blood and flecks of raw meat on her lips.

When she saw Grace she let go of the little boy's hand and drew a long, rusty but wickedly sharp knife from her belt and pointed it at Grace. Strangely, Grace felt no fear. She met the girl's eyes calmly, and was reminded suddenly of looking into the eyes of wild animals at the zoo; trapped, haunted, desperate.

The police whistle sounded again, closer. The girl, judging Grace to be no threat, thrust the knife back through her belt, grabbed the boy again and ran off, disappearing down a muddy lane still carrying the shin of beef. Deeply saddened by what she had seen, Grace turned towards home.

∽

I knew right away who she was. It was that nosy mort who'd watched us in the churchyard, back in the summer, after we'd nicked a loaf of bread. First meal we'd had in a day, too, and she came along and stared at us like we were animals. I didn't like that. I don't have parents or a home, but I've got dignity. Ask my knife, if you don't believe me.

She looked different this time. Proper square-rigged she'd been back then, dressed like a lady. Now she didn't look no different from anyone else. Her eyes were the same, though. I remembered them, all dark and serious. I pointed my sticker at her, but she didn't budge an inch. Just stood there, looking at my little brother and me.

I could have cut her, but I didn't see why I should. Apart from staring at me, she hadn't done me no wrong. So I grabbed

Joe's hand and we legged it. She didn't follow, and she didn't send the bluebottles after us, neither. I wondered why.

But never mind her. That was a good day. We lit a fire out in the fields where no one would follow us, not far from the railway, and we had our beef hot. Proper scran we had, first time in a long time. We filled our bellies, and then went out looking for trouble.

We found it, too, right where we hoped we would. There was a gang of little dollymops down in Deptford, who called themselves the Alloa Queens. They weren't queening by the time we'd done with them. Cut two of them, pushed the rest into the Surrey Canal, and sent them home crying to their mummies. They deserved it. They'd cut one of our girls a month back, and we'd been laying for them ever since. Nobody messes with the Angels.

It was a mild night for the time of year. We went back to Rotherhithe and slept out in the fields, in the open. It wouldn't be warm for much longer, though. Things aren't easy when it gets cold. I'd barely got little Joe through last winter. I wondered whether I could do it again.

Chapter 5

By coincidence, the vicar's sermon the following Sunday was based on a text from the Gospel of St Matthew, 'God blesses those who realise their need for him.' *Yes,* thought Grace, listening. *The Lord aids those who aid themselves. If the church will not help me found a school, I will help myself.*

She would not need much; desks and benches, chalks and slates, a few more books. She could acquire those. The main thing holding her back was space. She needed a room. Any room would do, anywhere, so long as it was large enough to accommodate twenty or thirty children.

The following afternoon, once George had returned to work, she went out to explore. The autumn wind sweeping across Rotherhithe was sharp. Watery sunlight struggled to penetrate the clouds of smoke and steam that hung over the docks and factories. The streets were slippery and further south the sunlight glinted off pools of water in the Rother Fields. When the tide was high and the wind was in the east, as it was now, the fields and even the area around the docks often flooded.

She walked through the old part of Rotherhithe along the riverfront, seeing the masts of schooners and coasters and barges on the river rising through gaps in the brick houses, passing taverns and wash houses and another church, St Mary the Virgin, the sailors' church and one of the oldest buildings in the parish. Further on was the seaman's mission and then the warehouses behind Albion Dock. To the south more clouds of smoke rose where the new dock was being dug, and where George was working.

Every building she passed was occupied, and carpenters and bricklayers were hard at work raising new ones, filling the gaps between existing houses. She looked longingly at these new houses, but knew she could never afford the rent. Retracing her steps, she walked down Lower Road, past the new factories going up on Commercial Road, then back past the engine works and the glue factory to Jamaica Row and along towards the Blue Anchor. Everywhere Grace found the same thing; every building full and new ones going up. She reached the border between Rotherhithe and the neighbouring district of Bermondsey, and wondered if she might have better luck there. Bermondsey was older and less prosperous, with many trades and industries shifting east to Rotherhithe, and the chance of finding an empty warehouse or even a shed was better, but she knew the streets of Bermondsey were even more dangerous than those of Rotherhithe.

And besides, she told herself, *this is a school for Rotherhithe children. I will not have them walking a mile or more to attend lessons. This school should be part of their neighbourhood, as familiar to them as home.*

She turned and walked over the waste ground south of Jamaica Road. At the moment this was open heathland, but soon it too would be covered in factories and houses. The wind began to blow harder, and a grey wall of cloud came sweeping in from the east, blotting out the sun and trailing sheets of rain. Caught in the open, Grace looked around for shelter. The nearest she could see was the railway viaduct, a short distance away. Composed of a series of heavy brick arches, the viaduct lifted the line about twenty feet above ground level.

Grace just managed to find shelter in one of the arches before the rain began to fall hard. A train thundered and rumbled overhead, steaming away towards Sevenoaks, and she was briefly reminded of her former life. She pushed the thought away and looked around. The brick arches were solid. The ground under her feet was firm earth but dry, even though a hard rain was falling. She saw some lumps of charred wood where someone had made a fire.

Seal off the arch to keep the weather out, she thought, and light a fire, put in a stove perhaps, and this would become a room more than adequate for her needs. And best of all, it would cost her nothing.

She stood still for a moment, staring around her as the rain fell outside. Was it possible? Was it simply too wild a notion to think that she could create a school, here, under the arches with the trains thundering past overhead? It was as far from the Clare School or the school in Sevenoaks as was possible to imagine.

On the other hand, she thought: *why not?*

That evening she sought George's advice when he returned home from work. She had expected George to be sceptical, but he surprised her. She knew that he had only a passing interest in education – taking lessons made his children happy and kept them occupied, but he hardly expected them to derive much benefit from it – but the challenge of turning this derelict space into something usable intrigued him.

'You'll need something to keep the wind out,' he said. 'It'll be perishing cold under them arches, otherwise.'

'What do you suggest?' asked Grace. 'I thought first of building a wall and putting in a door, but I am not certain we can afford the bricks and mortar.'

George shook his head. 'Sailcloth would do. They sell old sails for a song down at the docks. See, when the sails are worn out and no longer serviceable, they have to dispose of them. They send some of them to the workhouses, to be picked for rags.'

Grace looked at her fingers, half expecting to see them bleeding again. The workhouse had been a long time ago, but some memories died hard. 'A lot of the rest just get burned,' George said. 'I know one of the chandlers that disposes of them. We'll get the sheets from him, and Mickey Doyle and I will rig a frame for you.'

'Would Mickey be willing to help?' Mickey Doyle, Brigit's husband, was a deal porter, one of the dockers who unloaded timber from the big ships that came in from Canada and Russia.

'Of course. He's already proud to bursting about all their Bill has learned from you. I'm still worried, Grace. Even with the sailcloth, it'll still be right cold under that arch.'

'We'll need a stove,' Grace said.

'Stoves cost money,' George pointed out.

'I know ... But if I can find one, could you and Mr Doyle rig us a flue, to take the smoke away?'

'Nothing easier,' said George happily. 'Mickey and me will go over to the arch on Sunday and fit everything out. Just leave it to us.'

She wrote to Mela, telling her what she had decided to do.

What do you think? Is this even possible, or have I taken leave of my senses? Our local vicar thinks the latter, and has tried hard to talk me out of it. My dear friend, I need your wise counsel and advice. Reassure me that I am doing the right thing, or if I am completely and hopelessly cracked, talk me out of this venture before I go any further.

She posted the letter, expecting a speedy reply. Trains carried the post rapidly across London, and in some areas there were deliveries a dozen times a day. Sure enough, Mela's letter came the following morning.

Cracked? Grace, you are the most sensible and level-headed person I have ever met! And I knew you would

81

not be able to stay away from teaching for long. I think what you are doing sounds brave and wonderful. Pooh to your stuffy old vicar if he won't help you. I know someone who will. Meet me at Charing Cross tomorrow afternoon, and I will introduce you.

The sky was grey, and the November winds had stripped the last leaves from the trees, a sharp contrast to that brilliant June day when Grace and Mela had walked in the park and listened to Mr Forster speak about the Education Bill, and Lady Ringrose had offered Grace a job. An image of her nephew Walter's kind, intelligent face passed through Grace's mind. A man like that was far above her station, she thought sadly.

Outside the new railway station at Charing Cross the two women met and embraced. They had corresponded regularly over the past few months, but had not seen each other since Grace left for Sevenoaks. 'It has been too long,' said Mela.

'It has,' said Grace with feeling. She had been so busy that the time had flown, but seeing Mela reminded her of how much she missed her friend.

'The house feels empty now you are no longer there,' Mela said. 'Mother and Father say so too. Oh, Grace, it is so good to see you again.'

There were tears in her blue eyes, and the sight of them wrung Grace's heart. They embraced again, and Grace took out a handkerchief and dabbed at Mela's eyes, then her own. The latter giggled suddenly. 'That's the Grace I remember. Always prepared for everything. Even tears.'

'As a substitute mother, I have learned to prepare for plenty of tears, at frequent intervals,' Grace said with feeling. 'Mela, do you really think I can do this? Start and run a school, single-handed?'

'I think you can do anything you set your mind to,' Mela said. She smiled and hugged Grace again. 'I said I knew someone who could help you. Come, let me introduce you.'

They started to walk up the Strand. 'Where are you taking me?' Grace asked.

'To see a Ragged School,' Mela said. 'You know, of course, about Lord Shaftesbury and the Ragged School Union. They have already established schools in many poor districts of London, as well as places like Birmingham and Edinburgh.'

'I admire their work very much,' said Grace. 'And I confess I should have thought of them when considering my own school. I did not know you were involved with the Union, Mela.'

'I'm not,' replied Mela, 'although I have considered it. The son of one of Father's friends has started a school not far from here. I am taking you to see it.'

The Strand was busy with loaded wagons and gentlemen in top hats riding on fine horses. But the wealth of London, as

Grace knew only to well, was like a skin. Scratch beneath it, and you found something quite different.

York Lane was a narrow, dirty alley lined with dilapidated tenement houses, a block off the Strand and only a stone's throw from Charing Cross. Walking down the greasy cobbles with Mela beside her, Grace could hear the hooting of train whistles echoing off the brick walls.

They reached the door of what looked like an old warehouse and stopped. Mela knocked at the door. After a moment they heard the bar inside being lifted and a serious young man with dark eyes and a close-trimmed brown beard looked out at them. His face brightened when he saw Mela. 'Miss Clare! Do come in, do come in. To what do we owe the honour of your visit?'

His voice had a slightly drawling accent, and Grace guessed he had been to public school. He was about the same age as herself. She wondered what a man like him was doing in a place like this.

'I have brought a friend to see your school, Mr Hogg,' said Mela. 'This is Miss Perrow. She desires to know more about the Ragged School movement.'

'Does she?' Mr Hogg peered at Grace. 'Well, well, bless my soul. We've not been here long, only opened up shop a couple of years ago, so I daresay we're still stumbling about a bit. Making it up as we go along, don't you know. But it would be my pleasure to show you around.'

He led the way deeper into the building, and they followed a central corridor with several doors opening off

84

it. There was a strange scent in the air, like dried leaves. The first door opened into a classroom where about thirty boys sat on wooden benches, slates on the desk in front of them. They ranged in age from five or six to about thirteen Grace saw, and all of them were in rags; clothes patched and torn, with elbows and knees often showing through. Some had shoes with holes in them; most had no shoes at all, and Grace reckoned they must have been grateful for the cast-iron stove that sat in a corner, pumping out heat. Several had dirty faces.

That, Grace knew, was the definition of a Ragged School; where the children were so poor that they could not afford proper clothes or shoes. The school was their one alternative to life in the slums, or in the workhouse.

The boys were doing sums, instructed by a tall thin man in a black schoolmaster's robe. He smiled when he saw Mr Hogg, and then bowed to the two young women before carrying on with the lesson. 'Mr Kinnaird,' whispered Mr Hogg. 'Great chum of mine. Plays football for England, you know. When he's not teaching here, that is.'

They moved on to another class of boys chanting out the letters of the alphabet as a teacher pointed to them on a blackboard, and then two classes of girls, skinny, half-starved little things whose eyes seemed to bulge out of their sunken faces. 'We're setting up a kitchen too,' said Mr Hogg as they closed the door on the second class. 'No point in trying to educate them if they're too hungry to think. We'll give 'em all a good meal before lessons.'

'How many pupils do you have, Mr Hogg?' Grace asked.

'A hundred and twenty in the day school, and then we run a Sunday school as well. There's another ninety in that, though the numbers go up and down.'

He led the way into a small room at the rear of the building that served as an office. Another young man rose to his feet and bowed as they entered. 'This is another of our volunteer teachers,' Mr Hogg said. 'May I present Mr Walter Ringrose? Miss Clare, Miss Perrow.'

'W-we are are already acq-quainted,' said Mr Ringrose, stuttering a little. He seemed nervous, Grace thought. 'It is a pleasure to see you again, ladies.'

'And you, Mr Ringrose,' said Mela brightly. 'I didn't know you were teaching here.'

'I started j-just last month.'

'And are you enjoying it?' Grace asked with interest.

A look of intensity crossed the gentle young man's face. 'Very much so, ma'am,' he said. 'I think I may have found my calling. Like you, I find teaching children is vastly reward-ing. Your ambition seems to have become mine also.' He blushed a little and stepped back.

Grace smiled at him and said, 'I am sure that the children will learn a great deal from you. Where do the children come from?' she asked.

'Mostly from the rookeries,' said Mr Hogg. 'You know, the slums up at Seven Dials, and around Covent Garden. Nasty, ghastly places, full of poverty and every kind of vice imaginable. How these children manage to live, heaven only knows. Sometimes they just stop coming; there one day, gone the next. We never know what's happened to the poor little mites.'

Beneath the fashionable accent there was real sympathy, even sorrow in his voice. Grace spoke without thinking. 'Why did you do it, Mr Hogg? Why set up this school?'

Mr Hogg looked perplexed for a moment. 'We just had to,' he said. 'Look, all this came as a bit of shock to me, you know. I mean, Father is a lawyer, pretty well minted. I lacked for nothing when I was a little 'un, didn't even know poverty existed. Then I came out of Eton and . . . well. I started looking around. I saw what the world is really like. I remembered Eton was originally set up to educate poor children, even if things are rather different now. I had to do something.'

'I came here one day to look around and see what Quintin was up to,' said Mr Ringrose. 'Half an hour, and I was hooked. I knew I couldn't walk away. I had to stay and help.'

Grace noticed his stutter almost disappeared as his passion for the school took over and she found herself smiling at the man. She felt that she and Mela were in the company of kindred spirits here.

Mr Hogg looked around the building. 'This was an old tea warehouse,' he said, and Grace realised the smell she had noticed was tea leaves, engrained in the fabric of the building. 'I'm in the trade, along with my cousin. We don't use this building anymore, all the warehouses have shifted closer to the docks. So, two of my chums and I converted it into a school. We teach here when we're not working, and we also have good old Walter here, and a couple of lady volunteers. Smashing ladies, they are. Couldn't run this place without them.'

He looked at Grace. 'Do you mind my asking what your interest is, Miss Perrow?'

'I am starting my own school down in Rotherhithe,' Grace said.

Mr Hogg's serious face relaxed into a grin. 'Are you? By Jove. All I can say is, you must be mad. Take it from one who knows.'

Mr Ringrose laughed, and Grace smiled. 'Do you mind if I ask you some questions, sir?' she asked Mr Hogg.

'Of course not. Happy to help if I can. Fire away.'

'What is the hardest thing about establishing a Ragged School?'

'Oh, finding premises, beyond a doubt,' said Mr Hogg. 'We were so fortunate to have this place. Some schools really struggle. I know of schools in sheds and stables and upstairs rooms of pubs. Sometimes they get evicted and have to close down, which is very unfortunate. What about yourself, Miss Perrow? Have you found a place?'

'Yes,' said Grace. 'I shall use a railway arch.'

The two men stared at her. 'My word,' said Mr Ringrose. 'That really is roughing it. Are you certain there is no place else for you to use?'

'I fear that in a growing area like Rotherhithe there is little choice,' said Grace. 'My brother-in-law and his friends are going to make it weatherproof, and as soon as I can lay hands on a stove, we shall be snug as bugs. What about furniture? How did you acquire benches and desks?'

'The charity of our friends and neighbours,' said Mr Hogg. 'And, of course, we have dipped into our own pockets to pay for some things.' Mr Ringrose nodded in agreement. 'We didn't have benches and desks at first, and everyone sat on the floor. But gradually, things came trickling in.'

'What curriculum do you teach?' Grace asked.

'The four Rs,' said Mr Ringrose. 'Reading, writing, arithmetic and religion.'

Grace blinked. 'Religion?'

'Oh, yes. The Ragged Schools Union insist we have a religious education class every day.'

Grace thought that the vicar of All Saints would not be pleased if she started teaching religious education. 'How much help do you receive from the Union? Would they provide chalks and slates, for instance?'

'No,' said Mr Hogg. 'The Union has willing hearts and hands, but not a lot of money. We buy slates and chalk out of our own pockets. But the Union is very helpful with the curriculum. They provide reading materials and lesson plans free of charge, and plenty of good advice, too.'

'If I were you, Miss Perrow, I would get in touch with them straight away,' said Mr Ringrose. 'The sooner that you get to their notice the more help they can be, even if it is only with advice and lesson plans. The head of the Union is a good man.'

Grace nodded. 'What is the best way to reach them?' she asked.

'I'll give you the address before you go,' said Mr Hogg. The fellow to write to is Mr Raikes, Solomon Raikes. He's a bit of a dry old stick, but as Walter says his heart is in the right place. He'll see you right.'

Mr Hogg watched her. 'Well, you've seen the set-up here, Miss Perrow. Do you still want to carry on?'

'More than ever,' said Grace. 'It's as you said, Mr Hogg. I have to do something.'

Mr Hogg nodded. 'Then I wish you good luck, ma'am,' he said.

'Thank you, both,' said Grace. She looked around the plain bare brick walls of the warehouse. In the distance she could hear some of the girls singing a hymn. 'I think I'm going to need it.'

As they were leaving, Mr Ringrose came over to Grace and said, 'My aunt was so disappointed to lose you from her school, especially in such sad circumstances. I think what you want to do is marvellous. I sometimes have time to spare, so do write and ask if there is anything you think I could do to help.'

Grace blushed. 'It is very kind of you to offer, Mr Ringrose. I am sure that you have your hands full here though, without running down to Rotherhithe to help us.'

'Not at all,' he said. 'Yours is a noble enterprise, and I would be happy to help out. Please do remember that.' He smiled warmly once again at Grace, and then Mr Hogg came to see the two women out.

Back on the Strand Mela and Grace faced a whipping east wind, gritty with soot and harsh with the promise of rain. 'What did you think?' Mela asked.

'I am full of admiration,' said Grace. 'I only hope I can do half as well. I cannot hope to recruit as many pupils of course, but if I can get twenty or thirty, I will be very happy . . . And it was so pleasing to see Mr Ringrose there. He looked in his element, didn't he? I think the teaching bug has well and truly bitten him.'

'I think so too,' said Mela smiling. 'I think I might know where the bug came from, too.'

Grace blushed at the implication of Mela's words. 'Someone of Walter Ringrose's background and education is not likely to be influenced by me,' she said firmly.

'Mmm,' said Mela. 'What will you do next?'

'Go home and write to Mr Solomon Raikes,' said Grace. 'And then, start canvassing the merchants and shopkeepers of Rotherhithe for donations. I know Mr Hogg's pupils sat on the floor at first, but the ground under the railway arch will be very cold, even with a fire. I need benches and desks, and I need a stove.'

'And what about chalks and slates?' asked Mela. 'And books?'

'I still have some savings,' said Grace. 'Like Mr Hogg, I shall dip into my own pocket.'

'I think Mr Hogg's pockets are rather deeper than yours,' said Mela, laughing. 'Right, my dear. You need to come with me.'

'Where?'

'There is a cab rank at Charing Cross. We need to get a cab before it starts to rain.'

'But where are we going?'

'I am kidnapping you,' said Mela, laughing again. 'You will see when we get there.'

The cab took them to Hackney, back to the house where Grace had lived for nine wonderful years. She felt a lump in her throat as she stepped over the threshold, for she real-ised that this house and the people who lived here were very dear to her; more dear, perhaps, than she had realised up to that moment.

Mr and Mrs Clare were in the library, reading before an enormous fire. They rose when the two young women entered, exclaiming with pleasure when they saw Grace. They insisted she take a seat by the fire and Mrs Clare poured her a cup of tea, and they pressed her for news of her family in Rotherhithe. 'And what brings you back to us, my dear?' Mr Clare asked.

'Grace is starting a Ragged School,' Mela said proudly, before Grace could speak.

Mrs Clare's eyes opened wide. 'Why, that is wonderful news!' she said. 'Oh, Grace, my dear. I am so happy to hear you are returning to teaching, and what a noble venture you are embarking upon! I confess I am almost envious. Were I twenty years younger, I should follow in your footsteps.'

'My congratulations,' said Mr Clare, smiling. 'What can we do to help you, Grace?'

'She needs slates,' said Mela, again before Grace could respond. 'About thirty will do for a start. We have plenty of spares, don't we, Mother? And slate pencils and chalk as well, of course?'

'Of course,' said Mrs Clare smiling. 'What about furniture, Grace? You will need benches and desks.'

'I was thinking—' Grace began.

'There are some old desks and benches down in the cellar,' said Mela. 'We no longer use them. And I think I remember a couple of blackboards, too.'

'Yes,' said Mrs Clare. 'And the library can spare some books, I am sure. They will fit nicely into that oak cabinet in my office that I never use. Shifting it out will give me more space. I will make up a chest of medicines for you as well. You know how children come down with every complaint known to man.'

'No, really,' Grace said weakly. 'You must not go to so much trouble.'

They ignored her. 'Lamps,' said Mrs Clare. 'You will need oil lamps for light during the dark winter days. Wyndham, could your warehouse spare some lamps?'

'Of course,' said Mr Clare, 'and I will send over a couple of gallons of lamp oil too, to keep you going for a while.'

The three Clares sat and smiled at Grace. She thought, briefly, about refusing their offer, and then felt suddenly ashamed of herself. The truth, of course, was that they *wanted* to help, and it would be churlish in the extreme to refuse.

'You are wonderful,' she said to the Clares. 'Thank you, so much, for helping me to get started. I promise I shall make no further demands on you.'

'Nonsense, my dear,' said Mrs Clare. 'If ever you need help you must come to us.'

They made her stay for a while and then, reluctantly, as evening fell they let her go. Mela walked her to the door and they waited while the maid fetched Grace's coat and bonnet. 'Can I do anything?' asked Mela. 'Do you need another teacher?'

Grace smiled. 'You have more than enough work at the Clare School, and your mother would be furious if I stole you away.'

Mela kissed her cheek. 'If you change your mind, call me,' she said. 'And write often, and let me know how your school progresses. I shall expect to hear great things. And don't forget to take Mr Ringrose up on his offer of help. I am certain he was serious."

Crossing London Bridge with the city lamps twinkling around her, Grace felt a draft and wrapped her coat more tightly around her. Something rustled in the pocket. She reached inside, and found a sealed envelope had been placed in the pocket. Breaking the seal she took out several pieces of paper, which she realised with a shock were Bank of England five-pound notes. With them was a letter, and there was still just enough light to read it.

My dear Grace,

You have accepted only some slates and books and a few bits of furniture, and I understand why. Your independence of spirit is one of your noblest qualities. Nonetheless, I hope you will take this gift of £30, and use it well in the service of the project on which you have embarked. I have taken care, I hope, to give you enough money to be of use to you, while not giving you so much that you will feel compelled to return it.

Angela and I wish you every success with your venture. You know that wherever you go and whatever you do, our love and prayers follow you.

Yours faithfully
Wyndham Clare

The following morning Grace wrote to Mr Solomon Raikes at the Ragged Schools Union, and in the afternoon she called on Mr Jackson the ironmonger in Jamaica Row. She used part of Mr Clare's money to buy a cast-iron stove and several sacks of coal. The ironmonger promised to deliver them to the house on Saturday.

She was expecting a reply from Mr Raikes by post the following day, but what she got instead was Mr Raikes himself, driving a pony and trap into Bell Lane the next morning and stopping outside her door.

'It is a pleasure to make your acquaintance, Miss Perrow,' said Mr Raikes. He was tall and thin with long bony arms and a top hat that made him look like a scarecrow. Daisy was a little frightened of him, and hid behind Grace's skirts. Much to Grace's surprise and great pleasure, Walter Ringrose was sitting beside him.

'At the Ragged School Union, we were most pleased to hear of your new venture, ma'am,' he said. 'There are no Ragged Schools in this part of London, and very few south of the river at all. Mr Ringrose here contacted me to say that you would be in touch and asked to come along when I visited. Have you secured premises?'

Grace nodded. 'We shall use an empty arch, under the South Eastern Railway viaduct. The line is not far from here.'

'A railway arch?' Mr Raikes's eyebrows rose until they had nearly disappeared under the brim of his hat. Daisy clutched at Grace's leg. 'That is most unusual.'

'Will there be any objection?' Grace asked.

'Hmm. No. No, so long as you can keep your charges warm and dry. It will be of little use to educate them if they then expire of the flux.'

'We have the matter in hand, sir,' Grace said.

'Good, good. Now, we have brought you a few things to help you establish your school. To begin with, a bible.' He held up a leather-bound bible.

'I have little experience in the teaching of religion, sir,' said Grace.

'None is needed,' said Mr Raikes. 'Read to them from the Bible for twenty minutes every day and then give them a homily; we have a selection of tracts for you to choose from. Ensure they sing two hymns every day; our masters are very particular about this. In this way, so our masters believe, the spirit of the Lord will enter into them, and at least their souls will achieve salvation, no matter what distresses of body and mind the poor little creatures continue to encounter.'

'I shall do so,' Grace said, wondering again what the vicar would think.

'I have provided you with copies of Mrs Alexander's *Hymns for Little Children*,' said Mr Raikes. 'As to reading and writing and arithmetic, I have also brought you a selection of our standard lesson plans, and some exercises to give pupils who are just setting out on their journey towards numeracy and literacy. I trust you will find these useful.'

'Thank you, sir,' Grace said. 'I already have some experience as a teacher, but of course I value your expertise and wisdom.'

'Indeed,' said Mr Raikes. 'Your prior experience is one of the reasons why we are keen to offer our support. So many earnest, kind-hearted volunteers come forward with no experience of teaching. Mr Ringrose here is just one such, but he is throwing himself into the job with enthusiasm. You, ma'am, are a refreshing change. Even so, you will find this a very different proposition from teaching at the Clare School.'

'How is that, sir?'

'The needs of your pupils will vary greatly depending on their age and whatever ... circumstances they have encountered in their lives thus far. These are not the well-fed, well-nourished minds you encountered at your previous school. Many are children for whom everything in their lives, even existence itself, is a struggle. Thanks to the hardship they face in their everyday lives, many find learning even basic concepts like the alphabet and sums a slow and painful process.'

Mr Ringrose added, 'Even those keen to learn can find the regime of school very confining. They are unused to long periods of concentration. I have found this the most challenging element in my short time teaching. Although, of course, I have not your breadth of experience, Miss Perrow.'

Grace acknowledged the younger man's compliments with a smile and said, 'I believe I understand the problem, gentlemen.'

Mr Raikes looked at her very seriously. 'I hope so, Miss Perrow. Because teaching at a Ragged School is not like anything you will ever have encountered. The children are those whom decent society has rejected. They are too ragged, wretched, filthy and forlorn for any respectable school, such as those run by the church. Many have been torn from the arms of their parents, who have succumbed to gin, opium or disease. Even when still living, the parents often no longer care for their children, but let them roam the street like wild creatures. Some of these children have turned to crime, robbing and stealing in order to survive. Many do not wash because they have no clean water, with consequent grave injury to their health. In short, ma'am, you will be dealing with the very lowest forms of humanity.'

'I do not see it so,' Grace said steadily. 'All human beings, no matter how low their station, have dignity. I will read the Bible to them so their souls may be saved, Mr Raikes. But I intend to help them preserve their minds and bodies, too.'

Suddenly, surprisingly, Mr Raikes smiled. 'Mr Ringrose here said you were a strong-minded person and you seem to me to be a good young woman,' he said. 'I shall pray for your success. You have my address; if a situation arises where you think you might benefit from our help and advice, please write to me immediately. I cannot guarantee we can help you in every eventuality, but we will do our utmost.'

He looked at Albert, who stood watching and listening very seriously. 'Now, perhaps this young gentleman would care to assist us in unloading the cart?'

Suddenly, things were moving quickly. On Saturday Nicholas, the Clares' coachman, arrived at the house with a cargo of blackboards, slates, chalk, lamps, furniture and the cabinet full of books, all of which were crammed into the parlour of the little house, forcing the family to take refuge in the kitchen. Later that day the ironmonger arrived with his cart and delivered the stove, which was wedged into the narrow hall.

'Where are you taking all this lot?' asked Mr Jackson, the ironmonger.

'The railway arches,' said Grace.

'Auntie Grace is going to start a school,' said Albert proudly. 'And I shall be a pupil.'

'Will you now?' Mr Jackson took off his cloth cap and scratched his ear. Winter sunlight gleamed briefly off his bald head. 'And how are you planning to transport all this lot to the railway arches?'

'My brother-in-law thinks he can borrow a handcart,' said Grace.

Mr Jackson sniffed. 'He'll be all day, going back and forth. When do you want it shifted? Sunday? I'll call around after church with the horse and cart. No, miss, I don't want no payment.'

'You are very kind,' said Grace, a little overwhelmed by the offer. She had expected the charity of friends; the kindness of strangers was something out of the blue.

The ironmonger scratched his ear again. 'We're nonconformists, the wife and me,' he said. 'We're members of the Congregational chapel. The church school won't let our little lad into school, because they say we're heretics or some such. If we sent him along to you, would you give him lessons?'

'With pleasure,' said Grace, and she smiled.

Mr Jackson was as good as his word. He arrived with the cart at midday on Sunday, and he, George and Mickey Doyle loaded it and drove away to the railway arch, taking with them a big roll of sailcloth and some baulks of timber. Later in the afternoon Grace walked across to the railway line to look at the work, and found them just finishing.

Again to her surprise, she discovered Walter Ringrose was there. He had, it appeared, been there all afternoon helping George and Mickey. The open faces of the arch had been covered with sailcloth anchored firmly to a wooden frame, with a flap to serve as a door. Inside, the stove had been set up and the flue ran up and out the top of the arch, venting smoke from the room, and there was a basket of coal beside it. The cabinet sat at the front of the room, where it could also serve as a desk, and a couple of oil lamps hung suspended from the ceiling of the arch with another sitting on a sturdy oak table.

'Where did you get that table?' Grace asked.

George and Mr Doyle looked at each other. 'Mr Ringrose arrived with it,' said George.

'That is so very kind of you, Mr Ringrose,' said Grace smiling warmly at the young man.

'I-it is only a small gift,' said Walter. 'It was not needed at home and I wanted to mark the opening of your v-venture in some way. I do so admire your decision to start this school.' His ears had become a little pink.

'Well it is a delightful addition to our school, and very generous'. Grace blushed a little under Mr Ringrose's regard and looked around the room. 'It looks quite homely,' she said.

It did, too, she thought, if you ignored the bare earth floor and the sound of the trains rumbling overhead. She felt a sudden burst of pride and excitement. She turned and kissed George on the cheek then shook Walter and Mickey's hands and thanked them for all their work. Mickey Doyle grinned again.

'You've got your school, Miss Grace,' he said.

'Yes,' said Grace. 'Now all I need is some pupils.'

∞

'What are they doin'?' one of the girls asked.

'Don't know,' I said.

'That's our arch,' said another. 'That's where we been sleepin'. They've taken it.'

'There's other arches,' I said. Joe looked up with those big eyes of his. I knew he was hungry. We all were.

'It's that mort,' said the first girl. 'That one from the churchyard. She's doin' this. We should stick her.'

'Leave her be,' I said. 'She don't mean no harm.'

'Well, what's she doin' out here then? Why ain't she at home with her kiddies? What's she want to go messin' about over here? I'm tellin' you, this is our turf.'

'Oh, leave it out,' I said. 'Come on. We've got to find some scran. It's been two days. If we don't eat soon, they'll be shovelling us into the pauper's hole.'

I pretended I didn't care what she was doing, but I was curious all right. She puzzled me, that one. I still remembered the look in her eye when we raided the market. Cool and calm; looked me straight in the eye.

It was strange. She wasn't from around here, but at the same time, it was like she was familiar. I couldn't get used to the fact that I kept seeing her, and I couldn't get used to the fact that she kept seeing me. Cuz she saw us when she came out of the arch that day. She didn't say anything to the two men. She just looked up and saw me, and our eyes met again.

I didn't know what was going on. And I don't like it when that happens.

∽

Sitting at the kitchen table, Grace made a list of the pupils she had recruited so far. Albert, Daisy and Harry, of course. Rebecca Berton from next door, older than the others, but who needed an education if she was to fulfil her mother's dream and make a life for herself outside of Rotherhithe. Billy Doyle, Mickey's son. The two homeless boys from Cherry Gardens. Lettice, the match girl. Mr Jackson's son. And Jimmy, who was so hungry to learn. Ten in all, boys and girls. She had no qualms about teaching them together. In her view, boys and girls learned equally quickly, and she had no room to segregate them.

After lunch, once George had returned to work, she went out to knock on doors. Not everyone wanted to talk to her, or was happy at being interrupted. Several times, doors were slammed in her face before she had a chance to introduce herself or explain what she wanted. But as she worked her way through the streets of Rotherhithe, she found a few women, a few men too, ready to listen, and when she had finished explaining the purpose of the school, they nodded.

'Can't hurt,' said one man. He was on crutches, the lower part of one leg missing; the result, he explained, of an accident at the docks a year ago. Now he was at home, unable to work, his wife taking in laundry as a means of getting by, with two small children to feed. 'While they're at school, they're not in the streets getting into trouble. I'd be pleased if you'd look after 'em, missus.'

That's not exactly my purpose, Grace thought, but she didn't much care why children came to school, so long as they came. She added two more names to her list. In Paradise Row she found a boy begging in a doorway, and gave him a penny and told him where and when to find the school; it would be warm, she said. The lad nodded, shivering.

Grace walked on, thinking about the poor children on the streets and thinking too about the girls she had seen flitting across the flooded fields on the way back from the railway. It was the same group, she was sure; she recognised the girl with the little boy in tow. *Those are the ones I really want to get to,* she thought. *But they are so wild, so skittish. How do I get near them?*

Having covered the streets close to home, Grace approached the rougher area, nearer to the docks. Hanover Court was a mean, dirty alley running up from the river. The cranes of the Wapping docks on the far side of the Thames were like a forest in the distance; at the other end of the street lay Albion Dock, the first of the Surrey Docks, surrounded by hulking timber sheds. The smells of sawn wood and smoke filled the air.

The first two doors Grace knocked at yielded no answer. The third was opened by a thickset woman, with a blotched, unhealthy complexion; she smelled heavily of gin. Her apron was greasy and did not look like it had seen a laundry in weeks. She looked hard at Grace. 'What do you want?' she demanded.

'I am sorry to intrude,' said Grace. 'My name is Grace Perrow. I am starting a school in Rotherhithe, a free school with no fees. Lessons start tomorrow, and any child may join, anyone at all. I wondered if your children would like to attend, Mrs . . . ?'

The woman did not answer at first. She leaned nonchalantly on the doorframe and smiled. It was not a nice smile.

'Grace Perrow,' she said. 'Well, well, well. Little Grace Perrow. Look at you now, all grown up. Still the same lazy little cow, though. Won't do a job of proper work, not like the rest of us. Oh, no, she's too busy with her nose buried in her books. Thinks she's a *teacher*, now.'

Grace stared at her. 'Who are you?' she demanded.

'Don't you remember me?' taunted the woman. 'Maybe I should give you a clip around the ear. Perhaps that'd remind you, lazy-bones.'

And then, suddenly, Grace knew. This bloated, gin-soaked woman was Sara, her tormentor from the workhouse. Sara, the one who had caused her to be sent to the laundry, where Rosa had been injured and she herself had nearly died a horrible death in boiling water.

And then she saw something else. A face had appeared in the shadows behind Sara, a boy's face, small and frightened, but staring at Grace like she held out the promise of salvation. There was hunger as well as fear in his eyes, a longing for something he desperately wanted and was afraid he would never have.

It was Jimmy.

Chapter 6

Just for a moment she was back in the workhouse again, being pinched and punched and taunted by Sara, and she felt a wash of remembered fear. But the moment quickly passed. She was a grown woman now, and she was no longer afraid of bullies. She saw too the desperation in Jimmy's eyes. *What is he doing here?* she thought. *He looks like a prisoner.*

'Yes, I remember you now,' she said calmly. 'How good it is to see you again, Sara. And you too, Jimmy,' she said to the boy. 'Do you live here?'

'He's my son,' Sara snapped, before Jimmy could answer. 'And what's it to you? How do you know his name?'

Grace was silent for a moment. How could Jimmy, so quiet and delicate and shy, be the son of this woman?

'Well?' Sara demanded. 'What's he to you, lazy-bones?'

'Jimmy has been coming to see me,' said Grace. 'I have been giving him lessons.'

Sara's eyes, reddened by alcohol, glowed out of a face hard as stone. 'You!' she snarled at the boy. 'Stay inside! I'll attend to you later. Now, Miss Hoity-Toity Perrow, I want a word with you.'

She marched out into the street, slamming the door behind her. Grace stepped back as a waft of gin fumes washed over her.

'You stay away from my boy,' Sara said. 'We don't want none of your education, and we don't want none of your fancy ways, neither. You leave our children alone, do you hear? Jimmy is going to grow up a proper man like his father, not some milksop bookworm like you.'

'For heaven's sake,' said Grace. 'All I am doing is teaching him to read and write. What is wrong with that?'

'Read and write?' sneered Sara. 'Why? So he'll get ideas above his station? Well, I'm bloody well not having that. He'll know his proper place in life. He'll go to work down at the docks like his father did, and his father before him, cuz that's what boys like him do. Now, you stop messin' with him, and teaching him things he don't need to know, do you hear? Cuz if you don't, I'll batter him! And so help me God, I'll batter you, too!'

Her hands had balled into fists at her side. 'Very well,' Grace said calmly. She raised her voice a little, so the boy listening inside could hear. 'If you change your mind, the school is under the railway arches. Jimmy will always be welcome.'

'Get out of here!' shouted Sara. 'Piss off! Or by God, I'll make you wish you'd never been born!'

Grace turned and walked away. *Poor Jimmy,* she thought. Age and gin had done nothing to soften Sara's malevolence, and while Grace was no longer frightened of her, she strongly suspected that Sara bullied her son just as she had once bullied children in the workhouse. She remembered the look on Jimmy's face – like a trapped animal – and those desperate, appealing eyes, and felt terrible that she had given away his secret. She had only had to deal with Sara for a year before Aunt Edith rescued her and Rosa from the workhouse. Jimmy had known nothing else his entire life.

I've got to help him, she thought. *But how do I get past Sara?*

Monday morning brought a raw east wind reeking of smoke. Grace began to cough the moment she stepped outside, and her eyes watered. She wrapped scarves around the necks of the children and covered their mouths, then took Daisy and Harry's hands. Albert carried the leather satchel that held her plans for the day's lessons, pleased to be doing something important.

Another door opened and Rebecca Berton came out to join them, smiling and wishing them good morning. She had made an effort, Grace saw. The hem of her bonnet was frayed and the cloak she wrapped around her to ward off the wind was thin and worn, but she was neat and tidy. Billy Doyle joined them, drawing his hands up into the sleeves of his coat to keep them warm.

'This is exciting,' Rebecca said. 'Isn't it, miss?'

Grace smiled. 'Yes,' she said. 'It is.' In truth, she could hardly believe it was happening. Just a few short weeks ago, she had thought the idea of a free school in Rotherhithe was a dream. Now, it was real.

They walked through a shower of rain towards the railway, where the engines puffed and steamed. A big goods train passed overhead just as they reached the arches, and the roar of iron wheels on rails filled the air. Inside, Grace took a box of matches from her reticule and lit the oil lamps and then the stove. The mellow light of the lamps showed her the school, the neat rows of desks and benches, the slates and chalks, the cabinet and books. The air was chilly and she could see the steam of her own breath, but the coal fire in the stove soon began to warm the room.

Gradually the others began to arrive; Rufus Jackson, the ironmonger's son; Gabriel and Isaac from Cherry Gardens; Johnny, the injured docker's son; Lettice the match girl; the beggar boy, who introduced himself in a soft shy voice as Nathan. He had no coat and was shivering with cold, so Grace made him sit next to the stove. He had no shoes, either, nor did some of the others. *Truly a ragged school*, Grace thought. Her own three, Rebecca, and Rufus were the only properly dressed ones in the room, and only Rufus's clothes were new.

We shall make something of all of you, Grace promised silently. *With an education, you can go forth into the world. You need never know such poverty again.*

They waited a while longer, and a few more children arrived. Another train rumbled overhead, shaking the walls of the arch. Nathan pillowed his head on his arms on the desk and slept through the noise. Grace watched the canvas flap that served as a door. She was waiting for Jimmy, but there was no sign of the boy. Sara had won. Jimmy would not be coming to school.

Her heart bled for Jimmy, but there was nothing she could do. She took up her position, standing at the head of the class as she had so often done at the Clare School. 'Good morning, children,' she said smiling.

'Good morning, miss,' they chorused. Nathan woke and sat up, bleary-eyed.

'This morning we will begin with reading and writing,' she said. She took some of the reading sheets Mr Raikes had given her and began handing them out. 'Look at these, for a few minutes, and we shall go through them together. Those of you who can read already, help the others.'

∽

'Jimmy!' shouted Ma. 'You little rat! Where the bleedin' hell do you think you're going?'

Even this early, the smell of gin coming off her was horrible.

'I'm going out,' I said.

'Where?'

'I dunno. Down the docks, maybe.'

'Oh, yes. Thieving, no doubt,' said Ma. 'Well, steal us something for supper. Now, hop it. I've got things to do.'

Things meant the bottle of gin in the kitchen cupboard. There was never enough money for food, but there was always plenty of gin.

I hurried out before Ma could change her mind. I walked down Hanover Court all quiet-like, hands in my pockets like I was in no hurry, in case she was watching me. Then I turned the corner and started to run, past the market and the church and the glue factory and the engine works towards the railway line, praying I wouldn't be too late.

I saw the arch covered in canvas and ran towards it. A big goods train came roaring down the line and sprayed me with soot and cinders, but I didn't hardly notice. Inside I could hear voices. I was too late.

I almost turned and ran away again. But I wanted to be part of that school, oh, I wanted it so bad, and I could feel it pulling at me.

I opened the canvas flap and went inside. They all turned to stare. Albert smiled, and I saw his eyes light up. 'Look, Aunt Grace!' he said. 'It's Jimmy!'

And there she was, standing in the lamplight with dark eyes and a serious face. 'Jimmy,' she said, and her voice was quiet and gentle. She came over and took my hands. She didn't smell of gin. 'I was afraid you might not come.'

'I came as soon as I could,' I said. 'Please, miss, I hope I'm not too late.'

'Of course not. Sit down there by the fire. Albert, find him something to read. Now, children, we shall carry on with our lesson.'

I sat down. I was breathless from running and dirty with mud and soot. But I saw the letters on the blackboard and *smelled the chalk and looked at the printed reading exercise that Albert gave me, and I wanted to cry. I felt like I had come home.*

∽

That morning was the hardest teaching Grace could remember, even back when she was a young pupil-teacher just starting out at the Clare School. Mr Raikes had been right. Some of the children were quick learners. Albert, Rebecca and Rufus and especially Jimmy all excelled at reading and even the twins were picking it up. But Lettice had always been slow to learn, and Nathan the beggar boy simply did not understand what she was talking about. The crude scratchings of chalk on his slate bore little resemblance to the letters she had written on the blackboard. When she tried to correct him he simply shook his head wearily. Cold and hunger had ground the boy down to the point where he could barely think. Eventually, he put his head down on his desk and went to sleep.

Later, she listened to some of the children read aloud. She was particularly impressed by the progress Jimmy had made. His voice was clear and he read without stumbling, and he seemed to really know and feel what he was reading. Grace watched him, rejoicing once more at the progress he was making. A few weeks ago he could barely read at all; now he was probably the best in the class.

When she sensed they were growing tired, Grace took a book from the cabinet and began to read to them, not the Bible, but the first chapter of *Alice's Adventures in Wonderland*. She had read the book when it was first published two years earlier and had been captivated by it, and now she saw it work its magic on the children. They sat wide-eyed, listening with rapt attention, and at the end of the chapter they begged her for more.

'Tomorrow,' Grace promised them. 'You can have too much of a good thing.'

'I don't understand,' said Lettice. She had been one of the ones paying closest attention to the tale. 'Why would a rabbit have a pocket watch? He wouldn't be able to wind it with his paws.'

'And he wouldn't be able to button his waistcoat,' said Rebecca.

The other children were giggling. 'Not in the real world,' said Grace, smiling. 'But this is Wonderland, and anything is possible there. Now, my dears, I think it is time to sing. Shall I teach you a song?'

'Yes!' they chorused.

Smiling, Grace opened a copy of *Hymns for Little Children* and began to sing.

> *All things bright and beautiful,*
> *All creatures great and small,*
> *All things wise and wonderful,*
> *The Lord God made them all.*

'Now I shall sing it again,' she said, 'and this time you will sing it with me.' And all around, treble voices were raised up in song.

∽

'What's that noise, Mary?' one of the girls asked.

'They're singing,' I said.

'Singing? You mean, like in church?'

'Something like that,' I said. It did sound a bit like church. I'd stood outside churches sometimes, on Sundays, and heard people sing like that.

'Why?' said someone else.

I didn't have an answer. We stood outside the arch listening to them inside, eight or nine of us girls and Joe. The wind was evil that day. It was cold as iron and black with soot from the mills and trains. Poor little Joe was shivering beside me. We all were. I couldn't remember the last time I'd been warm.

'There's going to be trouble,' said one of the girls. She was called Ness.

'What do you mean?' I said.

'You know that boy who went in late? I know who he is. He's called Jimmy. His dad and brother run with that Bull Head Gang, the Captain's lot. Murderin' bastards, they are.'

'Nothing to do with us,' I said. We took care to stay away from the grown-up gangs, like all the street kids did. We were just trying to survive. They were criminals, proper hard.

My belly was gnawing at me something awful. It was probably the cold. 'No point in standing here,' I said. 'We need some scran. The baker's van will be doing the rounds. Missy, Ness, you distract the driver. The rest of us will break into the van. Grab everything you can, and we'll meet up in the fields.'

We started to walk way, moving silently in bare feet on the cold ground. I held Joe's hand. 'I reckon it's warm inside there,' said Missy. She was thin and miserable. 'They've got a fire.'

'You're going soft,' taunted Ness. She was a really hard little bitch, Ness. She had a big knife, longer than mine, and now she pulled it out of the sheath at her waist. 'Come on. Let's go stick it to that baker.'

∽

At midday when lessons were over, Grace walked home with Albert, the twins, Rebecca and Billy. Jimmy accompanied them. 'I'm so glad you came,' Grace said to him. 'Did you enjoy the lessons?'

'Oh, yes, miss!' said Jimmy fervently. 'I always enjoy lessons with you. I'm learning so much.'

Grace smiled, but she was also worried. 'Will you get in trouble at home?'

'No.' Jimmy was silent for a moment, and then he said, 'She won't hardly notice I'm gone.'

A thought struck Grace. 'So your mother isn't expecting you now? No? We are about to have our midday meal. Will you join us?'

'Oh, yes please, miss,' said Jimmy eagerly.

Dinner was bacon dumplings left over from last night, bulked out with more potatoes. George joked with the children as usual, while Jimmy sat at one end of the table and ate ravenously in utter silence. 'How did it go?' George asked Grace.

'Very well,' said Grace smiling. 'The children behaved themselves splendidly.'

'What? Even this little monkey?' George tickled Daisy, who squeaked and giggled. 'I can't believe it of her.'

'Even her,' said Grace. 'And Harry was very good at singing. Weren't you, Harry?'

'I was,' Harry affirmed. 'And Albert was good at everything. That's cuz Albert is clever. He and Jimmy are cleverest of all.'

At the end of the meal George returned to work, and Jimmy departed reluctantly for home. Grace wondered if she should let him go. *You can't help them all*, the voice of reason said in her head. *I know*, she thought, *but Jimmy is special. He has so much promise. If I help him, we might even be able to get him a free place at a grammar school.* With a good education he could go anywhere, and do anything he wanted.

She was still thinking about this when someone knocked hard at the door. Hurrying to answer it, she found the white-bearded figure of Reverend Hobbes, the vicar, standing on the doorstep. The expression on his face was more forbidding than usual.

'Good day to you, Reverend,' Grace said, as humbly as she could. 'How may I help you?'

'This . . . school of yours,' said the vicar heavily. 'I see you have gone ahead.'

'Yes, sir,' said Grace. 'I found I did not need the support of the church after all.'

'You are doing these children no good whatsoever, you know. They do not need education. They need correction, discipline, and hard work. They are fit for no other occupation than manual labour for the boys, or breeding in the case of the females. To educate them puts foolish ideas into their minds, teaches them to forget their station in life. What will happen to them then?'

What had Sara said? *He'll get ideas above his station*. It was shocking to hear the Reverend Hobbes saying almost exactly the same thing. But then the vicar, as she already knew, was just another bully.

'I don't know will happen to them, Reverend,' said Grace. 'But helping them to forget their station in life and rise above their background is exactly what I intend to do. These children don't need to remain trapped in poverty. With education and encouragement, each and every one of them can go on and do great things.'

'Sentimental rubbish,' snapped the vicar. 'Who put these ideas into your head? Some agitator, I am certain. Now, listen to me, young woman. This is my parish, and you are interfering in it. You will close this school at once.'

Reverend Hobbes leaned forward a little. 'Or else, I will close it for you,' he said.

Grace crossed her arms over her chest. 'And how would you do that, sir?' she asked.

'That railway arch occupied by your school is owned by the South Eastern Railway. You do realise you are trespassing on their land?'

'But sir, that is waste ground! No one was using it before we came. We are doing no harm!'

'Are you not? Let us see if the railway directors agree with you. One word from me and they will send the railway constables to close you down and evict you.'

Grace stared at him in horror. 'Sir, you are a man of God! How can you be so lacking in pity and compassion?'

'Compassion is for those who deserve it,' said the vicar. 'Close your school, Miss Perrow, and send those children home, or it will be the worse for you.'

'If you have us evicted, I will find someplace else,' said Grace, although she was not certain where. 'But I am not closing my school, Reverend. Not for you, not for anyone.'

'We shall see,' said the vicar, slapping his thigh in annoyance. 'We shall see,' he repeated, and he stalked away down the lane. Sighing, Grace went inside to the parlour, where she sat down at the little table and took up paper and pen.

Dear Mr Raikes,

You said I should write to you if I needed help. I am sorry to trouble you so soon, but I fear I do need your

*advice. The vicar of All Saints, Reverend Hobbes, objects
to the presence of my school as he does not approve of education for the poor. He is threatening to close my school.
Can you advise me as to what course of action to follow?*

    Yours sincerely,

    Grace Perrow

    Headmistress

    Rotherhithe Ragged School

Mr Raikes's reply came the next morning as Grace was just about to leave for school, informing her that he was coming down to Rotherhithe that day. Grace met him at the railway station that afternoon. 'Thank you for meeting me,' he said. 'I have certain things to say to your Reverend Hobbes, and I wish you to bear witness.'

They began walking towards the church, down roads busy with heavy wagons hauling timber and bricks. 'All is well otherwise?' asked Mr Raikes, raising his voice over the rattle of iron wheels.

'Indeed, sir,' said Grace. 'But you were right. No matter how ardently they desire to learn, some truly struggle. The spirit in them is willing, but their bodies are exhausted with hunger and cold. Their minds cannot function.'

'I know,' said Mr Raikes, and she heard the sympathy in his voice. 'I have seen it myself, many times. Be patient with them, Miss Perrow. Patience and kindness will win the day.'

At the vicarage, Mr Raikes rapped on the door with the handle of his walking stick. A maidservant ushered them inside, took Mr Raikes's card and went into the study. She was back in a moment, curtseying. 'The Reverend will see you now, sir.'

Reverend Hobbes rose from behind his desk as they entered. The buttons on his flowered waistcoat sparkled in the lamplight. 'Miss Perrow. To what do I owe the honour of this visit?'

There was no mistaking the irony in his voice. 'May I present Mr Solomon Raikes of the Ragged Schools Union?' Grace said.

'I see,' said the vicar. 'How may I help you, sir?'

'Miss Perrow has called on me for assistance,' said Mr Raikes. 'I am the secretary of the Ragged Schools Union, and we are supporting Miss Perrow in her endeavours here in Rotherhithe. She has told me, Reverend, of your objections to her school.'

'Then I hope she has also told you of the reasons behind my objections,' said the vicar. 'I disapprove of this school, sir, and I disapprove of your Union and your entire movement.'

'May I ask why?'

'Because you are disturbing the social order of the entire kingdom!' the vicar thundered. 'By encouraging the poor to uplift themselves, you are threatening to set them against their masters! Give them learning, and who knows what pernicious beliefs may spread among them? Leave them to their ignorance, sir. Ignorance is their lot in life. God has so ordained it, and let no man put aside the work of God.'

'Indeed,' said Mr Raikes, and he clasped his long bony hand behind his back. 'I congratulate you, Reverend, on your intimate knowledge of what God has ordained. It must be comforting to know God's will so clearly, but I cannot help wondering why he singled out you, of all people, for enlightenment while choosing to leave the rest of us blind. As for the social order, sir, I can only say that any social order which condemns the mass of society to live in ignorance, poverty and wretched vice deserves to be overthrown, and sooner rather than later.'

'Blasphemy!' shouted the vicar. 'You and the others like you, you are all socialist blasphemers! Well, you will receive your reckoning! God will take note of your impiety, and strike you down!'

'Others like me?' repeated Mr Raikes. 'Do you then include the Earl of Shaftesbury in our number, Reverend? Are you accusing his lordship of blasphemy? If so, then you will need to tread very carefully.'

Reverend Hobbes stood silent, his mouth open. Lord Shaftesbury, the president of the Ragged Schools Union, was well known as a pillar of the Church of England, and he was also one of the most powerful men in British politics. Antagonising him would be dangerous indeed, as the vicar knew only too well.

'I have acquainted Lord Shaftesbury with the facts of this situation,' Mr Raikes went on. 'I can inform you, Reverend, that he regards the foundation of the Rotherhithe Ragged School as a great step forward for our movement. He sends his personal congratulations to Miss Perrow for her initiative and courage.'

Now it was Grace's turn to stand with her mouth open. 'You will desist from your obstruction of Miss Perrow's school,' Mr Raikes said to the vicar. 'You will offer her no further opposition. If you do so, then I promise you, his lordship will come to hear of it. Am I clear, sir?'

'You are clear,' said the vicar, through clenched teeth.

'Then my business here is done. Miss Perrow, we shall take our leave now.'

Out in the street, walking back towards the railway station, Mr Raikes nodded with satisfaction. 'That was easier than I expected,' he said. 'With men like Reverend Hobbes, an appeal to their sense of self-preservation is generally all that is needed. As for the South Eastern Railway, you need have no fear of them. I shall have a word with their directors. I fancy that, once again, the mention of Lord Shaftesbury's name will bring them swiftly to heel.'

Grace was still full of astonishment. 'Did Lord Shaftesbury himself really say that about me?'

'I spoke with him last evening,' said Mr Raikes. 'He was not yet aware of your school's foundation, but he was most interested to hear of it. He said specifically that he admired your courage.'

'Goodness,' said Grace. She felt a little overwhelmed. 'But why should I need courage?'

'Because Rotherhithe is a dangerous place,' said Mr Raikes. 'Oh, we have schools in worse places still; Field Lane in Camden, for instance, the school about which Mr Charles Dickens once wrote so memorably. But none of these schools are run by a woman, let alone a young one, working all alone.'

Mr Raikes paused for a moment. 'Reverend Hobbes is not the only opponent you will face,' he said. 'There will be others, more threatening and more dangerous by far. And we will not always be able to help you stand against them, Miss Perrow. I hope that God in his mercy watches over you. For I think you will need His love and protection, before all is done.'

When they reached the railway station he turned and bowed to her again. 'Forgive me,' he said. 'I hope I have not alarmed you.'

'Not at all,' said Grace.

The next week went well. Nathan and Lettice and some of the others continued to struggle, but Grace remembered Mr Raikes's advice and was kind and patient with them. Jimmy continued to flourish. Every day his reading improved, and he began to memorise the multiplication table; by the end of the week he could recite from 1x1 to 12x12 by heart, without faltering. Grace's pride in her pupil grew along with his confidence.

On Thursday morning a bitter east wind blew a reeking sea fog up the Thames, shrouding Rotherhithe. The masts and cranes were like skeletons in the gloom, and the trains on the railway viaduct continued to belch steam and smoke, thickening the air still further. When Grace and the children arrived at the school she noticed the gang of girls huddling in one of the nearby arches, clinging to each other to keep warm. She noticed again the girl she had seen in the market, holding the little boy wrapped close to her, trying to impart warmth to him. On impulse, she turned and walked over to the girls.

'I am about to light a fire,' she said. 'Why don't you come in, and be warm?'

The girl who was holding the little boy looked back at her. 'Who are you?' she asked. Her voice trembled with cold, but she spoke in strong, firm tones.

'My name is Grace. I am a teacher, and this is a school. Don't worry, you don't need to take lessons. Just come in and be warm.'

They looked back at her without speaking. Grace smiled in what she hoped was a reassuring way then went into the school. The knives at their belts no longer worried her. These were children, desperate and homeless. They were no threat to her.

They did not follow her at once. Living wild as they did, every new thing was a source of danger. But the cold was stronger than their instinct for survival, and an hour after lessons began, the canvas flap opened and the first skinny, grimy child stepped cautiously into the arch, looking around in fear and wonder. Others followed, the girl leading the little boy last of all.

'Welcome,' Grace said kindly. 'You must be frozen. Come here, close to the stove. I'm afraid we have no more benches, you will have to sit on the ground, but at least you will be warm.'

Wordlessly they obeyed her, slinking among the other children like wild animals, then reaching the stove and sinking down onto the ground. 'We shall resume our lessons,' said Grace to her pupils, who were staring at the feral girls in wonder. Daisy in particular had eyes like saucers. But they resumed their spelling lesson, and within a few minutes the cold, exhausted girls were asleep on the ground.

All but one. She sat holding the little boy asleep on her lap, watching Grace steadily. Her eyes flickered back and forth between Grace and the blackboard covered in chalked letters. There was no expression in her face, not fear, not curiosity, nothing at all. Grace wondered what she was thinking; or indeed whether, numbed with cold, she was thinking anything at all.

Once, when the others were working on the slates, she turned to the girl. 'What is your name?' she asked.

'Mary.' She indicated the boy. 'This here's Joe.'

Joe's nose was running as he slept. Grace reached out with a handkerchief and wiped it gently. The little boy snuffled but did not wake. 'Your brother?' Grace asked.

Mary nodded. 'Stay here,' Grace said. 'Stay as long as you like. We will look after you.' Then she smiled and stepped back to the blackboard, and resumed the lesson.

∞

I couldn't tell what she was doing at first. Them marks she was making on the blackboard, they were like the marks birds make when they scratch in the dirt. But then as I watched, I saw there was more to it than that. She was making patterns. And then I began to listen, and I realised each pattern had a sound that went with it.

It was like magic. She wove those patterns together, like she was plaiting straw to make a basket, or weaving hemp into rope. And each time she did it she made a word. I didn't know all the words, but even the ones I didn't understand I could still hear, invisible in the air. It was amazing what she did. I didn't know what it was for or why she was doing it, but it was amazing.

Later she read to them out of some book. I didn't like that so much. It was all nonsense, about rabbits and lobsters and queens, but it made the kiddies happy, so I suppose something good came of it. Afterwards they sang. Missy woke up when the singing started and lay there listening. Her face was in shadow and I couldn't see at first, but after a while I realised she was crying.

I didn't cry. I just held little Joe close while he slept, and I felt the music making a big dark hole inside me, a hole that got bigger and bigger as the song went on, and I realised how little my life was, and how much I was missing.

Chapter 7

Grace knew she should wake the sleeping girls at the end of the lesson and ask them to leave, but she could not bear to do so. It was warm next to the stove, and turning them out into the cold would have been an act of wanton cruelty.

Back home, when she told George what she had done, he was horrified. 'I know them girls! They're a pack of little savages! And you let them in with our kids?'

'They're not savages,' said Grace. 'They're desperate, that's all.'

'Desperate! They held up the baker's van at knife point last week, didn't you hear? Threatened to stab him, and then stole bread out of the van and ran off. The driver was scared witless, poor soul.'

'I expect they were hungry,' Grace said. 'Honestly, George, there was no threat in them. They were too tired and cold to be a danger to anyone.'

'I wasn't scared of them at all, Daddy,' Albert said.

'I wasn't scared either,' said Daisy, and Harry nodded with his mouth full of food. 'They liked it when we sang,' he said.

Grace had seen one of the girls in tears during the music, and had felt a prickle behind her own eyes in response. 'Every one of those children is a walking tragedy,' she said. 'I can't do much to help them, George, but at least I can let them stay warm. I promise you, if ever I think they are becoming a danger, I will call the constables.'

'Fat lot of use the constables will be. I tell you what'll happen, Grace. You'll go back to the school in the morning and they'll have cleaned the whole place out, lock, stock and barrel.'

'Perhaps they will, perhaps they won't. I hope that kindness will be repaid with kindness.'

'Hope,' George snorted.

'Yes, hope,' said Grace. 'Without it, where would we be?'

As it turned out, she was right. She returned to the school the next morning with the children to find everything exactly as she had left it. There was no sign of the girls. Oddly, Grace felt vaguely disappointed that they were gone. But later that morning, as the pupils were doing sums and she was kneeling beside Nathan's bench teaching him his numbers, the canvas flap opened and the girl called Mary came in, leading Joe by the hand. One by one the other girls followed her.

'Can we come in?' asked Mary simply.

'You will always be welcome here,' said Grace. 'Come, gather around the stove and get warm.'

And so, life at the Rotherhithe Ragged School settled into a gentle routine. Every morning the pupils gathered in the railway arch to study, sometimes reading and writing, sometimes doing arithmetic, and afterwards Grace would read to them and then they would sing. The gang of girls were never there when they arrived – Grace guessed they were out hunting for food – but later each morning they returned, slipping like little ghosts into the schoolroom. Most paid no attention to the pupils or herself and simply fell asleep by the fire.

The exception was Mary. She never slept, at least not when Grace was there. Instead she sat holding her sleeping brother in her lap, soothing him a little if he woke, watching Grace with eyes that never seemed to blink. *She never lets her guard down*, Grace thought. She is always alert, waiting for danger.

November turned into December. The winter weather turned colder still. Often there was a skin of ice on the puddles as they walked to school. Their house, like all the houses on Bell Lane, had been built quickly and in a shoddy fashion; no matter how much coal they put in the stove, the house never seemed really warm, and the smell of damp was always with them. The children often had coughs, as did George, who suffered more working outside at the docks in the wind and weather. The spectre of the consumption that had killed Rosa returned to haunt Grace's mind. She covered the children in old blankets, and made hot poultices for their chests to keep the coughs at bay.

Very often Jimmy accompanied them back to the house and shared their midday meal. Feeding an extra person on a tight budget was not easy, especially when he ate as much as Jimmy did. 'I hope you don't mind,' Grace said once to George.

Generous as ever, George did not mind. 'He's a nice lad. I hope he's not making trouble for himself at home, though.'

Grace nodded. 'I know his mother. We were in the workhouse together. She was a nasty piece of work then, and still is.'

'She's a saint, compared to that fellow of hers.'

Grace was surprised. 'You know him?'

'No, but Jimmy told me his dad was a deal porter, so I asked Mickey Doyle about him. His name is Ben Wilson. Long Ben, they call him. He's a docker, all right, but he's also in thick with the Bull Head Gang. He's one of their insiders on the docks, says where the best cargoes are and which warehouses to rob and how to get around the night watchmen. There's a brother called Jake, too, older than Jimmy. He's a cutpurse, wanted by the law. Rumours say he's up at Jacob's Island.'

Jacob's Island on the Thames was one of the worst dens of crime and vice in all of London. Grace shuddered. 'Poor little boy,' she said. 'Oh, George. We are so lucky to have these three little ones healthy, happy, and safe.'

'Mostly thanks to you, Grace,' said George, and he kissed her gently on the cheek.

After that Grace tried a couple of times to ask Jimmy about his home life, with the vague idea of helping him in some way, but the boy refused to answer. He continued to attend school, never missing a lesson; unlike poor Lettice the match girl, who had to work in the market to make ends meet and was falling still further behind the other pupils. Jimmy, on the other hand, was a shining light. His reading, writing and sums were now well ahead of the others in the class, and Grace realised that soon she would have little to teach him. He needed a good school.

The question was, where to find one? She sat down one afternoon, after the children had gone to rest, and wrote a letter to Mrs Clare.

My dear Mrs Clare,

I hope this letter finds you very well, and Mr Clare too. Mela writes often, giving me news of the school and my former pupils, whom I very much miss.

I am writing in the hope that I might beg your assistance. I have a pupil, a talented young boy who comes from a very poor background. I believe he might flourish at a grammar school, not only intellectually but also spiritually. His parents are violent and unpleasant people. Removing him from his home can be a good thing. I am confident that if he receives a proper education he could get a good job, as a clerk or secretary, or even with the right encouragement and support, attend university. It would take him away from the hard world he inhabits now. I wonder, therefore, if you could recommend any schools to whom I might apply on this boy's behalf?

Thank you, dear Mrs Clare, for your kindness. I think of you often, and you are always in my heart and prayers.

Your ever affectionate,

Grace

Mrs Clare's letter came back the following day.

My dearest Grace,

What a pleasure it is to hear from you, my dear. We all miss you at the Clare School, and the boys and girls all send you their fond best wishes. It seems clear that your own school is thriving. I cannot tell you how proud we all are of you.

As for grammar schools, I can recommend no finer institution than Colfe's School in Lewisham. It is not far from you, and the headmaster, Mr Graham, is a fine and generous man. I heard him speak some months back at a meeting of the National Education League. I am certain he will give you a hearing.

Take care, my dear, and stay safe,

Your loving friend,

Angela Clare

Much encouraged, Grace wrote a letter to the Mr Graham, asking for an appointment. Receiving a positive reply, she went out on Saturday afternoon and took the train to Lewisham, just a few stops down the South Eastern line.

Lewisham was only four miles from Rotherhithe, but it belonged to a different world. Streets of fine houses and gardens gave onto meadows still green, even in the dead of winter, and leafless woodlands where rooks cawed amid the branches. When Grace rang the bell at the gate of Colfe's School, she could hear sheep baa-ing in the fields beyond.

Mr Graham was interested in her work and, despite her youth, treated her with respect. 'I have the utmost admiration for anyone who teaches in a Ragged School, ma'am. Your burden, I daresay, is far heavier than mine.'

'Thank you,' said Grace smiling. 'I confess I do not find it unduly heavy. Not yet, at any rate.'

'This boy you described in your letter, Jimmy Wilson. How old is he?'

'It is difficult to say, sir. I am not certain if he knows himself. I would guess he is about ten years of age.'

'Hmm. A little young, but . . . you say he has talent?'

'He has more than that, sir. He is a prodigy. In just a few months, he has learned to write fluently, and he is reading at a level much beyond that of a boy of his years. His ability to learn is quite astonishing. He has read nearly every tract I can supply, and is determined to start reading a book very soon.'

'Very soon? What is holding him back from starting straight away?'

'Indecision.' Grace smiled. 'He cannot make up his mind whether to begin with the Bible, or *Alice's Adventures in Wonderland*.'

'Both in their own way excellent examples of the art of storytelling,' said the headmaster, his eyes twinkling. 'And numeracy?'

'He can do his sums and knows his times tables, and is making progress with long division. Indeed, he knows as much about numbers by this point as I do.'

'Or I. But perhaps our maths master can make something of him. Very well, Miss Perrow. We will examine your young prodigy at the start of next term, and provided he is as good as you say he is, we will take him on. We will waive his fees, and he can board with myself and my wife until other provision can be made.'

Grace took the train back to Rotherhithe and walked home through the early winter dusk, the shadows lit by sparks from chimneys and flares from the engine works, her heart singing. She did not tell Jimmy what she had done. He loved school and she was certain he hated his life at home, but the prospect of uprooting him from the only home he had ever known would still come as a shock. She needed to work up to the idea slowly.

That evening after the children were in bed, she told George about her visit to Lewisham. He rubbed his chin, not saying anything. 'What is wrong?' she asked.

They were sitting in the little lamplit parlour, where the fumes from the coal fire competed with the smell of damp. 'You know I've never interfered in anything you do at the school, Grace,' George said. 'But, are you sure what you're doing is right?'

'What do you mean?'

'How are you going to get this boy away from his family? You can't just kidnap him, you know.'

'I wasn't going to,' said Grace, a little tartly. 'I shall persuade him to go of his own free will.'

'I reckon his parents will have something to say about that,' George said. 'Ben Wilson isn't going to let his son go easy, and from what you said about this Sara woman, I reckon she won't neither. And Jimmy is young. A magistrate would probably just send him back to his parents.'

Grace's heart sank. 'I have to do something, George,' she said. 'It's not enough for Jimmy to go to school, he needs to get out and away from his family. Otherwise, he'll end up in one of the gangs.'

George looked disbelieving. 'Jimmy, in a gang? He's too soft. He wouldn't last five minutes in a gang.'

'Yes,' said Grace. 'That's exactly what I'm afraid of.'

Two days later, Grace and a group of children, including Albert, the twins, Rebecca Berton and Jimmy, were on their way home from school. A group of boys, who had been gathered in a little huddle around the fence at the back of the factory, turned suddenly and began walking towards them, spreading out in a line to bar their way. The oldest was probably about thirteen, Grace thought, the youngest eight or nine, but there was nothing childlike about their faces, or the cudgels and rough-honed knives they held in their hands.

'There he is,' said one of the older boys. He wore a man's coat that hung down to his knees, the elbows worn through, and a shapeless cap on his head. 'Hullo, Jim. What you doin' here, then?'

Grace glanced at Jimmy and saw he had gone white with fright. 'Cat got your tongue?' the other boy jeered. 'Come on, Jim. Speak up. What you doin' with this bunch of babies? Or maybe you're a baby too. A little cry-baby, just like them.'

'Oh, for heaven's sake!' snapped Grace. 'Leave him alone, and get out of our way.'

The boys didn't move. 'That's big talk comin' from you, missy,' said the one in the long coat. 'You want to be careful talkin' like that. You need to show more respect when you talk to a man.'

'When I meet a man, I will consider it,' said Grace, and she took a couple of steps towards him. 'Meanwhile, *boy*, you will show *me* some respect and get out of my way. Or do I have to turn you over my knee and spank you?'

Some of her pupils sniggered. So did a couple of the gang boys, nudging each other and pointing at their leader who stood and stared at Grace, discomfited. After a moment he turned his head and spat deliberately on the ground, then motioned to his fellows and turned and walked away. The others trotted after him, some glancing at Grace and still laughing. Feeling much less calm than she looked, Grace turned to her charges. 'Come, children. Let us be on our way.'

When they reached Bell Lane, Jimmy refused to stay for lunch and ran off without another word. Upset, Grace ushered Albert and the twins inside and went to prepare lunch. The twins played happily in the parlour but Albert came into the kitchen and stood beside her, silently. He knew she had been in danger, and wanted to protect her.

She heard the squeal of delight as the twins ran to greet their father. A moment later George came into the kitchen, a giggling child tucked under each arm, but when he saw Grace's face he set the children down and came over to her. 'What has happened?'

Grace told him, and he nodded soberly. 'I know the lads you mean. Proper little thugs, they are.' He paused. 'Sounds like they were waiting for you, Grace.'

'Yes,' said Grace. 'I'm sure they were. They know Jimmy is at the school, and decided to bully him. If those boys know, it won't be long before his parents know too. George, I've got to get him away from here. I'm really worried for him now.'

'I'm not worrying about Jimmy,' George said. 'I'm worried about you. Who's going to protect you?'

'I will,' said Albert stoutly.

George smiled and ruffled his hair. 'You're a brave lad. But it'll need more than you.' He looked back at Grace. 'Perhaps we should get a dog. It could protect you, and the other kids and the school, too. Those little ruffians might try to get at Jimmy by attacking the school.'

'And how would we feed a dog?' Grace demanded. 'We can only just about afford to feed ourselves.'

George shrugged. 'It was just a thought.'

But what he had said about the gang of boys attacking the school worried Grace. That afternoon she asked Mrs Berton to keep an eye on the children and put on a coat and hurried back to the school. Most of the gang girls were still asleep around the warm stove. Mary was asleep too. It was the first time Grace had seen her eyes closed, but she sat up quickly when the canvas flap opened, moving her body around to protect her brother. She relaxed when she saw Grace, and took her hand away from the hilt of her knife.

'May I talk to you?' Grace asked quietly.

Mary nodded. She listened in silence while Grace explained about the bullies, her eyes never leaving Grace's face. 'I'm worried these boys might try to vandalise the school. Will you and the others keep watch? If you do, I am quite happy for you to continue sleeping here.'

Mary nodded again. 'We'll look after it. Me and the Angels.'

'The Angels?'

The girl gestured around at the others. 'The gang. That's what we call ourselves. It's by way of being a joke,' she added.

'I assumed as much,' Grace said dryly. She studied the girl for a moment. 'How old are you, Mary?'

The girl shrugged one shoulder. Grace considered. 'How many summers can you remember? Tick them off on your fingers as you think of them.'

Mary frowned and began to count slowly on her fingers. When she reached eight she stopped. *Add another two that she is too young to remember*, thought Grace, *and that makes ten. She looks older, but hardship does that to children. It hollows their cheeks and lines their faces, and makes them old before their time.*

'What happened?' Grace asked. 'How did you end up with the Angels?'

Mary shrugged again. 'My da worked at the docks, on the other side of the river. He was killed, some sort of accident; I don't know what happened. Ma was sick and couldn't work, so some men came and said we had to leave our home. We went to the workhouse. They wouldn't let Joe and I see Ma, and then one day they said she was dead. I think that place killed her.'

'Very likely it did,' Grace said softly. 'What did you do?'

'I grabbed Joe and we ran away. We crossed the river hoping no one would find us and bring us back. We met the Angels and fell in with them. We been living on the streets ever since. That's all there is to tell.'

'How have you survived?'

Mary looked perplexed. 'What do you do for food?' Grace asked.

'Steal it, mostly. Like that day in the market.'

Grace thought of Mr Hogg, establishing a kitchen to feed his pauper children. *What I wouldn't give for the money to feed these children as well as teach them,* she thought.

'What are you going to do?' she asked. 'When you grow up, I mean.'

'I want to join the Forty Elephants,' said Mary.

'And who are they?'

'A gang of flash morts from over west, round Elephant and Castle. They go up to the West End and rob society women and steal their jewellery. They're rich, and dress in fine clothes and never go hungry. If I join them, I'll be rich too, and I can look after little Joe forever.'

'That's all you want to do? Be a thief?'

'Why not?' Mary asked simply.

Grace could make no answer to that. 'Thank you for looking after the school,' she said, and turned to go.

'Why do you do it, miss?' Mary asked. 'This school, I mean. What do these kids matter to you?'

Grace paused. She thought about trying to explain the value of education and how it opened up doors and allowed people to be free of their past and go out and discover the world and themselves, but she was not sure how much of this Mary would understand. 'I'm trying to give them hope,' she said finally.

'Hope for what?'

'For whatever they want, Mary. For whatever they dream of.' Grace gestured towards the sleeping boy. 'What does Joe dream of, do you think?'

'I don't know,' said Mary. 'He hasn't spoken a word since Ma died. You're a good woman, Miss Perrow. But you can't help every kid. Jimmy's da and brother will come and take him, sooner or later. The gangs want him, you see.'

'Why would the gangs want a boy like Jimmy?'

'All the big gangs want kids, 'specially boys. They toughen 'em up, see, make 'em hard. They become soldiers in the gangs, ready to rob and steal and cut people up. Jimmy'll probably end up with the Captain's lot.'

Grace's heart sank. 'Do you mean the Bull Head Gang?'

'Yes, miss. They're always wantin' new soldiers. I expect Jimmy's da has already promised him, when he is older.'

'Well, he won't have him,' Grace said grimly. 'I shall see to that.'

But Jimmy did not come the next day, or the next. Grace walked to Hanover Court after dinner and knocked at the door of the Wilson house. There was no answer. She knocked several more times, but still the house remained silent, its windows dark in the December dusk. A neighbour looked out to see who was knocking. She slammed the door tight when she saw Grace.

'Jimmy,' Grace called quietly. 'It's Miss Perrow. Can you come to the door?'

She thought she heard a faint noise in the house, but when she listened again, all was silent once more. Worried sick by the thought of what might have happened to Jimmy, she turned and walked home.

Another week passed without any sign of Jimmy, and Grace was beginning to grow very worried about him. Then one morning, after George had left for work and as she was getting the children ready for school, there came an urgent knock at the door. When she opened it, one of the Angels was in the street, huddling up against the wall to stay out of the wind.

Grace was getting to know the girls now, and knew some of their names. This one, with a perpetually runny nose, was called Missy. 'What is it?' she asked.

'Mary asks you to come quick, miss.'

Alarm leaped in Grace's mind. 'What is it? Has something happened at the school?'

'Yes, miss.'

Leaving the children at home, Grace hurried to the school. When she arrived, she was horrified by what she saw. The sailcloth covering the arch and protecting them from the weather had been slashed to ribbons and part of it had been torn down. Inside, desks and benches were overturned, slates and chalk broken and hurled across the room, printed reading sheets torn up and scattered on the ground. The cabinet of books had been smashed open and the books thrown around the room too, some of them with covers ripped off. The stove had been knocked over and the chimney dangled from the roof of the arch, swaying a little in the wind.

Mary was there, holding her brother by the hand, and a couple of other girls with her. 'Who did this?' Grace asked. 'The boys?'

'No, miss,' said Mary. 'It was men that came and did this. Men from the Bull Head Gang. The same lot as Jimmy's da.'

Grace's heart sank. Sara must have discovered that Jimmy had returned to school and told her husband, and he and his mates from the gang had decided to smash up the school. 'We couldn't stop 'em, miss,' said one of the other girls. 'They told us to get out. Threatened to break our necks if we didn't.'

Mary looked steadily at Grace. 'I'm sorry,' she said. 'I promised we would keep it safe.'

'Oh, my dear child,' Grace said. 'I asked you to watch out for a gang of boys. You could hardly stand up to grown men.' She bent and began collecting books.

Mary let go of Joe's hand and came to help her. 'What will you do?' the girl asked.

'Rebuild it and start again,' Grace said. 'I'm not giving up.'

'You will give up, if you know what's good for you,' a man's voice said.

Grace straightened and turned sharply. The man who stood where the door of the school had been was powerfully built, nearly as broad as he was tall, and he wore a rough coat with a heavy leather apron and cap, the kind the deal porters used in the docks when carrying baulks of timber, to protect their heads and shoulders from splinters. He stood with his thumbs tucked into his belt, a knife in a sheath at his side.

'Who are you?' Grace demanded.

'None of your business,' said the man, and he hawked and spat at her feet. 'I've got a message for you from the Captain. Don't go messin' about with things that are none of your concern. Leave this school nonsense alone, leave the kiddies alone, and get back to that fellow of yours.'

'He's not my fellow,' snapped Grace. 'He is my brother-in-law.'

'Sure,' said the man, with contempt in his voice. 'Whatever you want to call it, dolly. But stay away from this school, and leave our kids alone.'

'Who are you?' Grace demanded again. 'Are you Jimmy's father?'

The man hawked and spat again. 'Nah,' he said. 'I ain't Long Ben. I'm just a friend, see. Now, I'll say it again for you, dolly. Keep away from kids like Jimmy.'

A sudden wave of horror flooded over Grace. 'Where is Jimmy? What have you done with him?'

'You ain't going to see Jimmy again,' said the man. He turned and walked away, leaving Grace standing and watching him, sick with fear.

Leaving the Angels behind, she hurried to Hanover Court as fast as her long skirts and the slippery, muddy streets would allow. This time the door was flung open and Sara stood in the doorway, her face and eyes red, her arms crossed over her chest.

'Why?' she shouted before Grace could speak. 'Why did you try to take him from us?'

'I didn't,' Grace said, though a guilty voice in the back of her mind told her this was exactly what she had been trying to do. 'I was only trying to give him what he wanted, Sara. Education, and a little hope for the future.'

'Why?' Sara shouted again. 'Why should he have hope when the rest of us don't? Why should he get to go free when the rest of us are stuck in this hellhole for the rest of our lives? Why, you little cow? You tell me the answer, and maybe I won't thump the daylights out of you.'

Grace realised that Sara was drunk, and also that she had been crying. That shocked her; she had not thought Sara capable of motherly feeling. 'Where is Jimmy?' she demanded.

'Gone,' said Sara. 'They've taken him away. Somewhere you'll never find him. Now get out of here! Get away from me, and stay away, do you hear? Or by God, I really will smash you.'

She raised her fists. Remembered fear washed over Grace, and she backed away, frightened while at the same time ashamed of her fear. 'He's gone,' Sara said. 'He's gone, and he'll never come back. What's done can't be undone. Leave it alone. For God's sake, just leave us alone.'

∞

'Maybe this time you'll learn to obey,' the Captain's voice said.

I was in a pit with a cover over the top, dark as hell. There was mud and water under my feet, and the stink was something awful. I pounded my fists on the cover, pulling at it, trying to shift it, but it was anchored solid. There wasn't a chink of light anywhere in the pit, just the dark, grabbing at me, trying to smother me.

'I promise,' I said. I was crying hard, blubbering and pleading. 'I promise. I'll do whatever you ask, but please let me out.'

'No, Jimmy. You'll stay there for a good long while, until you've truly learned to do as you're told.'

I couldn't think. I could hardly breathe. 'Please,' I said. 'Please.'

'Think,' the Captain said. 'Think about your future, Jimmy. You were promised to us, long ago, and we own you.'

I heard him walk away. I was alone, and the invisible fingers of the dark were around my neck, trying to strangle me. I sat choking, shivering, too frightened even to cry. My ma had cried when I was taken away. I was surprised, because I didn't think she cared enough to cry about me.

Now, I clung to the hope she might come and rescue me. I didn't really think she would, she was too scared of Da and the Captain, but I had to hope. Miss Perrow taught me how important hope is.

Oh, please, Mummy, please. Come and find me. I'm so afraid of the dark.

Chapter 8

Back in Bell Lane, Grace burst into tears. Albert and the twins watched her in concern, for she seldom cried in front of them. George, just returned from work, put a comforting arm around her and held her close for a moment, patting her on the back.

'I'm sorry,' Grace sniffed. 'But I can't help but grieve for him, George. It's so sad to think of all the things he could have had, and all the things he'll miss.'

'And maybe one day he will have them,' said George. 'Sara said they've taken him away. That means he's still alive, lass. And while there's life, there's hope. Remember?'

'But I'll never see him again,' said Grace.

'Don't be too certain of that, neither. Now, dry your eyes, lass. We've got work to do.'

Grace looked up at him. 'What do you mean?'

'We've got to rebuild your school. You're not planning on giving in to these bullies, are you? Because if you are, you're not the Grace Perrow I know.'

'No,' said Grace, taking the rather grimy handkerchief he gave her and blowing her nose. 'Of course not.'

'That's more like it,' said George cheerfully, and he turned and scooped up Daisy and tickled her. She giggled and the mood lightened. *He is right,* Grace thought. *I must get on with things.* Jimmy was one child; there are twenty others depending on me.

Yet Jimmy had touched her heart in a way that none of the others, save for her own family, had ever done. She vowed she wouldn't give up on Jimmy and one day she would find some say to help him, but in the meantime she was more determined than ever that the Ragged School would succeed.

The first step in rebuilding the school was to write to Mr Raikes at the Ragged School Union and see what help he could give. He arrived a day later, bringing with him a box of reading materials and some slates and chalk and slate pencils to replace the ones that had been broken. The latter was a particular relief. She had been thinking she would need to approach the Clares again, but that would mean telling them what had happened and she did not want to do that. They – and Mela – would only worry for her.

'You say this damage was done by one of the local gangs,' said Mr Raikes. 'Have you reported it to the police?'

'No, sir. My brother-in-law doubts it will do any good. The police here seem powerless to stop the gangs.'

'Let us try all the same,' said Mr Raikes firmly.

They rang the bell at the police house in Rotherhithe. A skinny young constable with bad skin opened the door and ushered them into the foyer. He listened to Grace's account of the damage to the school, shook his head dubiously, and then disappeared into a back office. They heard the faint murmur of voices.

Another officer came out, an older man with greying hair, clapping his blue helmet onto his head. 'I am Sergeant Bates,' he said. 'What's all this about a school?'

Grace explained again. The sergeant looked bored. 'I see,' he said. 'And what do you expect us to do about it?'

'We expect you to do your duty,' said Mr Raikes. 'This is a clear case of criminal damage, and the identity of the perpetrators is known. Will you arrest them?'

'Arrest them?' The sergeant's expression changed. 'Arrest the Bull Head Gang? Have you lost your wits?'

'I assure you I have not,' said Mr Raikes. 'This outrage must not go unpunished.'

The sergeant puffed his cheeks and then exhaled sharply. 'Outrage,' he repeated. 'Hardly that, is it? A few books damaged, a few slates broken, that's all. And my men are overstretched as it is. Sorry, can't help you. If you want to keep people out of your school, put a lock on the door.'

'Very well,' said Mr Raikes. 'If you will not take action, Sergeant, I shall have to go over your head.'

The sergeant's eyes bulged. 'Over my head?' he repeated. 'How dare you come in here and speak to me like that? Get out, now, both of you!'

Outside in the street a little watery sunlight was leaking through gaps in the clouds. A brewer's van splashed

152

past, the horses hock deep in mud. 'What now?' asked Grace.

'I shall write to the local division commander of the Metropolitan Police,' said Mr Raikes, 'and I shall also ask Lord Shaftesbury to have a word with the commissioner.' He sighed. 'However, I doubt that any good will come of it. My threat was an empty one, and Sergeant Bates knew it. The situation is clear.'

'And what is the situation, sir?'

'Bates is frightened. He was full of bluster, but I could see the fear in his eyes. And that means one of two things. Either he is frightened of the Bull Head Gang, who are threatening him, or he is colluding with the gang and is afraid it will come to light. Or both,' Mr Raikes concluded. 'Either way, even if his superior officers do put pressure on him, he is unlikely to take action.'

Grace digested this. 'Everyone has been telling me the police wouldn't help,' she said. 'Now I understand why. Can anything be done?'

'I very much doubt it,' said Mr Raikes. 'Knowing about police corruption is one thing, finding evidence of it and persuading the authorities to act is very much another. I am sorry, Miss Perrow. I fear this is not the outcome you were hoping for.'

'No,' said Grace. She thought again for a moment. 'Perhaps ... Perhaps it doesn't matter. The gang were angry because I was teaching a particular boy, Jimmy Wilson. His father has now sent him away.' She stopped for a moment, wondering where Jimmy was and fighting back another rush of emotion. 'Perhaps now they will leave us alone,' she said.

'I fear that is unlikely,' said Mr Raikes. 'I have seen these situations before. The local gangs dislike our schools, and resent their presence. They see us as interfering outsiders, and are opposed to the influence we gain over the children, the boys in particular. They regard the boys as their property. If we educate these poor lads, they will leave home to look for better jobs and new lives, and so will be out of the clutches of the gangs.'

'But why?' asked Grace. 'What do they want with the boys?'

'Put brutally, they are cannon fodder,' said Mr Raikes. 'The younger ones serve as watchers and lookouts, or are set to work as petty thieves and cutpurses. The older ones engage in armed robbery, large-scale theft, blackmail and a host of other crimes. Of course, many come to bad ends. They are killed in fights, or die of drink and disease, or less frequently, are arrested and put in prison. The gangs need a steady supply of boys to fill up their ranks. That is why they see our schools as a threat. Education is the enemy of poverty, and poverty is the close ally of crime.'

'They are soldiers,' Grace said, remembering what Mary had told her.

'Just so, Miss Perrow,' said Mr Raikes sombrely. 'And they come to the same end as so many soldiers do, a sudden death and a nameless grave. Believe me, it gives me no pleasure to say this.'

He turned to look at Grace. 'What will you do now?'

'Carry on,' said Grace, still thinking of Jimmy. 'I have come too far to turn back now.'

'Then I salute your courage,' said Mr Raikes.

That night Grace spoke again to George. 'We must make the school more secure. Can we brick up the archway, and put in a door with a lock?'

'We would never afford the bricks,' said George. 'But we might get some timber for free.'

'Oh? Where?'

George grinned at her. 'This is Rotherhithe, lass. Forty ships a day come into the Surrey Docks, from Canada and Russia and Norway, laden with timber. There's warehouses stacked with the stuff. Go to one of the importers and ask if they'll donate some from their stocks. Try Mr Gould at Five. He's said to have a good heart. He might be willing to listen.'

Grace thought about this. 'And if he does, what then?'

'Me and Mickey will get some of the lads together. We can knock up a wall one Sunday, and make a door too. And see if that ironmonger will give you a lock.'

George's employers would not give him time off work, so Grace went alone to find Mr Gould. She had never been down to the docks before, and when she walked through the gates, she stopped for a moment and looked around in wonder.

Behind her lay Limehouse Reach on the Thames, crowded with shipping. Ahead were the Surrey Docks, great ponds carved out of the boggy land bordering the river and connected to it by canals. There were ships everywhere; mighty three-masted sailing ships, smaller coasters and hoys, wooden-hulled steamers with smoke trickling from their funnels. Close at hand a tugboat, its funnel belching more smoke, slowly drew another ship through a canal towards Lady Dock. Logs floated in booms, enclosed by chains to keep them from drifting in front of the ships, and she watched men running across the logs, heavy iron hooks in their hands. She expected them to slip and fall between the rolling logs, but their feet were nimble and they never once stumbled.

A wagon pulled up, the driver looking at her in surprise. Unaccompanied women did not often come to the docks. 'Can I help you, ma'am?' he asked.

'Yes. Can you direct me to Acorn Pond?'

'You mean Five?' the driver asked. A few years ago the owners of the docks had renamed some of the ponds, giving them surprisingly delicate names, Lavender Pond, Lady Dock and the like, but the men who worked here still referred to them by their old names. Timber Pond Five was now called Acorn Pond.

'It's the next one along,' said the driver, pointing. 'What are you wanting there, ma'am?'

'I'm looking for the offices of Mr Gould.'

'Aye, that's where you'll find him. Go along the line of warehouses, and his office is in the second one from the end.'

Grace thanked him and walked towards Acorn Pond and the row of brick warehouses. George, she knew, was hard at work not far away, building similar warehouses at the huge new pond the company planned to call Canada Dock. The cold air was full of the scents of freshly cut wood, hot oily tar and the resinous scent of pitch all underlaid with coal smoke. Men hurried around her, pushing handcarts or carrying enormously heavy stacks of wooden planks and beams, and she wondered at the strength needed to lift such massive loads. Some of them turned and stared as she went past, and she could feel their gaze follow her as she walked past the long row of warehouses. A pack of dogs ran along the waterfront, chasing each other and barking.

Gould & Co.'s warehouse was one of the largest. Its doors were open and men were bringing in cargoes from two big steamships moored opposite, not just timber but also wooden barrels of pitch and bales of furs wrapped in canvas to protect them from salt water during the voyage. The spices of the tropics and exotic goods from the east all went to the London Docks north of the Thames; the commerce of the northern lands came here to the Surrey Docks.

Mr Gould's office was a small, rather plain brick hut next to the warehouse. A secretary in black frock coat sitting behind a desk looked up as she entered. 'Yes?' he asked abruptly.

'My name is Grace Perrow,' Grace said. 'I wish to see Mr Gould.'

'Have you an appointment?'

'No.'

The secretary clicked his tongue in annoyance. 'Very well. Wait here.' He rose and went through an interior door into another office. A couple of minutes later he returned. 'This way, please.'

Mr Gould was tall, with broad shoulders that stretched the seams of his frock coat. He had a rather hard, weathered face, and Grace wondered if he had once been a sailor. He laid down the sheaf of papers he had been studying and rose to his feet as she entered. 'Mrs Perrow,' he said abruptly. 'What can I do for you?'

'It's Miss Perrow,' said Grace, dropping a curtsey.

Mr Gould looked horrified. 'A single woman, walking around these docks on her own? What the devil were you thinking of? Have you no care for your reputation?'

'I do,' said Grace, 'but I also needed to see you, sir. The matter is urgent.'

Mr Gould pondered for a moment. 'Very well,' he said, his voice sharp. 'You may have two minutes. I am a busy man.'

If he had a kind heart, Grace thought, he was taking care not to show it. She explained about the Ragged School, the attack by the Bull Head Gang and her desire to build a stronger wall to make the school safe. 'I came to ask if you might donate some timber, sir, for building works. Our funds are very limited, you see. If you help us, you will be making a great contribution to the cause of education in Rotherhithe.'

'Education,' said Gould. 'Do you think the people of Rotherhithe really want education?'

'I'm certain they do, sir.'

'In that case, why are they attacking your school?'

'It's the gang, sir, the Captain and his men. They were behind this, I know it.'

'And the Captain pretty much owns Rotherhithe, young woman. And the bits he doesn't own yet, he soon will. You've made a bad enemy there. You really think a few bits of wood can make your school safe?'

'It's the best I can do, sir,' Grace said.

'It's utter nonsense. The Captain makes short work of any who stand in his way.'

Grace was quiet for a moment. 'Do you know him, sir?' she asked.

Gould made a sharp barking noise which Grace realised was laughter. 'Know him? Not personally, no. I've never seen his face. But my men have crossed swords with him, many times. He steals from my warehouses, every damned week. His gang have infiltrated the dockers, and probably the night watchmen too. The Captain's merry pranks have cost me thousands, and things are getting worse. And now, you expect me to give you my timber out of charity.'

'I'm sorry, sir,' said Grace after a moment. 'I did not wish to trouble you. I will make enquiries elsewhere.'

'No, stay a moment.' Gould sat down again, and Grace could see he looked tired. 'Why are you doing this?' he asked. 'I meant what I said. The Bull Head Gang won't give up, and no matter how strong you make your wall, it won't keep you safe. Why put yourself in harm's way?'

'Because they kidnapped one of my pupils,' Grace said quietly, 'and forced him into the gang. I can't save that boy, not now, but I'll do whatever it takes to protect the others.'

The timber merchant studied her for a moment. 'How old are the kiddies at your school?'

'The youngest is five, sir. The eldest is thirteen.'

Gould nodded slowly. 'I never had a proper education,' he said. 'I went to sea when I was a boy, same age as some of your pupils, and spent ten years before the mast. What little I learned about reading and writing and numbers came from a priest at the seaman's mission. It wasn't much, but it gave me a chance to get a shore job. Then I started night classes, and finally made something of myself. I articled as a clerk, saved some money, and built my own business.'

He paused. Grace waited to see what he would do next. 'I've got kiddies the same age as yours,' he said. 'And unlike some others, I do understand what education means. Also, you're about the only person in Rotherhithe who has the courage to stand up to the Captain. I think you're mad but . . . well. Good for you.'

Mr Gould nodded suddenly. 'All right, Miss Perrow. You'll have your timber. Tell me how much you need, and where you want it delivered.'

Walking back along the waterfront towards the gates, Grace had the sudden feeling that she was being followed.

She stopped and turned quickly. A pair of brown eyes regarded her at a distance of about twenty feet, warily but not without hope. The eyes belonged to a dog. At least, Grace assumed it was a dog, although it resembled no breed she had ever seen. It was not particularly large, about the size of a spaniel, with a rough matted coat that was a patchwork of different colours ranging from black through brown, several shades of grey and finally to dirty white. Each of its legs was a different colour. It had a long shaggy tail and upraised pointed ears, and a long pink tongue lolling out of its mouth.

Satisfied the dog was no threat, Grace walked on. She heard the pad of its footsteps, following her, and turned again. 'Go away,' she said.

'Grrr-*af*!' said the dog, and wagged its tail.

'Go away,' Grace repeated, fluttering her hands. 'Shoo!' She turned and walked towards the gates, and again it followed her. Every time she halted it stopped too, always about the same distance away. But as soon as she moved on, it followed her again, out through the gates of the docks and all the way back to Bell Lane.

Outside the house Grace stopped again. The dog stopped too. 'What am I going to do with you?' she asked.

'Grrr-*af*!' came the response, accompanied by another wag of the tail.

Albert, coming out of the house, heard the bark and ran up to Grace, seizing her hand. 'Oh, look, Auntie Grace! A dog!'

Harry and Daisy came rushing out too. 'He's a nice dog,' said Daisy. 'What is he doing here?'

'He followed me home,' said Grace.

'Why did he do that, Auntie?' asked Harry.

'I don't know,' said Grace.

Albert let go of her hand and walked forward towards the dog, kneeling down and putting his face close to the animal. 'Careful!' Grace said in sudden alarm. 'Oh, do come back, Albert! He might bite you!'

Far from biting, the dog opened his mouth and unfurled his pink tongue and licked Albert's face. Albert giggled. 'He likes me,' the boy said.

'He's our new friend,' said Harry happily. 'Can we keep him, Auntie? Oh, can we? Please?'

Those were exactly the words Grace had been hoping not to hear. Her heart sank. But she looked at the appeal in the three small faces, and knew this was an argument she could never hope to win.

And so it was that by the time George came home for the midday meal, the dog was ensconced in the kitchen chewing on a bone from yesterday's stew, his fur drying after a long bath and firm scrubbing to rid him of fleas. 'I have no idea what we're going to do with him,' Grace said. 'But I'm afraid if we turn him out in the street, the children will go with him.'

'I told you we should get a dog,' George said, bending to ruffle the dog's fur between its ears. 'Hey there, boy. You're a good boy, aren't you? Shall we keep you?'

'Yes!' chorused three small voices.

'But what on earth will we feed him?' Grace asked.

'Looks like he's doing pretty well already,' George said. He grinned at her. 'Come on, Grace. He'll protect you and the nippers, and he'll be good company too. What shall we call him, kids?'

'I think we should call him Radcliffe,' said Albert.

Grace and George both stared at him. 'Why Radcliffe?' asked Grace.

'I don't know,' said Albert. 'I just like the name.'

'Well then, welcome to Bell Lane, Radcliffe,' said George, scratching the dog's ears again. 'Right, you little rascals. Who wants to play piggy-back while Auntie gets the food ready?'

That afternoon Grace went to the market to buy bread and eggs and mutton, and then went to see Mr Jackson the ironmonger. He rummaged around in his stock and came up with a cast-iron lock, old but heavy and strong, and two keys. 'Happy to donate these to the cause,' he said. 'Rufus is fretting the day away. Doesn't know what to do with himself when he's not at school. Tell me when the rebuilding work starts and I'll come and lend a hand.'

December dusk was falling when she came out of the ironmonger's and almost ran into Mrs Hobbes. The vicar's wife was wearing a shapeless coat with a rabbit fur collar turned up, hiding her neck and making her look more than ever like a disapproving turtle. 'Miss Perrow!' she said. 'How good it is to see you.'

'And you also, ma'am,' said Grace. *What hypocrites we are*, she thought. *We cannot stand each other, and we both know it.*

'I was so sorry to hear of what happened to your little school,' said Mrs Hobbes, her voice resonant with insincerity. 'Not at all surprised, of course, but sorry. I don't expect you'll have the heart to carry on now, will you?'

'On the contrary,' said Grace. 'I intend to rebuild and carry on exactly as before. Indeed, I hope to recruit still more pupils.'

A look of vexation passed across the turtle's face. 'I am astonished,' said Mrs Hobbes. 'I assumed you would have learned your lesson by now. Miss Perrow, when will you not realise that these people do not want or need your help? They are content with their lot, and desire nothing further. Why do you persist in interfering?'

Grace felt the time had come to speak honestly. 'Because I do not agree with you,' she said. 'I don't believe they are content. They want something better, if not for themselves, then certainly for their sons and daughters. The children I teach are hungry for learning, Mrs Hobbes, and I intend to feed that hunger. Nothing you say will persuade me to change my mind.'

'Is that so?' Affronted, the vicar's wife glared at her. 'Well,' she said. 'We shall see about that. I bid you good day, Miss Perrow.' And, gathering her coat more closely about her, Mrs Hobbes marched away down the street.

Mr Gould was as good as his word. A wagonload of timber was dropped off at the railway arch and on Sunday, after church, George, Mr Jackson, Mickey Doyle and a couple of his fellow dockers, and Elijah Berton and some other men from the engine factory went to the arch and built a stout wooden wall nearly as high as the arch, covering the remaining gap with another sheet of sailcloth. The stove and chimney were refitted, and instead of a canvas flap there was now a sturdy pine door. Mr Jackson fitted the lock and gave Grace both the keys.

'Thank you,' Grace said to them. 'I am quite over-whelmed by your kindness.'

Elijah Berton shuffled a little and scratched his ear. 'It's us that's in your debt, ma'am,' he said. 'What you're doing for our kids. You can't put a price on that.'

Two weeks before Christmas, the school reopened and the children came streaming in, barefoot and ragged as ever but with faces bright with excitement. Grace's heart glowed with warmth when she saw them, but then she looked at the empty spot where Jimmy used to sit and felt again the pang of loss.

Nor was there any sign of the Angels. They had not come near the school since it was attacked, and not for the first time, Grace wondered why. Were they afraid the Bull Head Gang might return? She looked at the ground around the stove where they used to sleep, and realised to her surprise that she missed them, too.

The children were all talking at once, chattering like little birds. Even Nathan and Lettice seemed more lively than she remembered. She clapped her hands to silence them. 'Good morning, children,' she said.

'Good morning, Miss Perrow!' they chorused.

Grace smiled at them, and watched their faces beam back at her. 'Let us begin,' she said.

One morning before Christmas there was a knock on the new door and Walter Ringrose walked into the school. Grace was startled to see him, but felt a happy smile appear on her face as he came towards her. 'I hope I am not intruding,' he said. 'I wanted to see how your enterprise was prospering. I see that your fears about not having any pupils were unfounded. Would you mind if I stayed to watch you teach?'

'I would be happy to have you stay, if the children are content.'

He turned and said to the class, 'I am a friend of Miss Perrow's. Would you allow me to stay and take part in your class? I am always keen to learn and I hear that Miss Perrow is an excellent teacher.'

The children nodded. 'She is a wonderful teacher,' one of them said. 'You can learn lots of things from Miss Perrow.'

'I am certain I shall.' He settled himself into the space on a bench where Jimmy had once sat and spent the rest of the time helping the children in their tasks, giving every evidence of enjoying himself hugely. The children responded to his kindness and sense of fun and asked when he would be coming back.

At the end of lessons, when most of the children had left, he came to Grace to thank her for welcoming him. 'I heard from Mr Raikes that you had had some trouble,' he said. 'I wanted to come myself and see if you and your school were well.'

'It has been a difficult time,' agreed Grace soberly, 'but the children have been wonderful and have returned, as you see.'

They talked for some time about the progress of individual children and Grace welcomed this rare opportunity to talk to someone who understood the joys and challenges of teaching. Mr Ringrose had some excellent suggestions to make and they found themselves talking for over an hour. 'Oh, my goodness,' she said finally, realising the time, 'the family will be waiting for their dinner. I must go. Thank you so much for your visit, Mr Ringrose. It was a pleasure for the children and for me.'

She ran home quickly to discover that Albert had taken on the making of the meal; George asked where she had got to and when she explained he said, 'That Mr Ringrose is a kind man to come and check on you.'

'Yes,' said Grace absently, still mulling over the morning in her mind.

Hard work and the tensions with the gangs, her concern for Jimmy – and, if she was honest, for Mary and the still-absent Angels – had masked her deeper grief, but as Christmas grew closer Grace found herself thinking of Rosa more and more often. Christmas itself, she knew, would be hard for all of them.

What George was thinking, she did not know. Outwardly he remained as cheerful as ever, doting on the children and spending whatever time he could with them. He never spoke of Rosa, but Grace knew he missed her bitterly. She knew also that she herself was the rock he leaned on, the pillar of strength that helped him get through life and carry on.

The twins, on the other hand, often talked about their mother, sometimes as if she was still alive, and when they did it nearly broke Grace's heart. But they were sunny little souls, and the addition of Radcliffe to the household had helped them too. He was very gentle with the children, and Harry and Daisy spent hours playing with him. Albert was more like his father. Grace never heard him mention his mother, but ever since her death he had stayed close to Grace in a way that was partly protective and partly clinging on for comfort. He was, Grace knew, beginning to regard her as his new mother.

She was not sure what to do about this. She had come to live at Bell Lane in order to look after her sister's family. Somehow she had imagined it a temporary situation. She still hoped to someday marry and have her own children. Yet every day that passed she felt the bonds that tied her to the children becoming tighter.

They were in the market one afternoon, a raw, frozen day with clouds dark and low and a few snowflakes drifting on the wind. A barrel organ wheezed steadily, playing a tune Grace could just about recognise as 'God Rest Ye Merry, Gentlemen'. She held Harry tightly by the hand to keep him from running off after the organ grinder, and led him, Albert and Daisy through the crowds of people buying yule logs, festive wreaths and mince pies, Radcliffe trotting at their heels. Albert sniffed the air appreciatively as they passed the pie stall; he liked his food. Radcliffe looked interested too.

'Would you like a pie?' Grace asked.

The boy smiled and nodded. Grace set down her shopping basket and checked her purse. There were still a few coins left, and she pulled out a halfpenny and handed it to the woman keeping the pie stall. The latter crossed her arms over her chest and stared at Grace.

'You're that Grace Perrow,' she said. 'Rosa's sister. Aren't you?'

'Yes,' said Grace, puzzled by the woman's hostile tone.

'Then you can keep your money. I'm not serving the likes of you. Not now, not ever.'

Grace's jaw dropped. 'What on earth do you mean?'

'You know what I mean, you hussy.' The woman's voice had raised, and other people were turning to look. 'Your poor sister, not even cold in her grave, and there's you moving into her house, and moving in on her husband. It's disgusting! You're no better than a whore!'

People were staring now, and Grace felt her cheeks flame red with embarrassment. She took firm hold of Harry, who was still wriggling and trying to get away to find the barrel organ grinder. 'How dare you speak to me like that?' she gasped. 'In front of the children, too! Honestly, have you no manners at all?'

'Not when it comes to dealing with tarts like you,' the woman snapped, and she waved her arm, pointing down the street. 'Go on, hop it! Clear off!'

Grace wanted to respond, but then she saw Albert out of the corner of her eye and realised the boy was trembling, on the verge of tears. Clutching the rags of her dignity, she ushered the children away.

That night she told George what had happened. 'Mostly I was upset for the children,' she said. 'Poor little Albert. He's such a sensitive soul.'

'What are we going to do about this horrible gossip?'

'Ignore it,' said George. 'You don't want to be paying any attention to what people like that say. I'll have a word with Albert and calm him down.'

'What will you say to him?'

'The truth,' said George. 'That grown-ups can be horrible to each other sometimes.'

That this was true was further proven the following day when, in the middle of the afternoon, Grace answered a knock at the door. She had been making pastry for mince pies, determined to give Albert the treat he had missed in the market, and her hands and apron were covered in flour. Facing her in the street was a group of women in overcoats and bonnets led by Mrs Hobbes.

'Good afternoon,' Grace said politely. 'What can I do for you?'

'We have come to make our views known,' said Mrs Hobbes loudly. 'The situation is beyond tolerance. We are all in agreement on this. Are we not, ladies?'

There was a murmur behind her, with some heads nodded firmly, but others of the ladies looked rather mutinous, like they had better things to do with their time and had been dragged along against their will. One of them was Mrs Lane, the severe-looking woman who had been at the vicarage when Grace called to ask about the school.

'What situation?' demanded Grace, though she knew full well what this visit was about. 'Speak plainly, ma'am, I beg you.'

'Very well. We wish to protest, Miss Perrow, in the very strongest of terms, about the immorality of your living arrangements. It is not seemly that a single woman should take up residence under the same roof as a married man, even one who is recently widowed.'

'Yes!' said Grace. 'He *is* recently widowed, and his children recently orphaned. Their mother, his wife, was my sister. I have a right and a duty to take care of them. And my relations with Mr Turneur are entirely innocent.'

'Oh, please,' said Mrs Hobbes. 'Miss Perrow, what you yourself do is a matter for your own soul, and your own

171

conscience, if you have one. But you are exercising a malign influence on the Turneur children, and on all those children you teach at that wretched school of yours. Their lives are brutish enough, without you corrupting them still further.'

Two women at the back of the group shuffled their feet, clearly uncomfortable. 'Corrupting!' Grace went red again. 'You are accusing me of corrupting my pupils?'

'Of course you are, Miss Perrow. How can you be doing anything else, so long as you live in a state of harlotry?'

'Oh, Mrs Hobbes!' said one of the women before Grace could speak. To Grace's surprise, it was Mrs Lane who had spoken. 'That is too unkind! I'm sure Miss Perrow is only trying to do what is best for her family.'

'That is not a matter for you to decide, Mrs Lane,' said Mrs Hobbes firmly. 'My instruction to you, Miss Perrow, is to cease and desist with this unfortunate school, and to leave this house at once before your wanton behaviour causes any further damage. Go back to Hackney, or wherever it is you came from, and stay there.'

She made Hackney sound like one of the outer suburbs of Sodom and Gomorrah. 'And who will care for the Turneur children if I do?' demanded Grace.

'Rotherhithe folk will look after their own,' said Mrs Hobbes. 'We don't need the likes of you poking your nose in.'

Grace slammed the door in her face with such force that it woke up Radcliffe, who began to bark. Tears of frustration and anger rolled down her cheeks as she went back into the kitchen. *Why?* she thought. Grace had given up everything to do the right thing by Rosa, George and the children. Yet Mrs Hobbes seemed determined to find fault with her and turn people against her. Was it because the Reverend had been warned off and could not interfere with her work, but his wife was acting as his willing accomplice?

Was she spreading the rumours about me? Grace wondered. Good heavens; had she perhaps even *started* them? Whatever the case, ignoring the rumours would not be possible, not with the vicar and his wife both against her.

Chapter 9

If the vicar and his wife were trying to sabotage the school, the attempt had mixed results. Mrs Hobbes may have been able to bring a mob to Grace's door, but the next morning as the children were arriving at the railway arch, Mrs Lane appeared at the school door leading two boys, aged about eight and six, by the hand.

'I've taught them all I can at home,' she said. 'If you can take them in, Miss Perrow, I would welcome it. At the moment, all they are getting is Sunday school with the vicar.'

'And what will he and Mrs Hobbes say if I take in your boys?' Grace asked.

'I don't know,' was the tart response. 'And I don't rightly care.'

Mrs Lane was only the first. It seemed Mrs Hobbes had crossed a line, at least with the poorer women of Rotherhithe who disliked the vicar's wife for her snobbishness and overbearing ways. They came forward to support the Ragged School, and by the end of the week, the number of pupils had swelled to more than thirty, so that they were forced to sit two to a bench, sharing a desk and sometimes a slate as well. Some of the children, like the Lane boys, were reasonably well turned out and had received a little home schooling; others were shoeless in patched, threadbare clothes, and some even made little Nathan, the beggar boy, look respectable. The influx delighted Grace, but she worried that the show of support would only drive Mrs Hobbes to redouble her efforts to defame her and George.

'The way things are going, you'll need another class,' George said. He had started to take a real interest in the school now, to Grace's great pleasure. He would sit in the evening and listen to Albert read to him, or Daisy reciting her sums.

'I need one already,' Grace said. 'We could run another class in the afternoons, but I don't have a teacher. And I can't run both classes and look after the house and the children at the same time.'

'And me,' said George smiling. 'Write to that fellow Raikes and ask if they can find someone.'

'What a good idea.' Grace wrote to Mr Raikes at the Ragged School Union, explaining the situation and asking if another teacher could be found. Prompt as ever, Mr Raikes replied by post the following day.

My dear Miss Perrow,

May I offer you my warmest congratulations on the success of the Rotherhithe School. Your energy and zeal have clearly made their mark on the community, as I *expected they would. Alas, I fear that teachers are a little like gold dust, being both rare and hard to find. I can only suggest that you find a suitable person in your community and train them yourself. Are any of your pupils old enough to act as pupil-teachers? If not, you might apply for volunteers among your neighbours.*

I am sorry to have so little assistance to offer,

Yours sincerely,

Solomon Raikes, Esq.

Grace pondered this. She knew no one who fitted the bill. None of her pupils were yet old enough or literate enough to teach a class unsupervised. In a couple of years' time Rebecca Berton might be ready, but not now. And the friends she had made in Rotherhithe, people like Brigit Doyle and Louisa Berton, Rebecca's mother, had neither the time nor the education of their own to serve as teachers.

Perhaps the Clares could help, she thought. She had trespassed on their kindness enough already, and was reluctant to ask them, but her need overrode her reluctance. That afternoon she sat down in the kitchen to write a letter, but even before she began there came a knock at the door. Opening the door she found Mela Clare standing on the doorstep, wrapped in a long dark overcoat with a fur collar. Her cheeks were pink with cold and the wind had tugged wisps of her fair hair out of her bonnet.

'Mela!' cried Grace, drawing her into the house and embracing her. The two friends had not seen each other for a couple of weeks, not since before the attack on the school. 'Where did you spring from? I was just about to write to you, and now here you are!'

'I came to bring you your Christmas present,' Mela said, handing over a small box and smiling at the children. They smiled back at her. Mela was always a popular visitor, especially if she brought sweets. 'What were you going to write to me about?'

'Come into the kitchen, and I will tell you.'

In the kitchen Mela spotted the bundle of fur curled up on the floor next to the stove. 'What is that?' she asked.

'That is Radcliffe,' said Grace. The dog raised his head at the sound of his name, regarded Mela with a bleary eye, and then fell back to sleep. 'We adopted him, or more correctly, he adopted us. He's an extra mouth to feed, but the children adore him.'

Grace turned to put the kettle on for more tea. Her friend studied her. 'You look tired,' she said.

'I am, a little,' Grace admitted. 'Running the house is hard work, and the school grows busier by the day. We have forty-two pupils now, and I am running out of time to teach them, and room for them to sit.'

'Have you thought of two classes?' Mela asked.

'Of course, but I lack a teacher. That is why I was about to write. I don't suppose you know of anyone who would be willing to volunteer?'

'I will certainly ask around. I would gladly come myself, only I am busier than ever at the Clare School. One of our young teachers has left to get married, and now I am doing the work of two.'

'I certainly wouldn't ask you to come and teach here,' Grace said.

'Why ever not?'

'Things are quite different here, Mela. The children here are very poor, some living right on the line between life and death. One of my boys is a beggar, others are orphans who live in garrets or sheds, and the weather is so cold. When they leave each day, I do not know if I will see them again in the morning, or whether they will die in the night. It is not easy, Mela.'

'And yet you cope with it,' said Mela, 'and carry on.'

'I must,' Grace said simply.

After a moment Mela reached across the table and took her friend's hand. 'You are so brave,' she said, her voice soft. 'I admire you so much, Grace. I wish I were like you.'

Grace blinked. For years she had looked up to Mela and tried her best to be like *her*; to hear the sentiment returned now was something of a shock.

'Suppose I could come,' said Mela. 'Even for a few hours a day. Could I be helpful, do you think?'

Reluctantly, Grace shook her head. 'I cannot let you do it,' she said. 'It is too dangerous.'

Mela's eyes widened a little. 'Dangerous? What do you mean?'

Grace told her, for the first time, about the Bull Head Gang and the attack on the school and disappearance of

Jimmy. 'The gang is getting stronger and stronger. George told me a couple of days ago there is a rumour they are getting set to take on some the rival gangs, in Bermondsey and Deptford, and drive them out. If that happens, they'll own not just Rotherhithe but all this corner of London.'

Mela looked alarmed. 'Have they molested your school again?'

'No. I suspect they are too busy with their wars with the other gangs. But one day, they will come back. I'm certain of it.'

'Have you any protection?'

Grace smiled. 'I have Radcliffe. That's about it. The local police are probably in the pay of the gang. And I have lost my night watchmen, too.'

She told Mela about Mary and the Angels. 'They disappeared after the attack, and I've been so worried about them. Especially Mary. She can't be more than ten and she's also looking after her little brother.'

'How horrible,' said Mela softly. 'To be that young, and on the streets, alone.'

'Yes,' said Grace. 'As I said, things are different down here.'

'Yes,' said Mela slowly. 'I see that now.'

'And as if the gangs were not giving me enough problems, there is our vicar and his wretched wife. I am quite certain she is spreading slanderous stories about me and George in an attempt to force me to go.'

'Slanderous stories?' asked Mela. 'Whatever do you mean?'

'She tells people that we are living an immoral life together. That we are living in sin.'

Mela's eyes opened wide again, and her hand flew up to her mouth. 'Oh, Grace! Oh, my dear! What will you do?'

'Well,' said Grace. 'I have been thinking.'

She had, too, walking back from the school or while working in the kitchen or lying awake at night holding Daisy close to her and listening to the sounds of male breathing coming from the other bedroom. The thoughts had made her uncomfortable, but there was no escaping them.

'The way I see it, there are three things I can do,' Grace said. 'I can ignore the rumours and hope they go away.'

'They won't,' said Mela.

Grace shook her head. 'Especially not while Mrs Hobbes continues to stir the pot. I don't care for myself, but I'm worried it will affect George and the children. What if his employer decides he is a man of bad moral character? He could lose his job. And the children will suffer too. Albert has already heard how some people talk to me, and I know it hurts him. My second choice is to leave, go back to Hackney or perhaps find a position as a schoolmistress somewhere else.'

'But you would have to abandon your Ragged School,' Mela said, still shocked by Mrs Hobbes's vindictiveness. 'And your sister's children, too.'

'And I'm not willing to do either of those things. I left them once. I won't do it again,' said Grace. 'I'm not going to let Mrs Hobbes beat me, either.'

Mela looked worried. 'But Grace, what will you do? You said there is a third thing.'

'Yes,' said Grace. She looked down at her teacup for a moment, and then up at Mela again. 'George and I could get married.'

Neither of them spoke for quite some time. 'Is that possible?' Mela asked finally. 'He is your sister's husband. Would the church permit you to marry him?'

'I don't know,' said Grace. She forced a smile. 'Remember history lessons? King Henry VIII did it. Catherine of Aragon was married to his brother, before she married him.'

'But marriage,' said Mela. 'Oh, heavens, Grace. It is a big step.' She paused, and then asked quietly, 'Do you love him?'

'No!' said Grace hastily. 'No, lord no! We're fond of each other, and I know George needs my help, but we don't love each other. George still misses Rosa. She was the love of his life, and I don't think anyone will ever replace her. And I certainly don't intend to try. It would be a marriage of convenience only.'

'Your sister died five months ago,' said Mela. 'Would George be allowed to marry yet? Women are supposed to wait for at least a year after their husband dies.'

'I don't know,' Grace said. 'I expect things are different for men. You're right, Mela, it may not be possible. But it would sort things out. No one could complain about me living in the house if we were lawfully married.'

Mela's eyes were suddenly full of tears. 'Oh, Grace. But you had such dreams of finding someone as passionate about teaching as you are. A helpmeet to share your worries with late in the evening while the rest of the world slept.'

'Those dreams belonged to a different Grace. This is my place now. You're right, Mela, they are my family. George needs my help, and I think he always will. Albert and the twins need a mother. And there's the other children too, the ones at the school. For some of them, the school is all they have. I must stay, Mela.'

'You are sacrificing yourself,' said Mela. 'All the hopes and dreams you once had, the world at your feet, and you are turning your back on it.'

'Yes,' said Grace quietly. 'That is how it must be.'

Christmas was only two days away. The temperature had fallen more sharply still and the mud in the roads had frozen hard. In the morning Grace saw a robin tapping its beak on the ice in a puddle, trying to break through so it could drink. The bird flew off when Grace went over and broke the ice with her foot, but when she walked on it came back again, fluttering down to land beside the puddle.

At midday that day Grace dismissed the children until after New Year. Some of them, she knew, would have a very meagre Christmas. 'It breaks my heart,' she had said to George the previous evening. 'I wish I had the resources Mr Hogg has, and have a kitchen to feed our waifs and orphans.'

'One thing at a time,' George said. 'Get your school in order first, lass. Have you had any more thoughts about a teacher?'

Grace shook her head. She still could think of no one locally, and she had no real confidence Mela would be able to find anyone willing to uproot from comfortable Hackney and move south of the river. *Not everyone is as mad as me,* she thought.

But it turned out that someone was that mad. That day as Grace was finishing reading to the children there came a knock at the school door.

'Who is there?' she called.

'It's Mr Ringrose, Miss Perrow. I hope I am not disturbing you once more?'

'Not at all,' said Grace, hurrying to open the door. The children greeted him with smiles and said 'Happy Christmas'.

Mr Ringrose bowed to her and to them. 'It is jolly good to see you all again,' he said.

'And you too, sir,' said Grace. 'Please do come out of the cold. Children, the lesson is finished. God speed you all home, and I wish you a very merry Christmas.'

'You too, miss!' they chorused. Her own three waited for her while the others streamed out of the school, talking happily. 'How may I help you?' Grace asked.

'Well, I-I . . . I wanted to wish you a happy Christmas. And to see how things are going, you know. My word,' he said looking around. 'You seem to have more children than ever.'

'They keep coming,' Grace said smiling. 'I need a second teacher so I can open another class.' A thought struck her. 'Mr Ringrose, I don't suppose you know of anyone who might be willing to volunteer?'

'I will certainly ask around,' Mr Ringrose promised. 'It might not be easy to find someone, though. There are more and more rumours about the gangs hereabouts now. It sounds like these fellows have an animus against schools.'

'They know that by educating the children, we are encouraging them to move away and find good work, rather than staying here and becoming involved in crime. As you know, they have threatened me and attacked my school once. They may well try to stop you as well, sir.'

'If they try, I'll be waiting for them,' said Mr Ringrose with a young man's bravado. 'Well, thank you very much, Miss Perrow. I won't take up any more of your time. It was very good to see you once more,' and he blushed deep crimson, much less at ease than on his previous visit. He took his leave, walking back towards the railway station, and Grace collected the children and went out, locking the door behind her. She puzzled over Mr Ringrose as they walked home. He was a nice, charming young man, far above her in station of course, but perfectly friendly. Why was he so nervous?

The approach of Christmas affected the household on Bell Lane in different ways. Daisy and Harry were visibly excited by the preparations, especially the delicious smells that came from the oven when Grace was baking; but once, forgetting, Daisy asked when Mummy would be coming, and then remembered and burst into inconsolable tears. Albert came to help in the kitchen, rarely speaking, just watching Grace while they worked together with large solemn eyes.

George too grew more sombre. In front of the children he was always cheerful, but sometimes when he and Grace were alone he relaxed his guard, and she could see the sadness in his face and the lines around his eyes. She knew he was thinking of Rosa, the Christmases they had once had, and would never have again.

Despite her own sorrows, Grace did everything she could to lift the mood. Some of the fir and spruce trees that came as lumber into the docks from Canada and Norway still had boughs on them, and the dockers' wives made Christmas wreaths and sold them in the market for a farthing. Grace bought two and hung them in the parlour, where their sweet scent helped mask the damp. From another stall she bought – at an expense that made her wince – a nativity scene made of papier mâché, complete with sheep and shepherds and angels, and set this up on the side table in the parlour. The twins in particular were fascinated and wanted to play with the sheep, until Harry picked one up with fingers covered in sticky jam, rendering the sheep a peculiar shade of pink. Thereafter, handling the figures was gently forbidden.

On Christmas Eve George came home early from work with a goose tucked under one arm and a sovereign in his pocket, a bonus from his firm. Grace extracted the sovereign and marched off to the market again with Radcliffe escorting her, leaving George to play with the children, and spent the money on as many treats as she could find, walnuts, oranges, stick candy and a plum pudding to go with the small mountain of mince pies she had already made.

Coming back from the market in dusk, snowflakes drifting down and dusting her coat, she saw Mrs Hobbes in the distance. The vicar's wife saw her, too, and crossed the road to avoid her. Two other women had already cut her dead in the market, looking at her and then pretending she was not there. Grace ground her teeth. She had not spoken to George about her idea, although she was fairly certain he had heard the rumours too; she had been waiting for the right moment, and so far the right moment had resolutely refused to come. But she knew she could not delay much longer.

Back at the house, she showed George what she had bought. 'And I fetched you a bottle of porter. I know you enjoy it.'

'Oh, you're a good lass.' George opened the bottle and poured himself half a glass; unlike many of their neighbours he never drank to excess, even on the rare occasions when he had money in his pocket. Grace watched him, seeing again the sombre, faraway eyes.

'George,' she said softly.

'Yes.'

'We're going to have a good Christmas. For the little ones.'

'Of course.' George forced a smile. 'Don't worry. You know I'd do anything for them.'

'I know.' Her heart aching, she watched him settle back in his chair, glass forgotten in his hand, eyes dreaming, far away.

But despite the memories and the pain they did have a happy Christmas, largely because both George and Grace were determined that it should be so. After church where Grace avoided the eyes of the censorious, the morning continued with stockings filled with toys and good things to eat, and the smell of orange peel and of chestnuts roasting on the coal stove filled the air with a delicious perfume. Harry and Daisy both had toy horses on wheels – Grace had learned early on that giving the twins different toys was a recipe for arguments and tears – and Albert had a picture book with scenes from foreign lands; he sat rapt over it, turning the pages slowly, his face a study in dreams.

Rather awkwardly, George gave Grace a little parcel. Inside was a small locket on a chain. 'I'm sorry,' he said a little awkwardly. 'I know I shouldn't have spent the money.'

He was right, but Grace kissed him on the cheek. 'It's lovely,' she said. 'It was a kind, kind thought.'

'You do so much for us,' said George. 'I wanted you to have something in return.'

Later, Grace opened the box Mela had left for her and found, as expected, a selection of books; newly published works, straight from the bookbinder, their covers still smelling of calfskin. There was Mr Trollope's *The Last Chronicle of Barset*, and Mrs Braddon's new novel *Circe*, and the first volume of a new history of England. Firmly repressing the urge to sit down and start reading now, Grace went into the kitchen to begin preparing dinner. For a moment she thought of Rosa, and how many times over the years her sister had stood before this very stove and done the same things on Christmas Day, and she bit her lip to stop herself from crying.

Oh, Rosa, she thought. *I don't want to take your place. I don't want them to forget you. But I don't know what else to do.*

At dinner they gorged themselves on goose and trimmings, and Albert ate so many roast potatoes that George began to tease him. 'You'll burst if you eat any more,' he said, at which point Albert picked up another potato and crammed it into his mouth. 'Manners!' said Grace, but she was laughing. After the goose came the plum pudding, lit with a thimbleful of brandy Grace had found in a bottle in the back of the larder, and mince pies and a cup of mulled ale for herself and George. They played games, and sang Christmas carols, 'Once in Royal David's City' and 'See, Amid the Winter's Snow', Harry insisting on conducting them like he had seen bandmasters do and piping away in his treble voice.

At length, stuffed and tired out, the children were put to bed, where all three fell quickly asleep. Grace tiptoed downstairs and joined George again, who was sitting before the fire deep in thought. On impulse, Grace kissed him on the cheek and sat down beside him.

'That was a good day,' she said. 'Better than I dared hope.'

'Yes,' said George. 'All thanks to you, lass.'

Grace smiled. 'You should give yourself more credit,' she said. 'You're so good with the children, and they love you so much.'

George coughed a little. 'I dote on them. Sometimes when I look in their faces and . . . well, I see Rosa looking back at me. Especially when they're happy, like today.'

'You bore up very well,' said Grace.

George glanced at her. 'And you. I know how much she meant to you, and how you miss her too.'

'Yes.'

Silence fell in the little room. Grace sat and wondered where Jimmy was, and where Mary and the Angels were spending this cold Christmas night. Outside, a few snow-flakes came curling down.

∽

Missy was sick, bad sick. She couldn't stop coughing, and there was this sticky fluid coming up out of her chest. 'We've got to get help for her,' I said.

'Where you going to do that?' demanded Ness. We were a long way from home now, way over in Lambeth, wandering and wandering always, trying to find somewhere we could settle down. But always something happened; if it wasn't the traps moving us on or trying to round us up and put us in the workhouse, it was the local gangs who didn't like us on their turf.

I wanted to go back to Rotherhithe, but the others wouldn't have it. It was too dangerous. Those big bastards who smashed up Miss Perrow's school told us what would happen to us if they caught us. They'd break our necks, sure, but they'd do something else to us first. I knew a girl they'd caught once. She was never right again, died on the street a while later. So, maybe the others were right. But I still missed Rotherhithe. Not that for a moment I could have told you why.

Missy was coughing again. In the houses along the street you could see lights and green wreaths, and they were singing some Christmas songs. I held onto little Joe. He was too young to remember Christmas the way it had been at home, but I remembered it, just about. Mince pies and fruit and singing. There wasn't no singing on the streets. There was just cold, and slow death.

Missy wouldn't last much longer. We'd have to take her to the workhouse and leave her at the door, then knock on the door and run away so they didn't catch us. Hopefully someone would take her in and give her medicine. Even then, she probably wouldn't make it.

I knew my turn would come soon. I wasn't going to live long enough to join the Forty Elephants. I was going to die out here on the streets. I didn't mind much for myself, but who would look after Joe? That thought made me desperate. I didn't know what to do.

I heard the singing again. I remembered a line from a book Miss Perrow had read at the school, about a poor family who suddenly had plenty on Christmas Day. The last line of the book, it was 'God bless us, every one.'

Well, He wasn't blessing the Angels, not that Christmas night. I knew where the workhouse in Lambeth was, we had passed it earlier and I had smelled the misery in the air. 'Come on,' I said to Ness. 'I know what to do with Missy. Give me a hand.'

∞

In the warmth of the parlour on Bell Lane, Grace stirred. 'George,' she said, 'we must talk.'

George looked up from his mulled ale, which once again he had barely touched. 'About what, lass?'

'You and I,' Grace said.

There was a long pause. 'Ah,' said George quietly. 'You've been thinking about it too, then.'

Relief flooded through Grace; this was going to be easier than she had dared hope. 'I don't care about my reputation,' she said. 'But I do care about you and the children. It might be a way out of the problem.'

George sighed heavily. 'Yes,' he said. 'That's what I was thinking, too. Like you, I don't give a fig for what people say about me. But I'm worried about the nippers. And, there's no denying they need a mother.'

He looked at Grace. 'But it's asking an awful lot of you. I always assumed one day, when the kids were older, you'd go back to your old life, and do all the things you intended to do. And find a man of your own.'

'I supposed I assumed it too, when I first arrived,' Grace said. 'But George, I can't leave and there are no men on the horizon. The children will need me for years to come, and then there's the school. My place is here.'

George said nothing.

'I know I'll never be Rosa to you,' Grace said, 'and I don't even want to try. But I can be a good wife to you, in many ways.' She forced a smile. 'Most ways except one. If that's all right by you.'

'That's fine,' said George, and she saw the relief in his face. 'I'd never ask that of you, Grace, really I wouldn't. To me, you're still my sister-in-law and always will be. This is just a face we put on things, isn't it?'

'Of course,' said Grace. 'We're making ourselves respectable to the public eye. Inside this house, we go on exactly as before.'

Another silence fell. 'How do we explain it to the kids?' George asked.

'I don't think we'll need to explain much,' Grace said. 'They're wiser than we are, in some ways. Indeed, I think Albert may be expecting it.'

They looked at each other. 'So, that's it then,' George said.

'That's it, then,' Grace repeated, and she smiled suddenly. 'I didn't know how you would take to the idea. I've been waiting for days, trying to get up nerve to ask.'

'Me too,' said George, and he smiled too. 'Proper couple of duffers, aren't we?' The smile faded. 'Grace, are you really sure this is what you want? I know how much you gave up when you came to live with us. Marry me now, and you'll be giving that up forever.'

'I know,' said Grace. 'But I promise you, George, with all my heart. This is what I want.'

They said no more. They sat in silence in the low glow of the oil lamp and the fire, while outside snowflakes curled soft against the windowpane.

Chapter 10

They broke the news to the children the following day. Harry and Daisy were curious, but too young to understand how it would make any difference to them. All that mattered was that Grace would still be there. Albert sat and listened very solemnly while his father and Grace explained the situation.

'Are you doing this because of the bad things people say about you?' the boy asked.

'Partly,' Grace said honestly. 'But mostly, my dear, so that we shall be a real family, all together, now and forever.'

Albert thought about this. 'Auntie Grace,' he said, 'does this mean you will be my new mummy?'

They had thought this question might come, but had struggled to think of how to answer it. 'You must never forget your mummy,' said Grace gently. 'She was loving and kind and good. But if you want to think of me as a kind of second mummy, who looks after you, then you can do so.'

Albert gave the matter further consideration. 'The other children at the school might think it odd if you are married to Fa and I still call you Auntie Grace,' he said. 'So I think I ought to call you Mummy. Would that be all right?'

'If that is what you wish,' Grace said, thinking it might take her a while to get used to being called 'Mummy'.

Albert smiled. 'Then it is settled.'

Getting the children on side had been easier than expected. Finding a place to be married, however, proved rather harder. Coming out of church on the first Sunday after New Year, George addressed the vicar. 'Might we have a moment of your time, Reverend?'

Reverend Hobbes nodded reluctantly. George and Grace waited, the children fidgeting around them, while the last of the parishioners filed out of the church and the vicar finally turned to them. The day was clear and cold, the blue of the sky for once unstained by smoke.

'Well, Mr Turneur?' the vicar said. 'Make it quick, if you please, I am a busy man.'

'Yes, sir,' said George. 'Me and Miss Perrow would like to get married. We were wondering if you would marry us here at All Saints.'

Mrs Hobbes could be seen lurking in the background, staring at them, her wrinkled face framed by the fur collar of her coat. The vicar looked at them, his own face disbelieving.

'Marriage?' he said. 'Of course not. It's quite out of the question.'

'May I ask why, sir?'

'For heaven's sake, man. Have you not heard of consan- guinity? No man may marry his own sister. It is completely forbidden.'

'But she's not my sister, Reverend,' George protested. 'She is my late wife's sister, and even more than that, she was adopted. We're not related by blood, not at all.'

'In the eyes of the law, Mr Turneur, it does not matter,' said the vicar. 'According to both canon law and the Marriage Act of 1835, a man's wife's sister is deemed to be his sister also. And the fact Miss Perrow is an adopted child has no bearing on the matter. Any relations between you would be tantamount to incest.'

George looked appalled. 'Please, Reverend,' said Grace. 'It's to be a marriage of convenience, no more. It's only so I can stay in the house and take care of the children and to stop the rumours flying around.' *The rumours your wife has been circulating*, she thought of adding.

The vicar's eyes bulged. 'A marriage of convenience?' he repeated, in a tone of voice that suggested he had just stepped on something nasty. 'Do you not understand the purpose of marriage? A true Christian marriage is under- taken for the sole purpose of rearing children and giving them a loving home.'

'Yes, Reverend,' said Grace. 'That is what we are trying to do.'

'But they are not *your* children, Miss Perrow. And they never will be. For the good of your soul, and the souls of

Mr Turneur and his children, I strongly suggest you leave their house forthwith, and return whence you came.'

The vicar and his wife never give up, do they? Grace thought. She could feel her temper rising. 'Come, children,' she said shortly, and took George's arm. They walked away, the three children following, and Grace caught a glimpse of Mrs Hobbes's face as they passed. There was no mistaking the gloating look in her eyes.

'I never knew that was the law,' George said later that day. They were resting after dinner, the children asleep. 'Well, lass. What are we going to do?'

'We still need to get married, George. We may never win over Reverend and Mrs Hobbes, but at least it will stop other people from spreading rumours ... I don't believe what he said about adoption,' Grace said. I'm sure adopted children are treated differently in law.'

George looked dubious. 'How can we find out?' he asked. 'There's not many lawyers round here, even if we could afford one.'

Grace thought for a few moments. 'We could go to St Mary's and ask the rector there.'

The church of St Mary the Virgin was the oldest church in Rotherhithe, situated among the crumbling buildings that formed the core of the ancient village along the Thames, surrounded and all but swamped by the newer docks and warehouses. George shook his head. 'The rector there is a crusty old fellow, even more set in his ways than Hobbes. I doubt he'll give us the time of day.'

'All right,' said Grace, 'we'll go to Bermondsey. I remember the rector there, Reverend Soames. He conducted Aunt Edith's funeral service, and he was such a kind man. We'll go next week and talk to him.'

'You want to start going to church there as well?' George asked.

'Why not? It is a little further to walk, but I shan't set foot in All Saints again, not while that fat hypocrite and his horrible wife are there.'

That week the weather turned bitter, with freezing rain and lashings of sleet, but that was not the only affliction Rotherhithe had to endure. On Wednesday evening George came home from work, his face grim.

'You know that war between the gangs everyone's been talking about? Well, it's started. A bunch of toughs from Deptford came up to pick a fight with the Bull Head Gang. We were working on the warehouses, and we had to run for it to get out of the way. Proper nasty it was, hammers and knives and even a couple of shooters.'

'What happened?' Grace asked.

'Don't know for certain. We didn't hang around to find out. I heard there was a couple of folk killed, but I don't know who they were.' George looked at her in concern. 'You take care at school, lass, and any time you're going out. Make sure you have Radcliffe with you.'

'I always do,' Grace said.

The violence continued into the next day, and in the afternoon on her way to market, with Radcliffe trotting at her heels, Grace saw a fire engine go rushing past, bell clanging, mud flying from under the horses' hooves. Smoke was rising from somewhere down near Greenland Dock. 'It'll be the gangs, fighting again,' said a woman selling vegetables.

'The Deptford lot?' asked Grace.

The woman shook her head. 'Word is the Black Crows from Peckham are trying to move in while the Bull Heads are fighting the Deptford mob. And the police are sitting on their hands as usual, doing nothing. God help us poor people caught in the middle. There ain't no one to look after us, is there? We could all be murdered in our beds and no one would care.'

On Sunday the family walked to Bermondsey warily, keeping to the main roads, and went to church. Afterwards, filing out the door, Grace went up to the rector to introduce herself, but found there was no need.

'Bless my soul, it's Grace Perrow,' the rector said, eyes twinkling. He was in his sixties, with snow-white hair and beard and a gentle face with lines of laughter around his eyes and mouth. 'How good it is to see you again, my child.' He looked at George and the children. 'And who do we have here? Is your name Perrow no longer?'

'It is, Reverend,' said Grace. 'But in a way, that is why I am here. Sir, could we talk to you?'

A few minutes later they were seated in the study at the rectory, the children looking around in wonder at the big room full of books and politely taking the sweets the rector's wife offered them. 'What brings you back to these parts, my dear?' the rector asked.

'I came to Rotherhithe to look after my sister's children after she died last year. And then I got involved in things, and I have set up a Ragged School.'

'Ah, an admirable institution. I heard one had been established in Rotherhithe, though I did not know you were the mistress. Although I should have guessed.' The rector smiled. 'Even as a child, it was easy to see you would grow into a young woman of determination. Did you know we have a Ragged School here in Bermondsey now? It is in Potters' Fields, very near here.'

'Yes, sir. I am acquainted with the gentleman who has set it up. Reverend, we – that is, Mr Turneur and me – we have a problem. We're hoping you can help with it.'

Grace explained. The rector looked grave. 'I fear Mr Hobbes is right. The Marriage Act states quite explicitly that no man may marry his wife's sister. It is iniquitous, of course. All over London, sisters of deceased wives come to look after the children just as you have done. But they are prevented from entering into a state of wedlock that would regularise their union, and so are condemned to live in a state of sin. It is quite wrong, and many people are campaigning for a change in the law, but I fear it will be some time before their efforts bear fruit.'

'We have no intention of living in sin,' Grace said firmly, and George nodded. 'I wondered if my being adopted would make a difference.'

The rector pondered for a moment, stroking his white beard. 'Do you know,' he said finally, 'I think it might.'

'I don't understand, sir,' said George. 'Adopted or no, Grace was Rosa's sister, and there's an end to it.'

'Not in the eyes of the law, Mr Turneur, and it is the law that matters here. You see, adoption is not a legally recognised process. Your mother, Miss Perrow, God bless her soul, took you into her home and raised you as her daughter and Rosa's sister. But in the eyes of the law, you are no such thing.'

Grace was horrified. 'Then the law is callous and unfeeling!' she exclaimed.

'It is all of those things, Miss Perrow, and much more besides. Rest assured; in the eyes of all who know you, and in the eyes of God Almighty who watches over us, you and Rosa were sisters. And right now, be grateful for the law, for it works in your favour. There is a loophole here which I think we may be able to exploit. As you are not *legally* Rosa's sister, there is no impediment to you marrying Mr Turneur.'

Grace felt her heart skip with excitement. 'Then ... Reverend, would you do it? Would you marry us?'

'It would be my pleasure,' said Reverend Soames. 'You once lived in Bermondsey, after all; you are one of us. But we shall marry you by common licence, I think. There is no point in reading the banns as neither of you resides in this parish, and in any case, we don't want to give your Reverend Hobbes or his supporters time to object. I shall arrange for the bishop to provide a licence. No, no my dear, there is no question of a fee. I shall be pleased to do my part. Shall we set the date for a month from now?'

She told herself repeatedly that it was a marriage of convenience, but despite this Grace could not prevent a flutter of nerves as her wedding approached. She told their neighbours in Bell Lane, Louisa Berton and Brigit Doyle and a few others, with strict instructions not to spread the news. Reverend Soames was right, it would not do for Reverend Hobbes or, still worse, his wife to hear about it. They would almost certainly try to stop the wedding from taking place.

She thought long and hard about what to wear. Finally on the morning of the wedding she decided on a simple dark green wool skirt and blouse that she used to wear when teaching at the Clare School, and which was still in good order. No jewellery, she thought, but then she relented and put the locket George had given her for Christmas around her neck.

She put on her bonnet and coat and looked at herself for a moment in the mirror, seeing once again the serious dark eyes and level eyebrows. She disliked her eyebrows and always had. *Who cares*, she thought, making a face at herself in the mirror. *George is marrying me so I can look after him and the children. Eyebrows don't enter into it.*

She took a deep breath and went downstairs. George waited for her, looking a little sombre in his church suit. Albert looked at them both, his face equally solemn. 'You look nice,' he pronounced.

'Thank you,' said Grace. 'Be a good boy, and if you need anything, run next door and fetch Rebecca. We won't be away for long.'

They kissed the twins and then walked outside. January had passed while they waited for the marriage licence to arrive, and it was February now. The air was slightly warmer, but the wind from the west was raw and damp and brought with it the rich dark smells from the glue factory mingled with smoke from the railway. The streets were quiet, even though it was Saturday, and people walked past them quickly, heads down against the wind. The violence of the gangs continued unabated. The day before, two people had been stabbed to death in Jamaica Road. Both were gang members; one was fifteen years old. Grace thought again of Jimmy, and wondered a little desperately where he was now.

Outside the church in Bermondsey, George stopped and took Grace's hand. 'Are you sure, lass? You still want to go through with this?'

'I'm sure,' Grace said. 'This is the best thing for us all.'

George looked up at the grey late-winter sky. 'Do you suppose she's up there watching us?'

Grace smiled. 'I'm sure of it.'

George nodded. 'So am I.' He looked at Grace. 'I'll try to make you happy, lass. I can't promise I'll do it all the time, but I'll try.'

'You're a good man,' said Grace, and she kissed him on the cheek. 'Now, let us go and get married.'

Mela was waiting for them in the church porch, fair and bright in a handsome coat and bonnet. She kissed Grace and smiled at George. 'Come along, you two. This is a wedding. Do try to look as though you are actually happy!'

George grinned. 'How do you do, Miss Clare. Thanks for coming to stand up with Grace.'

'There is nowhere else I would rather be,' said Mela, taking Grace's arm.

Mickey Doyle, the best man, was waiting inside the church. Grace wondered how he had managed to get time off work. George's employers had grudgingly allowed him the morning off, unpaid, in order to get married but would not release any of his workmates. The only other people were a few women, Brigit and Louisa and, to Grace's surprise, Mrs Lane. *She must really have cut her ties with the vicar's wife*, Grace thought.

And there was Reverend Soames, white-haired and bearded in his white cassock, beaming at them like Father Christmas. 'Welcome,' he said genially. 'If you are ready, my children, then let us begin.'

Afterwards, Grace could remember little about the ceremony. She was aware of herself speaking the words required of her, mechanically and without emotion, and the murmur of George's voice beside her, and the rector's rich baritone pronouncing them man and wife. They moved through to the vestry where the parish clerk waited while they signed the register, Mela adding her signature in firm writing beneath Grace's own.

'Congratulations, Mr and Mrs Turneur,' the rector said smiling.

'Thank you very much, sir,' George said, and Grace repeated his words. She still felt rather distant and removed. *This is not how one is supposed to feel on one's wedding day*, she thought.

Outside the church Mela kissed her. 'I must get back,' she said. 'Unless there is anything you would like me to do?'

'No,' said Grace. 'Thank you for coming, Mela. I'm so glad you were here.'

Mela smiled. 'I meant what I said. I wouldn't be anywhere else. My dear Grace, I know it is your wedding day, but would you be willing to talk school business for a moment?'

At the mention of the school the mists surrounding Grace cleared a little. 'Of course,' she said.

'I may have found you a teacher. A lady called Agnes Korngold came to see us. Her real name isn't Agnes, it's something unpronounceable, and she comes from Poland. Poor thing, her husband was killed by the Russians and she came here seeking sanctuary. She's a teacher, and she speaks English very well; her mother was the daughter of an English cloth merchant. Papa knows the family, he has done business with them in the past. Anyway, to cut a long story short, she was looking for work at the Clare School, and we offered her a post for five half-days a week.'

'And?' Grace prompted.

'And, she teaches in the mornings but has afternoons free. I told her about your school, and she is interested.'

'I cannot afford to pay her,' Grace said.

'That's all right. She has a little inheritance on her mother's side, and with that and what we pay her, she says she gets by. She is willing to volunteer.'

'Does she know it is dangerous?'

'I told her about the gangs. She said it cannot be any worse than Zitomir when the Cossacks are on the rampage. I don't know where Zitomir is, but it sounds quite horrible. She wants to meet you. May I send her to you?'

'Of course. Oh, Mela, thank you so much.'

Mela kissed her and departed. The other guests had gone too, leaving them to their privacy. Grace took George's arm and they walked east towards Rotherhithe, the wind whistling around them. 'What were you and Miss Clare talking about?' George asked.

'She has found me a teacher,' Grace said.

'Oh, lass, that is good news. I know how you've been worrying.'

'It is wonderful news,' said Grace. 'Now I need to think about how to divide them up. Reverend Hobbes would doubtless insist that I teach the boys separately from the girls, but I'm not going to do that. They all need the same education. No, I'm going to have one class for more advanced pupils, like Rebecca, and another for the young ones and the ones who are struggling, like poor little Nathan. That way I can concentrate on them, and really help them along.'

'You're wonderful with them kids,' George said. He added wistfully, 'I wish I was young again, and could get an education.'

'It's not too late,' said Grace smiling.

'Yes, it is. I'm far too old a dog to be learning new tricks now.'

Back at home Grace put on an apron and prepared a meal while George went upstairs and changed into his work clothes. After he had eaten he kissed her on the cheek as usual and departed for work. Albert went into the parlour room to read by the fire, but in the doorway he turned suddenly and smiled at Grace.

'I think I shall like calling you Mummy,' he said.

They passed the evening together as usual, and the children departed for bed. George yawned and kissed her on the cheek again and went upstairs too. He had been coughing less today, but he was finding his work physically tiring. *He needs to eat more*, Grace thought. *I know he holds back at meals so the children have enough, but he mustn't let his strength run down.*

I must do more to look after him. I forget sometimes that he needs me too. And now I am Mrs Turneur . . .

Yes. It really is going to take time to get used to that.

After a while she started to yawn, and she closed the coal stove and went quietly upstairs herself, carrying an oil lamp to light her way. She could hear George breathing gently in his bed. Softly, she opened the door and went into the other bedroom, and stopped in astonishment. The twins were curled up together in the bed she and Daisy had been sharing, and Albert was fast asleep on the truckle bed.

There was no room at all for her.

Her first thought was to wake the boys and tell them to go back to the other room, but she stopped. *For heaven's sake,* she told herself, *I'm a married woman. I can share a bed with my husband.*

Quietly, she undressed and put on her nightgown and then, carrying the lamp, went through to the other bedroom. George stirred as she came in, and then opened his eyes and sat up, looking at her in surprise. 'Grace? What is it?'

'Were the boys here when you came up?'

'Yes, of course.' George looked around in wonder. 'What? Where have they gone?'

'To bed in the other room,' Grace said. 'They have decided that now that we are married, we must share a bed. I suspect the hand of Albert behind this. You know how he likes things to be organised and proper.'

'But . . .' George said, and she thought he sounded nervous. 'What are you going to do?'

'It looks like I'm sleeping here,' Grace said. 'If you don't mind, that is.'

George looked even more anxious. 'Will that be all right? I mean . . . You remember what we talked about?'

'Indeed I do. And nothing has changed,' Grace said. 'At least not for me.'

George shook his head. 'Me neither.'

They looked at each other for a moment, and then Grace started to giggle. 'This must be one of the strangest wedding nights ever.'

'I reckon it happens more often than you think,' George said. He moved over to one side of the bed, making room for her. 'All right, lass. Climb in.'

Grace extinguished the lamp and lay down on the other side of the bed, drawing up the covers and feeling the draught from the window as the wind moaned around the house. 'Goodnight, Mr Turneur,' she said gravely.

She heard the smile in his voice in the darkness. 'Goodnight, Mrs Turneur.'

After only a moment, George was asleep again. Grace lay and listened to his gentle breathing, feeling the warmth of him in the bed beside her. It felt very odd at first; she had shared a bed with Rosa when they were children, and then with Daisy since moving here, but this was different. After a while she found that his presence next to her was actually calming and rather soothing. Her body relaxed and she fell asleep, and slept deeply and well.

Chapter 11

Agnieszka Korngold was a round-figured woman dressed severely in black with steel-rimmed spectacles perched on her nose. Her age was impossible to tell; Grace thought she could have been anywhere between thirty and fifty. 'Please, call me Agnes,' she said when Grace tried to pronounce her first name. 'Back in Zitomoir, I was Agnieszka. Here, I am always Agnes.'

'Where is Zitomir?' Grace asked.

'Poland,' came the response. 'I was born there, and I lived there for many years. Then one day, the Cossacks came. They were like wild animals. They spared no one. They killed my husband and many others, women, even children, and then they burned our synagogue.'

'Heavens!' said Grace in horror. 'Why did they do these things?'

'Because we were Jewish,' said Agnes.

'That is surely not a reason to kill innocent people!'

'In Zitomir, it is,' Agnes said simply. 'After the attack, I realised there was nothing left for me there. I came to England to start a new life.'

'I am so sorry,' said Grace.

'Do not be. What happened is God's will.'

Perhaps, thought Grace, *but if it happened to me, I would not take it so calmly.* Aloud she said, 'I am so grateful to you for coming. Let me show you the school.'

They walked from the railway station to the school, and Grace unlocked the door and lit a lamp. Agnes stood for a while, looking at the rows of desks under the brick arch, the bare earth floor, the little cabinet of books. 'It's not much, I know,' Grace said.

Agnes smiled, and in a moment her face was transformed. She must once have been quite a beautiful woman, Grace thought, before her life was torn apart. 'Great things come from small beginnings,' she said.

'I hope so,' said Grace. 'You have seen how primitive everything is. Are you still willing to volunteer?'

'By God's grace I have my life,' said Agnes, 'and I am comfortably provided for. I wish to put something back, to give something to this country that has given me a home and sanctuary. 'When do you wish me to start?'

She started a couple of days later, once Grace had a chance to divide the children into two classes. As she had discussed with George, she sent Rebecca and some of the older children into the afternoon class where Agnes would teach them, and kept the younger ones including her own stepchildren – she was *still* not used to thinking of them as such – and the ones who were struggling, like Nathan and Lettice, in her morning class. Right from the beginning, the arrangement worked well. Grace had given Agnes her own key so she could come and go, and she always left the makeshift classroom immaculate when she departed in the evening.

She had been worried for Agnes's safety, and right at the beginning had warned her about the gangs. As Mela had said, Agnes was dismissive. 'I have no fears. I have seen far worse than a few street toughs. You must not worry for me, Grace. But have a care for your own safety.'

February turned into a cold windswept March, which in turn gave away to a damp showery April. The air grew a little warmer, and wildflowers began to appear in the marshes south of the docks. Just after Easter a strong east wind pushed the high tide up the Thames and most of Rotherhithe flooded; George and the other men building the new dock worked in a foot of water, and more water dark with silt lapped around the door of the houses in Bell Lane. The glue factory was flooded and had to shut down for several days, and for a while the air smelled almost clean. When the water receded, men began clearing the barren fields near the engine works and putting up a new factory. Rumour said this one was for weaving carpets and other textiles. The owners were the firm of Crompton and Rhodes, the same business that owned the garment factory where Rosa had once worked.

More factories meant more houses for workers, Rotherhithe was still growing apace. 'And that means more work for bricklayers,' said George cheerfully. 'It's all good news, lass.'

His cough had improved as the weather became warmer, and Grace's concern for his health had receded a little. 'Good,' she said. 'Maybe then you can get a job with a firm that pays better.'

He grinned at her. 'Is this you being a nagging wife?'

'Maybe,' said Grace, grinning back. 'I thought I might try it, and see if it suited me.'

Life at the little house in Bell Lane had settled into a gentle routine. Much to her own surprise, Grace had slotted easily into the role of wife and mother. She had been worried about superseding Rosa, but for George and the children there was no question of this. Life was like a story, moving on, and she was part of the next chapter. There were still times when someone addressed her as Mrs Turneur in the market or in the street, or at school, and it took her a moment to realise they were talking to her; there were still times when one of the children called her 'Mummy' and for a split second she looked around half-expecting to see Rosa standing there. Harry was the first to notice this, and he decided to clarify the situation using his own form of logic.

'Mummy was Mummy,' he announced, 'and now you are Mummy. I shall call Mummy Mummy, First Mummy, and I shall call you Second Mummy. That way when I say first mummy you will know I mean Mummy Mummy, and when I say second mummy you will know I mean you mummy, Mummy.'

He grinned up at her. 'I hope that makes sense to you, Harry,' Grace said. 'Because if so, you're the only one.'

News of their marriage spread through the community, and was met with a mixed reaction. The vicar's wife and her friends continued to cold-shoulder Grace in the street, and one or two women in the market still scowled at her. There was a rumour, too, that the vicar had preached a sermon railing against fornication and denouncing false marriages. On the other hand, kind Reverend Soames had preached another sermon about tolerance and understanding, and on the whole it seemed more people were listening to him. Most of Rotherhithe understood exactly why Grace and George had married. For them the marriage had corrected the situation that had so worried them. They knew how fine the line was between life and death, and how easily many of them could be in the same situation.

In the spring of 1868, death came easily to the crowded streets of south-east London. An outbreak of fever forced Grace to close the school for a week to prevent infection. More than thirty people died, though fortunately her pupils and their families were all spared. But even more ominous, rising like a shadow over Rotherhithe, was the ongoing war between the gangs.

'It's getting very bad,' George said, one evening after the children were asleep. 'The Deptford gang are finished, they say. The Bull Heads caught two of their leaders and . . . well, you don't want to know what happened to them. That was pretty much the end of it. The rest of the gang dispersed, or went over to the Bull Heads and joined them instead. But the Black Crows, now, they're a different matter. They've been moving in on Jamaica Road, demanding the shopkeepers pay 'em for protection, or threatening to burn them out if they don't. That's Bull Head territory, and they'll fight back.'

'Goodness,' said Grace. 'Is there no one who can do anything?'

'Don't reckon so,' said George. 'You saw for yourself how useless the peelers are, and no one from outside is going to step in.'

'Why ever not?'

George shrugged. 'Why should they? We're just poor working folk. If we get caught in the middle of it all, and stabbed or beaten, well, we're expendable, ain't we? There's plenty more who'll fill our places. That's how the high and mighty see it.'

'If we all stood up to these gangs, every one of us, they couldn't harm us,' said Grace. 'We're too many. If the gangs found every hand was against them, they would have to give up, or move away.'

'But who is going to be the first to stand up to them? That's the problem.' George rubbed his chin. 'Although I hear tell that young schoolmaster Ringrose over in Bermondsey is doing just that. The Black Crows came and demanded protection money, and he sent them away with a flea in their ear. Sounds like he knows how to look after himself.'

'If they come to me, they'll get the same response,' she said.

George looked worried. 'Have a care, lass. Those Black Crow beggars are dangerous, even more than the Bull Heads.'

'You said Mr Ringrose knows how to look after himself. Well, so do I.'

Late one morning a few days later, Grace was reading *The Ugly Duckling* to the children when she was interrupted by a knock at door. Radcliffe, asleep by the stove, woke up and began to bark. Grace hushed the dog, but he continued to growl, his hackles up. The knock was repeated. Frowning, Grace motioned to the children to be quiet and walked to the door, Radcliffe following her.

'Who is it?' Grace asked.

'I'd like to be having a word with you, Mrs Turneur,' came a man's voice. 'I've three little weans with me who'd like to enrol in your school.'

Grace unlocked the door and opened it, and then stopped in shock. Facing her was the largest man she had ever seen. He wore a black suit, the front of which was matted and sticky with grease, and his lank hair hung down over his shoulders. His nose at some point had been badly broken and not reset, with the result that it seemed to spread out across his face. Two enormous sheath knives hung from his belt.

'Good day to you, missus,' said the giant, bowing. He smelled like he had never washed in his life. 'May I introduce my little weans? Fine wee fellows, would you not say, now? Maybe a trifle old for schoolin', but I reckon you can whip 'em into shape.'

The three men behind him grinned. They were big, though nothing like as large as their leader, and they too carried knives. Grace's heart began to pound. 'Who are you?' she demanded.

'My name's Jack,' said the giant. 'People call me Rancid Jack, though for the life of me I've never known why. I'm a . . . a representative, you might say, of a business organisation. We're called the Black Crows. I expect you'll have heard of us.'

'Yes, I have heard of you,' Grace said. 'And whatever your business is, you are not wanted here.'

She started to close the door, but Rancid Jack took a step forward and blocked the door with one enormous boot. Beside Grace, Radcliffe snarled, baring his teeth. The giant ignored him.

'Not so fast, now,' said Rancid Jack. 'You've a fine little school here, Mrs Turneur. A trifle primitive and all, but I can see how you're proud of it. Are you not?'

'Yes,' said Grace, glad her skirt hid her shaking knees.

'We're here to help you, see,' said Rancid Jack. 'There's some people about, ill-intentioned folk you might say, who would like to see this school gone. They might try to damage it, perhaps even burn it down. We don't think that should happen. We're well-intentioned fellows, see. Very fond of education we are. Aren't we, boys?'

'Aye,' said one of the men, baring his yellow teeth in a grin. Radcliffe growled again.

'So here is our proposition, Mrs Turneur,' the giant went on. 'For a small consideration, we'll keep your school safe. Not a large fee, not at all. Just a trifle. Contribution to the parish funds, you might say. Does ten shillings a week sound fair?'

Ten shillings a week was half of George's wages. 'I don't have any money,' Grace said.

The giant grinned at her, looking her up and down in a way that sent tremors of revulsion running through her entire body. 'Well, now, Mrs Turneur, that's no obstacle at all. A fine, well set-up filly like you can easy earn ten shillings a week, maybe more. Me and the boys, we'll show how you can earn it.'

He leaned towards her, and lowered his voice. 'It'd be our pleasure,' he said.

Summoning all her reserves of courage, Grace glared at him. 'You'll not get a penny from me. Not now, not ever. Now, go away. You are frightening the children.'

Rancid Jack shook his head. 'It's not a good idea to say no to the Black Crows, Mrs Turneur. Not a good idea at all.' He motioned to his men. 'I think the lady needs a little demonstration. Show her what happens to those who don't co-operate with us.'

Radcliffe began to bark very loudly. The other men moved towards Grace, but stopped when the dog ran at them. Grace pointed across the fields to the place where workmen were building the new carpet factory. Some of them had heard the dog barking, and turned towards the sound of the noise.

'I'd be careful, if I were you,' she said to Rancid Jack. 'If there is any trouble, those men will send for the constables.

And the local constables, in case you didn't already know, are in the pay of the Bull Head Gang, and they will call on the gang for help. You can't fight both of them at once, can you?'

The big man glared at her. 'This isn't over, missus,' he said. 'We'll be back. That's a promise.' Then, motioning to his friends, he turned on his heel and walked away.

Grace called Radcliffe and then slammed the door shut and leaned against it for a moment, quivering. The children stared at her, faces full of fright; Albert was as white as a sheet. She forced herself to be calm.

'I think that's enough for today, children,' she said. 'And there will be no lessons tomorrow.' Nor would there be any more lessons, she thought, until this menace had gone away. She had thought she could face down the threat, but she knew now that she could not put the children in danger. The thought sickened her, but for the moment at least, the school would have to close.

Back at the house, her hands still shaking, she wrote a letter to Agnes, advising her that the school would be closed until further notice and then, taking Radcliffe with her and locking the door firmly behind her, went out to post the letter and then knock on the doors of the parents with older children to give them the news. Back at Bell Lane she called on Mrs Berton last of all.

'It's sickening, what's going on,' said her neighbour and friend. 'Elijah says the Crows have threatened to beat up the men working at the engine works, unless the company pays a ransom. But if they do pay, then the Bull Heads will attack them. We're caught between the devil and the deep sea.'

That was all too true, Grace thought. She remembered what George had said, and what the woman in the market had said too. No one would help them, because no one in power apart from a few reformers like Lord Shaftesbury and Mr Raikes cared about the lives of the poor. They were on their own. Their salvation, if it was to come at all, would have to come from themselves.

But she did have one potential ally; Mr Ringrose in Bermondsey, whose own school had been attacked. It would be dangerous to go there. The Black Crows were said to be all over Bermondsey, and she knew what would happen if she met Rancid Jack and his friends again. But something had to be done. Taking a deep breath, she called Radcliffe to her and then began to walk towards Bermondsey.

Potters' Fields was a narrow lane running off Tooley Street, not far from London Bridge railway station. Many of the buildings, including the station itself, still bore the marks of the big fire seven years ago which had swept through the area, destroying many houses and warehouses. Now most of the surviving buildings were used as doss-houses, or were abandoned entirely. But the last house on the lane, looking out over a field full of brambles and weeds, had new windows fitted, and a sign saying SCHOOL posted over the door.

All seemed quiet. Grace knocked at the door and waited. After a while there came the sound of bolts being drawn back, and the door opened and Mr Ringrose appeared in the doorway, carrying a cricket bat in one hand. He looked tense, but he relaxed when he saw Grace.

'Miss Perrow! What a pleasant surprise! Please, do come in.'

Grace followed him into the hall, watching him bar the door again. He seemed more flustered than ever, and yet she had heard from George that he had faced down the Black Crows. 'I say, would you like some tea or something?' he asked. 'I was just about to put the kettle on.'

'You are too kind,' Grace said. 'But I cannot stay long. My husband will be home soon, and I must get back.'

Mr Ringrose looked startled.

'I'm married,' Grace explained. 'I am Mrs Turneur now.'

'Oh.' The young man looked at her, and then suddenly lowered his eyes. 'M-my congratulations,' he stammered. 'I wish you every happiness.'

'Thank you,' said Grace. She looked around the hall. 'You've a fine big building here. I wish I had such luxury.'

'Oh, it was a fortunate chance,' said Mr Ringrose, recovering his poise a little. 'I happened to know the owner, and was able to buy the lease for a song. I live here as well, you see, partly in order to keep an eye on the place. Things have been difficult lately.'

'I heard you had trouble with the Black Crows,' Grace said.

'Yes,' said Mr Ringrose. 'They demanded I pay them for protection. If I didn't, they would burn my school down.' He looked at the cricket bat in his hand. 'I told them they would only do it over my dead body. The fellow that led them – big smelly chap – said that was the general idea. They told me to think it over, and went away. Have you had trouble too?'

'Yes.' Grace told him about Rancid Jack, and Mr Ringrose nodded. 'Sounds like the same fellow,' he said. 'What are you going to do?'

'I've closed the school for the moment,' Grace said. 'But I cannot stay closed forever. My pupils are depending on me. I came to talk to you and see if we could agree what to do next.'

'I have been thinking about it,' said Mr Ringrose. 'We're not strong enough to fight these fellows. I think we need to just keep our heads down, and wait.'

'Wait? For what? Surely the Black Crows will come back, and this time they'll do more than just make threats.'

'Not if someone else sees to them first,' Mr Ringrose said. 'Look, I'll tell you what I know. There's a public house along the way, the King's Arms. It's a fairly rough crowd who drink there, but one or two have children at the school, and they know me and trust me, enough to talk pretty freely when I'm around. The word is that there's going to be an almighty showdown between the Black Crows and the Bull Head Gang, probably quite soon. Now that the Deptford mob have been cleaned up, the Bull Heads are turning their attention to the Crows. And the smart money is on the Bull Heads to win.'

Grace shuddered. 'It is like living in a war,' she said.

'That's exactly what it is,' said Mr Ringrose quietly. 'Like I said, Mrs Turneur. I don't think there is much we can do, except wait.'

She waited, while showers of April rain swept over the city. Three days later, George came home from work looking – unusually for him – pale and rather upset. He kissed the children and then sent them to play in the parlour and drew Grace into the kitchen.

'It's bad,' he said. 'Very bad. The Black Crows approached Crompton and Rhodes and demanded protection money for that new carpet factory they're building. Mr Crompton refused, so this morning the Crows went in to burn the place down. Only thing is, somehow the Bull Head Gang had found out about it. When the Crows arrived, the Captain and his men were waiting for them. It was an ambush.'

Gentle to the core of his soul, George hated violence. So far as Grace knew, he had never raised his hand to anyone. 'What happened?' she asked.

'Six killed, they say, and Lord knows how many hurt. These people are animals, Grace. Wild animals, brutes and beasts, that's all they are.'

'Reverend Soames would tell you that even brutes have souls,' said Grace.

'His reverence can't have had much dealing with folk like the Captain or Rancid Jack. He's gone missing, by the way. Jack, I mean. No one's seen him since the fight. The

Black Crows are beaten, and the Captain's men are on top. They run all this district now, everything from London Bridge to the Surrey Canal.'

'If the Black Crows have gone, then something good has come of this,' said Grace. 'I'm going to re-open the school.'

George took her hand. 'Lass, I'm begging you; don't. The Bull Heads are just as violent and cruel as the Crows. They're just as likely to do you harm. Stay at home, and stay safe.'

'I can't stay at home forever,' Grace said. 'Yes, the Bull Heads attacked my school once, but that was months ago. You said it yourself, they're a big gang now, and they'll have plenty on their plates. I'm not a threat to them, not now. I'm sorry, George, but I must do this.'

Grace wrote to Agnes and asked if she was ready to return to work, and received a terse reply to the effect that yes, she was. A little apprehensively, Grace then approached the parents of her children – and, if they did not have parents, the children themselves – and asked if they were willing to return. All but one said yes. 'And if those swine give you any trouble, tell us,' said Mickey Doyle. 'We'll see you safe, Mrs Turneur.' He was a courtly man, Mickey, for all his size and strength, and he always insisted on calling her Mrs Turneur, even though she begged him to use her first name.

The school resumed and Grace went back to her old routine, teaching in the morning, returning home to prepare a meal and then housework or shopping in the market in the afternoon before George came home in the evening. April turned into May, and May to June. The skies were brighter, though the wind remained cold from the east, raw with smoke and fumes from the glue factory and vitriol works. At home Grace kept the doors and windows tight shut to keep out the stink, with the result that without ventilation the house became damper than ever.

July came, and still the cold persisted, making a mockery of summer. The anniversary of Rosa's death was hard for both her and George. That evening they sat before the fire for a long time, not saying very much, remembering. 'I loved her,' George said softly, staring out the window. 'But it was more than just love. She kept me going. Stopped me from doing foolish things, and reminded me of my responsibilities. I know I'm an idiot sometimes, but Rosa was always there to pull me out of whatever mess I'd got into.'

He shook his head. 'I still can't believe she's gone. I look at the kids sometimes, and I think, oh, she's not far away. She's just in the other room. She'll come to us in a moment, and then all will be right with the world again.'

'She's watching over you still,' Grace said softly. 'I do believe that, George. She's watching over us all.'

George forced a smile. 'Maybe so . . . She'd be proud of what you're doing now, that's for certain. She always said you were the clever one in the family.'

Grace smiled. 'And I always thought she was the brave strong one.'

'You're both of those things too,' George said, taking her hand.

'If I am, it's because I learned how to be both from her. I miss her so much, George. When I was little, she was the only family I ever had.'

'Do you remember anything, lass? About where you came from?'

Grace shook her head. 'I was adopted when I was a newborn babe, Rosa said. As for our parents, I remember little hazy moments, no more. I don't even know what they looked like. My first real memories are of the workhouse.'

'That's sad,' George said quietly.

'A little, yes. Rosa was my last link with my old life. Now, I'm the woman with no past.' She smiled and patted his hand. 'But at least I have a future, and a family too.'

'No regrets?' George asked.

'For Rosa, yes. We'll both miss her forever. For everything else; no, none. I think things have worked out for the best. I'm lucky, George, to have so much, when so many others have nothing.'

The following day the weather changed. The wind died away and the weather became warm and humid, the air sticky and reeking with smoke and fumes. The sun shone dull orange through the haze. In the afternoon once George had returned to work, Grace washed the dishes and tidied the kitchen and then, leaving the children to read or play, fetched her basket and called Radcliffe and went out to go to the market.

After the long spell of cold weather, the sun on her cheek felt positively hot. The market was crowded with people, and in the distance a brass band tootled away, volunteers from the London Christian Mission raising funds for the homeless. Grace was glad she had not brought Harry, for she would not have been able to keep him away from the band. She bought bread and cheese and fresh vegetables and a scrag end of mutton, and began to walk back towards Bell Lane.

A covered van drawn by a single pony pulled up alongside her. Two men jumped out, and before Grace realised what was happening, they were alongside her, seizing her by the arms. One clapped a rough hand over her mouth. She struggled, dropping her basket, but they were far too strong for her. Radcliffe was behind her, barking furiously, but the men ignored him. Dragging her between them, they threw her into the van and slammed the doors. Winded, she lay on the floor of the van and felt it lurch into motion. After a moment she crawled over to the doors and pushed against them as hard as she could, but to no avail; they had been securely locked from outside.

'Help!' she screamed. 'Let me out! Someone, help me! Please!' But there was no answer and the motion of the van never ceased or faltered. No help was coming, and there was no escape. She had been kidnapped.

Chapter 12

Even as George reached the house, he felt something was wrong. Taking out his keys, he let himself in the front door and then stopped in alarm. The children were huddled together around the shaggy form of Radcliffe, who lay on the floor with his head on his paws and his ears down, the picture of canine misery.

'What is it?' George asked. 'Is something wrong with the dog?'

Their faces stared back at him, pale with fright. 'Mummy went to the market,' said Albert. 'She took Radcliffe with her. Then Radcliffe came home without her. Mummy hasn't come back.'

To George, it was at once clear what had happened. Grace had been wrong. The Bull Head Gang had remembered her. Now, with their rivals defeated and their supremacy over the docklands unchallenged, they had come back to settle their score.

He drew a deep breath. 'Albert, run next door to Mr Berton, and then find Mr Doyle. Tell them I need their help.'

Doyle and Berton arrived a few minutes later. 'I think the Bull Heads have taken Grace,' George said. 'I've got to find her.'

The others nodded. 'We're with you,' Mickey Doyle said.

'Stay here,' George said to Albert. 'Lock the door and don't let anyone in until we come back.'

He bent down to the dog and snapped his fingers. Radcliffe lifted his head. 'Here, boy,' George said. 'Find Grace. There's a good dog now. Find her, boy.'

Radcliffe shook himself, rose to his feet and trotted out the door. The three men hurried after him. Five minutes later they were standing at the spot where Grace was taken, the abandoned shopping basket lying in the road. It was empty; hungry thieves had doubtless taken whatever food the basket had contained.

'What do we do now?' Elijah Berton asked.

'If it was the Bull Heads, they'll have taken her to Albion,' said Mickey Doyle. 'That's where their lair is now.' He hesitated, and then said what they had all been thinking. 'There's only three of us, George. We can't take on the whole gang.'

'We can't abandon Grace, either,' George said. He snapped his fingers again to summon the dog and set off walking towards Albion Dock. The other two followed him.

The room where they had brought Grace was lit only by shafts of sunlight coming through windows high overhead. The walls, she could dimly see, were rough brick. The resinous smells of pine and fir told her it was a timber warehouse.

There were other smells too; smoke, sweat, the sharp smell of the river.

She could feel the bruises on her arms where the two men had gripped her. They were still there, standing behind her. Another man walked into the room, a tall man with a livid red cut on his cheek and a bandage on one ear. The wounds looked recent. She wondered if they had been sustained in the fighting at the carpet factory, and shuddered.

'Well, well,' said the man. He walked over and stood a few feet away, crossing his arms over his chest. 'What have we here? A prime little pullet, ripe for the plucking.'

'Keep your hands off me!' she said sharply.

'You're in no position to make demands, my dainty.' The man considered her, slowly. 'Sara said you were a hoity-toity one. I see what she means. Well, I reckon we'll take you down a peg or two.'

'Sara . . .' Realisation dawned. 'Are you Jimmy's father?'

'Aye. I'm Long Ben Wilson. And you're the interfering little snipe who tried to take him away from us. I owe you for that.'

Shaking but determined to show no fear, Grace said, 'Where is Jimmy? Is he safe?'

'What's it to you?' Long Ben lowered his arms and walked forward until he was within touching distance of Grace. 'You've interfered enough in our business, lady. You and that bloody school of yours. We're closing that down, now.'

Grace swallowed. 'No,' she said. 'You'll not touch my school.'

In response, Long Ben raised his arm, fingers curling into a fist. Grace closed her eyes and waited for the blow to fall.

'*Stop!*' said another voice.

Slowly, Grace opened her eyes. Another man had come into the room, smaller, more slightly built, dressed in a long black coat despite the heat and with a broad-brimmed hat shading his eyes. Only the bottom half of his face could be seen. Something flashed and glittered with rainbows in the gloom, a diamond ring on the man's right hand. It flashed again as he moved forward.

'That's enough, Wilson,' he said.

Long Ben looked at him, and without a word lowered his hand and stepped back.

'Get out,' the man said curtly. 'I'll handle this myself. Wait outside, all of you. I'll have work for you later.'

The three men left in silence, not looking back. As the door closed behind them, Grace found her voice.

'Who are you?' she asked. 'Who brought me here, and why?'

'I gave the orders to bring you here,' the man said. He hooked his thumbs through his belt. A long, wicked-looking knife hung in a sheath at his waist. 'These are my men. As you may have guessed, they are from the Bull Head Gang, and I am their leader. I am the Captain.'

Grace felt herself growing cold. If she had thought she was in danger before, now she truly was in mortal peril. Standing before her was one of the most ruthless and dangerous men in London.

'As to why you are here,' the Captain went on, 'you already know, don't you? Like Ben said, we are closing your school.'

Grace swallowed. 'My school is doing no harm,' she said.

'No harm,' the Captain repeated. 'Stealing our children away from us, filling their heads full of useless ideas, teaching them to think they're better than their own parents. You don't call that harm?'

'I am teaching them so they can make a better life for themselves,' Grace said.

'A better life for themselves,' the Captain repeated, malice in his voice. 'A better life for themselves. It's a fraud, little Grace. A hoax, perpetrated on the poor by a few do-good reformers who want to pat themselves on the back and tell themselves how wonderful they are. Make a better life for themselves? There's no such thing.'

He walked around Grace, still speaking, his voice echoing a little in the high room. 'But if you give the poor hope, you see, tell them there is something better out there waiting for them, then they're quiet. They don't make a fuss. They obey the rules, they play the games the rich set out for them, in hopes that one day everything will come good, and they'll be happy and prosperous. But it never happens, does it? The hope that is fed to the poor is a delusion, a cheat, a sham. This life, what we have here and now; that is all there is.'

'I don't believe you,' said Grace.

'It doesn't matter what you believe, little Grace. I hold the cards here. I am the Captain, and in Rotherhithe *I* make the rules. Do you understand?'

'Yes,' said Grace.

'Good. Let's start with a simple question. Rancid Jack came to your school not long ago. He asked you to pay protection money. Did you agree?'

'No,' said Grace.

'Really? He threatened you, did he not? What reply did you make?'

'I told him to go away.'

Below the brim of his hat, the Captain smiled. 'Let's see if you're telling the truth.' He raised his voice. 'All right, Wilson, bring him in.'

There was a pause of about a minute and then the door opened. Ben Wilson and another man came in, dragging something between them. After a moment Grace realised to her horror that it was a man's body, and then realised with an even deeper shock that it was Rancid Jack. He was still alive, but he had been beaten savagely. His coat had been ripped away and there were bloodstains on his filthy shirt. His face was a mass of bruises.

'Jacky-boy,' said the Captain. 'Jacky, Jacky, Jacky. You really are a bit of a mess, aren't you?'

The giant said nothing. The Captain walked over and stood looking down at him. 'You're probably wondering why I've kept you alive,' he said.

The giant moved his battered lips. 'It crossed my mind.'

'My little friend here says that when you came to her school and demanded protection money, she refused you. Is she telling the truth? No lies now, Jacky. The truth and nothing but the truth, so help you God.'

'It's the truth,' said Rancid Jack. 'We were planning to go back and sort her out. Only you got to us first, you bastard.'

The Captain held up a hand. He clicked his tongue. 'Bad language in front of a lady,' he said. 'I'm not having that. All right, Wilson. Take him away and dispose of him. Do it however you like, but make sure he is never seen again.'

The two men dragged Rancid Jack out of the room, closing the door behind them. The Captain walked around Grace again, surveying her. 'Well,' he said. 'That makes things a bit different. Had you paid him off, you would have been fraternising with the enemy. My father didn't hold with fraternising with the enemy, and neither do I.'

Grace was still shaking. She tried not think about what was happening to Rancid Jack. 'The enemy?' she said. 'Was your father a soldier?'

'He was, little Grace. He was one of those poor sods who believed, like you, that it was possible to better oneself. He chose the Army as his way of making a new life, and he joined Her Glorious Majesty's 44th Regiment of Foot. Ten years he followed the colours and served his queen and country. *And what do you think it got him?*' the Captain shouted suddenly.

'I don't know,' said Grace.

'The 44th Regiment of Foot were sent to Afghanistan. Their generals were lords and toffs. They were blundering fools, but they were toffs, so they got to be generals. When the fighting started, all the generals were safe. And why, you ask? Again, because they were toffs, and therefore too important to risk their lives in the line of fire. Instead, the poor common soldiers of the 44th were sent to march through winter snow with no blankets, no boots, no ammunition, barely any muskets. At a place called Gandamack, they were sacrificed. The Afghans cut them to pieces with knives, butchered them like so many sheep. My father was one of them.'

'Oh, God,' said Grace, and now she could not stop her teeth from chattering. 'Gandamack. My Aunt Edith's husband died there.'

'Indeed he did, little Grace.' The Captain's voice was sombre now. 'Your Aunt Edith's husband. My father.'

'You're Charlie,' Grace said. 'The boy who ran away.'

'The boy who ran away,' the Captain repeated. 'The boy who realised that everything was a sham, a fraud. The glory my father died for was a lie. The idea of serving queen and country was a lie. The idea of advancing in the service and making a better life for himself was a lie. Life was a lie. So, I left and joined the gangs. In the gangs I finally found truth.'

He held up his hand, the diamond flashing and sparkling again. 'Beautiful, isn't it?' he said. 'Comes from Ceylon, I'm told. I cut it off a dead man's hand ten years ago. This is what life really means, little Grace. This is truth.'

Grace's head was spinning. 'If you are who you say you are, then you are my cousin,' she said.

The Captain walked over to Grace, studying her. She could see the gleam of his eyes now, under the brim of his hat. 'Don't count on family feeling to protect you, little Grace. I could kill you right now, and not shed a tear.'

I am going to die here, Grace thought. *Goodbye, George. Goodbye Albert and Harry and Daisy, I love you, and I am sorry you'll lose yet another mother. Goodbye, Mela, my dear friend. I am sorry that I'll never see you again. If I am going to die, let it at least be swift.*

She straightened her back and looked at the Captain. 'Do it, then,' she said. 'What are you waiting for?'

The Captain said nothing. 'Do it,' Grace said again. 'I'm not going to beg, if that is what you are waiting for. Get it over with.'

The Captain watched her for a little longer. 'It doesn't have to be like this,' he said. 'Agree to close your school, and you can walk out of here, free and unharmed.'

'Why?' Grace demanded. 'Why is the school so important to you?'

'Because it interferes with my plans,' the Captain said. 'I need these children to work for me, the boys especially. They are the gang's future. I was just like them. The gang took me, moulded me, and made me the man I am.'

'God forbid,' said Grace, and she shuddered.

'Oh, yes, let's talk about God,' the Captain said, mocking her. 'God will save your school and your children, God will punish me for my sins. Well, no, he won't, little Grace, because there is no God! Religion is another fraud, perpetrated on the poor to keep them in their place. Don't worry about your sufferings in this life, because you will be rewarded in the next? Only a fool would believe that.'

'I believe it,' Grace said.

'Then, you are a fool. I'll say it again. I need those children, and I don't want you filling their heads with rubbish about equality and a better life.'

Sudden anger flooded through Grace. 'And you accuse *me* of stealing children? You take them from their families like you took Jimmy Wilson, you corrupt them and turn them into thieves and criminals, drive them into an early grave, and for what? To make your gang stronger, to give you more power over innocent people so you can rob and steal and kill? You are a monster!'

'I don't deny it,' the Captain said calmly. 'I am a criminal. But I am honest about what I do. I don't hide behind patriotism or religion or some false and foolish notion of a better world, because I know a better world does not exist. And now I am telling you one last time. Close your school.'

'No,' said Grace. 'I won't. And you can do whatever you like.' She stared at the Captain. 'You could kill me right now, but you haven't done it. I don't believe even a monster like you would harm his own cousin.'

'Don't bet on it,' said the Captain. His voice was still calm. 'But, all the same, I find myself strangely hesitant. There is no denying you have spirit. Perhaps we are more alike than I had guessed.'

Silence fell. Grace listened to her heart thudding in her chest, wondering desperately what would happen next. *Thank God he doesn't know I am adopted*, she thought. *It might change his mind.*

'I will make you a bargain,' the Captain said finally. 'I took Jimmy Wilson with the consent of his father, by the way.'

'But not his mother,' said Grace.

'Sara is a drunken sot. Her feelings are nothing. I will continue to take boys when I need them, or when I hear of one who shows promise, and you will not stop me. The girls I will leave alone. If I am ever in need of drabs, there are plenty already on the market.'

'You won't take them,' Grace said. 'I won't allow it.'

'Wait until you hear the rest of the bargain. In exchange, you may continue your school. You may teach the girls and the younger boys whatever rubbish you see fit. You will not interfere with me, and I will not interfere with you. But you will allow me my tithe of the boys.'

'I do not accept,' Grace said.

'You have no choice. Go back to your school, little Grace. Go back and do whatever you like. But if you try to stop me or hinder me in any way, I will reduce your school to ashes, and cousin or no cousin, I will break your sweet neck. Is that clear?'

The steel in his voice made Grace quake again. She opened her mouth to say that she would never submit to his will, not ever, but then, suddenly, the door behind her crashed open and Radcliffe, barking furiously, came hurtling across the room towards her.

∞

I was on watch outside the warehouse when I saw them bring Miss Perrow in – I knew she'd got wed but she was still Miss Perrow to me. The gang had sent me out to act as a lookout. They hadn't treated me too bad after they let me out of the hole. I guess they knew I wouldn't try to run away again, and they were right. I did what they told me. I wasn't going back in the hole again, not ever.

But when I saw Miss Perrow I felt sick. All the memories came back, the classroom and the books and her voice, so soft, so kind and gentle. I knew they were going to top her. I just stood there watching them drag her inside, a sick knot of misery filling my guts and chest. I saw Da and the other two take Rancid Jack away to kill him. After that I wandered outside and sat down on a bollard, looking out over Albion Dock and seeing the ships moored along the waterfront, wondering what to do.

That was when I heard the dog running along the waterfront, hackles up and barking. Just some stray, I thought, but then I saw one of the men following him was Mr Turneur.

He saw me too. 'Jimmy,' he said quickly. 'What are you doing here?'

I tried to say something but it felt like my tongue was stuck in my mouth. 'Never mind,' he said. 'Grace has gone missing. Have you seen her?'

I pointed at the warehouse. The Captain would find out I told them, and I would go into the hole again, or worse. But I had to save Miss Perrow.

⤬

'Stay away from her,' George said to the Captain. Radcliffe stood beside him, growling. 'By God, if you've hurt a hair on her head, I'll—'

'She is unharmed,' the Captain said. 'And who might you be?'

'George Turneur,' George said. 'I'm her husband.'

'Her husband?' A little mocking smile played around the corners of the Captain's mouth. His hand rested, lazily, on the hilt of his knife. 'Riding bravely to the rescue, I see.' The Captain looked from Grace to George and then back again. 'Well,' he said mockingly. 'Let me not stand in the way of true love. You are free to go, Mrs Turneur. Think about what I said, and do not forget it.'

Relief washed through Grace like the incoming tide. She thought of the children at home, and wanted more than anything else in the world to see them and hold them, to feel their kisses on her face and smell their hair. 'Wait!' she said.

'What is it now?' asked the Captain.

'I was coming back from market when your men grabbed me. I lost my basket and all our food. What am I meant to feed our children?'

The Captain reached into his pocket. Something gold gleamed in the air and landed at her feet; a sovereign. 'Never let it be said that I am ungenerous,' he said. 'Farewell, little Grace. Let us hope we do not need to meet again.'

He turned his back on them and walked through another door at the far end of the room, closing it behind them. Shivering, Grace threw herself into George's arms, sobbing into his chest as he held her close. 'Come on,' said Elijah Berton. 'Let's get out of here before the others come back.'

They hurried outside and away down Albion Dock, quiet in the evening sun. Grace wiped her eyes and looked at the men. 'Did you really come alone? Just the three of you?'

She thought they looked a little embarrassed. 'We couldn't not come,' said Elijah Berton. 'I mean, not knowing that you'd been took. We had to look for you.'

'Three men and a dog, against the Bull Head Gang,' said Grace. 'I think that is the bravest thing I have ever heard of. Oh, George, thank God you came.'

'Are you sure he didn't hurt you?' George asked anxiously.

'No. But the things he said ...' She started to weep again. 'He'll let me keep the school going. But oh, George, the price he asks is awful.'

Chapter 13

The Captain kept his word. As the months passed, the Bull Head Gang cemented their control over south-east London, forcing businesses and some homes to pay protection money, and punishing those that refused to pay with burnings and beatings. But they never came near the school.

Grace had insisted on returning to work the day after the attack. She could see the look of awe in her pupils' faces as they came into the classroom under the arches. News of the kidnapping had spread quickly, and it was known that Grace had stood up to the Captain and refused to give in. And as the days passed and word spread still further, people began, quietly and sometimes a little nervously, to stop her in the street and thank her.

This embarrassed her. They praised her as a heroine, but she did not feel like one. Instead, she remembered all too clearly her terror and then relief when George and the others came into the warehouse. At night she often had nightmares, reliving that terrible afternoon, and when this happened she clung to George, begging him to hold her until she could sleep again.

George had told her that he had seen Jimmy outside the warehouse, and that had revived her hope that she might find the boy once more. Whenever she went out she scanned the street, hoping for some sign, but she never saw him. Once, summoning up her nerves, she went to the house in Hanover Court and knocked at the door, praying that Long Ben would not answer it. After she knocked she could hear someone inside the house, but no one came to the door.

Summer that year was one burst of heat and humidity lasting until late August, and then the clouds and rain closed in, bringing an early autumn. The marshes flooded again, but this time the docks were spared. Several men were killed when two barges collided in the Surrey Canal, and a man at the engine works, the father of one of the girls at the school, lost an arm in an accident. He survived, but was unable to work. The manager of the engine works turned him off without pay, and shortly thereafter the family were evicted from their home and sent to the workhouse. Grace never saw the girl again.

By this time, the sickness had begun. It came, regular as clockwork, every morning as she was getting the children ready for school. The spasms did not last long but they were violent and left her pale and shaking. She had little appetite, and began to lose weight, which she knew was a bad thing. Mela Clare, coming to visit one afternoon as she did every few weeks, noticed the change at once. 'Grace, whatever is the matter?'

They were seated as usual at the kitchen table, drinking tea out of the same chipped cups. Grace looked down at her hands. 'I don't know how to tell you,' she said.

'Tell me what?'

After a moment, Grace raised her head and looked her friend in the eye. 'I am carrying a child,' she said quietly.

To say that Mela was stunned was an understatement. She sat staring at Grace for a long time, the expression on her face unreadable. 'How long have you known?' she asked finally.

'About three weeks.'

'And you did not think to tell me?'

'I did not know if you would approve,' Grace said quietly.

'You said it would be a platonic marriage,' Mela said.

'And that is what I intended. That is what we both intended. Then, something happened.'

She told Mela about the kidnapping and her confrontation with the Captain. 'I don't think I have ever been more terrified. It was worse than anything that happened in the workhouse, far worse. I truly thought I was going to die.'

Mela herself had gone pale now. 'Oh, heavens, Grace. Oh, my dear.' She caught Grace's hands in hers and squeezed hard. 'Why didn't you tell me any of this?'

'Because I didn't want you to worry,' Grace said. 'You are my dearest friend, Mela, and I did not want to cause you distress. I'm all right, truly I am. I bounced back remarkably well, all things considered. But, one of the reasons I did recover so quickly is that I have a husband who cares for me.'

'Ah,' said Mela.

'Ah, indeed. That night, after I was freed ... We both needed something. We found it in each other.'

Mela continued to stare at her. 'We are, after all, man and wife,' Grace said. 'I don't love him, Mela, and he doesn't love me. But that doesn't have to stop us from giving each other warmth, and comfort.' She forced a smile. 'And Reverend Hobbes can no longer complain this is not a valid marriage. He insists the purpose of marriage is the procreation of children, and, well ... We have procreated.'

'You certainly have,' said Mela.

Another silence fell. 'I can see the look on your face,' Grace said quietly. 'I know this is hard, Mela. But it would mean a great deal to know I have your blessing.'

The silence lasted for a moment longer, and then Mela suddenly began to giggle. 'The look on my face? Yes, I probably do look like someone has smacked me in the face with a wet fish. I am ... astonished, and indeed I am worried for you. But, my blessing? Of course you have it, you sweet fool. How could you ever doubt it?'

Relief flooded through Grace, and she felt her eyes grow moist. 'Thank you,' she said. 'I'm so glad. And may I call upon you to fill the role of godmother?'

'I would have been most offended if you had not,' said Mela, smiling again. 'And you, my dear. Are you well?'

'The sickness in the mornings is hard. But my neighbours who have children tell me this will pass, and that I will regain my appetite. I have not noticed many other changes yet, though I daresay they will come soon enough.'

'When will the baby come?'

'April.' Grace smiled. 'A spring baby.'

'What does George think?' Mela asked.

'George is a mixture of many emotions. He is by turns worried for me, concerned as to how we will stretch his wages to feed another mouth, feeling guilty for getting me in this condition in the first place and, I think, secretly a little bit pleased. He loves children. I have told him it is all right to be happy, and he is to stop worrying and above all to stop apologising. I am just as responsible as he.'

She patted her belly lightly. 'I know childbirth is risky, and I know that feeding another child will be a stretch. But Mela, I would not have it any other way.'

'You are content,' said Mela.

'I have many concerns and cares. But, on the whole, yes. I am content.'

Mela smiled. 'Then I am glad for you. And the school? It is flourishing?'

'It is. Agnes has been wonderful. Thank you for sending her.'

'I am glad she is proving useful,' said Mela.

'Oh, she is. Because we teach at different times of day I don't see much of her, but she calls in once a week after teaching. The older children are very fond of her. Rebecca, the girl next door, says she tells the most marvellous stories about life in Poland and her travels in Austria and Russia.'

'So you have turned a corner,' Mela said. 'Your school is on its way to being a great success.'

Grace sighed. 'I hope so,' she said. She remembered, every day, the Captain's threat, and heard his voice in her mind. *You will allow me my tithe of the boys.* What if they came and took Billy Doyle, or Nathan, or Gabriel? What if, God forbid, one day they came to take Albert? How would she stop them?

'I don't think things are finished with the gang,' she said finally. 'I fear we will have trouble with them again one day.'

'Then get the community on your side,' Mela said. 'If everyone supports you, the gang will have to back down.'

'Yes. Someone else said that to me not long ago. Mela, do you remember Lady Ringrose's nephew, Walter? The one you admired at the summer party? He is running a Ragged School too, in Bermondsey.'

'So I heard,' said Mela. 'Have you met him?'

'Yes, I called on him when I heard he also was having trouble with the gangs. He is trying to rally Bermondsey people against them. I wish him luck.'

'So do I.' Mela smiled. 'Is he still as handsome as when we first met?'

'I wouldn't know,' Grace said with mock primness. 'I pay no attention to such things. *I* am a respectable married woman.'

She had told Mela the truth. It wasn't the future she had imagined for herself, but being pregnant had made her strangely content. The works doctor from Mr Clare's business paid her an unannounced call one afternoon and insisted on examining her, refusing any offer of a fee. Grace presumed the Clares had sent him, but did not ask.

'You are profoundly healthy, Mrs Turneur,' the doctor said, beginning to pack his bag. 'As a result, there is every chance that your baby will be healthy too. May I offer my congratulations?'

'Thank you, sir,' said Grace. 'Is there any reason why I should not continue to teach?'

The doctor considered the matter. 'Work is not generally considered advisable. Ladies in your condition need their rest.'

'And yet, many of the women around here work almost until the hour of childbirth,' said Grace. 'I can hardly do less.'

'You must do what you feel right,' the doctor said. 'All the same, Mrs Turneur, have a care. Your health is good, but the slightest upset could change that.'

To the fascination of the children, her belly began to swell. The twins in particular plied her with endless questions over the baby inside her, how it had got there, what it was doing, and how it was going to come out. 'Honestly, I don't know what to say to them,' Grace said to George one evening as they made ready for bed. 'Daisy asked me this morning if she could have a baby too, to keep me company. When I said she was too little, she said that was all right, she only wanted a very little baby. And then Harry wanted to know if Radcliffe could have a baby too, and didn't seem to understand when I pointed out the obvious problem.'

Gently, George touched her belly through the cloth of her nightgown. 'It's good they're curious. That means they won't be jealous of the baby when it comes. They'll want to help you look after it.'

'Oh, Lord,' said Grace. 'I'm trying not to think about what happens when it comes ... George, I just want to keep teaching as long as I can.'

He kissed her softly on the cheek. 'Of course you do, lass.' He repeated the doctor's words. 'Do what you think is right. I'll be right behind you, whatever you do.'

Her world shrank a little. The school, the house and her family, the baby inside her, these were everything to her now. Mela still came to visit at least once a month, and Grace always welcomed her with pleasure, but her life with the Clares was becoming a distant memory. She still thought of her time in Hackney with fondness, but she remembered those days less and less often.

Despite the winter cold and the damp, despite the poverty and the strain of eking out every last penny, she found herself surprisingly happy. George was as kind and gentle as ever and the need for skilled bricklayers had raised his pay by a small amount. As she told Mela, they did not have love and never would, but there had developed between them a kind of fond friendship that, she thought, would be good enough for a lifetime. Albert and the twins loved her, and she them. Radcliffe was her adoring shadow.

Every morning she walked to the railway arch to work with her pupils, the young and those who struggled to learn, and she taught them patiently, walking among the desks with a hand resting on her belly, coaxing and encouraging them in a soft voice, praising them when they got their sums right, soothing them when they struggled with spelling and urging them to try again. They rewarded her by working as hard as they could, and repaid her with a devotion that staggered her. They knew how much she wanted them to succeed, and they wanted her to be proud of them.

And still the Captain's men did not come near the school, nor did they touch any of her pupils. She began to wonder if the threat was not as great as she had feared. Perhaps the Captain had changed his mind and decided to let them alone.

There were other clouds on the horizon, of course. Mrs Hobbes, apprised of Grace's pregnancy and her determination to go on working despite this, poked her head out of her shell again and began another whispering campaign. It was, she declared, quite disgusting that a woman in Grace's condition would continue to work. Women who were *enceinte* should remain indoors, away from the gaze of the public. To go out in such a condition, and especially to work, was an offence against common decency. Indeed, she declared, Grace might as well expose herself naked.

This last was related by Mrs Lane, dropping her children off to school one windy morning when the coal smoke from the railway hung particularly thick around the arches. Everyone was coughing. 'I really do think she has gone too far this time,' said Mrs Lane. 'She is making herself ridiculous, and no one is listening to her. Well, no one except a handful of old biddies who spend their lives inventing spiteful gossip about people. The rest of us know you are a good person. You carry on, Mrs Turneur.'

Underneath her severe exterior, Mrs Lane had a good heart, and she and Grace were becoming friends. 'Half the congregation at All Saints has left,' she reported. 'People are going up to St Mary's, or over to Bermondsey or Deptford. It's further to go, but folk reckon it's worth it to avoid Reverend Hobbes's sermons.'

The weeks sped by. October was bleak and windy. In November the cold came early, blanketing the marshes with frost and turning the mud in the streets into a glutinous mixture crackling with ice crystals. Grace was grateful when Mr Jackson the ironmonger gave her a walking stick. 'It used to be my grandfather's,' he said. 'You use it, Mrs Turneur, and have care when you go out. Them roads is treacherous.'

Winter fastened its grip on Rotherhithe. George came home from work most evenings racked with coughing, and Grace made him sit as close to the fire as possible while she plied him with hot drinks. 'You should look for another job,' she said. 'Something indoors, out of the wind.'

George shook his head. 'Bricklaying is all I know, lass. I couldn't learn another trade, not now. I'm too old.'

'You're thirty-one,' Grace said. 'That's hardly over the hill. You could find something else if you wanted to.'

He grinned at her. 'Is this the nagging wife again?'

'Get used to it,' Grace said laughing.

Christmas, her second in Rotherhithe, passed happily. The ghost of Rosa was still in the room, but there was something light and bright about her presence now, as though her spirit was watching over them, happy to see them well and content. The new year 1869 dawned in a peal of bells. The newspaper vendors in the market cried headlines of skirmishes on the North West Frontier in India, and another battle in faraway New Zealand against people known as the Maori. Grace wondered how many British soldiers had died on these battlefields.

Early in February, Grace received a letter, hand-delivered by a ragged urchin who said he would wait for a reply.

Dear Mrs Turneur,

Please forgive the presumption of writing to you out of the blue. I write, I assure you, on a purely professional matter. Something worrying is happening at my school, and I would like to ask your advice. I would be very grateful if you could spare me a few moments of your time?

Might we meet tomorrow afternoon? I suggest Spiers and Pond at London Bridge station. If that is inconvenient, I beg you to name a time and place that are more suitable. You may send your response with Felix. He looks like a ruffian, but he is a good lad.

Your faithful friend,
Walter Ringrose

Walking into the Spiers and Pond café in London Bridge station the following day, Grace was reminded with a jolt of the world she had left behind. Stained glass windows, walls of polished oak, marble floor tiles, snow-white table-cloths and glittering silver and china all reflected back the light of elegant chandeliers. She stood for a moment, a little dazzled, and then spotted Walter on the far side of the room.

'It is all right,' she told the tail-coated *maître d'hôtel* who appeared at her elbow. 'I am joining the gentleman over there.'

The *maître d'hôtel* looked at her suspiciously. She had brushed and cleaned her coat and worn her best clothes and polished her boots and the brass ferrule of her walking stick, but she still looked down at heel compared to the other patrons. But if Walter thought she looked scruffy, he certainly did not let it show. His eyes lit up at the sight of her and he rose quickly to his feet and bowed. Then he noticed the stick, and the roundness of her figure. Unaccountably, he blushed bright red.

'I-I did not know,' he stammered. 'My dear Mrs Turneur, forgive me. Truly, I would not have dragged you all this way had I realised. Oh, I am such a fool.'

'There is nothing to forgive,' Grace said. 'It is a short train journey from Rotherhithe to London Bridge, and I am continuing to work and live my life as normal. I am pregnant, Mr Ringrose, not ill.'

'I say, that's the spirit.' He was recovering a little, though his cheeks were still pink. 'Er . . . may I offer my congratulations? When is the happy event?'

'April,' said Grace smiling. 'Do you think we might sit down now?'

'Of course, of course.' Flustered all over again, he seated her and leaned her stick carefully against the wall, and then sat down himself, nearly upsetting his cup in the process. 'I'm having coffee,' he said, straightening the tablecloth. 'Will you join me, or . . . ?'

'Coffee would be wonderful, thank you.' Mr Ringrose signalled to the waiter to bring another cup. Grace watched him, wondering why he was so flustered. He did not seem to be the sort of man who would be discomfited by the sight of a pregnant woman; there was something else, she thought.

The coffee arrived. She had not had coffee for well over a year, and it tasted delicious. 'Why did you want my advice, Mr Ringrose?' she asked.

The awkwardness vanished and he grew at once serious and sombre. 'Something bad is happening at my school,' he said. 'The boys are disappearing.'

At once Grace felt herself begin to grow cold. Of course, since the defeat of the Black Crows the Bull Head Gang now ruled Bermondsey as well as Rotherhithe. She had been wrong; the threat had not gone away. The Captain had decided to pick on the Bermondsey school for the moment, but her day would come.

'Do you know what is happening to them?' she asked, though she knew full well.

'Oh, yes,' he said. 'The fellows at the King's Arms know all about it. The gangs take the boys from the poorest families. Boys as young as ten or eleven are basically kidnapped and taken up to Jacob's Island, where they turn 'em into hardened criminals. It's absolutely vile, Mrs Turneur. It's no better than slavery.'

'I know,' said Grace quietly. 'Have they threatened you?'

'Yes, again. You too?'

Grace nodded and told him about her meeting with the Captain. 'He offered me a bargain with the devil,' she said. 'The school stays open, but he can take the boys whenever he wants. I refused, of course, but I don't know how to stop him.'

'We could try spiriting the boys away,' he said. 'Send 'em to another part of London, or out of the city altogether.'

She shook her head. 'All too often the boys are taken with the full consent of their parents. The fathers, at least, if not the mothers,' she added, thinking of Sara.

There was a short pause. 'Have you tried the police?' she asked.

'Yes. They're worse than useless. I reckon the local bobbies are in the pocket of the gangs.'

'That is likely,' said Grace. 'I don't know what to suggest, Mr Ringrose. We can let them take the boys, or we can oppose them, in which case they will destroy our schools and take the boys anyway.'

He regarded her for a moment. 'But you're not going to lie down in front of them,' he said. 'You're not going to let them have their way.'

Grace sighed and stirred her coffee. 'No. But ... It breaks my heart to say it, but I don't know what to do. Mela said we needed to get the community on our side to help fight for the boys, but in truth, I don't know if that is possible.'

She looked up. 'I am sorry. You invited me here hoping I could help you, and I fear I have nothing to offer you.'

'That's not true at all,' said Mr Ringrose. 'Now I know you're in the same situation, I don't feel so alone and help-less. We're in the same pickle together, aren't we? No, Mrs Turneur, what you have given me is hope. I reckon if you and I put our heads together, we can figure out how to use our communities to get the gangs off our backs.'

He realised what he had said, and blushed bright red again. 'That is ... er ... of course, if you would be willing to join forces. As it were.'

'I am willing to help in any way I can,' said Grace. 'We are in this together.'

The young man perked up, looking eager, his embarrass-ment once again forgotten. 'Well, by Jove, that's a start ... Perhaps we need to play King Log for a while. You know, keep our heads down, lie low and wait for an opportunity. I reckon that now they're running things, the Bull Heads will start to get cocky. With no other gangs pushing them, they'll grow arrogant and then they overreach themselves.

A chance will come, I'm certain of it. That's when we'll make our move. And we'll work together, won't we?'

'We certainly will,' said Grace, smiling.

'Do you mind if I ask another question?' he asked. 'Forgive me if I am being too personal, but what will you do when the baby comes? About your school, I mean? I understand you run two classes, Mrs Korngold taking one and you the other.'

Mr Raikes must have told him that, Grace guessed. She had notified the Ragged Schools Union that she was taking on another volunteer. 'I am not quite decided,' she said. 'I had thought of asking my friend Miss Clare, but if she cannot come, I'll have to combine the two classes and ask Agnes to take both for a few weeks, until I am up and about again.'

Mr Ringrose nodded. 'I'd be happy to take your class, if you like. I teach one class in the afternoon; I could easily come down and cover for you in the mornings.' He smiled. 'I would like to help, if I can.'

She gazed at him for a moment, meeting his eyes. He blushed suddenly. 'Thank you, sir,' she said, and smiled. 'That is a most generous offer.'

They parted, he thanking her profusely for coming and blushing again as he bowed. Riding the train back to Rotherhithe, she wondered about him. Gauche and flustered one minute, poised and certain of himself the next, she thought. What makes the difference? He was energetic and full of ideas when talking about the school, but the moment they strayed into any personal topic he became awkward.

Suddenly she put her hand to her mouth. *Goodness, do I make him nervous? Is he . . . Is he attracted to me?*

She told herself it was ridiculous, but the thought, once established in her mind, would not go away. For her part, she had to acknowledge that she found his eagerness infectious. It was impossible to be worried or unhappy in his presence. No matter how gloomy things might be, he would find a shaft of sunlight. He had energy, too, and quick wits. *He's the sort who will always walk into a room and make his presence felt,* she thought. *It is impossible to ignore him.*

Just for a moment, an invisible finger walked up her spine. She shook herself. *Don't be ridiculous, Grace,* she told herself. *Remember what you told Mela. You're a married woman, carrying your husband's child. And even if you weren't, he is beyond you. You are an orphan from the slums; his uncle is a knight of the realm. That's far too wide a gap ever to be bridged.*

A voice in a corner of her mind said, *but you are thinking about it.*

The train pulled into Rotherhithe. She shook herself and stood up, reaching for her stick, and then realised it wasn't there. She must have left it in the café. *Your wits are addled,* she told herself. *This is what you get for daydreaming.*

She stepped out onto the platform, seeing her breath steaming in the cold air, and made her way carefully down the icy steps to the road and began to walk toward home. The streets were slippery with ice and frost and she walked slowly, planting her feet carefully and missing the stick even more. But she made slow progress, walking out onto Jamaica Road and seeing the street almost empty in the dusk. Her boots crunched a little on the frozen ground. Her foot slipped briefly on a patch of ice and she stopped. *I must be careful*, she told herself. *If I fall, I might damage the baby.*

Taking a deep breath, she walked forward again, planting her feet carefully. A wall loomed up beside her, a drainpipe running down from the roof. She made for this, hoping to use the drainpipe for support, and then suddenly both her feet were sliding and she was falling. Crying out, she grabbed for the drainpipe and clung onto it, feet flailing on the ice – but she could not regain her balance. Slowly she slid down the pipe until she was kneeling on the ice, hanging on for dear life to prevent herself falling over.

This is undignified, she told herself, but then came a much more serious problem; she could not get up again. She raised one leg, then the other, but each time she tried to plant her feet on the ice, her boots slipped out from under her. Again and again she tried with the same result. She looked around for help, but could see no one in the shadows. Already the night cold was biting into her bones. Panic began to rise. *I cannot stay out here*, she told herself, *or I will freeze to death.* But still, hampered by the baby and the extra weight, she could not rise.

Then, suddenly, someone was kneeling beside her. 'Take my arm,' said a female voice. 'Lean on me. I will support you.'

The arm she took was thin and bare and very cold, but strong. Gasping again, feeling entirely undignified but at the same time grateful for the help, Grace managed to get up onto her knees and then, leaning on her helper, drew herself to her feet.

'Thank you,' she said, and then she looked at her saviour and stopped in shock. Despite the matted, tangled hair hanging over the girl's face, there was no mistaking her identity.

It was Mary.

∽

I didn't even think when I saw her go down, I just let go of Joe's hand and ran towards her. It was so cold I couldn't feel my hands and feet, but I was used to that. I knelt down alongside her and helped her up. She looked like she was all right, though I could see she had a baby in her, and falling couldn't be good for women who were carrying. But there wasn't nothing I could do about that, so once I was sure she could stand without help, I turned back to find Joe.

'Mary,' she said. 'Don't go. Stay a moment, please.'

I turned around again and faced her. She looked pretty much the same, except for the baby, of course. 'You can't stay out here', she said. 'The night is bitterly cold. Come home with me, and get warm.'

Joe's head turned. Someone was coming, hurrying along the street towards us. 'Mrs Turneur!' I heard him call, 'Mrs Turneur!'

I trusted her, a little, but I didn't trust no one else. For all I knew her friend might try to grab us and put us in the workhouse. I took Joe's hand and we ran, like we ran so many times before. I heard her calling me, but I didn't look back.

We didn't go near the school, in case it was a trap. We found an old bit of carpet on the side of the road that night, and pulled it over us as a blanket and we slept. In the morning I found some frozen bread someone had dropped. I was lucky I managed to get to it before the dogs did. We ate it, chewing it slow so it would melt in our mouths, and for a while the cramps in my belly eased a little. We made it through another day.

∽

'You left your stick behind,' called Mr Ringrose. 'I came to return it to you. I thought you might need it on a night like this. I say, are you all right?'

'I'm fine, thank you,' said Grace. 'I had a small slip on the ice, that's all.' Her hip ached, but she could feel no other pain. She had been lucky; the baby was safe.

'The roads are very slippery,' he said in concern. 'Here, let me see you home.'

Grace smiled in gratitude. 'That would be very kind of you.'

Mr Ringrose took her arm and started to walk with her, glancing after the fleeing children. 'Who were they?'

'A homeless girl and her brother,' said Grace. 'I used to let them sleep in the school, but they disappeared after it was attacked. I'd not seen them again until now.'

'Poor little creatures,' he said quietly. 'Wearing nothing but rags, and no shoes. My God, barefoot in this weather! It passes all imagination, doesn't it?'

'Yes,' said Grace.

Mr Ringrose nodded. 'We're not going to lie down and let the gangs walk over us. How can we, when children roam the freezing night without food, or home, or hope? We're going to change things, Mrs Turneur, even if it's the two of us against the whole world.'

'We won't be alone,' said Grace. 'We'll have other friends and allies, Mr Ringrose. We do already. You too were right, sir. We must wait, and our chance will come.'

Chapter 14

'My!' said Mela Clare. 'Look at dear little Edith! Isn't she a bonny lass? She has grown so much since I last saw her.'

It was early June, two months since Grace had given birth to her daughter. She had wanted to call the child Pamela, but her godmother had resolutely refused. 'It is the worst name ever invented,' she insisted. 'You cannot possibly inflict it on this poor innocent girl. Name her after your aunt instead.'

Now Mela leaned over the baby's cot, cooing and smoothing her downy hair with a gentle finger. 'And she looks healthy as a horse.'

'She certainly eats like one,' Grace said with feeling. 'George says she's like a drunk at last orders. *Not* the most elegant of comparisons, but I know what he means. She feeds like she's afraid supplies might run out, and she had better get as much into her as she can while it lasts.'

'That explains why she is growing so much,' said Mela laughing. 'How is George? Working hard as ever, I assume.'

'Oh, yes. He is as always a model husband and father.' Grace paused. 'I am worried about him, though.'

'Oh? Why is that?'

'He is in a melancholy mood these days. To the children he is sunshine and light as usual, but when we are alone I see the darkness descend. I fear he is missing Rosa very badly. The baby, I think, reminds him of her.' Grace stopped. 'I don't know for certain. I'm just guessing. The truth is, I don't really know what goes on in his mind. When I ask him, he just smiles and tells me not to worry. But I do worry. He is coughing more and more, like the winter chill won't go away.'

'Shall I ask Father to send the doctor?' Mela asked. 'He will gladly do so.'

Grace shook her head. 'I've already suggested he see a doctor, but he refuses. He says it's just the brick dust in his chest, and it will pass.'

She paused. 'I don't know whether to believe him,' she said.

'If we can help in any way, call on us,' Mela said.

Grace shook her head again. 'Mela, we can't live off the charity of your family, as much as I love them. I'm already greatly in your parents' debt. I can't take anything more from them. Really I can't.'

Mela regarded the child sleeping in the cot. 'Well, Edith,' she said. 'If you grow up to be half as pig-headed as your mother, you're going to be quite a handful . . . How are things at the Ragged School?'

'Very well,' said Grace. 'Mr Ringrose has done a very good job of looking after my little ones. Albert and the twins think the world of him. I am starting back to work tomorrow, but I suspect my pupils would prefer that I remained at home and he stayed on as teacher.'

'I doubt that very much,' said Mela.

Mr Ringrose had been as good as his word. After baby Edith was born, she had stayed at home and he had taken her class. She received regular reports of his progress from Albert, and was pleased to find that he was popular with the children. He had read to them from Captain Marryat's *The Children of the New Forest*, which they loved.

They moved on from talking about the Ragged School to Mela's work at the Clare School. Grace thought Mela sounded dissatisfied. 'Out with it,' she said finally. 'What is wrong? Has something happened?'

'Not at all,' said Mela. 'Mother runs the place like a well-oiled clock. Everything ticks along very satisfactorily.'

Grace watched her for a moment. 'You're bored,' she said. 'Aren't you?'

'Perhaps I am, a little,' Mela confessed. 'My life seems rather . . . humdrum. You're the one having all the adventures. Marriage, a baby, running your own school, facing danger, confronting gangs . . .'

'That is not an adventure I wish to repeat,' Grace said.

'I know, but all the same, you're doing something wonderful. And Mr Ringrose, too, giving up his comfortable life to come down here to teach. It is exciting, whereas my own life just plods along. I suppose I just feel I'm not doing enough.'

'Have you spoken to your parents?' Grace asked.

'No. I'm not sure they would understand. I'm not sure *I* understand. I have everything I could possibly want in life. So why do I feel as if something is missing?'

The baby stirred, waving her tiny hands in the air, and began to wail. Grace rolled her eyes. 'I'm on duty in the taproom again,' she said. 'It will only take a few minutes.'

'No, I should go, and get out from under your feet.' Mela rose and picked up her gloves, and kissed Grace on the cheek. 'Take care, my dear friend. I will call again soon.'

After she had gone Grace sat for a while in the parlour, holding Edith while she nursed happily, making little snuffling noises from time to time. The thought that Mela might envy her life was odd, to say the least. As her friend said, she had everything she could want. She had her work, to which she was devoted, and had seemed content. What had changed?

Grace's mind wandered. For no particular reason she found herself thinking, as she often did, about Mary. She had not seen the girl and her brother since February; they had not come near the school. It was quite possible, of course, that something had happened to them during the winter and they were no longer alive, but she felt that this was not true. Mary was tough, a true survivor. She would always find some way to stay alive, even if only for her brother's sake. But what a terrible life she lived! Even Grace's own orphan pupils, Gabriel and Isaac and Nathan, had somewhere to sleep at night. But in the midst of a great and civilised city, Mary and Joe lived in a wilderness.

The baby had fallen asleep. Gently, Grace laid her back in the cot. In an hour or so George would be home; it was time to get the dinner on. Quietly she moved into the kitchen, putting on her apron and shovelling more coal into the stove. *Everything is calm now,* she thought, *calm and quiet. How long can it last?*

The following day she returned to work, and wrote Mr Ringrose a long letter thanking him for his help and inviting him to call at the school at any time. She and the children would always be ready to make him welcome. His reply was short and cheerful and, she thought, summed up the man.

My dear Mrs Turneur, there is absolutely no need to thank me. It was an honour and a pleasure to help you. I am deeply fond of your boys and girls, and I like your railway arch. It has a nice homely feel to it, more than my battered old house, and I grew to quite enjoy the sound of the engines puffing overhead; I imagined each one as a train of thought! Do please call on me again if I can ever be of assistance.

She thought about the letter as she dismissed her class, and it made her smile. Albert and the twins helped her to tidy the schoolroom, chattering cheerfully. Albert was nearly eleven now, and growing in height. Grace thought he was going to be tall, like his father. The twins were seven, bright and happy as they had always been but growing into proper little people.

They heard the rumble of a train passing along the line over their heads. Then, as the noise began to fade, someone outside rapped hard on the door.

The mood in the classroom changed at once. Radcliffe's hackles rose and he growled. The children went silent, staring at her. *The Captain's men*, thought Grace, full of sudden dread. *Please Lord, let it not be them . . .*

'Who is there?' she called.

The voice that answered was comfortingly familiar. 'It's Walter Ringrose, Mrs Turneur. May I come in? I have some news for you.'

The children relaxed at once. Letting out a sigh of relief, Grace opened the door.

'I . . . I hope I didn't startle you,' he said anxiously.

'Only a little,' said Grace smiling. 'Say good morning to Mr Ringrose, children.'

'Good morning!' they chorused happily. Radcliffe wagged his tail. Mr Ringrose grinned and bowed to them, and then turned back to Grace, his face serious. 'I'm so sorry to intrude on you, but I had to see you. May we talk in private?'

They walked to the far end of the schoolroom. The brick arch next to them began to vibrate a little as another train approached. 'It's gang trouble,' he said quietly. 'I had a delegation around early this morning, telling me to close down or they would burn me out. They said I had ten days to pack my bags. Then they were coming back. I damned their eyes, of course – oh, do pardon my language – but I reckon they mean it. I've closed the school and sent the children home, just in case. I don't want to put the little ones in danger.'

Grace's heart sank once more. 'Was it the Bull Head Gang?'

'Yes, and no. According to the locals at the King's Arms, some of the Captain's men have turned against him. The Captain has grown drunk with power, it seems, and his men are resenting his high and mighty ways. A faction led by someone called Long Ben and his son, Jake, are rebelling against him.'

Grace nodded. 'Ben Wilson,' she said. 'I know him. Go on.'

'It was Long Ben's men who came around to threaten me today. They're trying to carve out their own territory. But why close me down? Why not just ask for protection money, like the Black Crows did?'

'Wilson has a particular hatred of schools,' Grace said. 'Do you remember the boy I told you about, the one taken by the gang? It was Long Ben's son.'

'And if he threatened me, he might well threaten you as well,' Mr Ringrose said soberly. 'Once again, it seems, we're caught in the middle.'

'What will you do?' Grace asked. 'Earlier, you said we should wait for an opportunity.'

'And I think one may have come,' he said. 'The community are fed up with the gangs, the violence and the killing. I think it's time to get the people behind us.'

'What are you going to do?'

'First of all, I'm going back to my pals at the King's Arms and ask them for help. I think I can get enough volunteers together to help protect the school. If we can stop Long Ben quickly, it will show his followers how weak he is. And I reckon the Captain will step in, and crush them.'

Grace shuddered. 'And then we'll be at the mercy of the Captain again,' she said. 'Honestly, of the two of them, I am not sure which is worse.'

'Well, Long Ben is the man threatening me right now,' said Mr Ringrose. 'And if he makes a move towards you, Mrs Turneur, let me know at once. If your own neighbours can't or won't help, I'll bring my friends from Bermondsey.'

Grace nodded. 'Thank you for seeing me, Mrs Turneur,' he said, and there was no hesitation or diffidence now, but a calm authority in his voice that she had never noticed before. 'I shall take my leave now. But have a care for yourself. I fear we live in perilous times.'

After Mr Ringrose departed, Grace rejoined the children and Radcliffe. The books and slates had all been tidied away. She put the baby into her basket and they fetched their coats and made ready to depart. Just as they did so there came another knock at the door, softer and quieter this time, almost timid.

'Who is it?' Grace asked.

'It's me,' said a girl's voice. 'Mary.'

'Oh, good heavens,' Grace said, and flung the door open. Mary stood before her, grimy and ragged as ever with her matted hair falling over his face. Her brother was slumped on the ground by her feet, his eyes closed.

'He's sick,' Mary said, and Grace could hear her desperation. 'I don't know what to do.'

Swiftly, Grace knelt beside the boy. His arms and legs were like sticks and his belly was distended. His little face was sunken, and his eyes were dull and seemed to have trouble focusing. 'When did you last eat?' Grace asked.

'Three days ago,' said Mary. 'We've been hiding. Didn't dare go out.'

'*Three days*!' Grace gasped. 'What happened?'

'I tried to steal some bread and nearly got caught. They set the traps after us. We been holed up ever since. I don't know what to do,' she repeated. 'He's never been this bad.'

'Take him inside,' Grace commanded. 'Then, wait here and I will bring you food.' She saw the wary look come back into the girl's eyes. 'Please, Mary, stay here. Don't run off. I can't help you if you do.'

After a moment Mary nodded, and she took her brother under the arms and helped him stumble to his feet and go into the schoolroom. Picking up the baby's basket once again and summoning the children and dog, Grace hurried back to Bell Lane.

'Can you look after Edith?' she asked Albert. 'If she cries, rock the basket gently. I'll feed her as soon as I get home.'

The boy nodded, pleased to be given responsibility. Grace went into the kitchen where she found some bread, a couple of cooked potatoes and a sausage, and put them in a basket along with a stone jar of water and returned to the school. She found Joe sprawled on his side, his eyes closed, while Mary sat and watched him, a haunted expression on her own thin face. Grace knelt down beside them and broke off a piece of bread and handed it to Mary, but the girl shook her head. 'Let Joe eat first. I'll take what he doesn't want.'

It took some effort to rouse the exhausted little boy, and when he did sit up he ate slowly, chewing mechanically and from time to time sipping at the water Grace offered him. He ate part of a potato as well as some bread, and half the sausage, and then sat back exhausted.

'That's enough,' Grace said. 'He mustn't eat too much after so long without food. Now you must eat, Mary.'

The girl ate, chewing her food like she was barely aware of what it was. Usually a hungry person would eat ravenously, stuffing food into their mouth, but it dawned on Grace that both of them were so exhausted that even something as simple as eating was almost beyond them. She watched them, her heart wrung with pity.

The girl ate the last of the bread and sat for a moment, her eyes closed, swaying with fatigue. 'Mary,' said Grace gently. 'You can't go on like this. You need a home.'

The eyes opened again. They were, Grace noticed for the first time, a bright and vivid blue. 'We're not going back to the workhouse,' Mary said.

'No,' said Grace. 'A real home, with a family to look after you. If you stay on the streets you will die.'

'I know,' Mary said bleakly.

Grace watched her again for a while. She had reckoned Mary to be about ten years old when they first met, which meant she was now perhaps twelve. Joe might be six, though it was hard to tell.

'If I found a home for you, would you go and live there?' she asked. 'Would you give it a try, at least?'

Mary considered this for a long time. 'No,' she said finally. 'If they decided they didn't like us, they would send us to the workhouse.'

'Even if I made them promise not to?' Grace asked.

Mary shook her head. 'Can't take the chance,' she said.

There was no need to ask why Mary was determined not to go back to the workhouse; Grace remembered, all too clearly, the bullying and beatings and hard, unrelenting, dangerous work. 'Rest here,' she said. 'Sleep as much as you can. I will come back in the morning with more food. Don't run away.'

'No,' said Mary. Her voice was full of deep exhaustion. Her eyes closed again. Sorrowing all over again for their lost childhood, Grace let herself out of the school, closing the wooden door softly behind her.

'We've got to do something,' she said to George that night. 'The poor things are half dead. They must have somewhere to live, where they will be safe and looked after.'

273

George sat silent for a moment, staring into space, and Grace wondered at first if he had heard her. The melancholy mood had not left him. If anything, it had deepened as the days passed. But then he stirred and looked at her, sitting by the window and rocking Edith in her arms.

'You have something in mind,' he stated.

It was Grace's turn to pause, bracing herself to tell him the idea that had been crowding her mind all afternoon. 'Yes,' she said. 'I was thinking we could bring them here. We could adopt them.'

Again she wondered if he had heard her, but after a moment he shook his head slowly. 'Wouldn't do, lass. They're wild children off the street. Who knows what they might do, or how they'll behave?'

'They trust me,' Grace said. 'I think I might be the only person they do trust. They didn't let me down before, when they were sleeping at the school, and I don't think they'll let me down now.'

'What will the other children think? Albert, and the twins?'

'They already know Mary and Joe, from before. Albert, poor little soul, was very upset when he saw how hungry they were. He's asked me what could be done to help. I think it will be all right, George. Children are often wiser than we think they are.'

'All right. Suppose you're right. We've already got four kids to feed. How are we going to feed two more?'

She said firmly, 'I can eke things out. I promise you, George, I can manage. It won't be easy, but I'll find a way. I simply cannot bear the thought of those poor little things out on the street, starving.'

'There's plenty of homeless waifs in Rotherhithe,' George said. 'You can't adopt them all.'

'I know that. But . . . I have a connection with these two. I've seen them over and over, ever since I first came here. It's like I'm drawn to them somehow, or they to me. George,' she pleaded softly. 'Let me help them.'

George gazed down at his hands for a while, and then suddenly raised one to his mouth, covering a yawn. 'Lord, but I'm tired,' he said. 'I'm going to bed, lass. Let me sleep on it. I'll give you an answer in the morning.'

His reasons for not taking in Mary and her brother were good ones, and Grace was quite prepared for him to say no. Instead, just before he departed for work the following morning he stopped and kissed her and said, 'Gracie, you're about the wisest woman I've ever met. You're even wiser than Rosa, and that's saying something. If you think we can do it, then go ahead. I trust you.'

Astonished, Grace threw her arms around him and kissed him. 'George! You are the kindest and best man I know. Thank you. I promise you won't regret it.'

'I'll hold you to that,' he said, smiling a little.

Elated, worried and nervous all at once, Grace packed a parcel with more food and water and gave it to Albert to carry, picked up Edith's basket and, with the three children and the dog, made the usual journey to the railway line. Her heart was pounding as they approached the school. Would the two children still be there? Would they come with her? What if they suspected a trap and ran away? She would have lost them for good; they would never again come near her.

Just before they reached the railway arch she stopped. 'Albert,' she said quietly. 'Harry, Daisy, gather round. Now, children, I want to ask you a question. You know Mary and her brother, don't you?'

'Yes,' said Daisy. 'They're sick.'

'Yes, my dear. I want to persuade them to come home with us, so I can make them well. Would that be all right?'

'They need our help,' Albert said. 'They are poor and sick. Mummy, I think we must help them.'

I was right, Grace thought. *Children are wiser than we are sometimes. They see what must be done, and not the million and one reasons not to do it.*

'Thank you,' she said. 'Harry? Daisy?'

Two bright little faces nodded. They didn't fully understand what she was talking about, but they trusted their big brother. Grace bent and kissed all three of them, and then drew a deep breath.

When she opened the door she saw a shadow move in the gloom. It was Mary, sitting up quickly, and reaching for her knife. She relaxed somewhat when she saw Grace. 'I brought you more food,' Grace said, unwrapping the parcel. 'Remember, not too much at once.'

The two children began to eat. Grace watched them as she laid out the lessons for the morning, and saw them eating more hungrily now, and less mechanically. They were beginning to recover a little, but they were so thin and dirty. *Heavens,* she thought. *Cleaning them up will be like one of the labours of Hercules. Can I really be thinking of taking them into our home?* But she saw Joe's face as he ate and knew there was no other way. This was a battle she was determined to win.

She waited until the end of the lesson to talk to Mary. Edith had begun to grumble, and Grace picked her up and held her, rocking the baby in her arms as she approached Mary and knelt down on the ground beside her.

'I have found a home for you, Mary,' she said. 'A home with someone you can trust, who won't send you to the workhouse.'

Mary's eyes were quietly wary. She waited. Grace drew another breath and then took the plunge. 'We want you to come and live with us. We can look after Joe, and you.'

She was aware that Joe was regarding her with great intensity. He may not be able to speak, she thought, but he certainly understands. Mary continued to watch her too from behind the curtain of dirty hair, weighing her up, trying to decide if this was a trick.

'No,' the girl said finally.

'Are you certain?' Grace asked calmly.

Mary nodded. On impulse, Grace reached out a gentle hand and rested her fingers on Mary's cheek. The girl flinched and shied away, but then gradually she stilled.

'Think about it,' Grace said gently. 'I will bring more food tomorrow, and we will talk again.'

Three more days went past. Each day Grace spent a little more time, talking gently with the girl, not pressing her or asking her for reasons for her refusal, just letting her think. On the morning of the fourth day she brought another basket of food, bread and cheese she could scarcely spare from her own larder; but, she knew, the food was slowly nourishing the two children back to something approaching health. She sat the basket down in front of them and straightened, holding Edith on her hip. Joe looked up at her, his face solemn. His eyes were the same vivid blue as his sister's.

'I want,' he said.

Mary stared at him, her mouth open in silent shock. 'There is plenty of food there, Joe,' Grace said softly. 'Help yourself.'

Joe shook his head and stood up. He took two steps forward and seized hold of Grace's skirt, clinging to the fabric with surprising strength and looking up into her face. 'I want,' he said again.

'What does he want?' Grace asked.

'I don't know,' said Mary. Her voice was barely above a whisper. 'I've never heard him speak before.'

'Oh, heavens,' said Grace softly. She looked down at the little boy, and with her free hand caressed his face. Edith squirmed and wriggled and let out a little cooing noise.

'I want,' Joe said again.

And then Grace understood. Joy exploded like a sunburst in her heart, and she wanted suddenly to sing and dance. She smiled at Mary.

'I think Joe has made his choice,' she said. 'What about you, Mary? Will you come with him? Joe still needs you. I think we all do.'

Chapter 15

They must have thought they'd brought a wild animal into the house. I went around every room, sniffing the air, trying to see if there was danger somewhere. I smelled coal and dampness, and sickness too. But I could also smell food, and a strange smell that took me a long time to remember, cuz it had been a long time since I had smelled it. Soap.

'Time for a bath,' she said.

She put a cauldron of water on the kitchen floor next to the stove, and she took off Joe's clothes and asked him to get into it. He put his foot in the water than drew back all confused, cuz it was warm and he wasn't expecting that, but I told him it was safe and he stepped in and sat down. She scrubbed him all over with a bar of soap and brush, and after a while he started to giggle when it tickled him. I hadn't ever heard him laugh before, either.

Afterwards she dried Joe off with a towel, then wrapped him in a blanket and put him to bed in the parlour room,. He fell straight to sleep. 'I'll find him some of Harry's clothes when he wakes,' she said. 'They're about the same size. Now, Mary, it's your turn.'

She refilled the cauldron with clean water and took off the rags I had been wearing. She took my knife too, and put it away, and I didn't like being without it. I'd been carrying that knife for as long as I could remember. It was all that stood between me and the world that wanted to hurt me.

But I made myself be calm, and climbed into the water and sat down. The hot water, the smell of the soap, the brush scrubbing my back brought back another rush of memories, and all of a sudden I remembered my mother doing the same thing to me, long ago. So long ago . . . I couldn't remember her face anymore, or the sound of her voice, but I remembered that same gentle touch, and the feel of the soapy lather on my skin, and I sat still for a moment, suddenly realising all the things I had lost.

'I don't know what to do about your hair,' she said. 'I don't think I can get a brush through the tangles and knots. We'll have to cut it off, Mary.'

'I don't mind,' I said. I really didn't. It felt like, for the first time I could remember, someone else had taken charge of me. I was used to being the one making the decisions, about looking after Joe. Now I didn't have to do anything. It felt strange, but I decided I liked it. At least, for the moment.

She cut my hair off short all over my head, and lathered it and then scrubbed me hard for a long time. Finally I stood up and she dried me off with another towel. 'I feel lighter,' I said.

'I'm not surprised. I've taken about five layers of grime off you.'

She was right. When I looked at my arm it seemed paler than I remembered. She brought me some clothes, including a

281

dress that was so long I tripped over it. 'I'll hem it up,' she said. 'This used to belong to the girl next door. Do you remember Rebecca, from the school?'

'Yes,' I said. 'What happened to her? Why doesn't she need the dress?'

'Nothing happened to her,' she said smiling. 'She grew, that's all. The dress doesn't fit her anymore. You'll grow too, with regular feeding.'

That evening we all sat around a table in the kitchen. Joe was uncomfortable and kept sliding off his stool, but she just picked him up and put him back again. The food was hot, and it tasted wonderful. We started to eat with our hands like we always did, so George, her husband, tried to teach us to use a knife and fork, like they were doing. We both made a mess of it and kept dropping things. I got annoyed. I couldn't see why they wanted us to do this. Why couldn't we eat with our fingers? What was wrong with that? Maybe coming here was a mistake.

They made beds for us in the parlour, blankets laid down on the floor. Everything was soft, so soft I couldn't get comfortable. I finally rolled up the blankets and laid down on the hard floor, and lay there for a while listening to Joe snore. I couldn't sleep. I was waiting for a trap to spring, waiting to be locked in the house, so we couldn't get out. Once I got up and tried the door, but it was unlocked. I could go out any time I wanted. That reassured me, a little.

I lay back down again and started thinking about all the food there was in the house. My belly was full, but on the streets you learn to eat whenever you see food, in case you don't see it again. After a while I got up and went into the kitchen. The dog was asleep in a corner, and he raised his head and looked at me and then went back to sleep again. I opened the larder door. There was a big sack right there in front of me, huge, nearly as big as Joe, absolutely full of potatoes. I picked one up and started chewing on it. Raw potatoes don't taste of much, but they fill you up.

I was so busy eating I didn't hear the movement behind me at first. I turned around fast, reaching for my knife, but of course I didn't have it anymore. She lit the oil lamp on the table and stood and looked at me with the potato in my hand, and bits of mush and skin on my face around my mouth.

'They're much better cooked,' she said. 'Would you like one?'

I nodded. She was offering food, and like I said, I wasn't going to turn it down. She put some water in a pot and put it on the stove, which was still hot, and put my potato into it. When it was cooked she took it out and mashed it up with some butter and salt, and then sat me down at the table and taught me, ever so slow and patient, how to use the knife and fork, guiding my hands until I could hold them on my own. I still didn't see the point, but it made her happy.

'Why did you come back to Rotherhithe?' she asked.

'It's what I know best,' I said. 'I didn't like the other places we went. People were always hunting us, trying to capture us and put us in the workhouse.'

'What happened to the other Angels?'

'I don't know.' I tried to pretend it didn't matter. 'I was tired of being with them anyway. Ness and the others, they think they're tough, but they're not really.'

The truth was we'd got separated one wild night in Lambeth when a bunch of other girls came down on us like mad things, knives flashing everywhere, and we had to run for it. Joe and I looked for them but couldn't find them, and finally we decided to cut out altogether and come back to Rotherhithe. I didn't know what had happened to the rest. I didn't know if they were still alive. They probably weren't.

'And what are you going to do now?' she asked.

'It's like I told you before. I'm going to become a thief, and join the Forty Elephants.'

She smiled at me. I didn't know why, because I was deadly serious. That was my ambition, to become the best thief in London and get rich.

'Would you like to go to school?' she said.

I ate some more of my potato. 'What would I want to do that for?'

'Even thieves need to know how to read and write,' she said. 'And if you do steal lots of money, you'll need to know how to count it.'

That made sense. 'Will you read some more books to us?' I asked. 'Not that silly one about Alice and the rabbit. But I liked the other books.'

'Of course,' she said. 'Good, then it is settled. You and Joe will come to school with us. I am glad. I wouldn't want to think of you sitting around the house with nothing to do.'

I ate a bit more, thinking. 'Your husband ... Does he like us being here?' I had seen the expression on his face last evening when he came in.

'George is worried that there won't be enough food for us all,' she said gently. I started to push my plate away, but she pushed it back. 'No, Mary. Eat. You need to regain your strength. Only, when next you are hungry, my dear, ask me. I will always find food for you.'

'Your husband won't want to put us in the workhouse?' I asked.

She smiled. 'No. He is a good and kind man, and you can trust him as you trust me.'

'And what about the other man,' I said. 'The one who came after you when you fell that time. Who is he?'

'He is another teacher,' she said. 'He came to return something I had left behind, that is all.'

I wondered if she knew how her face changed when she mentioned the other man. Her eyes went open a little wider, and there was a little touch of colour on her cheeks in the lamplight. I wondered if she even realised it was happening.

I wondered, too, if she knew how sick her husband really was.

∽

Always crowded, the house on Bell Lane was now full to bursting, with six children and two adults crammed into four small rooms. On Sunday, George and Elijah Berton built a cot for Mary and Joe to share in the parlour room.

To Grace's mild annoyance, Mary refused to use it, preferring to sleep on the hard floor.

'She told me that's what she's used to,' George said.

Grace was surprised. 'She talks to you?'

'A little, now and then. She's trying to figure out if she can trust me, I think.'

Joe was happy to sleep on the cot, but then, Joe would sleep pretty much anywhere. Grace thought she had never seen a more malleable child. He did whatever she asked of him – he didn't always do it very well, but he never stopped trying – and he was also utterly good-natured. If he had a temper, she never saw it.

For Joe, everything was new and exciting. Life on the street had come close to killing him, but he was young and impressionable and he adapted quickly. He adored Grace and tended to follow her around the house tugging at her skirt and asking constant questions about what she was doing. As time passed and he put flesh on his bones, he began to talk more, and more, and still more, about anything and everything under the sun: what they were having for dinner, what Radcliffe had done this afternoon, what colour the sky was. Words came out of him like water spilling over a dam. Joe had spent years locked in silence, and now was doing his level best to make up for it.

Mary was different. Her memories of the violence she had seen, and perpetrated, had left deep scars on her mind. She wore proper clothes now, but refused absolutely to wear shoes. Sometimes when she looked at her, Grace could see the feral child still there beneath the surface, waiting, watching. The girl was often tense, and she jumped at every unfamiliar sound. At school she was not a good pupil. She was easily distracted, and if pushed to perform a task that was beyond her ability, she became frustrated and angry.

At home, too, she was restless and flighty. Once, when asked by Grace to wash some pots, she made a mess of the task, and Grace's request that she do it again led to a screaming fit that ended when Mary pulled a knife out of the block and pointed it at her. Grace crossed her arms over her chest and stared her down, at which point Mary threw the knife on the floor and burst into a shattering flood of tears.

She avoided Grace for the rest of the day, and was silent and sullen through dinner, clattering her knife and fork clumsily against her plate. After dinner, George went through to the parlour room and then called Mary. She hesitated but then went, dragging her feet. Joe remained in the kitchen, crouched on the floor having a long and necessarily one-sided conversation with Radcliffe, whom he found fascinating. Grace washed the dishes and cleaned the table and went cautiously through to the parlour, and stopped in surprise.

George was sitting in his chair next to the stove. It was July and the evening was warm, but he still had not shaken off the winter chill, and needed the heat. Mary was sitting on his lap, leaning back against him, sound asleep while George slowly stroked her hair.

'How did you do it?' Grace murmured.

'I just talked to her,' George said softly. 'I told her the story of my life. She still doesn't really know me, you see. So I told her who I am, about going to work young when my father died, and the brick works, and all the houses and warehouses we built, and the work at the docks. She just sat and listened, and then after a while she came and sat on my knee, and then she fell straight into sleep.' He stroked the girl's hair again. 'She doesn't really understand what it is to be loved. And yet she craves it much.'

'And is she loved?' Grace asked softly.

George smiled at her. 'For years, she looked after that little boy on the streets. Gave him everything she had to keep him alive, and she nothing but a child herself. How do you not love someone with a heart like that? You know I had my doubts, Grace, but that's all gone now. You did the right thing bringing her here, and mark my words, one day all the kindness you're showing her will be repaid.'

'I don't care if it isn't,' said Grace, watching the sleeping child's face. 'It's enough to know that both of them will live and grow.'

The road ahead was still far from smooth. Mary continued to struggle to adapt to her new world, and the frustration and tension were still there, but now when she blew up she was at once contrite, apologising often tearfully for her behaviour and begging them to forgive her. And, of course, they always did. That edge of anger would always be there, Grace thought. How could one expect otherwise, when the

288

world had treated her so cruelly? But there was hope, now, that she could turn the corner and leave her old desperate life behind her. *I'll keep her out of the gangs*, Grace told herself, *if it is the last thing I ever do.*

And yet, the gangs were always there, lurking in the shadows. Agnes Korngold called one afternoon in late July, on one of her weekly visits. She had become friendly with Walter Ringrose when he had substituted for Grace at the school, and sometimes called on him too, in Bermondsey. She was old enough to be his mother, so there was no hint of impropriety.

'He has great spirit, that young man,' Agnes said. 'He is what we call a *mensch*. He said he would stand up to the gangs, and so he has.'

Grace felt a pang of fear. 'What happened?'

'He persuaded some of the local men to help him. Long Ben came to burn the Bermondsey school, as he promised to do, and Mr Ringrose saw him off. He had twenty of his friends with him, and Long Ben did not dare to attack.'

She looked seriously at Grace. 'But Ben threatened you as well. He promised he would get the better of Mr Ringrose and you too, and he would burn both your schools to the ground. Mr Ringrose replied that if Ben or his men hurt so much as a hair on your head, he – Mr Ringrose, that is – would hunt him down and exterminate him.'

To her astonishment – indeed, to her horror – Grace felt herself starting to blush. 'Is Mr Ringrose all right? Is he hurt?'

'He is as well as you or I,' said Agnes. 'It will take more than a few bullies with knives to stop that one … But, I mustn't stand here gossiping when you have work to do. I shall be off.' She glanced at Mary, who was sitting and listening, and then looked back at Grace. 'Mrs Clare often asks after you. Shall I tell her you are well?'

'Tell her we are all very well,' said Grace, who was still blushing.

She was annoyed with herself for blushing, and that evening she was curt with George for absolutely no reason, which annoyed her still further. The truth, she finally admitted to herself, was that she was thrilled that Mr Ringrose had indeed stood up to the gangs, but she was also worried for his safety. Long Ben wasn't likely to be put off. He would try again, and his next attack was likely to be more deadly.

Two days later, as she was locking up the school at midday and gathering her little flock of Albert, Daisy, Harry, Joe, Mary, Edith in her basket and Radcliffe trotting at her heels, she saw the familiar figure of Mr Ringrose himself come walking across the wasteland past the carpet factory. She stopped and realised her cheeks were warm again. She wished Mary would stop looking at her like that.

'Welcome, sir,' she said smiling. 'To what do I owe the honour of your company?'

He smiled back but his usual stumbling, stammering manner was quite absent. He looked preoccupied, and like he had not been getting much sleep. 'Please forgive me for intruding,' he said. 'I know how busy you must be.'

'What is it?' she asked.

'My school was attacked. Did you know?'

She nodded. 'Agnes told me of your heroic defence.'

'It was a near-run thing,' he said with feeling. 'We only just persuaded them to back down without bloodshed. We had numbers on our side, but even so, I don't know how things would have turned out. And they have threatened you also.'

'Yes,' she said. 'Agnes told me that as well.'

'Mrs Turneur, Long Ben means business. If he defeats the Captain, he'll run this entire district. And he'll enslave every boy he can lay his hands on, and drag them into his gang. The schools stand in his way, and he'll do anything to get rid of us. I came here today because I am greatly concerned for your safety.'

His eyes met hers. They were warm and brown, she realised, and she felt again that little frisson down her back, a prickling sensation that this time lingered and stayed. Suddenly furious with herself, she shook her head.

Mr Ringrose saw the gesture and misunderstood it. 'I assure you the threat is real,' he said. 'You are in danger, Mrs Turneur.'

'Everyone in Rotherhithe is in danger,' she said shortly. 'The gangs are a threat to us all.' She needed to get away from him, away from those warm eyes and the gentle planes of his face and that serious voice, and those ever-so-capable hands that had gripped a cricket bat in defence of his school.

'I have a proposal for you,' he said. 'May I beg you to hear me out?'

'Go on,' Grace said reluctantly.

'I suggest that we merge our two schools. We could find a single location, midway between where we both are now, still in easy walking distance for the children. We could get a house, a strong sturdy house that could be fortified and defended. Some of the local men would help us guard it. There's plenty who hate the gangs, and know the threat to their own children. They would be happy to assist us.'

'And how would that help?' she countered. 'Should we barricade ourselves in this house, never to come out? Perhaps you can afford to do so, sir, but I have a husband and family to care for. And our pupils, what about them? Will you lock them up in the school too, for their own safety? I am sorry, Mr Ringrose, but what you propose is quite impracticable.'

He looked down at his hands for a moment. He had not expected such complete rejection. 'I meant only it would be easier to protect a single school, and the schools are what seems to be the object of Long Ben's ire,' he said.

'But if Long Ben can no longer attack the schools, he will turn his attention to us in person,' said Grace. 'Schools can be replaced, Mr Ringrose. Bricks and wood, books and slates are all that we should lose, and more of these can be found. But lives are irreplaceable.'

'Yes, of course. You are quite right. It was a foolish notion.' She could see the disappointment in his face, and suddenly she felt guilty for hurting him, and meanwhile that insistent nagging finger continued to brush up and down her spine.

On impulse she said, 'I am sorry. I did not mean to suggest the idea is entirely without merit. There might well be advantages to sharing premises.' She smiled a little. 'I should miss my draughty, smelly railway arch, but it might be nice to have a proper roof over our heads. Will you let me think about it?'

His face lit up again. 'Of course,' he said smiling, and he bowed. 'I shall detain you no longer, Mrs Turneur. Good day to you. Good day, children.'

She stood and watched him walk away, unaware that her lips were parted a little. Behind her, Mary said, 'Long Ben won't win.'

'How do you know?'

'I hear things about him on the street. He's tough, but the Captain is tougher, and he has more men. Long Ben won't last much longer.'

Mary paused, watching Mr Ringrose disappear behind the carpet factory. 'Do you like him?' she asked.

'Like? Like whom?' Grace asked.

'Him.' Mary pointed. 'You like him, don't you?'

'He is a good man,' said Grace. 'I like and respect him as a teacher.'

She was blushing again as she said it, and she knew she was lying. Unconsciously, she had tried to bury her feelings, but they had refused to stay down and now they were bursting and boiling to the surface. She was attracted to him. How long this had been happening, she could not say, but although she could deny this to Mary there was no longer any denying it to herself.

It is a foolish infatuation, she told herself as they walked home, *and I must get rid of it. I am not a silly girl anymore. I am a married woman, a mother with children. I shall put him out of my thoughts entirely.*

And I shall not see him again. The idea of our schools joining forces is impossible. I need to be away from him, as far away as possible. Out of sight, out of mind. If I do not see him or speak to him, then I shall cure this disorder of my mind and get back to my real life.

At home she prepared the midday meal absently, her mind on other things. She barely spoke to George or the children while they ate. After George returned to work, coughing in the dust and wind outside, she nursed Edith and put her down, and then sent Daisy and Harry and Joe for their afternoon nap. Albert sat reading in the parlour room next to the baby's cot while Mary, in one of her restless moods, prowled around the house. Upstairs, Grace gathered laundry and brought it down to the kitchen, put a cauldron of water to heat on the stove, and then began sorting the clothes for washing.

She picked up one of George's handkerchiefs, and stopped. The fabric was dotted with dark brown flecks and blotches. She could not think what it was at first, and then with a sudden stab of horror, she knew.

It was dried blood.

When George coughed, he always covered his mouth with a handkerchief, which he then folded carefully and put in his pocket. Feeling sick, she wondered how long he had been coughing up blood, and how long he had been concealing it from her.

She realised someone was watching her, and turned around. Mary was standing in the kitchen doorway, staring back. 'He's sick, isn't he?'

'Yes,' said Grace. She staggered a little, putting one hand on the table to support herself as the full force of what was happening began to hit her. 'Oh, Mary,' she said, her voice faint. 'What are we going to do?'

'When Joe and I were sick, you looked after us,' said Mary. 'Now George is sick, and we'll look after him. For as long as we need to.'

∞

'Come here, Jimmy,' the Captain said. 'I want to ask you some questions. Have no fear, boy, I'm not going to hurt you.' He paused. 'Unless, that is, I don't like your answers.'

I took a couple of steps forward on legs like jelly. He watched me from under the brim of his hat. We were in the big room in his warehouse, and it was dim, with just a single oil lamp burning. I was mortally scared. I was scared of many things, I was scared of the dark, I was scared of the hole, but most of all I was scared of the Captain.

'Your father betrayed me,' he said, soft-like. 'Your brother too. You know what happened to them, don't you, Jimmy?'

'Yes, sir.' I said.

'So that leaves you,' the Captain said. 'The last of your family. Well, there's your mother, of course, but she's of no account.'

'What will happen to her?' I asked.

The Captain raised a finger, and I quaked in my boots. 'I'm the one asking the questions. Now then, Jimmy. Speak truthfully. Have you also betrayed me?'

'No, sir,' I said.

'And now, Jimmy? Will you follow my orders, without asking questions or doubting me? Will you do everything I ask?'

'Yes, sir,' I said.

He watched me for a long time 'All right,' he said. 'You asked about your mother. I tell you what, Jimmy. I'll let her live. I'll pay the rent and buy her all the gin she can drink so long as you do what I tell you. If you ever give me cause to doubt your absolute loyalty, I will kill her before your eyes. Is that clear?'

'Yes, sir,' I said again.

'Good. Now, Mr Gould is refusing to pay protection. Tomorrow night I'm going to burn some of his cargoes, to show him who's the master here. In the afternoon I want you to go along and scout out Acorn Dock.'

He nodded. 'You're a good boy, Jimmy. You made the right choice. You stick with me. I'll make a man out of you, so I will.'

Chapter 16

By the middle of August it was evident to everyone that George was seriously ill. He began to fall behind in his work, and because he could no longer keep up, his employers docked his wages. The deductions were not large, usually only a shilling or two a week, but in that overstretched household every penny counted. Typically, George's first thought was for his family, he felt humiliated that he could no longer look after them.

'You mustn't feel badly,' said Grace, kissing his cheek. 'No one could do more than you have done.'

George shook his head, covering his mouth while he coughed. 'I have failed you all,' he said.

In early September his health took a strong turn for the worse. Racked with spasms of coughing that brought up bloody sputum, on some mornings he struggled to even get out of bed.

Without George's wages, the family would go hungry. There was only one thing for it, Grace thought; she herself would have to find work. That afternoon she wrote out a series of cards advertising her services as a seamstress and laundress, and then went out and posted them in shop windows around Rotherhithe. At first nothing happened, but after a while some of the more prosperous house-wives in the district began sending her sheets to be washed and shirts to be mended, and a little more money began trickling in. Grace put aside as much of this money as she could, saving it for the inevitable day when George could no longer work at all.

At the end of September there came a spell of cool, calm weather, when the smoke that belched into the air from factories and mills descended and hung like a shroud over Rotherhithe, blurring the masts of the ships in the docks. The smoke ravaged George's decaying lungs still further, and one afternoon he came home from work early. He did not say anything; he did not need to. The look of despair in his face said everything. No longer able to work, he had been fired from his job.

'What shall we do?' he asked after a while. 'How will we get by?'

'What you are going to do is rest,' said Grace. 'I shall find a way to look after us.'

The days and weeks that followed always remained rather blurred in Grace's memory. Her routine was one of steady, unceasing work from dawn until dusk. Rising each day, she lit the stove and cooked porridge for the children and George, and then, leaving her husband in his chair in the parlour, wrapped up against the cold and damp, she took the children away to school, carrying Edith in her basket. Returning from lessons she gave the others a meal and then did laundry and repaired clothes all afternoon. The water and coarse soap dried her hands until the skin cracked and sometimes bled, and she was reminded of her days picking rags in the workhouse, but she could not stop.

Each evening she went out with Radcliffe as her escort to return parcels of clothes to their owners and receive her meagre fee. Back at the house she cooked dinner and then put the younger children to bed before finally sitting down exhausted in the parlour with Edith, George, Albert and Mary for company. Edith was still nursing, which added to her fatigue. She had tried the baby on porridge, but Edith had made her displeasure clear in a very vocal manner. She went through her days wrapped in a cocoon of weariness.

Mela called one afternoon, and saw at once how thin George had become and heard him racked with coughing. She drew Grace into the kitchen. 'Did the doctor come?' she asked.

The Clares, hearing of George's illness, had pressed Grace to accept the services of their doctor, and Grace had finally persuaded George to see him. But, as with Rosa, there was nothing the doctor could do.

Grace nodded, fighting back tears. 'Oh, my dear,' said Mela, embracing her, and then the tears did flow and she cried silently into Mela's shoulder for a few minutes. She had thought weeping might make her feel better, but in fact she felt more wretched than ever.

'Oh, Mela,' she said. 'What am I going to do?'

Mela looked at the piles of laundry on the kitchen table. 'Is this how you are making a living?'

Grace nodded. 'Let us help you,' Mela said. 'We can lend you money until you find something else.'

'No!' Grace said emphatically. 'This is my family, and I am going to look after them.'

'You are making ends meet?' Mela asked doubtfully.

'Yes,' said Grace. 'I am.'

Mela looked at her. Her pretty face was sharp with concern. 'Grace, why will you not accept help?'

Grace hesitated, struggling to find words. 'Ever since Aunt Edith died, I have lived dependent on someone else. Not until I came here and married George did I ever stand on my own feet. I love your parents, Mela, and I always shall, for their goodness to me, but I cannot live forever on their charity. I must see this through, and I must do it alone.'

'Will you at least let us send the doctor again?'

Grace shook her head. 'It would do no good. He is very sick, Mela, and has been for a long time, and now he is declining fast. I don't think the end is far away.'

Again they clung to each other, both weeping now. 'I feel so helpless,' Mela said. 'Standing here and watching you suffer is agony. Is there nothing I can do?'

'There is nothing anyone can do,' Grace said.

Each day seemed to bring about a worsening of George's health. He lost his appetite almost entirely, and would eat no more than a mouthful or two of the porridge and savoury stews she brought him. 'Give the rest to the kids,' he said one evening. 'They need it more than me.'

'You need to keep your strength up,' Grace said.

George shook his head. The fight was going out of him. In his mind, he was already preparing for death. 'There is one thing you can do for me,' he said.

'Oh? What is that?'

A ghost of a smile crossed George's face. 'You know I never had much use for reading and writing. But I see the kiddies all reading, and I think I might have missed something. Grace . . . would you teach me to read proper?'

And so, because there was nothing else she could do, she sat in the evenings and taught her husband to read while she watched him die. The effort of concentration took George's mind away from his illness and pain, at least for a little while, and although she worried that she was tiring him too much, he insisted on continuing the lessons. 'I want to read at least one book before I die,' he said, and he grinned at her and for a moment she saw the old George once more. 'It might have to be a short one.'

After a couple of weeks he had progressed to the point where she brought one of the children's lesson books home and gave it to him. He read it slowly, sitting by the stove wrapped in blankets, head down, coughing from time to time. But he finished the book in an evening, and he smiled with real pleasure when it was ended.

'Now for a real book,' he said.

'Give him the Alice book,' Mary said.

'I thought you said it was silly,' said Grace.

'Maybe I was mistaken,' Mary admitted. 'Let's read it together, George. We can help each other with the words we don't know.'

And so it was that for the last few weeks of his life, George Turneur and Mary the wild girl from the streets sat together by the fire and read *Alice's Adventures in Wonderland* aloud to each other, and watching them, Grace did not know whether to laugh or cry. Sometimes she did both. Mary was a comfort to George in those dark weeks, and gradually Grace found herself handing over more of his care to the girl, allowing her to work and look after Edith. She saw a gentle, even tender side of Mary begin to emerge, and after a while she realised that this side had been there all along. It was the side of her that Joe saw, she thought; the caring and compassionate side, allied to a steely will, that had kept them both alive on the streets.

As the illness tightened its grip, George could no longer be left alone. Grace debated with herself about whether to close the school, and thought briefly about sending some of the children, at least, to Mr Ringrose. That brought back memories of her last meeting with him, and her feelings, and that in turn provoked a wash of guilt and shame. Her husband was dying, and she was thinking about another man. No; she would not go near Mr Ringrose.

It was Mary, again, who solved the dilemma. 'You don't have to close the school,' she said. 'I can stay home in the mornings and look after George. I know how to make him hot drinks, and we can read together. It will pass the time for him.'

'What about your lessons?' Grace asked.

Mary pulled a face. 'I don't mind. I only go because you didn't want to leave me at home in case I ate all the food.'

'That's not true.'

'You were right, though, I probably would have. And all I do at school is cause trouble.'

'You don't,' said Grace.

'I do. I threw a slate at Gabriel last week, remember?'

'I don't think you really intended to hit him,' Grace said. 'And he shouldn't have teased you . . . Mary, are you sure?'

'I said we would look after him,' said the girl. 'Please, Grace. Let me help. I want to.'

It was the first time she had ever heard Mary say please. She bent and kissed the girl, ruffling her hair which had largely grown out again. 'Thank you,' she said.

In October the cold deepened, and rain once again turned the streets of Rotherhithe to mud. Beyond the docks, the marshes were sheets of water. George was slipping away fast now. In the evenings, when Edith was asleep and the other children had gone to bed, they talked quietly about their short life together. 'I'm sorry,' George said once.

She kissed his cheek softly. 'You have nothing to be sorry for.'

'Yes, I do. I'm going off and leaving you with six kids to look after, and nothing more than a few shillings of laundry money to live on. I'm worried for you and the kids. How will you get by?'

'Don't concern yourself, my dear,' Grace said softly. 'We will manage.'

Silence fell for a while. 'You must find someone else,' George said. 'You're young and pretty, and you deserve to be happy. Find a fellow who will love you and look after you.'

Privately Grace doubted she would ever find a man who was willing to take on six children, but she was not going to upset George by saying so. 'Let's not talk about it now,' she said gently. 'It's getting late, George. You should rest.'

'I'll have plenty of time to rest before long,' he said, staring at his hands. 'I've been thinking a lot recently. About Rosa.'

'I know,' Grace said. She could see it in his eyes sometimes, a look of dreaming and yearning as death drew near.

'I should have been a better husband to you, Grace. I should have loved you. But I've never been able to stop thinking about her. I've missed her so much.'

'I know,' Grace said again. 'We both have. Loving her is one of the things we share.'

The final week was terrible. George was in constant pain, coughing over and over and retching up blood, and Grace realised that watching this was taking a terrible toll on Mary. 'You mustn't bear this alone,' she said. 'I'll close the school and stay home with him until the end.'

'I can do it,' Mary said. 'I can look after him.'

'No, my dear. You are too young.'

Mary looked mutinous. 'Instead of closing the school, why not ask that other man to take it? Like you said he did when you were carrying Edith? I'm sure he'd do it again. He likes you.'

'I can't,' Grace said.

'Why not?' asked Mary. 'Because you like him, too?'

'Yes,' said Grace finally.

Mary planted her hands on her hips. She had grown at least an inch since she had joined them, and her face had become firmer too. 'That makes no sense,' she said. 'Ask him. Write him a letter, and I will take it to him. You know the school needs to stay open. And it gets Albert and the twins and Joe out of the house for a while.'

Grace bit her lip. 'All right,' she said finally.

Mary carried the letter over to Bermondsey, and brought back a reply from Mr Ringrose.

My dear Mrs Turneur,

I am so sorry to hear of your husband's illness. I shall pray daily for his speedy recovery. Meanwhile, I am more than happy to cover your morning class as before. Please do take good care of yourself.

Your faithful friend,

Walter Ringrose

Grace read the letter without emotion. The old frisson of excitement was gone, her tired mind had no room for it. There was nothing in her life now except work, and George.

Downstairs, the clock chimed two. George lay in the bed they had shared, the same bed where Rosa had died, his head propped on a pillow. An oil lamp glowed with smoky light. His face was hollow, the lines of his cheek and jaw and nose in sharp relief in the light, his sunken cheeks full of shadow. He had stopped coughing, and his breath came slow and shallow and ragged, bubbling a little in his chest. Grace listened with horror, remembering how Rosa had died two years before.

'I hope I've been a good man, Grace,' he whispered. 'I tried to live a good life, and I tried to be a good husband to you. Truly I did.'

'No woman could have asked for a better man,' said Grace, weeping.

He turned his head slowly to look at her, and his hand brushed her wet cheek. 'Dry your tears, lass,' he whispered. 'I'm going to a better place. And mayhap I'll find Rosa there, waiting for me.'

'I'm sure you will, George. I'm sure she's waiting right now.' A fresh flood of tears streamed down Grace's face. 'She'll smile when she sees you, my dear. Remember how lovely her smile was? You'll be seeing it again before long.'

'Yes.' George closed his eyes. 'Rosa,' he whispered. 'Rosa . . .' Softly he called her name, whispering over the bubbling sound in his chest, and half an hour later he called her name one last time while Grace held his hand. Then his breathing stopped and the soul of a good and generous man took flight and set out on its lonely journey to the better place that awaited him, far away. In the room the clock ticked softly, the only sound to break the silence of death.

Grace sat beside the bed for a long while, still holding his hand clasped in hers, sobbing quietly. He had been the best man she had ever known, and now he was gone from her life. She sat there in the light of the oil lamp, caressing the dead hand, mourning the things she had lost and the things she had never had, feeling the shadows close in around her. Never before had she felt so utterly alone.

She would remember George to the end of her days. She would have Edith, of course, always to remind her of what they had shared, and Albert and the twins would be his memorial too. When she looked at them she would remember his kindness and gentleness, the love he bore his children, the bond he had formed with Mary who had taken such fond care of him. *Oh, poor Mary,* Grace thought, weeping again, *she will be devastated . . .*

On the heels of the thought she heard the stair creak, and then the door opened and Mary came in, her newly grown hair flowing over the shoulders of her nightgown. 'Is it over?' she asked.

'Oh, my dear,' Grace said quickly. 'You shouldn't be here.'

'I wanted to see him one last time,' the girl said. Her eyes were dry, but Grace could see the sorrow in them. 'He was so good to me.' She came closer to the bed, staring at the silent figure under the blankets. 'Why, Grace? Why do the people who love us get taken away? Why is the world so cruel?'

'I don't know,' Grace said, and she drew Mary to her and held her close, and then the girl did start to cry softly, and they held each other weeping until the oil lamp began to flicker and die.

Chapter 17

'I am sorry to hear of Mr Turneur's death,' said Reverend Hobbes, stiffly. 'He was not always the most responsible of men, but I believe his heart was in the right place.'

'He was a good father and a good husband,' said Grace.

A frigid silence fell. They were sitting in the vicarage study at All Saints, just as they had sat two years earlier after Rosa died. Outside, rain tapped on the windows. *Even the clouds are weeping for George,* she thought.

The vicar, of course, had never accepted that she and George were legally married, and he and his wife were still opposed to the Ragged School. 'I need the money from the burial fund so that I may arrange his funeral,' Grace said. 'And I would like him to be buried in the churchyard, next to his first wife.'

Reverend Hobbes stirred a little in his chair. 'You may have the money, of course,' he said. 'You are entitled to it. But as for the burial, that is quite impossible. I know you went through a form of marriage, but so far as I am concerned, you and Mr Turneur were living in a state of sin. I cannot bury a man in consecrated ground unless he died in a state of grace.'

Grace's temper, frayed by sorrow and weeping, snapped. She rose to her feet. 'A form of marriage?' she demanded. 'We *were* married, sir, by Reverend Soames the rector of Bermondsey, under licence. That licence was granted to us by the Bishop of Southwark himself! Shall I go to His Grace, and ask him to confirm that our marriage was legal and honest in the sight of God and man? I am sure he will be pleased to do so.'

The vicar stared out at the rain for a moment. He knew when he was beaten. 'Very well,' he said. 'I will sanction the burial, but my conscience will not allow me to perform the service. For that, you must look elsewhere.'

Conscience, thought Grace. *As if you have one, you pious old hypocrite.* 'Reverend Soames will officiate,' she said shortly. 'If you would be so good as to count me out my money, sir, I will detain you no further.'

After that came the usual sad details: arranging for a death certificate and a burial licence, finding and paying the gravediggers and making the arrangements for the funeral with Mr Jevons the kindly undertaker. 'You'll have the black plumes for the horse free of charge,' he said. 'No, Mrs Turneur, this is my gift. It is the very least I can do, for someone who has done so much for our community.'

Through the haze of fatigue she realised he meant her-self, not George, and she wondered what she had done to deserve this. But everywhere she went that morning she found hands outstretched ready to help her. The physician also refused his fee, and under their rough exterior even the gravediggers were sympathetic. Several people stopped her in the street to say how sorry they were, watching her with anxious eyes. At the rectory in Bermondsey, Reverend Soames was so kind that she burst into tears again.

'That's good,' the white-bearded rector said, offering her a handkerchief. 'Let it out, my child. Do not be afraid to be emotional. It is good to release feelings, and not keep them bottled up inside.'

'I don't know what I am feeling,' Grace said honestly. 'Ours was a marriage of convenience, as you know. I didn't love him, but I was deeply fond of him. He was such a good man. Everyone says so.'

'You say you were fond of him,' the rector said. 'Surely that is enough? There are many kinds of love, my child. Think of the love of a baby for its mother, the love of a child for a kitten or a toy, the love of brothers and sister, the love of friends who care for and look after each other. All are very different in nature, and yet all are the same, for they are all of them part of God's plan. All love comes from God, and all love goes back to him.'

Back at the house in Bell Lane she gathered the children around her. It was her turn, now, to comfort them.

Each of them was taking the loss quite differently, she saw. Daisy was tearful, desperately missing her father and clinging to Grace like she was the only anchor left in her life. Harry was silent and bewildered. Albert knew he was now the man of the household and was doing his best to be responsible and brave, though his eyes were red and his lip quivered from time to time. Mary was pale and silent. Strangely, it was Joe who seemed to be taking it best. He hugged both Harry and Daisy tightly, like he was trying to impart strength to them, and after a while it seemed to be working.

'We will have the service in a little while,' she said to them, keeping her voice soft. 'Then your daddy will be taken to the churchyard, and he will be laid to rest beside your mummy.'

'Beside First Mummy,' said Harry, determined to get the facts straight.

'That's right,' said Grace. 'And they will be together for all eternity, and they will be happy.'

'What does eternity mean?' Joe asked.

'Forever and ever,' said Grace.

'Then that is good,' said the little boy. 'They will be happy forever and ever. And when we die, will we go and be with them?'

'Yes,' said Grace, and she added firmly, 'but that will not be for a long time yet. Now we must get on with living. We'll remember them always, every day of our lives, but we must also remember the precious gifts they gave us, of cleverness and good health and strong bodies and clear minds, and use those gifts wisely. That is how we will honour those who have gone.'

Mary's head came up at this and she gazed at Grace with those clear, disconcerting blue eyes. 'Do you believe that?' she asked directly.

'Yes,' said Grace. 'We are not put on this earth solely to please ourselves. We are here to give service to others. You of all people, Mary, should know that.'

They came, the friends and neighbours, crowding into the little parlour beside the coffin, the Bertons, Mickey and Brigit Doyle, a dozen others, all that would fit in the room. None of his fellow workers from the building firm came. The firm's managers had refused to let them have time off to attend the funeral, and had threatened to fire anyone who failed to show up for work. George was right, Grace thought; we're just tools to be used. And when one tool breaks, you throw it away and replace it with another.

The door opened and someone else came into the room, a fair young woman in a long dark coat with a black armband. Grace gasped. 'Mela! How did you know?'

'Reverend Soames sent a message,' Mela said. 'I came at once. I was afraid I would not be in time.'

'I am sorry,' Grace said. 'I should have written to tell you, but I had so much to do, with arranging the funeral and everything . . .'

Her voice faltered and tears began to flow. Mela kissed her on the cheek. 'Hush,' she said. 'I understand everything. I am here now, and that is all that matters.'

Reverend Soames read the service in his beautiful rich voice, and they sang 'Abide With Me', the hymn George had requested. He had always loved the tune, but he had learned somewhere, Grace never knew how, that the composer had also died of consumption not long after writing the hymn. He wanted his family and friends to take comfort from the words. *That's George*, Grace thought, weeping silently and holding Mela's hand tightly in her own. *Even in the afterlife, he is still thinking of other people.*

At the end of the service they followed the coffin out to the hearse where Mr Jevons waited, and they began the procession to All Saints. As they walked slowly, following the hearse, Grace became aware of doors opening and closing behind them, and more people coming out to join them. She saw Mrs Lane and several other parents of her children, and to her astonishment, she saw the pie seller from the market place who had once refused to take her money. The little group of mourners swelled to twenty, then thirty, forty.

'Why?' she said to Mela. 'Why are they here? Some of these people didn't even know George.'

'They're not here for George, my dear,' said Mela, squeezing her hand again. 'They're here for you.'

More people waited for them at the church. They filed into the churchyard, Reverend Soames leading the way followed by the coffin and the mourners. Once Grace glanced over at the vicarage, and saw the curtains open at one of the windows. They twitched shut again, but not before she caught a glimpse of Mrs Hobbes's wrinkled face looking out at her. Then they gathered around the grave, and Reverend Soames read the service in his beautiful voice.

We have but a short time to live.
Like a flower we blossom and then wither;
like a shadow we flee and never stay.
In the midst of life we are in death . . .

It was over. George Turneur was at peace now, laid to rest beside the woman he loved. Grace straightened her back and turned away from the grave. Around her the people of Rotherhithe watched, extending her their silent sympathy. One day she would remember them, and draw strength from the support they gave her. For the moment, all she could feel was the empty hole in her life.

'My parents send you their love,' said Mela when they returned to the house on Bell Lane. 'They are very sad for you, and worried too.'

'Tell them they must be neither,' said Grace, and she smiled, hoping Mela would not see how forced the smile was. 'I am sad, of course, but I have much to keep me occupied and all my little ones to care for. And I shall find a way to support us all.'

'How?' demanded Mela.

'I have had an idea,' Grace said. The thought had occurred to her that morning, walking back from the rectory and passing the entrance to Potters' Fields. She was uneasily aware that her last conversation with Mr Ringrose had been one of the sparks that gave rise to the idea.

'Our biggest item of expense as a family is rent,' she said. 'If we can reduce that, we can get by much more easily. And I think it is time the school moved out of the railway arch. Even with two classes, we have too many pupils now and we need more space. I am going to find a building where we can relocate the school, and which will also be big enough to house us all. It will be our home as well as our school. Indeed, if it is a big enough building, I might be able to house some of the homeless children too, and have a kitchen to give them meals.'

'And how will you pay for this building?' Mela asked.

'I intend to ask some of the local businessmen for help. There is Mr Crompton, for example, of Crompton and Rhodes. Rosa used to work for him; he might be willing to help. Or there is the friendly timber merchant, Mr Gould. I shall appeal to them both. If they will provide me with financial assistance to acquire the lease on a building, as Mr Ringrose has done in Bermondsey, then in exchange I shall offer to teach the children of their workers for free, which will benefit the children and their families. That way we would acquire both a school and a new home without needing to pay for it.'

'And what will you live on?' asked Mela.

'With the rent paid for, we can live on very little. I will keep doing laundry in the afternoons, and that will bring in enough money for us to get by.'

Mela looked doubtful. 'Father would help you acquire the lease,' she said.

Grace shook her head. 'No,' she said. 'I won't ask it of him, and I beg you promise me you will not mention it to him. Really and truly, I can take no more favours from your parents. Even if I worked every day of my life, I could not repay what they have done for me. I will not add further debts to the ledger.'

Mela leaned over and tickled her god daughter who was lying in her basket waving her arms, oblivious to all that was going on around her. 'Pig-headed,' she said. 'And stubborn as an ox. Grow up quickly, little Edith, so you can come and help me talk some sense into your mother.'

'This is sense,' Grace said. 'The Bull Head Gang is still threatening our schools and our children. If I can persuade some of the local businessmen to stand up to them, then we have a chance to rally the whole community. This is not just a matter of securing my family's future. We're going to make Rotherhithe safer, if it is the last thing we do.'

George was gone, but the grinding burden of work went on. She wrote to Mr Ringrose the following day, thanking him for his assistance and telling him she was returning to duty. Mary was sceptical. 'You can't teach all morning and work all afternoon and look after the little ones at the same time. You'll work yourself into the ground. Let him keep the school.'

'No,' said Grace. 'That is my school, and I am not letting go of it.'

Through a growing haze of exhaustion she worked on. Teaching the children was her inspiration, the rock of foundation to which she clung. Going into the classroom under the railway always invigorated her, no matter how tired she might be. But the afternoons and evenings of laundry and sewing were sheer drudgery, and the money she made never quite repaid the effort she put in, nor did it quite manage to pay the rent and put food on the table. She was glad she had saved some money before George stopped working, for she had to dip into those savings time and again. But they would not last forever.

She took a break from her work one afternoon and went to see Mr Crompton at his office in the new carpet factory. Sitting outside his office and listening to the thump and clack of the power looms on the workshop floor, she was conscious that her clothes were tattered and the leather of her shoes had begun to crack. She needed new shoes, but there was no money. She had set a little sum aside to buy shoes for Mary as soon as she could persuade the girl to wear them; her need was more important.

Mr Crompton was a thin, pale, rather harassed look-ing man. 'Yes, I recall your sister well,' he said. 'A very fine worker. We missed her very much when she left to get married. How may I help you, Mrs Turneur?'

Grace outlined her scheme for the school. 'I'm hoping some of the other employers will also back me, sir, so the cost of the lease would be spread around. In return, I will be happy to take in the children of your employees as pupils, free of charge.'

'I see. And how will you yourself earn a living?'

'I have other employment as well,' Grace said.

Mr Crompton looked dubious. 'I will give it some thought. I have concerns, however. Your school, like that in Bermondsey, has received attention from the Bull Head Gang. If I support you, they might decide to attack my business as well. I already have enough trouble from that quarter.'

'I have received an assurance from the leader of the Bull Head Gang that my school will be allowed to continue,' Grace said, trying not to think about the other part of the Captain's bargain.

Mr Crompton's eyebrows rose. 'I am not certain that any promise made by that scoundrel is likely to be kept. Nonetheless, I will consider it.'

At Acorn Dock the following day Mr Gould was similarly doubtful. 'One of my warehouses was burned to the ground a couple of months back, and they have also made threats against my employees and their families. I'd like to assist you, Mrs Turneur. But you could end up by putting us all in greater danger.'

'But will you consider it?' Grace pleaded.

'Of course. And if I can see my way forward, then I will surely help you.'

It was not what she had hoped for. That night, Mary came into the kitchen while Grace was washing the dishes after dinner and found her in tears. Wordlessly, Mary embraced her and they held each other close for a moment. 'It will be all right,' the girl said.

'Yes,' said Grace, drying her eyes. 'It will.'

'I've got something to say that will make you feel better,' Mary said.

'What is it?'

'I think I might be ready to try wearing shoes.'

They stared at each other for a moment, and then from nowhere, Grace started to laugh.

Autumn turned to winter, Grace's third since she came to live at Bell Lane. The grinding routine of life in Bell Lane went on. Try as she might, she could not bring in enough work to pay the rent and put food on the table, and her little stock of savings ebbed away. By December, it had vanished entirely. Logic dictated she should either give up the school, or approach the Clares for financial assistance, but Grace rebelled against both ideas. *I will not admit defeat*, she told herself. *I will find a way. I am not giving up.*

There were, she realised reluctantly, other things she could do to raise money. For a start, there were George's clothes, which were no longer needed. It would be years yet before Albert was tall enough to wear them. Swallowing a lump in her throat, she packaged up his clothes and boots and took them to the pawn shop on Jamaica Road, a grimy establishment that dealt in every known commodity. The owner was not interested in lending money against the clothes, but he offered instead to buy them outright, and Grace had little choice but to agree. His work boots, which were strong and of good quality, fetched a good price, but the owner would pay no more than a few shillings for the rest. Still, that would buy a few more meals for the children.

Life has come to this, Grace thought as she walked home through the freezing wind. *I am selling my dead husband's clothes to feed our children.*

She wrote to Mr Crompton and to Mr Gould to ask if they had considered her idea, but received no response. A week later she called at the carpet factory and was told by an unsympathetic secretary that Mr Crompton was away in Germany on business. When she went to Acorn Dock to find Mr Gould she learned that he too was away. His father had died after a long illness, and he had gone to Dorset to arrange the funeral and sort out the family affairs. No one knew when he might return.

The next step was to go through Rosa's clothes, which she had packed away after her sister's death, and begin selling these too. Somehow this caused her even more pain than disposing of George's things. It was like she was erasing the presence of them both from the house. When that money too ran out, she turned to her own wardrobe and pawned as much as she could. She had bought no new clothes for herself since coming to Bell Lane, and as a result most of her own things were tired and worn, but there was a fine thick overcoat which she pawned for a good price. She walked home shivering in the freezing wind, teeth chattering, but knowing she had enough money to get the family through to the other side of Christmas.

But tragedy was not yet finished with Bell Lane. A week before Christmas while a ship from Norway was being unloaded at Lavender Pool, a heavy baulk of timber crashed down from its deck onto the dock below. Two deal porters were killed outright and Mickey Doyle just failed to get out of the way. The timber fell onto his leg, trapping him. His fellow workers cut him free and the doctor provided by the Surrey Commercial Docks Company managed to save the leg from amputation, but the bones were crushed below the knee. Mickey would never work at the docks again, and indeed it would be a long time before he would even walk. Brigit Doyle came to Grace in tears.

'I don't know how we'll get by, Grace. My bobbin and thread won't keep us for long. The rent is already in arrears.'

Mickey's salary had never been as much as George's and Brigit worked as a lace maker, earning a pittance by weaving fine lace intended for decorating ladies' gowns and hats. As well as Billy, she had two smaller children to feed.

'Come and work with me,' Grace said. 'You can do some of the seamstress work. I'm wretched with a needle. You do that work, I'll take the laundry and we'll split the fees.' She smiled. 'With both of us together, we can take on more work.'

She knew, of course, that the work would bring money in for both their families, but not enough to save them, yet she could do nothing else. She would not be responsible for putting another family onto the street, or into the workhouse. She had not told anyone how desperately overstretched her own resources already were, and she never would. Mela had been right to call Grace stubborn, and on top of that she was also very proud.

The days before Christmas were sombre. There was no goose this year. The best Grace could manage was a salmon purchased from the fishmonger in the market. Salmon was cheap – in grand houses, servants often complained that they were fed salmon too often – and so she could spend a little extra money on trimmings, and even managed to buy some small wooden toys for the children and a book for Mary, to keep up appearances.

Then on Christmas morning a parcel arrived, sent by special messenger. Grace recognised Mela's writing on the label, and knew it contained gifts.

'Shall we see what is inside?' she asked the children.

'Yes!' came a chorus of voices.

There were books for herself, *Lorna Doone* by Mr Blackmore, and *The Wyvern Mystery* by Mr Le Fanu, and an essay entitled *The Subjection of Women* by Mr Mill that reminded her of bygone days when she and Mela used to play how they would set the world to rights. For the children there were more toys, and a small mountain of sweets, oranges, walnuts and at the bottom of the box, a plum pudding. The note that came with the parcel said simply, *A gift for all my loved ones in Rotherhithe. M.* Exhausted and strained, it was all Grace could do to hide her tears.

At Christmas dinner she made the children eat as much as they could, taking only a modest portion for herself. Afterwards they sang Christmas carols in the parlour, with Harry conducting the others, while Edith crawled around on the floor by their feet and attempted to stand up. The mood lasted for a while, but then Daisy remembered her father was not there, and burst into heartbroken tears. Grace sat holding the girl on her lap, rocking her gently as if she was a baby, until she fell asleep.

Later, when Edith had been fed and put to sleep and the younger children had gone to bed, Mary came into the kitchen and, without a word, put her arms around Grace's waist and hugged her tightly. 'You still miss him too, don't you?' Grace said.

'Yes,' said Mary. 'He was so patient with me, even when I didn't deserve it.'

Once again Grace was reminded of how Mary, at twelve or thirteen, was older than her years. Now she looked up at Grace. 'Are you all right?' she asked. 'I can see in your face how tired you are. Let me help with the laundry, and maybe one day you could teach me to sew. With three of us, perhaps it will be enough. '

'Perhaps,' Grace said, and she bent and kissed the girl on the forehead. 'but you must not do too much, for you are still not as strong as you should be. Now, go to bed, my dear. You need your rest.'

After Mary departed, Grace sat for a while at the table, head in her hands. Behind her, the cast-iron stove ticked quietly as it began to cool. The clock chimed in the parlour, and in the distance she could hear the ringing of church bells.

There was still no word from Mr Crompton and Mr Gould. She had pinned her faith on them, and nothing had happened. And now, too, it was not just her own family that were in trouble. With Mickey unable to work, the Doyles were on the edge. Whatever plan she came up with would have to include them as well.

Briefly, she thought about taking Mela's advice and contacting the Clares for help, but once again her mind revolted from the idea. Her plan had failed. Very well, she would have to come up with another one.

Only, for the life of her, she could not think what it might be. She sat there on Christmas night in the light of the oil lamp, listening to the little sounds of the night, and never before in her life had she felt so alone.

Chapter 18

I knew if someone saw me in Rotherhithe, she would find out. So I struck out west, over towards Southwark where I hadn't been since the Angels split up, carrying a basket under my coat and wearing my new shoes. I hated those shoes, they pinched my feet something horrible, but I had to admit that wearing them made me warmer.

I remembered Borough Market, over by the cathedral, was a good place to scavenge for scran, so I went there. I picked up some cabbages that had fallen off a cart – they really had fallen, I didn't have to nudge the cart more than a little bit to make them roll off onto the ground – and some parsnips and potatoes that didn't have anyone looking after them, and then I whipped a loaf of bread off a table when the baker's back was turned. I used a hook on the end of a bit of line, an old trick I had learned with the Angels, to drag some sausages off another stall and then grab them before the dogs could get them, and I even managed to get half a cheese and hide it under my coat. I was feeling pretty good. I still had my old skills.

I walked back towards Rotherhithe carrying all this in my basket under my coat and thinking about the Forty Elephants and the jewellery I would buy when I was rich, and that's when I spotted him. He'd grown a bit, but then, so had I. He was scrawny, though, and he had a patch of bad skin on his neck. He hadn't been eating too good. He had his back turned to me, staring at something in the street, so I walked up behind him and tapped him on the shoulder. He jumped about a foot in the air.

'Jimmy,' I said. 'Jimmy Wilson, ain't it?'

'Yes,' he said. 'Who are you?'

His eyes looked like he had seen a lot of ghosts. Or maybe he was still seeing them, and maybe they never left him. I knew the look; I used to have it myself. 'I'm Mary,' I said. 'From the Angels. Remember?'

He looked at me kind of dazed, but I reckoned he did remember. 'Sorry to hear about your da,' I said.

He didn't say anything to that. I looked down the street towards the pawnbroker's he had been staring at. It was a big one, probably full of gold and stuff, unlike the scruffy one in Rotherhithe where Grace pawned her coat so she could feed us.

'You're on lookout, aren't you?' I said. 'The Bull Head Gang must be about to rob that place.'

'Keep your voice down,' he hissed. 'What are you doing here, anyway?'

'Stealing food,' I said. 'George died, and Grace is trying to look after her kids and me and my brother. I'm helping out.'

I saw the look in his eyes change. For a moment, the ghosts stepped back a little. 'Is she all right? Miss Perrow? I mean, Mrs Turneur?'

'No,' I said. 'She's going hungry so she can feed us kids. Things are hard for her.'

Again he didn't say anything for a while, but then he said, 'Things are going to get harder. I overheard the Captain talking. They're going to take some of the boys from the Ragged School. Not right away, but later, maybe in the spring or summer.'

'Why?' I asked.

'The Captain is building up the gang. He wants to take over Southwark now, maybe even Lambeth too. One day, he wants to rule all London.'

'And you're staying with him.'

He clenched his hands into fists and put them up to his eyes, and for a moment I thought he was going to cry. 'I don't have a choice,' he said. 'I can't do anything else. Please, Mary. Don't tell her you've seen me.'

'I won't,' I said. 'I don't want to worry her.'

I watched his face for a moment. 'What would happen if you had to choose, Jimmy?' I asked. 'Between the Captain and her. What would you do?'

'Don't make me choose!' he cried. 'Please don't make me!' Then he went running off down the street. I watched him turn the corner, and then he was gone.

⁓

Grace was just finishing ironing sheets on the kitchen table when Mary walked in and dumped her basket of food on a chair. Radcliffe woke up and raised his head, nostrils twitching at the scent of sausages.

Grace looked at the food and then at the girl. 'Where did this come from?' she asked.

'Here and there,' said Mary.

Realisation dawned. 'Mary,' Grace demanded. 'Have you been stealing?'

'Of course,' Mary said simply. 'We need food.'

Grace stared at her in horror. 'Mary! You must not do this! Take it all back, at once.'

'I can't,' Mary said. 'The market will have closed by now. I don't even remember where I got most of it. Anyway, I took it all from Borough Market. No one around here will know anything about it.'

'I will know!' Grace planted her hands on her hips. 'Mary, stealing is wrong.'

'It's better than starving,' Mary said. She was looking mutinous again, like she had in the days when she first arrived and they tried to make her do something she didn't want to do. 'Is that what you want?'

'No one is going to starve,' Grace snapped. 'And we are not eating stolen food. Take it away, get rid of it, I don't care how or where.'

Mary did not move. 'I'm only trying to help,' she said. 'I know stealing is wrong. But which is worse? A butcher misses a few sausages? Or Daisy and Harry and Joe go hungry? Or you? I know you're missing meals, and giving your food to the kids. What did you have to eat yesterday, Grace? A bowl of porridge and a piece of bread. You can't do this. I know what hunger does to a person, how tired it makes you. If you go on like this you'll kill yourself, and then where will the rest of us be? Do you want to see Albert and the twins and little Edith in the workhouse?'

They looked at each other for a long while, Mary's blue gaze never wavering. 'Don't throw good food away,' she said. 'Let's eat it for dinner. And since it upsets you so much, I promise not to steal food again.'

'I will hold you to that promise,' said Grace, resuming her ironing.

'Why?' asked Mary. 'Food is food. Why does it matter where it comes from?'

Lord, thought Grace, *how do you explain morality to a twelve-year-old who has lived most of her life in the jungle?* But, of course, it was not just a matter of morals. Deep in her heart, Grace knew the real reason she was angry was that she felt like a failure. She had sold her family's clothes and pawned her own, and still she could not make ends meet, to the point that this child felt she had to go out and steal in order to help. Her plan to rescue them all had failed.

She tried again. She wrote to some of the other factory owners and importers in the district, using her dwindling stock of Penny Red stamps, and received not a single reply. Hope began to dwindle and fade.

Somehow they made it through January of 1870 without falling behind on the rent, but Grace grew thin and hollow-cheeked, and the effort of doing laundry began to tell on her. Her hands, when she looked at them, were cracked red claws worn raw with effort. At school she was listless, and sometimes when reading to the children she lost her place and had to start over again. When not teaching she worked every hour of the day, sometimes alone, sometimes with Brigit Doyle for company. Mickey's leg was improving, but he still could not stand for very long. One afternoon Brigit came into Grace's house in floods of tears.

'I couldn't pay the rent last week. The agent says he will give us only one more week to find the money, and then if we can't, he'll turn us out. Holy Mother, Grace, I can't look after Mickey and the children, not without a roof over our heads. What am I going to do?'

Grace embraced Brigit and dried her eyes. She was weak and shivering with exhaustion and hunger. She had given all the porridge that morning to the children. Little Edith had wanted more, and had broken into wails of distress when her bowl was empty; Mary had fed the baby from her own bowl until she stopped crying. Things were desperate.

'What we're going to do,' she said to Brigit Doyle, 'is work even harder than before, and make enough money to pay your rent.'

For the next several days they sat sewing late into the evening, straining their eyes in the light of the oil lamps, and somehow managed to earn enough to pay off the Doyles' arrears. It had saved them for a week, but it would not last. The Doyles owed money to the doctors who had looked after Mickey's leg, too, and the pharmacist for ointments and salves for his slow-healing wounds, more money than Brigit could earn on her own. *We are trapped*, Grace thought, *trapped in this terrible circle of debt and poverty, and the only way out is through death*. She told herself in one wild moment of despair that George and Rosa were the lucky ones. They at least were at peace, and no longer had to dwell in this vale of tears.

To make matters worse, a letter from Mela arrived.

My dear friend,

I am so sorry not to have visited you of late. The truth is that I have been ill; nothing serious, nothing to worry you at all, just a chill in my chest. But the dreary doctors have warned it could turn into pneumonia, and have ordered me to stay indoors and rest. Mother concurs, and has told the servants to ensure that I do not go out. Can you believe it? I feel like a prisoner in my own home.

And, to my distress, I have had to give up teaching, at least for the moment. A substitute has been found and the Clare School carries on perfectly well without me, but I miss my charges and their faces. They were, and are, my delight. I cannot wait to be fully recovered so I can resume teaching and then, my dear, I will come once more and call on you. Give precious little Edith a kiss from me,

I remain your beloved friend,
Mela

And so now, along with all her other cares, she was worried for Mela. Her fear was that Mela was more seriously ill than she claimed. Could that 'chill in the chest' be the beginnings of consumption? She wrote to Mrs Clare seeking reassurance, and Mrs Clare wrote back saying only that Mela had been in bed for several weeks, but seemed to be recovering. She asked after Grace's own situation. Grace did not reply.

Two things helped her get through that bitter winter. The first was her own family, her children, and that included Mary and Joe. They were no longer guests in the house. She loved them as her own, and she knew they were beginning to love her too. The strength and power of that love was her foundation, and she drew strength from it. No matter how exhausted or weak she felt, when she looked at them – Joe talking to the dog, the twins crouched on the floor playing with their toys, Albert in a corner explaining something in a book to Mary, Edith toddling across the floor waving her arms in the air for balance – she felt a surge of strength, and knew she could carry on.

The other was the Ragged School. She had thought about closing it, but every day that passed made her more and more glad that she had not. She arrived at school each day, shivering in the wind without a coat, and looked at the shining hopeful faces of her pupils as she gave them their lessons and moved among them, gently correcting their work, or watched them listening rapt as she read to them, and she knew it was all worthwhile.

But as time passed and the slow descent into abject poverty deepened, Grace realised that there would be a day when she could no longer carry on. If she fell ill or was unable to work, then that would be the end. She would lose the house, and be forced to move away or go into the workhouse. And then the Ragged School would die, and her dreams and the dreams of all her boys and girls would die along with it. The Captain would have won.

Winter began slowly to fade. Spring arrived, dreary under the smoke from the mills and docks, the mud of the streets stinking of ooze and salt water, the new flowers in the marshes stained with soot. More buildings were going up in Rotherhithe, more houses, more people moving into the area, many of them poor working people hoping to find prosperity in the factories and warehouses that sprang up around the docks. The streets were full of wagons laden with timber and bricks and tiles. In Bell Lane they worked and waited and hoped, but for Grace Turneur and her family, no hope came.

The East London Railway Company's new line offered travellers, for the first time, the chance to cross the Thames from north to south by train. It took Mela Clare only a few minutes to travel from Wapping station on the north bank through the old tunnel dug under the river by the Brunels, father and son, to Rotherhithe. Stepping out onto the platform she wrapped her scarf around her neck, remembering her mother's instructions to stay well bundled up – it was early April now and the sun was warmer, but the wind from the north still had a bite – and walked to Bell Lane.

She had written to Grace several more times since the letter announcing her illness, but had received no reply. Apart from the short letter to her mother asking after Mela's health, there had been no word from Rotherhithe, and all three of the Clares were growing worried. As soon as the doctors had announced that Mela could go out once more, she had dressed in her warmest woollens and travelled down to see her friend.

She knocked at the door. There was no response at first, but then the door opened and she saw the street girl Grace had adopted standing and staring at her. 'Miss Clare,' the girl said, and Mela thought she sounded disapproving. 'Grace is in the kitchen. I suppose you had better come in.'

Ignoring the rudeness, Mela walked into the kitchen and found Grace surrounded by piles of laundry. Her smile when she saw Mela was her old brilliant smile of delight. But Mela could not help noticing her sunken cheeks and the circles under her eyes, and when they embraced she could feel how thin Grace had become.

'My dear!' she exclaimed. 'You are skin and bone! What have you been doing with yourself? Don't tell me you too have been ill?'

'I am perfectly well,' Grace said, still smiling. 'Sit down, if you can find a chair, and I will put the kettle on. Tell me, are you fully recovered?'

'I have been recovered for weeks,' Mela said, watching Grace fill the kettle from the water butt and put it on the stove. 'But I couldn't persuade those wretched doctors. Honestly, they were worse than gaolers.'

'I'm sure they were trying to look after you,' Grace said. 'You were never a good patient.'

'Fiddlesticks. There was nothing wrong with me. You, on the other hand, are working yourself to the bone.'

'I am a little busy,' Grace admitted. 'I have taken on a partner.' She explained about Brigit Doyle, and Mickey's injury, taking a tea tin out of the larder and spooning tea into the pot. 'With the doctor's bills to pay, the poor things are only just scraping by.'

'And you're trying to help them, of course,' Mela said. 'But Grace, you can't help other people if you don't look after yourself.'

'I am all right.' Grace returned the tin to the larder and closed the door, standing for a moment with one hand resting on the doorknob. 'Truly I am.'

She had started to sway. 'You don't look fine,' said Mela sharply. 'You look— *Oh, Grace!*'

Grace's knees had begun to buckle. She clutched at the larder door for support, but her strength failed her and she slumped to the floor, falling onto her side. Mela hurried around the table and bent over her, and saw to her shock that Grace was unconscious.

Mary rushed into the kitchen. 'I heard a noise. What is it? What is wrong?'

'She has fainted,' said Mela. 'Help me get her into the other room.'

Mary was strong for her years, and Grace was so thin that she weighed very little. They carried her into the parlour room and laid her down on Mary and Joe's cot, and the other children gathered around, looking frightened. Even little Edith, standing and clutching Albert's hand for support, was concerned.

'When did she last eat?' Mela asked Mary.

'Two days ago,' said Mary. Her hands were clenched into fists. 'She gives all the food to us. She says we need it more than her, as we are growing.'

Grace's hand was cold and clammy to the touch. 'Why is there no food?' demanded Mela.

'Because there is no money,' said Mary, adding, 'and she won't let me steal.'

Mela reached into her reticule and took out a shilling. 'Run to the market,' she said, 'and fetch me a boiling fowl.'

'Do you know how to cook it?' asked Mary.

'No,' said Mela, who had grown up with servants all her life. 'But I will work it out.'

'I know how to cook,' said Albert.

'Good,' said Mela. 'Go, Mary, as quickly as you can.'

By the time Mary returned, Albert had put a pot of water on the stove. Mary had helped Grace in the kitchen before and knew how to clean and joint the chicken. She did so now, handling the knife with a skill that Mela found both impressive and faintly worrying. Albert fed the stove until the water was boiling hard and they plunged the fowl into the pot and stood for a while, watching it cook.

'We'll make some broth,' Albert said. 'That will be good for Mummy.'

Mary looked at Mela and suddenly planted her hands on her hips. 'You're her friend,' she said.

'I am her closest friend in the whole world,' said Mela.

'Then why?' said the girl fiercely. 'Why have you let her do this to herself? Why would a true friend let her work herself and starve herself? She has pawned her coat and most of her clothes, and she gives us food she should be eating herself. Much more of this and she will be dead. You do know that, don't you?'

Mela stared at her in shock. 'I didn't know,' she said after a moment. 'I have been ill myself, so I could not come. I wrote to her, but . . . she never replied.'

'She ran out of stamps,' said Mary. 'She used the last one to write to your mother, because she was worried you might have consumption. She worries for everyone, all of us, all the time, but no one ever worries for her. She would take care of the world, if she could. But who takes care of her?'

'What do you want me to do?' Mela asked.

'Help her,' said Mary. 'I know she doesn't want help, I know how stubborn she is. But someone has to step in. I would do it myself, if I were older. But someone must help her now.'

Their eyes met. From next door they could hear the baby wailing, and Grace's weak voice calling to her. Mela

Clare reached into her reticule and took out two more coins, gold this time, and laid them on the table.

'Give her the chicken broth when it is ready,' she said. 'Meanwhile, here is money. Buy food and coal and lamp oil, pay the rent, do whatever must be done. This will tide you over until I return.'

'What are you going to do?' Mary asked.

'What I should have done long ago,' Mela said. 'You are right, Mary, I am her friend, and I should have done more to help her, whether she wanted me to or not. I promised her I would say nothing about her situation, and I was wrong. But it is not too late. I will see you all safe and well, if it is the last thing I do.'

That evening, in the library of the comfortable house in Hackney, she told her parents what had happened. Mr Clare shook his head in despair. 'I should have foreseen this,' he said. 'A woman on her own looking after six children was never going to find things easy, but I trusted Grace when she said she did not need help.'

'We all did,' said Mela. 'You must not reproach yourself, Papa. We have offered her help, many times, and her response has always been that she cannot take charity from us.'

'But it would not be charity!' protested Mrs Clare. 'We love her, and want to help her. Can she not see that?'

Mela shook her head. 'She loves you too, Mama, and Papa. But she has this ludicrous notion that she is somehow in debt to us. I don't know how to persuade her otherwise.'

339

Mrs Clare dabbed at her eyes with her handkerchief. 'I am wounded to the quick,' she said. 'How could she even think of herself as a debtor, or us as creditors? Does she not know that we regard her as our own?'

Mr Clare patted his wife's hand. 'She is an honourable young woman,' he said. 'Her aunt, and we, raised her and educated her well. Perhaps too well. She believes so strongly in her duty to others that she does not think of herself.'

Mela remembered Mary's words. *She would take care of the world, if she could.* 'And if we try to help her now, it will be the same,' she said. 'I know her mind. Even weak and ill as she is, she will insist on continuing to teach her school and look after her family – and her neighbours, the poor Doyles – all on her own.'

'What can we do for Grace?' asked Mrs Clare. 'For surely we cannot sit by and do nothing.'

'No,' said Mela. 'But whatever comes to her must not come from us. At least, not directly.'

'What do you suggest?' Mr Clare asked.

'She had a plan,' Mela said. 'She told me about it after the funeral. She wanted to move her school out of the railway arch and find a building to house it. She also wanted to set up a kitchen to feed homeless children, and perhaps even create a dormitory where some of them could live, a combination of school and orphanage. She was much inspired by the plight of this girl Mary and her brother, the ones she adopted. It would also give her own family a rent-free home.'

Mr Clare rubbed his nose. 'And how would she raise the money for the lease?'

'She intended to approach some local merchants to sponsor the venture,' said Mela, 'in exchange for which she would teach the children of their workers.'

'Hmm. An interesting plan,' commented Mr Clare. 'And an ambitious one, too. How typical of our dear Grace, who never does anything by halves . . . Of course she could also have approached us.'

Mela sighed. 'I did suggest it. But she said she wanted to ensure that local men and local firms were involved. As you know, the gangs have been threatening the Ragged Schools, both Grace's school and Mr Ringrose's establishment in Bermondsey. She wanted to use her school as a way of bringing the community together against gangs.'

Mrs Clare had dried her eyes, and now she reverted to her usual practical self. She nodded in approval. 'That is a sound idea,' she said. 'These local merchants. How did they respond to her approach?'

Mela sighed. 'They did not respond at all. She has not heard from them.'

'Do you know who they are?' asked Mrs Clare.

'She mentioned Mr Crompton, of Crompton and Rhodes. And also a timber importer, Mr Gould, who helped her once before.'

Mrs Clare looked at her husband. 'Giles Crompton? You know him well, my dear.'

Mr Clare nodded. 'I saw him only last week, newly returned from Germany, and we discussed this recent unpleasantness between Prussia and France and what effect it might have on trade. He is a nervous man, but at heart a good one.'

'Then you must go and speak to him,' said Mrs Clare firmly. 'And this Mr Gould.'

'But what will I say to them?' asked Mr Clare. 'Angela, we must do more than just put a roof over the heads of Grace and her family. We must find a way to give them some sort of financial security.'

'Of course,' said Mrs Clare. 'And I know how we shall do it. As chance would have it, I saw Lady Ringrose in Town earlier this week. She told me that her nephew is also seeking to expand his school, despite the threat from the gangs. Young Walter's father is a clergyman, and poor as a church mouse; it is Hector who has the money in the family. Walter had approached him for a loan to buy a larger building, just as Grace wishes to do.'

Mela clapped her hands together. 'Yes! I see it! And you want to invite Sir Hector to join forces with Mr Gould and Mr Crompton, and with us too, I hope, and jointly buy a building to house both their schools!'

'Exactly,' said Mrs Clare with satisfaction. 'In the morning, I shall seek out Sir Hector, while you, Wyndham, track down Mr Crompton and Mr Gould.'

'What about me?' asked Mela.

'I have a role for you too, my dear, if you are willing. But it would mean you giving up your role at the Clare School, probably for quite some time. I shall miss your support, but Grace needs you.'

Mela smiled. 'I know how you feel about Grace, Mother. I know how we all feel. If she needs my help, why then I shall walk across hot coals to give it to her. Now, tell me what you intend.'

Chapter 19

A week had passed since Grace's collapse. She had spent most of it in bed, being looked after by Mary and by Brigit Doyle, who came in at least twice a day to make sure all was in order. When she was not there, Mary took charge of the house, with Albert in support. They went together to the market to buy food and came home to prepare meals, and when the landlord's agent called for the weekly rent, Mary paid him. Where she got the money, she would not say, but she promised Grace she had not stolen it, and Grace had to believe her.

Gradually, Grace began to regain her strength and a little colour returned to her cheeks. She began to get up and move around the house and do a few chores, though she still did not feel well enough to resume either her laundry work or teaching. Her mind was cloudy, and she grew dizzy if she stood for too long, but most of all she seemed to have lost her impetus, like a clock that had been allowed to wind down. Outside the spring sun was bright, but nothing could lift the gloom from her spirits. Mary, watching her, asked what was wrong.

They were in the kitchen, the other children were playing in the parlour, out of earshot. 'I think we are about to lose everything,' Grace said quietly. 'The house, the school, everything I have worked for. I thought I could do this on my own, teach and work and support all of you, but I was wrong. And now . . .'

She paused, leaning on the table while another dizzy spell passed. 'Yes, you were wrong,' said Mary with her usual directness. 'One thing I learned on the streets is that you can't do anything on your own. So long as Joe and I were with the Angels, we could survive. But once we were on our own, that's when things got really bad.'

She faced Grace, looking up at her. 'You have to let people help you,' she said. 'That's another thing I learned. And what's more, I learned it from you, too. Now you need to heed your own lesson.'

'But who is going to help us?' Grace asked.

'Wait and see,' said Mary, wondering where Mela Clare was. *I will see you all safe and well, if it is the last thing I do*, she had said, and Mary believed her. But she hoped that whatever Mela was planning, she would be quick about it.

She need not have worried. An hour later there came a knock at the door, and Grace opened it to find Mela standing on the doorstep, smiling brightly. She looked like a ray of sunshine, Grace thought.

'How are you feeling?' Mela asked.

'Better,' said Grace. Her own smile was rather wan and forced. 'Thank you for rescuing me.'

'Do you feel well enough to go out for a while?'

Grace hesitated. 'You won't have to walk far,' Mela promised. 'The coach is waiting for us at the end of the lane. And I have brought you a coat.'

Grace looked at the overcoat Mela held in her hands. 'That is mine,' she said slowly.

'I know. I bought it out of pawn. You can repay me later.'

I don't know how, Grace thought, but she let Mela help her put on the coat. 'Where are you taking me?' she asked.

'It's a surprise,' Mela said smiling. 'Mary, will you look after everyone? I will bring Grace straight back, I promise.'

'Please do,' said Mary severely. 'She still needs her rest.'

'Honestly, there are times when I am not sure who is the mother in this household,' Grace said to Mela as they walked slowly down the lane towards the waiting coach. 'Where we are going?'

'Not far,' said Mela. 'It is just a short ride to Paradise Row.'

Paradise Row was a street of older buildings just off Jamaica Road, a mixture of cottages and larger brick houses. The coach pulled up outside one of these and they stepped out into the sunlight. Mela led the way up the steps and inside, into a large hall with a polished wood floor, and then into a room that might once have been a drawing room.

Grace stopped in the doorway, looking around. The original furniture had been cleared out and now there were rows of school desks and benches, each desk already laid out with slate and chalk. Books stood in a shelf next to the fireplace. She recognised some of the books as her own, from the school under the railway.

Her mind was refusing to work properly. 'What is this?' she asked.

'It is a school,' said Mela proudly. 'Do you like it? Agnes and I spent all day yesterday arranging the place and supervising the workmen. All your furniture has been moved from the railway arch, and we have bought more. There are three other classrooms like this on the ground floor, and upstairs there is an office and a comfortable flat. At the back there is a kitchen, and the workmen are turning the stable block and mews house into a dormitory. It is everything you wanted, I think.'

'I don't understand,' said Grace.

'Perhaps we can explain,' said a voice behind her.

Grace turned slowly. Mr and Mrs Clare stood in the hall, smiling at her. Sir Hector Ringrose was beside them, and Mr Crompton the carpet manufacturer and Mr Gould the timber merchant. With them too was Mr Solomon Raikes from the Ragged Schools Union. They were all smiling too.

'Allow me to introduce the board of trustees of the Paradise Row Charitable School,' said Mr Clare. 'Mr Gould has kindly agreed to serve as chairman.'

Mr Gould bowed. 'And I owe you an apology,' he said. 'My father died recently, and I had to go down to Weymouth for the funeral. Then I was detained sorting out our family affairs, which took much longer than I anticipated. I had intended to contact you once I returned, but unfortunately

I only arrived home a few days ago. Before I could write to you, Mr Clare sought me out and informed me of the proposed project. Needless to say, I was happy to become part of it.'

'And I also,' said Mr Crompton, though Grace thought he still looked worried.

'I still don't understand,' said Grace.

'It is quite simple,' said Mrs Clare. 'We heard that Mr Ringrose was seeking new premises so he could expand his school. From Mela, I knew that you were contemplating a similar project. What could be more natural than to bring them together? We then approached Sir Hector, Mr Crompton and Mr Gould, who also were happy to join forces with us.'

'And I, hearing of the proposal, approached one of the benefactors of the Ragged School Union and explained the situation,' said Mr Raikes. 'I am pleased to say that Baroness Burdett-Coutts has made a substantial donation towards the capital cost of the project, including helping us to acquire the lease on this building and fitting it out as a school. Thanks to her beneficence, we have been able to move quickly.' He nodded towards the others. 'Strictly speaking, this is now no longer a Ragged School, but your aims are so strongly aligned with our own that we are happy to continue our support. Lord Shaftesbury himself has consented to this.'

'As well as a school, the house is also being fitted out to provide meals and accommodation for your homeless pupils,' said Mr Clare. 'And, as mentioned, there is also a flat. You and your family may live there, if you wish to do so.'

The wheels of Grace's mind began to turn, albeit slowly. 'A caretaker will be needed,' she said, 'to make meals and care for the homeless children.'

'Indeed,' said Mr Clare.

'May I ask a favour? My neighbour, Mr Doyle, has been injured in an accident, and can no longer do heavy work. But he and his wife could serve as caretakers. Would you give the flat to them?'

Beside Grace, Mela smiled. 'We rather thought you might say that,' she said.

'I know of Mr Doyle from the docks,' said Mr Gould. 'The trustees would be happy to employ him and his wife. That brings us to you, Mrs Turneur. We know you are still convalescing. When do you think you might be well enough to take up your post?'

'My post?' said Grace blankly.

'Yes,' said Mrs Clare. 'As headmistress of the Paradise Road Charitable School.'

Suddenly Grace felt weak at the knees. 'Do you mean . . . this is all for me?'

'Yes, silly,' said Mela, laughing. 'What did you think?'

Grace did not know what to think. 'I . . . I have to work,' she said, thinking of the laundry.

'You will be working,' Mrs Clare assured her. 'We have made one small modification to your earlier plan. You will still teach the children of our employees, Mr Crompton's and Mr Gould's and several other firms we have recruited to the scheme, but you will not do so for free. For each pupil, the companies will pay a small fee to the school in exchange for lessons, which will be free of charge to the children and their parents. This fee will enable you to pay a salary to both your caretakers and yourself. The board of trustees has proposed that your salary be set at £100 per annum, to be reviewed and increased as the school grows.'

Mr Clare smiled. 'As, under your guidance, it most assuredly will.'

One hundred pounds a year was nearly twice what George had earned as a bricklayer. 'Oh, my stars,' said Grace faintly.

'Do you accept?' asked Mr Gould.

Suddenly the mists in her head began to clear. 'I accept,' said Grace. 'How could I possibly refuse?'

'Excellent,' said Sir Hector Ringrose. 'And now, perhaps you would like to meet your teaching staff.'

A door opened and three more people came into the hall. Walter Ringrose, young and handsome, smiling and bowing. Agnes Korngold, beaming. And Mrs Lane, her normally severe face lit up with a smile. 'I don't have much education,' she said. 'But I know enough to teach reading and sums to the little ones, and I'll pick up more as I go along. If you'll have me, Mrs Turneur.'

'Gladly,' said Grace, fighting down a rush of emotion.

'And I certainly hope you'll keep me on,' said Mr Ringrose, smiling.

'Of course,' said Grace. She had vowed once to avoid his company, to never see him again, but somehow none of that seemed to matter now. They were all entering a new world.

'The Clare School have allowed me to take an indefinite leave of absence, to serve you,' said Agnes.

'And me likewise,' said Mela, moving over to join them and then turning to face Grace. 'I said I wanted some adventure. I think I have found it.'

A little silence fell. Everyone stood looking at Grace. She gazed around the hall, into the immaculate classroom where sunlight poured through tall windows, and then back at these wonderful people who had just given her the chance to make her dreams become real.

'I don't know what to say,' she said. 'Thank you seems so . . . inadequate.'

'No need to thank us,' said Mr Gould. 'Just do a cracking good job, and make us all proud. That's thanks enough.'

The others took their leave, Mr Clare departing last of all. Grace hurried after him, putting an arm on the sleeve of his coat as he reached the door. 'Sir,' she said, 'I know I have you and Mrs Clare to thank for this. I had promised myself I would not trespass on your charity anymore than I already have. But now that it has come to this . . . I am glad.'

'So am I,' said Mr Clare gently. 'Grace, my child, there must never be any talk of charity between us. What Mrs Clare and I and Mela did, we did for love. Do you not realise how deeply we care for you? You are one of our own, and you always will be. We are not your benefactors, my dear,' he said gently. 'We are your family.'

Chapter 20

Spring turned into summer, gloriously warm with the sun shining nearly every day, although the smoke of the factories and mills still hung heavy over the city. Grace walked the short distance to work each morning with her little brood surrounding her, Edith toddling and clasping her hand and Radcliffe trotting behind them, her nostrils full of the thick air. *This cannot be good for the children's lungs,* thought Grace. *It cannot be good for any of us.*

The streets were busier than ever, crowded with heavy wagons, and she kept the children close beside her while they walked. But Paradise Row was quieter, the sound of the main thoroughfares only a distant murmur. The masts of ships moored at the wharves along the river rose over the rooftops. Grace opened the door of the school and went inside, followed by the children. Some pupils had already arrived, and more were coming in, ragged waifs from the streets mixed with the tidily if plainly dressed children of factory workers and dock hands. The smell of porridge drifted through from the kitchen, where Mrs Doyle was feeding the homeless ones. The children greeted her, their voices reminding her of a flock of birds. She smiled at them, glowing with pure happiness.

Two months had passed since the school opened its doors, and all was going well. They had five classes now, running six hours a day, ranging from Mrs Lane working with the very smallest and teaching basic reading and arithmetic, up to Mr Ringrose and Mela taking the more advanced classes and teaching them mathematics and music. Grace and Agnes took the intermediate classes, with Grace reserving to herself those who struggled hardest to learn. This group still included Lettice the match girl and Nathan the beggar boy although, with proper accommodation and food, both were beginning to grow both physically and mentally; no longer did they struggle with their lessons thanks to pure exhaustion. They had a hundred and sixty pupils now, and every week a few more came to enrol.

She sent her own children away to their classes, and then met as she did every morning with her staff, including Mr and Mrs Doyle. Despite his impairment, Mickey had proved to be an excellent caretaker, tending to the fabric of the building and doing running repairs while his wife looked after the kitchen and the children in the dormitory.

'All is well?' Grace asked.

'Nothing to report,' said Mickey cheerfully. He looked out the window. ''Tis a fine day out. Reminds me of summer days back home in Galway. Only, perhaps rather more smoky.'

Grace smiled. 'You have seen nothing suspicious? No one hanging about in the street?'

She asked this question every morning. 'No one at all,' said Mickey. 'Are you still worried about the gang, Grace?'

'I am,' she said. 'They are the one shadow on my present happiness.'

'I reckon we've seen the last of them,' said Mr Ringrose confidently. 'They know how big the school is now, and how the communities are behind us, Bermondsey and Rotherhithe both. They won't touch us now.'

Grace shook her head. 'Our success has been wonderful to see,' she said, 'and you have all played such a great part in making our dreams come true. But that same success also makes us more visible; and indeed, more of a threat to the Bull Head Gang. The Captain may tolerate us for the moment, but he will not do so forever. We must all be watchful.'

They nodded, sober for the moment, but nothing could dent their good mood for long. Mr Ringrose was whistling when he went off to take his class. Agnes Korngold looked ten years younger, and Hermione – as Mrs Lane now insisted Grace call her – had changed character almost out of recognition. The old stiff, severe poise had gone. The other day she had even made a joke.

Mrs Doyle took charge of Edith. She had offered her services as baby-sitter during the day, and Grace had gratefully accepted. Almost overnight, Edith had gone from being a clumsy toddler to a creature rather like a cross between a rabbit and an eel, capable of remarkable speed and able to wriggle out of just about any restraint placed on her. Fortunately Edith liked Mrs Doyle, whom Grace suspected spoiled her rotten. Smiling, Grace went up to her office and collected her papers, and then came downstairs to her own classroom in the old drawing room. Thirty children sat on benches, hands clasped solemnly in front of them on their desks, looking at her with bright expectant eyes. Joe was one of them. 'Good morning, children,' she said, smiling again.

'Good morning, Mrs Turneur!' they chorused.

'It is indeed a very good morning,' Grace said. 'Now, today we shall attempt our multiplication tables. Let's see who has managed to learn them. Nathan, you shall go first.'

She had said the gang was the one thing disturbing her happiness, but that was not quite true. The other source of disquiet, buried deep for the moment but threatening to bubble to the surface, was her feelings for Walter Ringrose.

That she *had* feelings for him was something she could no longer deny to herself. Just being in the same room with him made her feel warm and brought a faint blush to her cheeks. Being alone with him – something she tried very hard not to do – was even worse. Her heart began to beat more quickly. She became tongue-tied and could no longer remember what she wanted to stay. She reminded herself of him when they first met. She became aware of physical longing. She wanted to touch his hand or his cheek, to know what his skin felt like. He used Pear's soap, and she could smell his scent so clearly that she knew he had entered a room even before she saw him, or heard his clear, melodious voice.

Get hold of yourself, she told herself sharply. *You're a widow, still technically in mourning. You are the mother, to all intents and purposes, of six children, and you are a busy schoolmistress. There is no time or place in your life for a man, and especially not that man. His uncle is a knight, and you are the illegitimate daughter of a seamstress. Stop these foolish dreams and fantasies and get on with your work.*

But the dreams and fantasies refused to stop, and she did not know how to make them disappear.

Away from the school, life at Bell Lane continued as usual. The house was still far too small for all of them, but Grace was glad she had not moved to the school; apart from the fact that the Doyles needed a place to live, she was still reluctant to uproot the twins in particular from the only home they had ever known. But they were growing fast now, as was little Joe, and Albert was bidding fair to become a big strong lad.

Mary was growing too. She was about thirteen now, and her temper had changed completely. The tantrums and anger had gone; she worked hard, and Mr Ringrose reported that she and Rebecca Berton were his star pupils. At home, she was Grace's faithful lieutenant, helping her to keep the crowded household running and get the youngest children fed and dressed each morning. She and Albert put dinner on the table in the evening. As time passed, Grace found herself depending on Mary more and more.

Going to the school one day, Grace found Mr Ringrose reading a newspaper. Usually he was unfailingly positive, but today his mood was sombre. 'What is wrong?' she asked. 'Has something happened?'

'Yes, in a manner of speaking.' He looked up from the newspaper. 'Mr Charles Dickens has died,' he said quietly.

'Oh!' Grace gazed at the newspaper, lips parted in astonishment. 'I did not know he was ill,' she said.

Mr Ringrose nodded. 'He had a stroke last month, apparently, and has not been well since. He was a great man. A fine writer, of course, one of the very best, but I admired him most of all for his campaigns against poverty and in support of education. He was our great ally and supporter, and we shall miss him.'

'I read *A Christmas Carol* to the children every year,' said Grace. 'You are right, it is a terrible loss.'

Mr Ringrose smiled a little. 'It was his letter describing his visit to the Ragged School in Field Lane that first determined me to be a teacher, and to work with poor children if I could. He was one of two people who have inspired me. Come to that, they still continue to inspire me to this day, and probably always will.'

'Who is the other?' Grace asked.

Mr Ringrose's mouth opened, but no sound came out. He closed it again, looking down at his hands. 'Sorry,' he said. 'I'm blethering, as usual. I should probably go and prepare for class.'

'No, please,' said Grace. 'Will you not tell me who the other is? Perhaps I too share your admiration for this person.'

Mr Ringrose smiled suddenly. 'I doubt it,' he said. 'You're not that sort, thank God. Modesty is just one of your many virtues.'

'I don't understand,' said Grace.

Mr Ringrose looked at her. Their eyes met. 'The other person is you,' he said.

Quite a long time passed before Grace regained the power of speech. Even then, to her embarrassment, her voice came out as a kind of strangled croak. 'Me?' she said.

'You,' said Mr Ringrose. 'When I heard from the Clares what you were doing in Rotherhithe, I was full of admiration. To start a school under a railway arch in one of the toughest and most lawless districts of London, to start from nothing and face down the gangs and build it up until it became one of the most successful schools in the entire Ragged School Union . . . Well, I came down to Bermondsey and started my school because I wanted to emulate you. And I still do. You're my lodestar, Mrs Turneur. What I am as a teacher, what I have become, is all down to your example.'

Before Grace could think of anything to say, Agnes Korngold entered the room, looking from one face to the other. 'Forgive me,' she said. 'Am I intruding?'

'Not at all,' said Grace hastily. 'We were just talking about poor Mr Dickens. It is so sad that he has died.'

'Indeed, his death is a great loss to literature,' Agnes said gravely. She looked at them both again. 'But it is another fine day, no?'

'How long do you think it will take?' Agnes asked Mela Clare later that day.

Mela giggled. 'I have no idea. I was wondering whether to start a sweepstake.'

Agnes shook her head. 'To use one of your English sayings, it is plain as the nose on your face what is happening. Why can they not see what the rest of us can see? Even some of the children know.'

Mela laughed again. 'Walter Ringrose is an old-fashioned gentleman. He won't want to put himself forward. He also idolises Grace, which is why he is often diffident around her. And I love Grace dearly, but she is so dedicated to her duty that she never thinks of herself. It could be years before they come to their senses.'

Agnes looked at Mela. 'You are her friend. Do you think it will be a good match?'

'Honestly, I think they were made for each other. He's brave and handsome, but he wants a good woman to manage him, and Grace will do that better than anyone I know. And she needs someone who will cherish her. She needs love.'

Mela paused. 'Also, while he is not exactly well off, he does have a little money, enough for them to move to a better home. I understand why Grace is reluctant to leave Bell Lane, but they are living on top of each other in that damp little house. The children need light and air. Come to that, so does Grace herself. So, yes, I think it is an excellent match. I just wish they would get on with it.'

Agnes smiled. 'And you? Is there no young man on the horizon for you? No future husband waiting to sweep you off your feet?'

'I have promised myself I will never marry,' said Mela. 'I shall devote my entire life to education.'

'Then you are foolish,' said Agnes with her usual bluntness. 'Your friend has shown the way. One can devote oneself to a cause and still be happy. Let me give you a word of advice, Miss Clare. Never say never. You do not know what is waiting around the corner for you.'

And so they carried on, Grace happy in her new role as headmistress and the others, teachers and pupils alike, following her like the wake of a comet. The local trustees, Mr Crompton and Mr Gould, called in every so often to see that all was well, and once a month Mr and Mrs Clare took the East London Railway through the tunnel under the river and called in too, admiring the school and the progress Grace had made. 'I hope I have justified your faith in me,' Grace said during one visit in late June.

'Our expectations of you were high,' said Mrs Clare, kissing her cheek. 'And you have exceeded them. You are an inspiration to our entire movement, Grace. Everyone is talking about you. Lord Shaftesbury mentioned you and the Paradise Row school in a speech just the other day.'

'He did?' said Grace, feeling once again at a loss for words.

Another frequent caller was Reverend Soames, the kindly white-bearded rector of Bermondsey. As chance would have it he called in at the school just after the Clares departed. Grace was in her office packing up for the day, Mary and the other children waiting for her downstairs.

'I have some news for you,' he said. 'I have been offered a new parish, at Orpington out in the country. I shall be departing soon.'

'I shall be sorry to see you go, Reverend,' Grace said. 'You have been a good friend to us.'

The rector smiled. 'Do not fear, my child, I shall not be a stranger. Orpington is only a dozen miles away. It is a poor parish, or rather, there are many poor people in it. Many of my new flock are agricultural labourers and there is a large population of Romanies. I want to start a free school to educate their children, and I shall want your advice on how to do so. Would you be free to travel down to Orpington from time to time and assist me?'

'I should be honoured,' said Grace. 'Reverend, I will do anything I can to help you.'

After the rector left, Grace stood for a moment, looking out the window at the street bathed in afternoon light. *Goodness*, she thought. *It is all a long way from that little handful of children I used to teach in Bell Lane, or the railway arch with Mary and the Angels curled up around the stove.* How proud George and Rosa would have been to see all this.

It was nearly three years since Rosa had died, and eight months since George had followed her. She still thought of them every day, but her grief was no longer sharp. They were here; she could see them in the children's eyes and smiles. Most of all their spirits were always with her, like familiar, friendly ghosts. Mr Dickens was right, she thought. There are invisible presences that remind us of what has gone before, and what is now, and what will be.

She gathered her papers and walked downstairs to greet the children. Edith was squirming, trying to get away from Mary's controlling hand, and Grace scooped her up. 'My, but you are beginning to be a weight,' she told the baby. 'You are going to be a big strong lass when you are grown.'

'Perhaps she will be an Amazon,' said Albert, who had started reading Greek myths.

They walked home and Grace made Edith some porridge and fed her and put her to sleep while Mary started preparations for dinner. Grace joined her in the kitchen a few minutes later. They worked together happily, hearing Harry singing in the parlour room, attempting to teach Daisy and Joe a song he had just invented. This was rather difficult, as the words made no sense, and Daisy quickly grew distracted and came wandering into the kitchen.

'Second Mummy,' she said to Grace, 'may I have a biscuit?'

'Of course, my dear.' Grace opened the Huntley & Palmer's tin and handed Daisy a ginger biscuit. *What bliss it is,* she thought, *to be able to feed them without worrying about every penny, and to have little luxuries like biscuits . . .*

Someone knocked hard at the door. Grace heard Albert answer it, and then Brigit Doyle's voice outside. She sounded alarmed and worried. Wiping her hands on her apron, Grace hurried through to the parlour.

'Brigit? What is it?'

'Oh, Grace, I don't know what to do! I sent Billy to the market to buy cabbage for dinner, and he hasn't come home! It's not like him to go off. Holy Mother, what can have happened to him?'

Leaving the children with Mary, Grace hurried to the market, Brigit quivering with anxiety beside her. They talked to every trader in the street, but no one had seen Billy Doyle.

'Perhaps he lost his way,' Grace said finally. She knew this was unlikely. Billy had been born in Rotherhithe and knew its streets well. 'Let's go back to the school. Perhaps he has made his way back there, and the alarm is all for nothing.'

But as they started to walk towards Paradise Row, an anxious looking woman in a faded blouse and skirt and tattered bonnet came up to them. 'You're Brigit Doyle, ain't you?' she said. 'I seen your son. I don't know his name, but I seen him around with you.'

'You saw him?' gasped Brigit. 'Where? When?'

'About an hour ago. Oh, missus, I wish I had better news for you, truly I do. There was four men, big fellows, and they took your boy off the street and put him in a wagon and drove it away.'

'Holy Mary!' wailed Brigit. 'Oh, my Billy! Oh, Jesus, Mary and Joseph bring him back to me, I beg you!' She was ready to collapse, and Grace put a steadying arm around her. 'These men,' she said to the woman. 'Who were they? Did you get a look at them?'

'I seen them,' the woman said. 'And I know who they are, too. Missus, them what took your son, they're in the Bull Head Gang.'

You will allow me my tithe of the boys, the Captain had said. And now, he had come to collect.

She took Brigit back to the school, and broke the news to Mickey, and saw the look of desperation on his face. 'This blasted leg of mine. I tell you, Grace, if wasn't for that I'd be out there looking for these fellows right now.'

'And getting yourself killed,' said Grace. 'Stay with Brigit, Mickey. I will find Billy and bring him back to you.'

How she was going to do this, she did not quite know. There was little point in going to the police. She hurried instead to Bermondsey, where Walter Ringrose still lived. He could have gone back to his aunt and uncle in north London, but he said he had grown used to Bermondsey, and would miss his friends at the King's Arms.

He answered the door when she knocked, and stood looking at her in wide-eyed surprise. 'Mrs T-Turneur,' he stammered. 'Wha-what a surprise. Do come in.'

'I am sorry to intrude, Mr Ringrose,' she said quickly, 'but we have an emergency. Billy Doyle has been kidnapped by the Bull Head Gang. Do you think you might talk to your friends, and find out where they could have taken him?'

Instantly he was alert, the stammer gone. 'Of course,' he said. 'I'll fetch my coat.'

'I'll come with you,' Grace said.

Mr Ringrose shook his head. 'The King's Arms is no place for a lady.'

'I'm not a lady,' Grace said.

They looked at each other. 'You are in my eyes,' Mr Ringrose said quietly. 'Mrs Turneur, I suggest you go home. Your family needs you. I will find out where Billy is, but I might need to go to some rather dark and unpleasant places. Meet me at the school in the morning, and I will tell you what I have learned.'

She did as he asked. There was no mistaking the brisk authority in his voice. In the morning they met at the school as usual while the pupils came streaming in off the streets. The Doyles were pale, Brigit still looking like she was about to faint. Mela, Agnes and Mrs Lane were quiet and tense. Walter Ringrose came in last of all, his eyes lined with red like he had not had much sleep.

'My friends managed to trace the Bull Heads,' he said. 'They took Billy to Jacob's Island, the thieves' haunt in Bermondsey.'

Brigit let out a wail of fear. 'We went up and had a look,' Mr Ringrose went on. 'We thought we might be able to slip in, but there's no chance. The place is surrounded by a stinking ditch full of water and heaven knows what else.

There's only one bridge across it and plenty of mean look-ing fellows guarding it. All of 'em loyal to the Captain, no doubt. And even if we did get across the bridge without being spotted, the place is a warren. We could look forever and never find Billy.'

'So what do we do?' asked Grace.

'If I were you, ma'am, I would send the children home for the day, and ask their parents to keep them indoors and under close watch, especially the boys. You do the same with yours. I reckon Albert is old enough to be a target. Meanwhile, I'm going to start a fire.'

'What do you mean?'

'I'm going to organise a demonstration,' said Mr Ringrose. 'I'll raise every man I can, and we'll march through the streets as a show of force. My friends are already out there spreading the word. We'll show the Bull Heads that they will have to fight us all. If they start stealing our children, we'll come after them. For the moment, this will be a peaceful protest. But if Billy Doyle isn't released unharmed, why then, we'll storm Jacob's Island and every other Bull Head haunt until we find him. And woe betide any beggars who try to stop us.'

She wanted to stop him, to beg him to hold back from such a dangerous path. Instead she said, 'Mary can look after the children. I am coming with you.'

'As am I,' said Hermione Lane, and there was iron in her voice. 'The streets of Rotherhithe are fouled by these Bull Head filth. It's time we cleaned them out, and made our homes safe. I'll bring every wife and mother in Rotherhithe, and set them marching alongside you. Give me two hours, and I promise you we'll be there.'

Grace looked at Mela and Agnes. 'Try and stop us,' said Mela, her fair face pale but determined.

'Then let's go,' said Grace.

She knew Walter was determined and vigorous, and she knew too by now that Hermione Lane had a will of steel, but all the same she was still amazed by what happened next.

From the docks came the deal porters, big men with heavy leather caps around their heads armed with baulks of timber. From the construction sites came the bricklayers, walking off the job without a word to their foremen, and quite often the foremen downed tools and followed them. From the carpet factory came the weavers and mechanics, Mr Crompton looking nervous as usual but marching with determination at their head and brandishing a walking stick. From the engine works and vitriol factory and all the other mills came more workmen, and pouring out of the houses in a steady stream came the women of Rotherhithe, some still in their aprons, carrying pots and pans and beating on these with spoons, setting up a clangorous timpani that echoed off the walls of the buildings. A sea of humanity flowed down Jamaica Road and then down Lower Road towards the police station and magistrates' court, singing and chanting

'This is magnificent!' Mela called over the din. She and Grace were marching near the head of the procession, following their leaders, Mr Ringrose and Mrs Lane. 'I wasn't expecting half this many people!'

'Neither was I,' said Grace. 'But I think Hermione is right. People have had enough. Billy's kidnapping was the tipping point.'

'And Mr Ringrose was right, too,' Mela said. 'We're going to take on the Bull Heads, and we're going to win!'

It won't be that easy, Grace thought. *And if we don't get Billy back, this will all be for nothing.* But she could not help but share Mela's excitement.

On Lower Road the police station was shuttered and silent. Of the police themselves there was no sign. The procession stopped outside the magistrates' court, singing and chanting still, the hammer of pots and pans roaring like a drum beat. Walter Ringrose stood on the top step of the courthouse, holding up his cricket bat and waving his arms for silence, and the crowd quietened a little.

'My friends!' he shouted. 'People of Rotherhithe and Bermondsey, this is our moment!'

'Yes!' they roared back at him, and the pots clanged and clattered. Mr Ringrose waved his arms again.

'This is our moment!' he repeated. 'This is the hour when we stand up to the Bull Head Gang, and their corrupt accomplices in the police! This is the moment when we say: *enough is enough*! We will no longer tolerate your bullying and violence! We will no longer pay your protection money! We will no longer hide in our houses or walk our own streets in fear of you, and above all, we will no longer tolerate you stealing our children! You are finished!'

Again the crowd roared. *I don't care*, Grace thought. *I don't care if my cheeks are flushed, I don't care if my eyes are shining, and above all, I don't care who sees me and guesses the truth. He is wonderful. There; I have said it, and I will say it again. He is wonderful, and I love him.*

'Captain!' Mr Ringrose shouted. 'I know you are listening, or that you have listeners amongst us. Here is my message to you. You have until midnight to release Billy Doyle unharmed, and clear off out of this district. If you do, you will come to no harm. If you fail; if by morning Billy is still held captive and your men are still on our streets, we will come for you! Fear our vengeance, Captain! For you may be strong, but we are stronger! You have scores of men, but we have *thousands*! And we are coming for you!'

The roar that went up shook the skies. Grace clasped her hands to her breasts and found there were sudden tears on her cheeks. 'Oh, my,' she said. 'Oh, my stars.'

'Are you all right?' asked Mela.

'I have never been better,' Grace said, smiling through her tears.

She was still shaking with emotion when the crowd began to disperse, returning to their work and their homes. Walter walked up to Grace, Mela and Mrs Lane, removing his hat and wiping perspiration from his forehead. The invisible finger played a dance up and down Grace's spine, and she resisted the temptation to throw her arms around him and kiss him. 'That was splendid,' she said instead.

'We have sent our message,' Mr Ringrose said. He looked flushed and triumphant. 'The Captain will hear soon enough what has happened. Now we wait for him to make his move.'

Back at Bell Lane, Grace found the younger children playing happily, supervised by Mary and Albert. 'What happened?' Mary asked. 'We heard the noise.'

'Mr Ringrose has challenged the Captain,' Grace said. 'Release Billy, or face the consequences.'

'That is dangerous,' said Mary. 'It could be especially dangerous for Mr Ringrose.'

'But he is a brave man,' Grace said happily. 'The others have gone back to the school to wait, to see if the Captain will release Billy, and I should join them. Can you look after everyone here? Be sure to lock the door.'

'Of course,' said Mary. 'Good luck, Grace. I hope you find him.'

'Billy will come home,' Albert predicted. They were close friends. 'He is clever. He will find a way.'

Back at the school Grace joined Mela, Agnes, Hermione, Walter and Mickey. Brigit was in bed. Mickey had given her a sleeping draught, one of the medicines he used when his leg pained him.

A knock at the door a few minutes later made them all jump. Grace opened the door to see Mr Crompton, still with his walking stick, and Mr Gould with what looked like a revolver tucked into his coat pocket. 'We thought we should be here,' the timber merchant said with a slight smile. 'After all, we have an investment in this place.'

'You are very welcome, gentlemen,' Grace said.

They sat quietly, waiting, and once or twice Grace closed her eyes and uttered a silent prayer of hope. Walter prowled around the school with cricket bat in hand, restless and fidgety. Agnes was motionless, staring into space, and Grace suspected she was reliving memories of the Cossacks riding into Zitomir. Mr Crompton took a book from the library and read patiently, showing more fortitude than Grace would have expected. Mela sat at a table and played patience with an old deck of cards.

The day wore on. Afternoon turned to evening, the sun sinking into a dull red haze of smoke in the west. Someone knocked hard at the door, and they all jumped. Heart in her mouth, Grace hurried to unlock it, Walter at her elbow. She opened the door to find a small boy standing on the step. His clothes were wet and torn and stank repulsively, and there was a bruise on his face, but it was unmistakeably Billy Doyle.

'Billy!' she cried. 'Oh, come in, child, come in!' She pulled the boy quickly inside and slammed the door and locked it. From the classroom where they had been sitting came Mickey's voice.

'Billy? Son, is that you?'

'Dad!' screamed Billy, and he hurtled into the room. Grace followed to find Mickey, tears streaming down his face, clutching his son to his chest and hugging him tightly. 'Oh, son! Where have you been?'

After a time Billy calmed enough to tell his story. 'They put me in a wagon, Dad. There were four of them, and I couldn't fight them off. They told me because I had been bad, they would put me in a pit. Then they made me go into this deep hole with water and rats and all, and closed the top so I couldn't get out. I was really scared, Dad, but after a while I realised the ground was soft and I had some coins in my pocket, the ones Ma gave me to buy cabbages. And I found the ground was soft around the top of the pit, and I used one of the coins to dig a hole under the cover so I could crawl out, and there wasn't nobody around cuz they thought I couldn't get out of the pit, and I ran straight here and now I'm home.'

Mickey calmed him and took him upstairs to be reunited with his mother, and they all heard Brigit's heart-rending cry of joy and the screams of the younger children when they saw their brother. 'Well,' said Mr Gould thoughtfully. 'That puts a different complexion on things.'

'It does,' said Mr Ringrose. 'When the gang finds out Billy has escaped, they'll come looking for him. And the first place they will come is here.'

'Then we need to get the Doyle family to safety,' said Mr Crompton. 'If the Captain's men can't find Billy, they may well attack others in the family.' He rose to his feet. 'Advise them to pack, if you will, and I shall fetch my coach to carry them away. They can stay at my house for the moment, though I feel they would be safest if they left the district altogether. The Captain has a long arm.'

'I will organise some men to protect the school building,' said Mr Gould.

'I'll help you,' said Walter. 'My friends from the King's Arms will come and join us. They're stout fellows.'

'What should we do?' asked Grace.

'I should go home if I were you,' said Mr Gould. 'I'm sorry, ladies, but I'm afraid this is one of those situations where brawn is required, not brain. There will be a confrontation, of that there is little doubt. I don't think the Captain will give in easily. And I think it best that you are safely out of the way when trouble comes. Mr Ringrose, I think we should send some of our men to protect Mrs Turneur's home, too.'

Agnes and Hermione departed. Mela looked at Grace. 'I don't want to go home,' she said. 'May I stay with you?'

'I'm sure it won't come to that,' said Grace smiling. 'And yes, you are welcome. I would be glad of the company while we await . . . events.'

'May I call on you later?' Mr Ringrose asked Grace. 'I'll come back and spend the night here, but I'd like to discuss tactics for tomorrow, if I may. We'll need to organise another demonstration, I think.' Grace nodded, her heart suddenly pounding again.

They walked home together through the ruddy light. The streets, usually so busy, were nearly empty, and the usual knots of men standing outside the public houses were absent too. The air was full of foreboding, and Grace was reminded of the calm before a thunderstorm. At Bell Lane, Mary was waiting for them, her face tense. She could feel the atmosphere too.

Briefly, Grace told her about Billy's escape. 'We don't know what the Captain will do next,' she said.

'It will be vicious,' said Mary, 'and it will be something you do not expect. That much I know for certain.'

On the heels of her words came a hard knock at the door. Instinctively, Mary pulled a knife from the block and stood waiting. 'It is all right,' Grace reassured her. 'Mr Gould promised to send men to protect the house. This will be them.' She moved to the door and laid her hand on the latch. 'Who is it?' she called

'It is me,' said a man's voice. 'Open the door.'

The shock was so great that Grace's knees went weak. She knew that voice, knew it very well, it had haunted her nightmares for a long time. The man standing in the street outside her front door was the Captain.

'What do you want?' she asked. Mela and Mary had come through to the parlour and were staring at her.

'I want to talk to you,' the Captain said. 'I am alone, and I will not hurt you. You have my word on that. Now, open the door.'

'No!' whispered Mela, but Grace shook her head. 'I must,' she said.

Shaking like a leaf, she opened the door. The Captain stood in the falling twilight, dressed much as he had been when she last saw him, in long coat despite the evening heat and with the same broad-brimmed hat pulled down over his face. The diamond ring on his finger sparkled a little.

She stepped out into the street and closed the door behind her. The protection Mr Gould had promised had not yet arrived, and she faced the Captain alone. She crossed her arms over her chest in a gesture of bravado that she did not really feel. 'What do you want?' she asked again.

'You know perfectly well what I want,' he said. 'I want Billy Doyle.'

'You can't have him,' Grace said.

The Captain sighed. 'I have had a long and trying day,' he said. 'First your friends organising that ridiculous demonstration and trying to set the district against me, and then that wretched child escaping. In due course, I shall give your friends a little demonstration of my own, a lesson in what happens to those who defy me, but meanwhile, I want the boy. Where is he?'

'We sent him away,' Grace said, praying that Mr Crompton had acted swiftly. 'Billy and his family are on their way to another part of the city.'

The Captain clicked his tongue. 'I saw a coach leave the school, so I suppose that was them being spirited away. It won't save him, Grace. I want him, and I mean to have him. Remember our bargain.'

'I made no bargain with you,' Grace said. 'You imposed your terms on me, but I did not accept them. And I will never accept your right to kidnap children. You can burn my school, or at least you can try; I promise you it is well defended. But even if you do succeed, I will simply rebuild it again. My school will rise from the ashes, stronger than before.'

The Captain's lips curled in a smile. 'I very much doubt that,' he said. 'I am about to whip Rotherhithe and Bermondsey like I might whip a dog, and when I am done the people will come crawling to me, begging for forgiveness. No one will support your school after this. And, I demand my tithe. I want Billy. And for good measure to punish *you* for defying me, I want more. I want Albert and Harry, and that little street boy called Joe.'

A wave of dark horror washed over Grace. 'No!' she gasped. 'Never!'

'I will not bandy words with you,' the Captain said. 'Give me the children or you will suffer as you have never suffered before. You have until this time tomorrow to make up your mind.'

He turned on his heel and walked away into the gathering dusk. Sick with dread, Grace opened the door and stumbled inside, sinking to her knees. Mary and Mela were with her at once, the other children crowding around in concern. 'What is it?' Mela asked.

'Albert,' said Grace, 'take the younger ones upstairs. Take Edith too. Keep them there, and keep them away from the windows. Do it, my dear. I'll explain why later.'

When the children had gone, Grace rose to her feet and, still fighting down a wave of nausea, told Mela and Mary what had happened. 'What are we going to do?' she asked.

'The man is an utter monster,' Mela whispered.

'He shall not have the boys,' Mary said fiercely. 'I'll stab him first.'

'No one is going to stab anyone,' said Grace, recovering a little. 'Oh, God, where are the men Mr Gould promised ... What is that noise?'

From further down the street came the sound of a man's voice upraised, then suddenly choked off. Another wave of fear washed over Grace, for she had recognised the voice. She looked around wildly for a moment, then picked up one of the oil lamps and ran towards the door.

'No!' cried Mela. 'Grace, it isn't safe!'

Grace paid her no heed. Throwing open the door, she held up the lamp and saw something that looked like a bundle, lying near the entrance to the lane. Others had heard the noise too, and more doors were opening. She saw Elijah Berton with a lamp in one hand and a hammer in the other. Ignoring them, she ran down the street and knelt beside the bundle, holding up her own lamp to see.

Walter Ringrose lay on his side in the street, blood streaming from a wound to his head and more seeping out of a hole in the back of his coat where he had been stabbed. His eyes were closed, and he was not moving.

Chapter 21

Numb with shock, she knelt beside Walter's body and took his hand, her fingers pressed against his wrist. There was no pulse. *No!* a voice inside her screamed, *he cannot be dead, he cannot be!* Panicked, she pressed again, and this time she found it, a faint, irregular beat. Walter was still alive; but only just.

Elijah knelt beside her, and others of their neighbours crowded around. 'He is badly hurt,' said Elijah.

'I know,' Grace said. 'Please, help me get him inside. And send for a doctor.'

A boy went running to find the doctor. Some of the men brought a makeshift litter, a sheet of canvas stretched between two poles, and laid Walter gently in it and carried him into Grace's house. Mela, her face white with shock, helped them lay him on the cot in the parlour room. Louisa Berton, who as a millworker's wife was used to tending injuries, came to join them and showed Grace how to cut away Walter's clothing so the wound in his back was exposed. The stab wound was oozing blood, but Louisa pressed a wad of cloth against it and gradually the bleeding slowed. The head wound they left alone. It was important, Louisa said, to wait for the doctor. Grace knelt beside the stretcher, one hand on Walter's wrist, feeling the faint pulse like the ticking of a clock as the unconscious man fought to stay alive. Mela sat beside her, her arms around Grace, silently lending her friend her strength.

The doctor arrived an hour later, not long after the men sent by Mr Gould to guard the house finally showed up. The doctor knelt beside the cot, his face grave as he examined the wounds. 'In one respect, Mr Ringrose has been very fortunate,' he said finally. 'The knife was meant for his heart, but it was deflected by one of his ribs. The wound is not serious, and provided it does not become infected, it will heal. The head is another matter.'

'Tell me, please,' Grace said quietly. 'I must know.'

'He was hit with a very heavy object, perhaps a hammer or something similar. The skull is fractured.'

Grace gasped. 'That in itself is not necessarily serious,' the doctor said, hastening to reassure her. 'The fracture is a simple one, and will heal with time. The problem is that we do not know what has happened below the surface, whether there is bleeding on the brain.'

He stood up, wiping his hands and reaching into his bag. 'I shall bandage the knife wound. You will need to change the bandage at intervals, and watch for any sign of infection. Keep the head wound clean, but touch it only very gently, so you do not disturb his head. Then, wait. If he regains consciousness soon, within a few hours, then he should make a good recovery. If not . . .'

'If not, then what?' Grace asked.

'Then I fear the worst,' the doctor said finally. 'Indeed, we must face the possibility that, if the bleeding is too severe or there is other damage to the brain, he might not wake at all.'

He might die. Grace felt tears welling behind her eyes. Mela hugged her tightly, her own eyes damp. 'Is it safe to move him?' Grace asked. 'I would like to at least put him to bed.' The parlour room was damp, he would be healthier upstairs where the air was cleaner.

The doctor shook his head. 'Moving him now could increase any bleeding on his brain. Leave him still. If he recovers consciousness and his mind does not seem too disordered, then you may move him, but not until then.'

After the doctor departed, Grace sat beside Walter, holding his hand. *Walter*, she thought. *That is how I think of him now, not as Mr Ringrose.* Mela hugged her again. 'Is there anything we can do?'

'No,' said Grace. 'You heard the doctor. There is nothing to do but wait.'

'I will stay with you,' said Mela.

'You mustn't. The hour is late. You must get some rest. I will look after him.'

'I'm not leaving you,' Mela said quietly.

Mary came in from the kitchen and looked down at the body, her young face still. 'Will he live?' she asked.

'I don't know,' said Grace.

Mary nodded. 'Have the children eaten?' Grace asked.

'I fed Edith earlier and put her down. The rest were waiting for you.'

Of course, Albert, Joe and the twins were still hiding upstairs. 'There is some rabbit stew you can heat up,' Grace said, 'and there is bread and cheese and biscuits. Can you look after them, Mary?'

'Of course. I'll get Albert to do it, he's a better cook than I am. Shall I bring something for you and Miss Clare?'

Grace had eaten nothing since breakfast, but her stomach revolted at the idea of food. She shook her head. Mary departed in silence and Grace heard her calling Albert and the others down to dinner. A murmur of voices came from the kitchen, and she realised Mary was explaining to them what had happened. She heard Albert's voice, steady and firm, and the twins and Joe chattering away. *They are all right,* she thought. *Trust Mary to handle things sensibly.* Yet again, she blessed the kindness of Providence that had sent Mary to them. *I thought I was taking in one more soul to be cared for. Instead, it is she who cares for us.*

Later the children went up to bed. Mary washed the dishes after dinner and prepared to go to bed herself. For a moment she paused at the foot of the stair and looked through the door where Grace sat in the lamplight, look-ing down at the wounded man's face. Mela was in a chair behind her; exhausted by the strains of the day, she had fallen asleep.

A single tear rolled softly down Grace's cheek. Quietly, Mary closed the door and went up to bed, leaving Grace to her vigil.

It had been a long day, full of emotions swinging from one extreme to the other. Eventually, exhaustion claimed her too and she fell asleep sitting up. For how long she slept she did not know, but a sudden gentle motion woke her. She sat dazed for a moment, recollecting where she was, seeing Mela still dozing in her chair, and then she realised what was happening. The man on the litter was stirring, his arm moving under her hand.

She sat up quickly, staring at his face, waiting and praying. Then, like a miracle, the response came. His eyelids flickered twice, and then opened.

Still she waited, holding her breath, and she saw his throat move as he tried to speak. No sound came out at first, but he tried again. 'Where am I?'

'In my house,' said Grace. Tears flowed steadily down her face, but they were tears of gratitude. 'In Bell Lane. You were attacked in the street, and we found you and brought you here.'

'Attacked in the . . .' His voice was weak. 'Wait a moment. It's all confused . . . No, I have it. I was coming to see you . . . And they jumped me, three of them. I don't know what happened next.'

'You were stabbed and hit over the head,' Grace said. 'They left you for dead.'

'Stabbed . . . Yes, I remember now. In the back, too. Beastly cowards . . . to stab a man in the back . . . How bad is it?'

'The knife wound will heal,' Grace said. 'But the doctor says you have a fractured skull.'

'Do I? That sounds exciting . . . Does that mean I am badly hurt?'

'It means you have to get a great deal of rest and let your wounds heal. Do you think you can stand?'

'I'm weak as a kitten, but I'll give it a go.'

She woke Mela, who sat up quickly. It took a long time for the two of them get Walter to his feet, and several times he collapsed and fell back, but he was determined to move. Eventually he stood, leaning heavily on them for support. They managed to get him upstairs to her bedroom and ease him down gently onto the bed and take off his boots. The effort of moving had exhausted him and he fell at once straight into sleep.

Grace sat down on the edge of the bed, taking his hand again and watching him sleep, seeing the handsome, slightly sunken face, the bare arms and body wrapped round with bandages to keep the knife wound closed. The enthusiastic, energetic, passionate young man of this morning looked vulnerable now, but that only made her love him the more.

All through that long night she sat with him, holding his hand, not knowing or caring what the future might bring for either of them but silently pouring out her love for him, willing him to live and be strong once more.

Morning came, the sun shining low and orange in a hazy sky. Grace had dozed once or twice in the night, but now she was fully awake. Walter was still deeply asleep.

Someone knocked at the door and she jumped, her heart in her mouth, dreading that it might be the Captain or his men, but then she head the reassuring sound of Elijah's voice. Mela came upstairs and looked into the bedroom. 'Mr Berton would like to see you,' she said.

Walter was peaceful, his pulse still weak but much stronger than before. Grace touched his forehead and found no sign of fever. He was safe. 'Of course,' she said. 'I will come down at once.'

Elijah looked like he too had not had much sleep. 'How is Mr Ringrose?' he asked.

'He is sleeping,' Grace said, 'but I think he will recover.' She felt the explosion of joy around her heart as she said the words.

'I'm right glad to hear it,' said Elijah, and his face showed his relief.

'What about the school?' Grace asked. 'Was it attacked?'

'All is quiet there. I reckon they thought if they did for Mr Ringrose, the rest of us would fold up. But if they thought that, they were wrong.'

'What is happening?' Grace asked.

'I went out last night and spread the word about what happened. Folk were furious when they heard about Mr Ringrose, angry and ready for a fight. Mrs Lane has been organising the womenfolk, too. There'll be another march today, bigger even than yesterday. We'll show the Captain what we're made of.'

He smiled at her. 'Don't you worry, Mrs Turneur. We'll carry on the good work, and we'll run these rats out of Rotherhithe.'

After he departed, Grace sat down slowly in a chair. Mela went into the kitchen to help Albert and Mary prepare breakfast. Weariness crept over Grace like a fog, and yet she knew she had to stay awake; Walter was not yet out of danger, and might need her. She heard the voices of the children in the kitchen, and then she remembered with sudden horror the Captain's threat.

'It won't do any good,' she said, half to herself.

'What won't?' asked Mary, who had been listening to her conversation with Mr Berton.

'The demonstration. The Captain will ignore them. Worse, he might attack Mr Berton or Mrs Lane, or some of the others. And then . . . Oh, God, Mary. Tonight he will come, and he will demand we give him Albert, Harry and Joe.'

Grace buried her face in her hands, her earlier happiness quite gone. Tears erupted, tears of exhaustion and fear, flowing from her reddened eyes. 'I can't bear it, Mary. I cannot bear the thought of losing them. I love them so much.'

'No,' said Mary, and for a moment the spirit of the feral child who had wandered the streets fighting for survival glowed in her blue eyes. 'No one is taking them anywhere.'

Grace raised her head, her own eyes still streaming. 'How can we stop them?' On the heels of the words an idea came. 'We must get them away, like we got the Doyles away. All of you, we must get you all away to a safe place.' She sat up suddenly. 'Yes. I will send to Mr Clare at once and ask him to help us. He will know of places we can hide from the Captain.'

And we save Albert, Harry and Joe, Mary thought, *but the Captain wins. He takes all the other boys and makes them his own.* She knelt and put her arms around Grace, and brushed the tears from her face. 'I am going out for a while,' she said.

'Out?' said Grace, blowing her nose. 'Where?'

'Just out,' said Mary.

'Why? What are you going to do?'

'I have an idea,' Mary said.

'The streets are dangerous. I am coming with you.'

Mary shook her head. 'No, Mother,' she said. 'This is something I need to do on my own.'

They gazed at each other. The word had escaped, unbidden and unawares, from Mary's lips for the very first time. She looked at Grace for a long moment, and then she smiled a smile of pure brilliance, like a ray of hope in a dark night.

'You stay here and look after Mr Ringrose,' she said. 'I won't be long.'

∽

I'd been living in a civilised house for a year and a half, but the street was still strong in me. I knew how the gangs lived and moved, and where their haunts were. I reckoned the Bull Heads were keeping their heads down, trying not to attract the attention of the mob gathering in Rotherhithe, while the Captain planned his next move. And I knew too that the boys in the gang would be out acting as lookouts.

It didn't take long to find him, less time even than I thought it would. He was sitting on a stack of timber not far from the entrance to the Albion Dock, carving something from a piece of wood. I took off my shoes so I could go silent, then circled around behind him and came up and tapped him on the shoulder.

He jumped about a mile in the air. 'You!' he said. 'What are you doing here?'

'Sneaking up on you. You're not a very good lookout, Jimmy.'

'What do you want?' he snapped.

'Remember last time we met?' I said. 'I asked you what you would do if it came to a choice between the Captain and Grace.'

'And I told you not to make me choose,' he said.

I shook my head. 'That ain't possible. Not anymore. The Captain is threatening to take her two sons, and my brother, and put them in the gang. You've got a choice, Jimmy. You can stay with the Captain and see Grace suffer. Or you can help her, and me, and get the Captain off your back at the same time.'

There was a long silence. 'I can't do it,' Jimmy said, and he sounded like a frightened child.

I wasn't letting him off that easy. I stabbed one finger against his chest. 'You can. You know you can.'

'How?'

'I reckon you know quite a lot about what happened last year, when your da and your brother rebelled against the Captain, and got killed. Am I right?'

'What makes you think that?' he asked, but I saw the change in his face.

'Back in the winter, I said I was sorry to hear about your da getting killed. You didn't say anything at all, you just looked away. I reckon you know what happened. Is that about right?'

He was still frightened, but he was angry too, now. 'It wasn't right, what they did. I hated my da, and Jake, but they were killed like dogs. It wasn't right.'

'Then make it right,' said Mary. 'Come with me.'

He hesitated. 'If they find out I betrayed them, they'll hurt my ma.'

'Your ma, who didn't lift a finger when your father sold you to the gang? Like I said, Jimmy, it's time to make a choice. Grace, or the Captain. You choose.'

∞

There was a carriage sitting outside Bell Lane, and Mary recognised it as belonging to Mr Gould the timber merchant, one of the governors of the school. Frowning, she opened the door and went into the parlour to find him talking with Grace. Mr Clare was there too.

'How is he?' she asked Grace.

'A little better,' Grace said. 'I tried him on some broth and he was sick. He is still very weak.'

She looked at the two men. 'We must get the children away to safety. But I don't know what to do with Mr Ringrose. I don't think we can move him any distance. Perhaps I should stay here with him, and send the children away.'

'We can arrange for the children to be taken to my house at once,' said Mr Clare. 'But Grace, I don't like the thought of you remaining here. As I understand it, the gang are threatening to return this evening. If they find the children have gone, they will attack you and Mr Ringrose. We have guards watching the house, but it will still be dangerous.'

Mary had seen the guards outside, workers from the docks armed with cudgels. She didn't think they would be able to stand up to the Bull Head Gang. 'I think I know what to do,' she said.

They all looked at the girl. 'There is someone waiting to see you,' she said to Grace. 'May I show him in?'

'Of course,' said Grace, puzzled.

Quietly, Jimmy Wilson opened the door and walked into the room.

Grace gasped. 'Jimmy!' she cried, and she rushed to the boy and embraced him. 'Oh, Jimmy, my dear boy! I thought

I would never see you again! Where have you been? What are you doing here?'

'I persuaded him to come,' Mary said. 'Mr Clare, sir, and Mr Gould, I am glad you are here, because I think you can help us. Jimmy has something he needs to say.'

Jimmy gave a little shiver, but then his chin came up. His eyes were bright in his thin, grimy face. 'Last winter my da and my brother led a revolt against the Captain,' he said. 'It went wrong. Da and my brother and two of the others were ambushed in Bermondsey. The Captain had them taken to Albion Dock and he killed all four of them himself. Their bodies were buried out in the marshes.'

'I see,' said Mr Clare. 'Did you witness this, boy?'

'No, sir. But I can give you the names of two men who did. If you arrest them, they'll talk, provided you promise to keep them safe. They will give evidence against the Captain.'

'I see,' said Mr Clare again. Mr Gould nodded grimly. 'Will you accompany me to the police and tell them what you told me?'

Jimmy nodded.

'The police are no use,' said Mr Gould. 'They are in the pocket of the gangs.'

'In Rotherhithe, perhaps,' said Mr Clare. 'I mean to go to Scotland Yard. And by heaven, I will knock on the door of the commissioner himself if I must, but I will see justice done. Boy, come with me.'

Mr Gould, Mr Clare and Jimmy departed, the latter with a backwards glance at Grace. After they had gone

Grace stood in the middle of the parlour floor, astonished and agitated. 'What did you do?' she asked Mary.

'I thought I knew where I could track him down. And I told him how much Mr Ringrose means to you, and how much you mean to Mr Ringrose, and I asked him to help us.'

There was a little pause while Grace digested her words. 'How much I mean to him?' she said blankly.

'Oh, Mother!' said Mary in exasperation. 'Are you really that blind? He is head over heels in love with you, and you with him. Will the two of you please get on with it?'

They stared at each other. Mary started to giggle. 'Now I sound more like *your* mother,' she said.

'Not for the first time, either,' Grace said, recovering. 'Never mind, my dear. It is the function of daughters to order their mothers about. That is the way of the world . . . Oh, *Mary*! Do you really mean it?'

'Yes,' said Mary. 'I really mean it. Go see him, Mother dear, and tell him Albert and the twins are looking forward to having a second Fa, very soon.'

Her heart thundering in her chest, Grace went up to the bedroom. Walter stirred and opened his eyes as she came in. For a moment he looked around, his wits still cloudy. 'What time is it?' he asked.

'Just before noon.'

'I see . . . And where am I?'

'In my house,' said Grace. 'In my bed.'

'In your bed? Ah. It's not quite how I imagined it would be.'

There was a long pause. 'If I had the strength I would blush with shame,' Walter said. 'Mrs Turneur . . . I'm sorry, my wits are addled. I don't know what came over me.'

Grace found herself giggling. 'But you admit you have imagined it,' she said.

'I've imagined quite a lot of things . . . Oh, Lord, that is even worse. I have let the cat out of the bag now, haven't I?'

Grace waited. 'Would it be all right if I sat up a little?' Walter asked. 'I've something to say to you, but I'd like to be able to see you when I say it.'

Gently, Grace helped him sit up a little, carefully minding the wound on his back, and tucked another pillow in behind him. He sank back, weak and grateful, his eyes fixed on her. 'It's like this,' he said. 'I've been thinking of you ever since we first met, that day at the picnic in the park. You, and no one but you.'

The pounding of her heart increased. 'No,' Grace said. 'It was Mela you were looking at.'

'Dear old Mela. I'm very fond of her, in a brotherly sort of way. But it was you that stole my heart. And then, before I could work up the nerve to do anything about it, you were married, and I felt like all my hopes had been shattered. But I couldn't stop my feelings. I knew it was you, or no one. You were the only woman I would, or could, ever love.'

Stunned, Grace stood and stared at him. 'You don't know what you are saying,' she said. 'The doctor said the blow to the head might have disordered your wits.'

'I assure you, my wits are in the best order they have ever been. Let me guess. You think we come from different walks of life, me from the gentry, you from the working class, as I believe Mr Marx and Mr Engels call them. The chasm between us is too wide to be bridged, you say.'

'Not my exact words, but you have the sentiment,' said Grace. 'I am the adopted child of a factory worker, and I spent a year in the workhouse. I am no one.'

'That is complete and utter rubbish,' said Walter. 'You are brave and honourable and true. You are noble, Grace Turneur, in the finest sense of the word. Where and how you were born are of no account. It is who you are that matters; and to me, you are the finest woman alive.'

'I also have six children,' Grace pointed out.

'Who's counting?' said Walter.

Tears started to flow again. *I have done nothing but cry for the last two days,* Grace thought. She wiped her eyes. 'Your wits really are disordered,' she said.

'Then I hope they remain so for a long time to come. For a lifetime, in fact. Because that is what I have in mind. I know you are still in mourning for your husband. I know I have to wait until the pieces of my skull grow back together. But when I'm better, and you feel you are ready; well, when that day comes, Grace Turneur, will you marry me?'

She was weeping and laughing all together now. 'I guess I'll have to,' she said. 'You need someone to keep you out of trouble . . . Walter, tell me this is not a dream. Tell me you really mean it.'

'I intend to spend the rest of my life showing you how much I really mean it,' he said. 'Meanwhile, though, you haven't told me if you love me.'

Slowly Grace bent and brushed her lips against his, and in a moment, all the agitation of the past few days vanished and a sweet peace descended around her. 'Does that answer your question?' she asked softly.

'Very much so. I'll need you to keep kissing me quite often, of course, once we are married. I'm an anxious sort of chap. I need constant reassurance.'

His eyes were heavy. 'You also need sleep,' Grace said, kissing him again. 'Rest now, my dear, and get well.'

Walter's eyes closed. Grace stood for a moment, looking down at his sleeping face. She still felt she was dreaming, and yet at the same time she knew beyond doubt she was not. They were not safe. They were surrounded by storms, but they would come through, and out on the other side a new life was waiting for them.

'Well,' she said quietly. 'I must tell the children.'

Through the long afternoon she waited. Outside, men armed with cudgels patrolled the street. Hermione Lane called in after the demonstration had ended to see how Walter was faring. She gasped when Grace told her about Jimmy's decision to turn against the Captain.

'Is it really possible? At last, the police will intervene?'

'Mr Clare said he would go to the highest levels if necessary', said Grace. 'And in my experience, when he wants to do something, it gets done.'

The time passed slowly, with Grace torn between the wonder of love and dread at the thought of the immediate future. What if Mr Clare had failed? What if Scotland Yard was too slow, and the Captain got away? She and the children, and Walter, were still in danger.

Mr Gould thought so too. As evening drew on, he knocked at the door. 'I've brought a carriage,' he said. Let me take your children away for the night. We can keep them safe, far safer than you can here.'

'Thank you,' said Grace with relief. She called the children to her and explained. 'You must do everything Mr Gould tells you to do,' she said. 'Be good, and I will see you again, soon.'

'Yes, mummy,' the younger ones said in chorus, but Mary looked mutinous. Then came another knock at the door.

For an agonised moment Grace thought, *too late. He is here.* But the knock had been a mild one, with no hint of threat. She shooed the children into the kitchen where Mary would look after them, and then answered the door herself, Mr Gould close and protective behind her. They both sighed with relief when they saw Mr Clare on the doorstep.

'The police have taken the Captain and his accomplices,' he said. 'It is done.'

'They are asking you to come to the police station,' Mr Clare said to Grace. 'Can you be spared?'

Mary came into the room, smiling at Mr Clare. 'For a little while,' she said. 'But not for too long. She is needed here.'

'I shall return her promptly,' Mr Clare said.

Mr Gould came with them – there was no need to send the children away now – and while they rode in his carriage to the police station on Lower Road, Mr Clare explained what had happened. 'I spoke to Inspector Franklin at Scotland Yard and told him your story, and then introduced Jimmy. The boy did very well, spoke honestly and truthfully, and Franklin was quite persuaded. He came down with a team of armed constables and they went into Albion Dock. I gather there was something of a fracas, but they managed to take the Captain alive.'

'And why do they need me?' Grace asked.

'Jimmy was right. Two of the gang members arrested have agreed to given evidence against the Captain. Franklin has charged him with the murders of four men, including Wilson and his older son, but he also intends to add a range of charges relating to the threats to you and your school, and the kidnapping of Jimmy Wilson and Billy Doyle. He will have a few questions for you about what happened.'

He watched Grace curiously. 'The Captain claims he is your cousin. Is that true?'

'He had already left home by the time we went to live with Aunt Edith,' Grace said. 'I never knew him.'

The police station was guarded by two constables in blue uniforms with long-barrelled rifles in their hands. They saluted Mr Clare as he handed Grace out of the carriage, Mr Gould following close behind. Inside the station there were more policemen, looking busy and determined. There was no sign of Sergeant Bates or any of the other officers Grace had seen when she and Mr Raikes had called.

A tall man in uniform hurried up, saluting. 'Mrs Turneur? I am Inspector Franklin of the Yard. Glad to see you, ma'am, and thank you for coming. If you would follow me?'

They seated her in a small office, Mr Clare standing behind her, another constable sitting to one side taking notes. 'Could you please repeat the threats the Captain made against you and your family and pupils?' the inspector asked.

Grace did so, and went on to describe the events surrounding the kidnapping of Jimmy and then later of Billy. 'What will happen to Jimmy?' she asked at the end.

'You mean, because of his involvement with the gang? He is still a boy, and it is quite clear that he was coerced. No action will be taken against him. He is free to go where he wishes.'

'And the Captain?' Grace asked.

'I'm afraid there's not much doubt about it, ma'am,' the inspector said. 'The charges relating to his threats to you and the kidnappings are serious, but they're window dressing compared to the charges of murder. The evidence from the two thugs who confessed is already overwhelming, and I have men out searching for the bodies now.' He looked at Grace, with sympathy in his eyes. 'I hope this does not cause you distress,' he said. 'I understand there is a family connection.'

'Is he here?' Grace asked.

'In a cell downstairs. You may see him, if you wish.'

'Thank you,' said Grace.

She knew Mr Clare and Mr Gould were puzzled, and she was not sure herself why, but she needed to confront the Captain one last time. Inspector Franklin led the way down to the cells, her two companions and another constable following. The inspector pointed into one of the cells. 'There he is,' he said.

Grace looked through the bars. She saw the Captain, manacled hand and foot, his clothes torn and ripped. His hat was gone, and he had a black eye and bruises around his mouth. He had clearly put up a fight before being arrested.

Slowly his head came up, and he saw Grace. A smile played around his battered lips. 'Little Grace,' he said. 'Have you come to gloat?'

'No,' said Grace. 'I just wanted to be sure that it was real. I'll sleep much safer, knowing you are behind bars.'

The smile deepened. 'Don't be too sure. The Bull Head Gang has been dispersed, but the bluebottles didn't catch all of us, not by any means. The gang will reform, and it will begin again.'

'But you will not be leading them,' Grace said.

'And for you, that is a pity. I spared you out of . . . family feeling, shall we say. Another leader might not be so accommodating. No, little Grace. You're not out of danger, not by a long way.'

The Captain paused. 'There is one thing that might help. Even behind bars, I am not without influence.'

'What do you want?' Grace asked.

'You could intercede on my behalf,' the Captain said. 'Inform the authorities that you forgive me for my crimes and have no wish to see me hang. The judge might listen to a plea from a cousin, who has lost so many of her family already. She would not wish to see her only surviving adult relative die as well.'

There was a long pause. Then, slowly, Grace shook her head. 'Once, I might have done so,' she said. 'I could forgive the threat to my school. I might even forgive you for the attack on Walter Ringrose, because he is going to live. But you crossed over the line when you threatened to take my sons. No, Captain. Those are *my* children, and I will defend them to the death.'

She stared at the manacled man from under her dark eyebrows. 'You are no kin of mine,' she said. 'I will not intercede for you, Captain. Indeed, I hope you hang.'

Chapter 22

'This is a bad business,' said Walter. He was sitting up in bed reading a newspaper, a bandage around his head and a frown of concern on his face.

'What is?' Grace asked, arranging the breakfast tray on his lap.

'France and Prussia are at war. I suppose we've been expecting it, but I reckoned it would just be a few border skirmishes then common sense would prevail and they would negotiate a peace. Instead, it looks like the French are getting badly knocked about. Uncle Hector won't be happy. He does a lot of trade with France.'

'As Mr Crompton does with Germany,' said Grace. 'I do hope Britain won't be drawn in.'

'Oh, no fear of that. Old Gladstone is too smart to get us into that mess.' Walter lowered the newspaper. 'Look at us,' he said. 'Chatting over breakfast like an old married couple. Is it starting to sink in yet?'

Grace laughed. 'Which? That the Captain is gone, or that we are going to be married?'

'I was thinking of the latter, but yes to both.' Walter dug his spoon into his bowl of porridge. 'How long will the doctor keep me here? I'm dying to get back to the school. Have you been coping all right without me?'

'You ask that question every day,' Grace said, 'and every day I give you the same answer. We have been coping just fine without you. Rebecca Berton has been appointed a pupil-teacher. She is fifteen now, and more than ready. Agnes has taken over your class, and Rebecca has taken Agnes's class. All is well, and you are not well enough yet to go home, let alone back to work.'

'And there have been no more threats? I'm still worried about that, to tell you the truth.'

'So am I,' said Grace quietly. The Captain had been right. The arrest of himself and the other leaders had caused the Bull Head Gang to splinter, but not to disappear entirely. Different factions had emerged, fighting a short but violent war for territory that led to several groups being pushed out, but the signs were that the remaining groups were starting to consolidate. Rotherhithe's interval of peace after the Captain's arrest would be short-lived.

'So, when do you think I might be up and about?' Walter asked.

Grace smiled at him. She could not remain downcast these days. 'If you are a good boy and eat all your breakfast,' she said, 'I will take you in tomorrow. The trustees are meeting, and they will be glad to see you. Now, Louisa will be here at midday as usual to give you a meal. Until then, do you have everything you need?'

'Yes,' said Walter, 'except for one thing. Your smile. Would you mind leaving it with me when you go? I get awfully lonely without it.'

'Flattery will get you nowhere,' said Grace, kissing him.

'Won't it? Blast. I was counting on it to get me out of quite a few scrapes, once we are married.'

Still laughing, Grace gathered the children and went off to the school, escorted as ever by the faithful Radcliffe. At school she was greeted with warm smiles by her fellow teachers and squeaks of delight by her pupils. She went through her day in a haze of happiness. In the afternoon she gathered the children and walked home, delighting in the world around her. Even the smoke of the factories hanging in the air could not dampen her spirits.

Walter was sitting in a chair in the parlour when Grace walked in. She stared at him. 'What are you doing?' she demanded. 'Why are you up?'

'Because it is time I got up,' he said grimly. 'The gangs are back.'

They looked at each other. 'How do you know?' Grace asked. The children stood behind her, silent.

'Someone put a letter under the door this morning. Mrs Berton found it when she came in, and gave it to me.' He handed over the paper. 'Have a look.'

The letter was written in crude handwriting. Grace read it, her heart sinking.

To Master Walter Ringrose, and the woman who calls herself Grace Turneur. You impeached our Captain and you sent him to hang. This letter is to give you fair warning. Your time will come.

Yours faithfully, the Albion Gang (formerly known as the Bull Head)

'The problem is, I don't know how serious this is,' Walter said. 'Is this Albion Gang a real gang, or is it just a few bully-boys nursing a grudge?'

'Even if it is the latter, they could be dangerous,' Grace said.

'I know. Blast! After all our hard work, all we've been through, why can't these pests let us alone? Well, it doesn't matter. We're not going to let them stand in our way. Paradise Row School will go on, and we'll jolly well make it the best free school in London.'

'We will,' said Grace smiling.

But Reverend Soames had other ideas. He called that evening, when a west wind swept smoke and cinders across the city and poisoned the air with fumes from the glue factory; even though it was summer, he had a scarf over his face. 'Good evening,' he said cheerfully, white beard wagging as he smiled at the children. 'I shall not detain you for long. I merely called, Mr Ringrose, to see how your recovery is progressing.'

'Very well,' said Walter, smiling. 'My nurse has promised to let me out tomorrow.'

405

'I am sure you are in capable hands,' said Reverend Soames.

'Er,' said Grace. 'While you are here, Reverend, there is something we would like to ask you.' She felt herself blushing, and reached for Walter's hand. 'We wish to be married. Not right away, but in a couple of months, perhaps. And we wondered if you would perform the service.'

'I would be honoured,' said Reverend Soames, bowing. 'You are the most gallant couple I know. And this time we shall call the banns.'

Then his voice grew more sober. 'I confess there is another reason for my calling,' he said. 'Word has reached my ears – in part thanks to your friends at the King's Arms, Mr Ringrose – that the gangs are reforming.'

'Yes,' said Walter. 'We heard that too.'

'It was to be expected, of course. Nature abhors a vacuum, and in the absence of an effective police force in this part of the city, the gangs were bound to return. But I am concerned for your safety, my children.'

Grace picked up the letter from the side table and handed it to the rector. 'This arrived today,' she said. 'We were wondering how seriously to take it.'

Reverend Soames looked even more grave. 'I think you should take this very seriously indeed.'

Silence fell. 'We cannot give in,' said Walter.

'I understand your sentiments,' said the rector. 'And I am sure that the resistance to the gangs within the community, which the two of you so ably led, will continue. But you must consider yourselves, and your family. This is not a threat against the Paradise Row School, or the community, but against the two of you in person. You nearly lost your life once already, Mr Ringrose. You might not be so fortunate a second time.'

'What do you suggest, sir?' Grace asked.

'I have had an idea in mind for some time, but have been hesitant to mention it because I knew how deeply committed you were to Paradise Row. However, I think the time is right. You may recall, Mrs Turneur, my decision to found a free school in my new parish of Orpington, where I go in a few weeks' time. I had asked if you would advise me on its establishment.'

Grace nodded. 'Would the two of you consider instead coming to run the school for me?' asked the rector. 'I think you would find teaching in a poor agricultural community every bit as challenging, and rewarding, as your work here. You would be contributing to the greater cause of education, just as you are here.'

Grace and Walter hesitated, looking at each other. 'I would pay you a salary, of course,' the rector said. 'And a house would be found for you. A house with a garden, and green space and clean air for your little ones. The health-giving benefits of country air cannot be overstated.'

Even inside with the doors and windows shut, they could smell the stench of the glue factory. 'Perhaps,' said Walter doubtfully. 'In my experience, the countryside has plenty of smells of its own.'

'It does,' acknowledged the rector. 'But they are on the whole good honest smells, not coal and tar and chemicals that sting the eyes and rot the lungs. For my part, I shall miss the people of Bermondsey, but not its smoke and reek.'

'It is a very kind and generous offer,' said Grace. 'May we think about it?'

'Of course.' The rector smiled and bowed again. 'Bless you, my children. I look forward to your wedding day.'

'Not half as much as I'm look forward to it,' said Walter when the rector had gone.

But the jest was lost on Grace, who was deep in thought. 'What do you think?' she asked.

'I don't know,' said Walter. 'He's right, it would be a challenge, and a jolly good one. Some of these farming villages really are quite desperately deprived. But . . . leaving would feel like giving up.'

He looked at Grace. 'What do *you* think? Could you really give up the school, after having worked so hard for it?'

'My first thought was no,' said Grace. 'I have stood by my school against all threats, but . . . I confess I am tempted. Before, if I gave in the school would close, but the Paradise Row School is strong and thriving now. I love it, and I always will, but it no longer needs us. Mela or Agnes or someone else could take over and run it equally well. The threat this time is to us, not the school, us and the children. And if we leave, the gang might let the school alone.'

Grace paused. 'And, I confess, like you I think Reverend Soames has presented us with a challenge, something new and interesting to do. I am intrigued.'

She smiled. 'When we are married, we shall start a new life. Why not start a new adventure as well?'

'How do you think the children would feel?' Walter asked.

'Let's ask them,' said Grace.

They canvassed opinion over the dinner table. She had been prepared for Albert and the twins to dig their heels in, for Bell Lane was the only home they had ever known. She was surprised to find they were looking forward to the idea.

'I want to travel and see the world,' said Albert. 'I know it is only ten miles, but that is a start.'

'I want a garden,' said Daisy. 'I want to plant things in the ground, and watch them grow, and then eat them.'

'Will there be music in the country?' Harry asked.

'There will,' said Walter. 'Brass bands and silver bands and fiddle players and all manner of music.' Harry clapped his hands with delight.

'What do you think, Joe?' Grace asked.

'I think Radcliffe would like the country,' said Joe.

Grace smiled. 'Edith is too young to have a vote. That leaves you, Mary.'

Mary's smile was warm in return. 'I've never seen the country,' she said. 'I think it sounds interesting. Let's go.'

'Welcome back, my boy,' said Mr Gould, shaking Walter's hand warmly. 'How are you?'

'On the mend, sir,' said Walter. It was the following afternoon; classes had just ended and the trustees had gathered for their monthly meeting,

'We have asked the other staff to join us,' Grace said. 'Mr Ringrose – Walter and I have a couple of announcements to make.'

They waited a moment while Mela, Agnes, Hermione, Rebecca, Mickey and Brigit came into the room and sat down. 'The first announcement,' said Walter, 'is I have asked Grace to be my wife. I am pleased to say that she has done me the great honour of accepting.'

There were cries of delight from the other teachers and smiles from the trustees. 'I hope we have your blessing,' Grace said to Mr Clare. 'And yours, Sir Hector.' She looked at Mela. 'And yours, my dear friend.'

Mr Clare smiled. 'I speak for Sir Hector and myself when I say that we are both delighted that this happy – and keenly anticipated – event has finally taken place. Congratulations to you both.'

'I'm just cross that I lost the sweepstake,' said Mela, to general laughter.

'It looks like everyone knew we were getting married except us,' said Walter dryly. 'The second announcement is much harder . . . The two of us have been offered a chance to run a free school in Orpington, under the sponsorship of Reverend Soames. After much painful deliberation, and not a little heartache, we have decided to accept.'

There was silence in the room. 'This was not an easy decision,' said Grace. 'But as you may know, Walter and I have received threats against our persons. Were it only our own lives that were at stake, we would defy the gangs to do their worst, and carry on. But there is our family to consider as well. Five of them have been orphaned at some time in their lives, and we are not willing to put them through this again. For their sake, and for the sake of the school, we have decided it is best that we should go.'

Mr Gould nodded slowly. 'You decision is quite timely,' he said. 'I should tell you that the return of the gangs has left us, the trustees, more than a little concerned about your safety.'

Mr Crompton nodded. 'We can protect the school,' he said, 'but we would find it harder to protect you and your family. We cannot guard all of you, all the time.'

'As your kin, we are delighted to see you take any steps that will increase your safety,' said Sir Hector, and Mr Clare smiled and looked at Grace. 'That goes for me also,' he said.

Grace smiled back at him and turned to Mr Raikes.

'You have been my guide from the beginning,' she said. 'Time and time again, I have turned to you for help, and you have never failed me. I would value your opinion, sir.'

Solomon Raikes rubbed his jaw for a moment. 'I think,' he said, 'that you have contributed a great chapter to the history of education in London, Mrs Turneur, and you too, Mr Ringrose. People will remember you as the pioneers, the ones who first brought schools to these poor districts south of the river, and stuck to your task against all odds and made those schools succeed.'

He gestured around the room. 'Now, we have this fine building, an excellent teaching staff, and nigh on two hundred pupils. By any measure one might care to name, you have succeeded. I believe it is time for you to close this chapter, and move on to the next.'

'Thank you,' said Grace, swallowing the lump in her throat. 'I suppose the next question is, who will take the post of head teacher? Do you wish to appoint someone from outside, or do you wish to promote one of the current staff?'

Hermione spoke first. 'I don't know if this is a democracy,' she said. 'But if it is, I vote for Miss Clare.'

Agnes nodded. 'Beyond doubt, it must be Miss Clare,' she said.

'Miss Clare,' said Rebecca.

'Miss Clare,' repeated Mickey, and Brigit nodded vigorously.

'But what about the Clare School?' Grace asked. 'You were supposed to take over that, one day.'

'And perhaps I will, eventually,' Mela said. 'But Mother still shows no signs of slowing down and besides . . . I like it here.'

'Then far be it from us to deny the will of the people,' said Mr Gould. 'Miss Clare, on behalf of the trustees, I offer

412

you the role of headmistress. May God bless the Paradise Row School.'

'And all who sail in her,' said Mr Ringrose happily.

When Grace left school that evening someone was waiting for her, a ragged barefoot boy standing in the shadows. He was taller than she remembered, and had filled out a little. She saw with a lump in her throat that he was growing up.

'Jimmy,' said Grace softly. 'I am so glad to see you. Are you well?'

Jimmy nodded. 'I've left the gang,' he said. 'I wanted to come and tell you that.'

'I'm so glad. But Jimmy, are you safe?'

The boy nodded again. 'I still hear from some of the others. They know you peached against the Captain, but they don't know it was me who told you. Otherwise, I would be dead.'

'You must be careful all the same,' said Grace. 'Jimmy ... just before they took you, I had arranged a place for you at a grammar school in Lewisham. I could write to the headmaster. I am sure he would still be willing to give you a place, free of charge, and he will find accommodation for you too.'

'That's very generous of you, miss,' said Jimmy. He corrected himself. 'Sorry, missus.'

'It is the very least I can do,' Grace said. 'You have such talent, Jimmy. I have never seen a pupil with such ability. You could go very far in the world, if you want to.'

Jimmy smiled and shook his head. 'I can't,' he said. 'I have to look after my ma.'

'Sara? She let the gangs take you, Jimmy.'

'She didn't want to do it,' Jimmy said. 'When she tried to argue with Da, he hit her. After Da got killed, the Captain paid her rent. But now he's gone, there's no one to support her, and she's too ill to work. I've got to work and look after her.'

What a waste, Grace thought, but then she stopped. Jimmy was doing his duty by his family, just as she had done. She took the boy's hand and kissed him softly on the forehead.

'If you change your mind, come and find me,' she said. 'We're moving to Orpington to open a school. There will always be a place for you there.'

'I will. And I'll never forget what you taught me. Good luck, missus.'

'You too, Jimmy.'

The boy turned and walked away down the street. Grace stood motionless, watching him until he disappeared from view.

❧

And so, the orphans of Bell Lane, Joe and me, Albert and Harry and Daisy and Grace herself, went out to live in the country. Reverend Soames performed the marriage and we settled into our new home. Everyone was happy. The twins played out of doors and Daisy got her garden. Albert's new father has taught him to play cricket, which he is actually quite good at, and he still enjoys cooking, too, lots more than I do. Joe and Radcliffe go out into the woods and chase rabbits. They never catch anything.

The new school is going well. They have won over the local farmers and even the Romany labourers, who aren't always best mates with each other, but they are teaching the kids of both in the same school side by side. I've made some good friends among both groups. I never had proper friends. I don't think I can really count the Angels. It feels good to be liked.

My life has changed, forever. I'll never be a thief now. I'll never join the Forty Elephants, and in some ways that's a pity, because I think I'd have been a very good thief, maybe even one of the best. But I don't want that life anymore. I've got something better now, something I never expected to have again. I have a father, a kind, clever, funny man whom I love and respect. And most of all, the blessing that fell from the skies one night like something out of one of Mr Dickens's books, I have a mother.

That's good enough for me. I'm getting on with life. I'm studying hard and learning, and I'm starting to think I might follow in my parents' footsteps and become a teacher too. In a few years I might go up to Rotherhithe again, and see if Miss Clare would take me on. She's not fooling anyone; she won't go back to the Clare School. She'll stay at Paradise Row and she'll carry on the fight, just like my parents did. It's in her blood now.

She's a good woman, Miss Clare. I just wish she'd give up that nonsense about never wanting to marry. I reckon there will come a time when she regrets saying that. I found a poem in a book the other day. I couldn't understand all of it, but I understood the first part well enough.

> *No man is an island,*
> *Entire of itself,*
> *Every man is a piece of the continent,*
> *A part of the main.*

I guess it was written by a man, because he didn't mention women, but it is true of us too. I have learned that all of us, man or woman, need someone to love us, someone to care for us and keep us, to give us comfort when things go bad, and love and hope when they go well. I didn't learn that on the streets, either, or from any book. I learned it from her. And I will never forget.

Acknowledgements

First of all, many thanks are due to Tara Loder from Zaffre without whom this book would never have seen the light of day. She was a major inspiration for this book and she has been its enthusiastic supporter and champion all the way. Thanks to the Royal Literary Fund for all their support during the process of writing this book. At Zaffre, Claire Johnson-Creek and Katie Lumsden's help and guidance and patience throughout the editing and production process has been great, and Laura Gerrard's excellent copyediting made many big, helpful improvements to the text.

The usual (and very fulsome) thanks are due also to Heather Adams and Mike Bryan for their excellent, calm agents' advice. It is always welcome and always helpful.

Advice from Suzie Stevens of St James' Primary School about education for children from traumatised backgrounds was really valuable (I still owe her a drink!). Other teachers have also provided helpful comments and information, even if they were not aware of it at the time, including Janine Cook, Hazel Fox, Adam Hills, Hugh Lee, Dierdre Petersen and Phil Whittley. Other really helpful education-related 'stuff' has been forthcoming from Derek Brett, Daryll Chapman, Jane Lake, Kelly Hoggins, Tania Skeaping and, latterly, Craig Griffiths. My fellow governors and trustees have also been a great source of useful information. Through discussions with these educators and teachers, I have gained a greater insight into the complexities of teaching which has been invaluable when writing *The Orphans of Bell Lane*.

Thanks are due to Michelle and Morwenna for providing a musical break from writing – it was a pause that always refreshed. Thanks also to the letting agent who led me to live (albeit briefly) in a corner of south-east London full of history, but much less famed than the east end north of the Thames.

Finally I would like to thank my grandparents, Alice and Arthur Holbrook, and my several great-grandparents (and step-great grandmother) for providing the inspiration for parts of this book. Though they are long gone, *The Orphans of Bell Lane* owes much to their personal stories.

Welcome to the world of *Ruthie Lewis*!

Keep reading for more from Ruthie Lewis, to discover a recipe that features in this novel and to find out more about Ruthie Lewis's inspiration for the book . . .

We'd also like to introduce you to MEMORY LANE, our special community for the very best of saga writing from authors you know and love, and new ones we simply can't wait for you to meet. Read on and join our club!

www.MemoryLane.club

Dear Readers,

Thank you for choosing *The Orphans of Bell Lane*. The story of Grace and Rosa and their family was wonderful to write and touches on things close to my heart. Behind the book are a few different strands of inspiration: personal, coincidental and strongly linked to my non-writing activities. Shall I tell you what these are?

Some elements of the plot of *The Orphans of Bell Lane* are an adaptation of my family history. Parts of the childhood of my maternal grandparents, Alice and Arthur, were a key inspiration for Grace, Rosa and George Turneur. Alice was born and brought up in Rotherhithe in a small road (much rebuilt since WWII) next to the London Bridge railway line. Alice's father was a bricklayer and died young. Her mother remarried and the family eventually moved out of unhealthy Rotherhithe to the clean air of Hornchurch in Essex.

My grandfather Arthur's family history is even more crucial to the plot. His mother died of tuberculosis in the early 1890s when Arthur was young and her sister moved in to look after the three children (sound familiar?) She and my great-grandfather married and had three more children before he died of TB when Arthur was just twelve. My family was more fortunate than Grace's. My great-grandfather's employer was a decent man and allowed the family to stay in their tied cottage (my great-grandfather had worked at a market garden in Essex).

When my grandmother's family moved from Rotherhithe to Essex, Alice and Arthur met and married. They emigrated to Canada the day after their wedding. All six of my great-grandmother's 'blended' family lived into ripe old age; the youngest, Great-Aunt Nellie, lived to 104. Her 100th birthday party was attended by dozens of family and friends.

When I first moved to London in 1987, I was surprised and pleased to find myself living not far from my grandmother's birthplace. Although I lived there only briefly, I travelled into London for many years on the same railway line that Grace would have taken from Sevenoaks. I often looked down from the train into the street where my grandmother was born. This connection inspired the novel's setting novel in Rotherhithe at a time then the area was undergoing big building projects and great change.

Finally, the education background (thanks to Tara Loder for the idea!) fits so well with one of my main non-writing activities. The child of a high school teacher, a sister and aunt to others, I have been a governor for over ten years, first at a small village primary school and then for a group of six primaries and one secondary comprehensive. I am also a trustee of a multi-academy trust with a strong co-operative/church ethos. Much of my 'free' time is spent in schools, talking to teachers, children and school leaders about how to improve our schools and ensure pupils have a safe, balanced and enjoyable education. While many things have changed in education over 150 years, there are many things that today's schools have in common with those of the past. Not least of these is the need to help our most disadvantaged pupils achieve their best and enable them to improve their life chances. Many of Grace's Ragged School challenges are familiar to today's teachers. Sadly too, the struggles of children like Jimmy Wilson would be all too familiar to some of our pupils today.

The Orphans of Bell Lane draws together many threads of my life and that of my family (I am one of seven children and know about living in a house full of children). I hope you have enjoyed reading it as much as I enjoyed writing it. If you did, please do share your thoughts on the Memory Lane Facebook page ⓕ Memory Lane Club.

Yours sincerely,
Ruthie Lewis

Bacon 'Dumplings'

This recipe was taught to me by a cook in a laminated chip-board factory in west Kent in the late 1980s; she called it Kent Bacon Roly-Poly Pudding. I have since discovered that it has a much more ancient history and was a good way for poor people to eke out small amounts of bacon or other meat to fill up hungry stomachs. Vegetables such as potatoes or swede are added to bulk out the expensive protein element! It serves six or seven healthy appetites and goes well with carrots and cabbage.

You will need:

2 onions, finely chopped
200g shredded suet
500g plain flour
2 tsp baking powder
a little cold water
12 rashers of streaky bacon chopped up (smoked or not as to your taste – I prefer smoked)
salt and pepper to taste
sage (optional)
2 potatoes, peeled and grated
2 dessert spoons swede, peeled and grated (or more if you like)

Method:

1. Sauté the onions, adding a little salt to help them sweat down. Try not to get too much colour on them to avoid a burned onion flavour. (Sometimes a little water or white wine helps to sweat them down.)

2. While the onions are cooking rub the shredded suet, flour and baking powder together in a bowl until like breadcrumbs, and then, a little at a time, add enough cold water to make a stiff dough. Roll this out into a rectangle about 3cm thick.

3. Add the chopped bacon to the onions for a few minutes and then season to taste. Some crumbled sage leaves can be added.

4. Spread the onion and bacon mixture along with the shredded potato and swede across the suet pastry.

5. Moisten the edges of the pastry and roll up like a Swiss (or jelly) roll.

6. Wrap in two layers of greaseproof paper and a clean cloth and steam for 2 hours 15 minutes. Unwrap the roll and put in the oven on a baking sheet to brown for another 45 minutes.

7. Serve with either a mustard sauce or with gravy.

8. Enjoy!

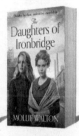